# Sweet
# REVENGE

# Sweet REVENGE

Sugar Rautbord

*Villard Books*

NEW YORK

1992

Grateful acknowledgment is made to the following for permission to reprint previously published material:
WARNER/CHAPPELL MUSIC, INC.: Excerpts from the lyrics of "Like a Virgin" by Tom Kelly and Billy Steinberg. Copyright © 1984 by Billy Steinberg Music, Denise Barry Music. All rights reserved. Used by permission.
GRUBMAN INDURSKY SCHINDLER GOLDSTEIN & FLAX, P.C.: Excerpts from the lyrics of "Vogue" by Madonna/Shep Pettibone. WB Music Corp. (ASCAP), Bleu Disque Music Co., Inc. (ASCAP), Webo Girl Publishing, Inc. (ASCAP), Lexor Music (ASCAP). All rights on behalf of all parties administered by WB Music Corp. (ASCAP). All rights reserved. Reprinted by permission.

Library of Congress Cataloging-in-Publication Data

Rautbord, Sugar.
Sweet revenge/Sugar Rautbord.—1st ed.
p.    cm.
ISBN 0-679-41387-1
I. Title.
PS3568.A827S94    1992
813'.54—dc20          92-3228

Manufactured in the United States of America

9  8  7  6  5  4  3  2

First Edition

*Book design by Richard Oriolo*

*For Virginia,*
*who finds no fault in her*
*daughters*

*For Michael,*
*who enthusiastically embraces the notion*
*that his mother is as regular*
*as apple pie*

*For Robert Clark,*
*who deserves a master's degree*
*in friendship*

*For the Tycoon who taught me*

Sweet is Revenge—especially to women.

—*Lord Byron, 1818*

In revenge and in love,
woman is more barbarous than man.

—*Friedrich Nietzsche, 1885*

Heaven has no rage like love to hatred turned,
nor hell a fury like a woman scorned.

—*William Congreve, 1700*

A woman who doesn't use perfume has no future.

—*Coco Chanel*

# ACKNOWLEDGMENTS

I wish to gratefully acknowledge the chief perfumeurs and Geoffrey Webster at Givaudan-Roure, who create some of the world's most beguiling fragrances; fashion photographer Victor Skrebneski, who renders models more beautiful and makes perfume visible in his Estée Lauder advertisements; Sgt. William Napolitano, who dissects the underbelly of New York homicides; IFAR, which analyzes art forgeries; Patricia Dey-Smith Fleming of Warrenton, Virginia, for ushering me into the private parlors of modern-day Southern Society and finding me an appropriately gentle horse on which to ride to the hounds; gentleman agent Sterling Lord; superwoman editor-in-chief of Villard, Diane Reverand; assistant and friend Karen Patterson; and Allan Grubman.

Thank you Gael Love, Diane DeWitt, Wayne Anderson, Tina Sawchyn, Cindy Lewis, Frank Zachary, David Grafton, Amy Einhorn, Maureen McMahon, Jacqueline Deval, Shelly Wanger Mortimer, William Bartholomay, Bob Zeff, Arnold Scaasi, Bob Mackie, James Galanos, Ralph Paterno of Gianni Versace, Terry Burns, William Norwich, Revlon, Kip Forbes, Peter Sharp, Bruce Leadbetter, Bill Zwecker, Ann Gerber, Maureen Smith, Gaetana Enders, Melvyn Klein, Mel Dultz, Robert Clark, and Fling!

# *Sweet* REVENGE

# PROLOGUE

*G*arcia gently dabbed at the twenty-four-year-old girl's flawless skin with a damp sponge. He deftly applied pressure to the cruel bruise under her eye and over her chiseled cheekbone. There was another smaller contusion over the full, petulant mouth. As he rapidly reached for another swab, Garcia blinked his bloodshot eyes. Even for someone who had made up stand-up comedians and fall-down drunks for *Late Night with David Letterman*, *Vogue* cover girls who had come straight from all-nighters to their photo shoots, and was rumored to have made up Imelda Marcos for her trial, this was his toughest assignment to date. He had been up almost all night, standing over the broken body of one of the most beautiful women he had ever worked on; if you were to believe the hyperbole of this week's *Time* magazine cover story, "The Most Beautiful Face in the World."

He wished he could use the new French cover-up in his makeup kit, perched on the straw mat neatly lying over a layer of sheets. Unfortunately the model's contract clearly stipulated that she be made up with only Carmen cosmetics. Garcia sighed. No sense messing with a lawsuit now. He put down his brush and examined his handiwork. The fine curve of her nose and her naturally deep set eyes did not need any shadowing. She was exquisite. He slowly moved the magnifying glass over her face and shuddered. He knew what had to be done.

The constant wail of sirens outside in the street did not deter him from his craft. He was used to working under pressure, with myriad distractions. His own brand of legerdemain, his skillful sleight of hand, made him the highest-paid makeup artist in New York, commanding eight hundred dollars an hour for his time. Now he was hard at work on his masterpiece. He wiped the sweat from his own brow with a fresh sponge, even though the room was icy. When the white-uniformed woman appeared carrying a tray of cold steel surgeon's implements, he motioned her over to the gurney. They still might want to close the cut on her forehead with a few more stitches, to conceal the deep indentation at the hairline. She had to be perfect before her public could see her. The "surgery" done, Garcia applied his finishing masterstrokes. He patted on the heavy pancake makeup to erase any final visible imperfections. Next he feathered her eyebrows with a gray pencil, brushed them up, and set them with gel so that her expression would be framed into a permanent arch of innocent expectation. At any moment he was expecting her to throw back her heavy honey-blond hair, laughing, and to hoot in her hokey Texas accent, as she always did when he made her up before a photo shoot, "Okay, darlin', make me to die for!"

He packed up his brushes and powders and proudly stood back to survey the final result. Magnificent! She looked exactly like the Carmen ad they had done together for the cellular night cream, the one that showed her sleeping in a peaceful, untroubled beauty; *their* world of make-believe and perfection. Garcia had never worked in a funeral parlor before, but the lighting at Frank E. Campbell's Funeral Home on Madison Avenue hadn't been half bad. Not bad at all. Fling would be pleased. Truman Capote had always joked that a certain ghoulish society lady had her makeup done daily by the morticians at Campbell's. Garcia had done well. Fling looked as if she were ready to step out on the runway and into the lights, dazzling the world with her thousand-karat face. She looked radiant. Just in the bloom of youth, fresh, dewy skinned, almost alive!

But she wasn't. The most beautiful girl in the world was dead. The newspapers were saying she had killed herself. He knew different.

# 1

*I*f Kingman Beddall had been a holy man, he couldn't have had loftier connections. Even now, standing deep in thought in the chairman's office of the award-winning Beddall Building, his hands clasped reverently behind him, the Manhattan midday sun throwing a filtered spotlight onto his dark-suited frame, he looked more like a man of God than a man of Mammon. The image could not have been farther from the truth. The fact that he publicly called himself a Catholic and had had a private audience with the pope, colorfully reported in the current copy of *New York* magazine lying open to the page on the vast expanse of his desk, had more to do with public relations than holy devotion. Conspicuous wealth was his religion, and New York City in the eighties had been the Gospel according to Kingman Beddall.

The popular press had been thrilled to draw attention to this enigma of a man who had meteorically eclipsed the reigning financial takeover titans and corporate raiders, taking Wall Street by storm in one colorful, greedy, yet somehow passionless sweep. The fact that he was devilishly handsome, with a full head of luxurious Irish black hair, made him even more the stuff of folklore. He was the modern J. P. Morgan, bowling other men over with his booming presence and power, playing Monopoly for real. He was John D. Rockefeller in the early days, manipulative, accumulative, and acquisitive; or Henry Ford arrogantly sailing for Europe on the *Oscar II* in an attempt to prevent the United States from fighting in World War II leaving a wife and mistress behind, or ruthlessly quashing the unions with thugs and murderers. He even owned a pair of cuff links that had once belonged to Ford. Kingman Beddall was a provenance man: if somebody rich and famous once possessed it, Kingman had to have it.

He brushed off a piece of lint from his custom-tailored Anderson & Sheppard Savile Row suit that had been magnified by a shower of twinkling sun dust pouring into his office from a huge triangular skylight. The architectonics of the Beddall Building when it was first constructed changed the New York skyline, according to the legion of critics who applauded it. Some of the Beddall collection of medieval illuminated manuscripts, displayed in vitrines of heavy burled wood and beveled glass, were further illuminated by the unimpeded sun beaming in through the arched skylight throwing strong slivers of light into the room. All the silver Cartier picture frames glittered, causing him to squint his heavily hooded slate-gray eyes. There were three picture frames on the million-dollar Ruhlmann desk, one holding a photograph of Kingman Beddall on his yacht with the president of the United States; one of the two Annes from years ago; and

Fling, a very much alive Fling in a startlingly beautiful photograph from her first Carmen advertisement. Someone had pinned a black-and-saffron ribbon onto Fling's frame in a funereal gesture of respect. Kingman lightly flicked it aside. He was annoyed by the tension her death had caused him and the havoc it had wreaked on the company. The death-defying leap off the Beddall Building by his wife, Carmen Cosmetics' model, could destroy the company, his cash cow, as quickly as her face had built it up.

The *New York Post*'s front-page headline had screamed FLING! FLUNG! SPLAT! announcing the supermodel's suicide from the roof of the Beddall Building. Only two days ago. Kingman had just arrived from the airport; all he knew was what he had read from the stack of newspapers in the limo or what he had been told by his driver. Rumors and facts were whirling in his exhausted brain. He hadn't had time to sort it out. Fling. How could she have done this to *him*? Not now. Not with the stakes so high. Two days ago he had stood on the precipice of unfathomable riches and fame. Now Fling had apparently hurled herself over the brink like a pouty human sacrifice. Fling. Whoever gave her that name at the agency apparently knew what he was doing, he fretted. It had captured the imagination of an American generation. Now it was an irony.

He glanced at her photograph. The perfectly chiseled face with the purest sky-blue eyes stared back at him, innocent, curious, sensual. He turned away. What could the girl have been thinking? He clasped his hands tighter behind his back. Was she trying to ruin the company? Was she getting even with him for leaving? He nervously ran his darkly tanned fingers through his curly hair and knitted his brow. Thank God the dog had the sense not to jump with her and had escaped from Fling's death grip just one story below the roof garden, where he had safely landed on one of the zigzagged terraces off the Beddall Building—or the Babylonian Tower, as it was called. Pit Bull had landed on all fours on a canopy, rolling into a petunia patch—Ed McNulty's petunia patch, to be exact—off Carmen's development office. Kingman pursed his lips and scooped the dog into his arms. He let out a long whistle, resigning himself to a very tough day. Today was Fling's funeral, and he was psyching himself up for the highly publicized invitation-only service at St. Patrick's Cathedral.

They were turning out in droves to the most sought after social event of the season. The funeral of the wife of the richest man in New York, who just happened to be as famous as Marilyn Monroe. Indeed, for years after, New Yorkers and aspiring models in Des Moines could tell you where they were when they heard the news that Fling, who needed only one name, had flung herself from her husband's building, the tallest building in the world, lying dead as the eighties on Fifth Avenue across the street from Bergdorf Goodman, where larger-than-life Fling! mannequins were prominently displayed in the windows.

Fling would have been thrilled. Thousands of people were already lining Fifth Avenue as if it were Macy's Thanksgiving Day Parade. Damn her. A speck of something must have gotten into his eyes, causing them to tear. He had loved her, once. He still loved her. He had just gotten tired of her, that's all. He was moving up farther in the world and needed someone more suitable for his ever-sophisticated and growing tastes. He had not meant to hurt her. The beautiful damn fool. Why hadn't she just gone to a shrink and not off the roof! He would have paid for it. Where was Dr. Corbin? He was the one who treated the two Annes! His first wife, Anne Randolph Beddall, and their daughter, Anne II, whom Kingman had always referred to as "Also," since both women in the house had the same name, had seen Corbin for years. Some sort of cockamamy Southern aristocratic custom, naming the daughter after the mother, he thought, nuzzling Pit Bull closer. Dr. Corbin, he should have treated Fling if she was crazy or depressed. He could have prescribed something, for God's sake! Lithium, Prozac, anti-PMS medicine. Corbin should have been on top of things! He paid him enough, didn't he? Kingman was fuming. Taking her own damn life and jeopardizing his prize dog as well. Blast Fling! He paced back and forth with his head bent in a prayerful pose like a high-rise Saint Francis.

She had just been too much in love with him and you do not fall in love with the Kingman Beddalls of this world. If you're smart, you marry them if they want you to, but you must always keep a distance, not entirely surrender yourself to men like him. Like Babe Paley and Jacqueline Kennedy Onassis had learned to do, Kingman thought. Didn't great men need longer leashes? Didn't great men's wives have to look the other way sometimes? Hadn't Dr. Corbin told all that to the Annes? Kingman spun around and looked at the important Impressionist painting hanging behind his desk.

"It's not my fault." He kicked at Pit Bull's rubber bone and then spit on his finger before he smoothed the smudge on his custom-made crocodile-hide shoe.

"C'mon, Pit Bull." He was pale in spite of his heavy Mediterranean tan. "We gotta go to a funeral."

In the high-tech marble-and-bronze antechamber, his secretary, Joyce Royce, pinned a black ribbon to his lapel.

"Archbishop says a big *no*. He just can't, and what with all the press . . ."

The question of an *accidental* death was a little much for the Church to deal with. J. P. Morgan might have been able to swing it, but then again, he hadn't had to deal with minicams and the six o'clock news, had he? But accident it was and accident it would be.

"But he is going to bend church law and allow the casket to be viewed like a state funeral."

Joyce marched him to his private elevator, upholstered in

burgundy leather and studded with brass buttons. He hesitated for a moment: there was the huge framed photograph of Fling—in nothing but fur and Fling! perfume—from the Carmen Fling! campaign, hanging in its proper place like nothing had happened.

"Do you want your sunglasses, Boss? It's such a beautiful day, the paparazzi are all out. I'm afraid it's going to be a real circus." She shared a sympathetic silence with him and, then, business as usual. "You're sitting in pew number one on the left," she said as efficiently as if she had told him where his scalped theater seats might be—section A, row six, seats seven and nine.

"The two Annes are supposed to be in the pew behind you, but Also doesn't know if her mother is well enough to come," she continued. "Virginia will be with her, of course. The Belzbergs are in town and this might be a good time to patch things up with them. The Solid brothers are here too." Suddenly Kingman was impressed. Gordon Solid must have flown in all the way from his Jackson Hole vacation house just for the funeral.

"I've put them with the Annes. There's no reserved seating, of course, but the ushers have been briefed to seat some of the more important mourners. McBane is coming and I've arranged for the Secret Service," she said, referring to the newly appointed secretary of state.

She was taller than he and twice as efficient. He looked up at her, startled. Apparently she had seen to everything. After all, he had been out of the country when the "accident" had taken place.

Joyce hurriedly hit the button for the third floor, where there was a small executive garage. No need to walk through the massive Philip Gladstone lobby with its sculpted arches and four fluted entrances. Even with all the Beddall security, no telling where the press would be lurking.

Joyce flipped a page on her memo pad. "Baroness von Sturm is in the pew directly across from you." She rolled her eyes. "You better be careful." Her tone was nonjudgmental. Kingman was beginning to feel a wave of anxiety overtake him. Two sleepless nights and a nonstop trip to Beaulieu-sur-Mer, in the south of France, from Tokyo and then directly home, had seemed endless. He felt as if he had been in the air for days. And now Freddie von Sturm, to boot. He was like Sisyphus pushing the rock up the never-ending hill, only to have it roll down again. He could feel his shoulders sag from the weight of his worries.

"The mayor, the Trumps, the Basses, are all in pews five, six, seven, and eight. We're doing our best to keep TV cameras out of the church. Oh, and the models: the girls have cooked up some sort of memorial ditty. They're singing one of Fling's favorite songs."

His eyes took on the look of a condemned murderer going to the gallows. She shot him a sympathetic look. She was worried. Her heart ached for Fling, who had tragically gone off the roof. Now it looked as if the stalwart Kingman Beddall might go off the deep end while a conga line of model beauties auditioned for MTV around his wife's bier.

"Steady, Boss," she said as she straightened his dark blue Hermès tie emblazoned with little coronets.

He looked feverish with dark shadows under his piercing eyes. As he ducked his head and climbed into the limousine, he was more the little boy than the mogul.

"Damn Fling," he mumbled. Joyce, laden with briefcases, followed him into the car.

"It's my fault. All my fault. I did this to her." Kingman was shaking with sudden guilt and remorse by the first stoplight. "I'm not fit to be in the same church with her. *I* should be in the box. That sweet baby. Dead!" He put his head in his hands.

"Now, King, don't." Joyce was fifty-six years old, eight years older than Kingman. "It's not entirely your fault." Her voice was maternal and soothing. His head was up like a bolt.

"You mean there was someone else? Who someone else? Who hurt Fling?"

"No, King." She patted his expensively tailored sleeve. "Not someone else. *Something* else. Fling was more complicated than even you knew."

He looked puzzled. He didn't want there to be something else. People, he could deal with people. And numbers, he was a genius at those.

"What kind of box did you get? Did you get the best coffin? A Hurlitzer. She would have liked a Hurlitzer." He put his grief somewhere else, where he wouldn't have to deal with it now.

"Yes. A bronze Hurlitzer with a black velvet lining."

"Good, good." He nervously nodded, remembering how good she looked in black. So who's going to see her in black? . . . "Is it open? The coffin's open! Oh, my God! After the fall! How could the coffin be open?"

He hadn't even seen her. His plane from Nice had arrived only two hours ago. He had spent the last four weeks shuttling back and forth between Tokyo, London, and the South of France. Jet-lagged, grief-stricken, and preoccupied, he couldn't even remember the last time he'd seen his wife's face.

"Her face is fine. Only the body . . . and Garcia's done the makeup," Joyce assured him.

"Carmen cosmetics?" the businessman asked, his grief conveniently tucked away to some other part of his brain.

"Yes, Boss," Joyce sighed. "She looks terrific." There were real tears in her eyes.

"Damn Fling! Damn this traffic," Kingman shouted as the limo moved through the Fifth Avenue gridlock of cars, much of it caused by Fling's fans and the morbidly curious. Kingman nervously peered out the window at the scene, which was on a par with the aftermath of the Yankees winning the pennant. Outside St. Patrick's Cathedral, in the sticky July heat, the press, four deep, were noisily jostling and elbowing one another, creating greater Bedlam for the funeral goers trying to make their way up the steps to the imposing Gothic edifice. The heavy bronze center doors, adorned with bas-relief saints, were swung open periodically to let in the invited. Paparazzi scampered up the lampposts like urban jungle monkeys or stood on tops of cars stuck in traffic going nowhere. The shameless blue-jeaned photographers who got paid by the picture shouted and punched just beyond the crowd-control police barricades. Human barriers were formed by policemen linking arms to form their own male fence. Finality and festivity were in the air. Cold-beer vendors and purveyors of *faux* Chanel handbags mingled with thousands of sorrowful mourners amid a cattle drive of black limousines.

"This way, Liza. Give us a smile," photographers yelled from a dozen different directions as the star tried to make her way to the vaulted church doors.

"Where's your ticket?" shouted the burly bouncers at the top of the steps to those who weren't instantly recognizable. Famous faces were never questioned. The owner of the city's hottest disco, Clyde Sangster, who had spent two years in prison for tax evasion, guilty of skimming off the top of his posh club, where Fling used to hold court in the first banquette, sipping fruit juice, was now pushed through the door along with the attorney general. All in all, it was an excellent "A" crowd: one ex-president, two ex-governors, and four ex-cons. It was highly improbable that any of these people would be gathered together under one roof for any reason other than the funeral of the world's most famous model-star married to New York's most powerful and visible businessman. No one had believed the news of Fling's death at first. It couldn't be! People grouped together, clustered in saddened silence on the street, the way a nation had done when the first rumblings of President Kennedy's assassination were broadcast piecemeal by weeping newsmen. After Fling's fall, when the incredulous had made positively certain she was dead, that she couldn't be revived or repaired, they hurried away to call their friends, who wouldn't believe it either until they saw it for themselves on CNN or read it in *The New York Times*.

Now Wall Street's brightest brokers were crowding into the cathedral, converting it into an active stock market in the aisles. Rumor mills were whirling. The high-society columnist Suki was saying Fling's death symbolized the end of the eighties.

An all-seeing photographer from *Women's Wear Daily* who had surreptitiously sneaked in seated himself in the third pew to record the solemn-looking social brigade. The socials were not auditioning like the leggy models, so they did not have to look both bereaved and beautiful. The politicians looked serious but not depressed—no telling where these pictures might turn up in an election year—and many of them waved and smiled. When the mayor walked in with the architect Philip Gladstone, the crowd outside broke into polite funereal applause. *Time* was covering. The Forbes brothers were seated in the fourth row. The tweed-clothed cub reporter from *The Economist* was squeezed in next to the colorfully Versace costumed editor of *Rolling Stone*. Of course, the whole extravagant procedure was being featured in this week's *OBIT* magazine, the country's hottest new periodical for the nineties. The sleeping-Fling picture from the cellular night cream ad graced the cover of Time-Life's newly launched magazine *OBIT*, the hot new publication that colorfully chronicled the newsworthy who had died since the last issue published bimonthly.

Joyce Royce had done her job well. As Kingman Beddall's private secretary, she had made the arrangements, consulted with Kingman's "women," and made out the guest list for the saddest social event of the summer. She had even persuaded Sirio, the owner of New York's posh Le Cirque restaurant, to man the church door, seating some of the more important guests as he had done at Malcolm Forbes's funeral. Joyce Royce and Gael Joseph, president of Carmen Cosmetics, had actually become friendly these days, both of them committed to the "Carmen Cover-Up," as it would later be called.

Joyce turned to Kingman. "I think it might be better if we went in the side door, don't you?" She instructed the driver to the Fifty-first Street entrance as Kingman sat in stunned silence.

"What the hell are these people doing here?" He hadn't seen Fling in over a month. Had she been busy signing up half of New York to come to her funeral in case she fell off the roof? He lowered the window an inch to let some of the pandemonium in. The city was alive with the excitement of the news of Fling's death.

"What a shame," he heard. "What an absolute utter shame" that Fling was dead at twenty-four years old. How could that be? She was so famous, she had to be thirty. Dead. Either self-propelled or accidentally fallen from the top of the Beddall Building. The rumors flew through the steamy streets. Fling had jumped off the roof of the building on the Fourth of July with her husband's pit bull terrier in her arms, and a suicide note pinned to her sweater as if she were a little girl coming home from kindergarten, they said. Pit Bull, Kingman's favorite dog, had panicked upon their descent. Using all his might to free himself from Fling's desperate clutch, the dog had landed on a canopy over a balcony only one floor below the roof garden. Kingman had always bragged that Pit Bull could tear out a cow's throat and had the strongest jaws of any animal four times his size. And poor Fling, going over the edge in despair, plummeting in a drugged cloud of sadness, was no match for the survival instincts of a dog bred for fighting.

Kingman picked up his dog from the glove-soft leather car seats, the very dog that had been profiled on *60 Minutes* when the borough of Manhattan had tried to outlaw the breed on the grounds that they were dangerous and vicious. The very same Pit

Bull that had been the focus of an entire *Lifestyles of the Rich and Famous* segment when Kingman Beddall and his beautiful wife, Fling, had cruised into New York Harbor after their honeymoon on their 260-foot yacht, the *Pit Bull*, with the new cigarette racing boats, christened the *Bullshit I* and *II*, moored to its side. The newlyweds had happily posed for the cameras straddling their matching Harley-Davidsons, secured to the upper deck, the photogenic dog between them.

At the Fifty-first Street entrance to the church, Kingman Beddall bolted out of the car and up the stairs, not a hair out of place, his pocket handkerchief pressed into three perfect points, and Pit Bull cowering under his arm. His Ray-Ban sunglasses were shoved into his pocket. He had nothing to hide. Kingman's cold gray eyes were so narrowed, they were only small slits under his dark bushy brows. With eyes that narrow, no one could really tell where he was looking or what he was thinking, a trick that had served him well in warlike negotiations. The sprig of jasmine Joyce had placed into his lapel with the black silk ribbon was suddenly yanked off by two lanky teenage models standing at the side entrance of the church like a pair of stage-door johnnies.

"I heard she was murdered. Murdered and pushed," the taller one said to the thinner one, twirling the jasmine in her fingers like a prize souvenir.

"I know. My makeup man said there were strangle marks on her throat, and her hands had been tied behind her back. They had to use a lot of Carmen cosmetics to cover that up . . . took 'em all night." She stretched her reed-thin neck up from her black spandex top and cracked her Trident gum.

"No way the prettiest, richest girl in the world would kill herself. What for?"

Inside the church the air was filled with heavy incense billowing up from two thuribles at either side of the altar, mingling with the heavier scents of Joy, Giorgio, and Fling! The guests, who were not in grief, were nonetheless in a heady, ethereal state induced by a rich combination of scents, aromas, and perfumes inside the stone-cooled cathedral on Fifth Avenue. A blaze of flickering votive candles gave the church a shimmering, surreal aura.

"I won't have it! I simply won't have it! Unheard of!" the Baroness von Sturm, throwing back her mourning veil, shrieked like a coutured harpy at Gael Joseph and Garcia. They were huddled in the Lady Chapel, just behind the High Altar, out of sight but not entirely out of earshot of most of the mourners. The Baroness was furious with her two old friends. How dare they display Fling like a Carmen commercial in church! An open casket in the cathedral! What was Gael trying to do, boost sales?

Even in this sea of models, Fredericka von Sturm stood out with her ramrod posture and European elegance, in a tall black Christian Lacroix hat, puce suede gloves, and a black satin-lapeled riding suit adorned only with the famous Von Sturm emerald, in its platinum winged-eagle setting. The epitome of nobility was shouting and gesticulating in the back chapel while her dearest friend in the world lay in an open Hurlitzer set on an extravagantly floral covered bier in front of the massive cathedral's sacrosanct apse, aglow in candlelight. Others were so busy gawking and appraising the pew directly in front or back of them, bedecked with bunches of ylang-ylang and jasmine (the floral ingredients of the fragrance Fling!), they barely noticed the Queen of European Society—the double entrendre title that Suki had bestowed upon her—stomping her feet in some sort of ritual dance. In the first pew, where the Beddall women were gathered, Anne II poked her grandmother to whisper in her refined ear that on the rarefied ski slopes of St. Moritz, Fredericka was referred to simply as the Baroness Sturm und Drang, in recognition of her legendary fits of high drama.

Garcia, his comb and makeup brush jutting out of his Armani jacket pocket, quietly stared defensively through the pillars at his masterpiece.

"She is now beautiful for eternity. Let them all see. They'll remember her final exquisite grace forever." He shuddered, still horrified at the *Daily Sun*'s blurred but burning images of a broken and bloodied Fling splattered all over the front page.

Baroness Fredericka von Sturm, designated keeper of Fling's flame, was apoplectic. "Are you mad? Nobody displays an open casket in church!" Tears rolled down her pale sculpted cheeks.

"You're bringing out a new fragrance, aren't you, Gael? 'Ghost!' I'll bet." The Baroness's hands were on her slim hips.

"You're selling her out, aren't you?" In her rage she nonetheless spied Calvin Klein swaggering down the nave. "Ah ha!" Her finger pointed to the creator of Eternity perfume. "You're going to do an ad campaign to compete with Eternity!" She whirled around in demonic rage.

Gael was the voice of reason. She adored Fling but she wasn't about to let Carmen Cosmetics go down the drain and into the grave. She was giving Fling a send off the only way she knew how.

"She looks fabulous. Terrific. She was the most visible woman in the world and she would have *wanted* her public to see her in death." Gael gazed lovingly at Fling. Over the years, the rough-talking head of Carmen had grown to care and be protective of the guileless Fling. She thought Fling looked like a young Grace Kelly with her golden hair swept up and pulled away from her face, her head gently resting on the small black satin pillow.

"This is not a public mourning. This is a vulgar, anonymous media circus." Fredericka was wild with grief. "Close this coffin! Close it and nail it shut!" Her lashes were so heavy that the tears hung onto them like slowly falling syrup.

Gael held her ground. She wasn't about to be intimidated.

She remembered Baroness Fredericka von Sturm when she was just plain old Fred.

Their rising voices caught the attention of the hard-nosed press surreptitiously sitting on the edges of the middle pews, who picked up their pens to take notes. Most of the Baroness's diatribe was drowned out by the gaggle of girls whose telephone numbers were listed only in Eileen Ford's private directory, or Elite's or Zoli's top-model lists. The models were making little sounds like children crying, Carmen mascara streaking down their collectively high cheekbones, sobs shaking their tall, willowy bodies.

The lid and base of the coffin were festooned with a blanket of white roses, baby's breath, and queen's tears, while the voices in front of it were escalating to such a degree that those respectable and high-powered businessmen lined up to give eulogies were afraid that they might be pulled into some sort of burial brawl. The sibilant echoes of the Baroness's voice were finally drowned out when the Greater Manhattan All Boys Choir suddenly rose to life at the direction of a tactically clever archbishop.

Sergeant Buffalo Marchetti of the New York Police Department carefully scrutinized Kingman Beddall as the tycoon loped down the side aisle to attend his wife's funeral as if he were coming in late to the theater, scurrying to his seat before the lights went down and the play began. Suddenly, all eyes were upon him, especially Sergeant Marchetti's, as he went to take his seat, hesitantly changed his mind, and then strode up to the casket with the dog strutting freely at his side. Kingman poked his handsome head deep into the coffin until he was almost nose to nose with Fling. There was no smell of death on her. The crowd was evidently too big for Campbell's to handle, so the viewing was smack-dab in St. Patrick's, along with his final farewell. He peered at his wife's perfect features. How could anything so beautiful be dead? Even after the fall, her beauty was intact; cheekbones high, perfect nose presiding over perfect lips, the poreless complexion creamy even in the pallor of death. He wanted to touch her again, shield her from this cheap sideshow. He lightly grazed her cheek with his hand, quickly pulling it back.

"She's ice cold!" he whispered accusingly to Joyce over his shoulder, as if he had just realized she was really dead. He looked bereft, and Joyce thought for one frantic moment he would do something crazy. But when he finally straightened himself and turned to face the congregation, his demeanor was one of perfect composure. Sergeant Marchetti studied his face. Kingman was clearly in charge. The business moguls, corporate chiefs, and captains of industry now knew why they were here: they were here to pay tribute to the financial success of one of their own. Most of them sat on one another's boards. It would have been bad business, as well as bad etiquette, not to pay their respects. The church was reverentially hushed at last. The crowd in the street stopped its uproar.

Everyone strained to get a look at Kingman Beddall. He was the real star now, and beautiful Fling just an extraordinary stage prop, except to all the millions of young women who worshiped and emulated her. Joyce had been worrying for two days that if they didn't quell the suicide rumors, young girls would be flinging themselves from roofs in droves all over the country, in a whiff of Fling! perfume, just as they had emulated the model's every move in life. A whole nation of teenage girls in Fling! perfume, Fling! sweaters, and Fling! scarves, flinging themselves off roofs in united grief. Joyce watched, pained, as her usually cocky boss faltered and looked to her for direction. Kingman finally took a seat.

"Close the coffin," he whispered to Joyce in a voice breaking with emotion. "I want the damn thing shut!"

# 2

*S O H O*

*A U T U M N 1 9 8 9*

he scent of success had come to Fling in the shape of a frosted crystal bottle she could hold in her hand. She slowly pulled the stopper and applied it lightly to the insides of her elbows, the pulse points at her wrists, behind her knees, and in the crevice of her full, young bosom—just as she had been instructed by the chief perfumer at Carmen Cosmetics. Sensual. The fragrance was decidedly sensual, she thought laughing, just like a narcotic. She tucked her nose into the bend of her elbow for the fiftieth time that day.

The top note of Fling! was bergamot—as fresh and green as the girl. Like mad musicians working with absolute pitch, the perfumers had added jasmine, ylang-ylang, and orris to the middle note. The powdery base note, the lingering note, included myrrh, amber, vetiver, and olibanum. These exotic spices, oils, and floral components were the major ingredients of the fragrance, her very own fragrance, which came in a saffron box and carried her name. She was so excited she could barely catch her breath.

At twenty-one, Fling was so much the girl of the moment that many designers had created a "Fling" gown for each of their fall collections—a ball gown reserved for the finale of the fashion show, when a fantasy gown inspired by a fantasy girl would leave the audience of buyers, reporters, and society women awestruck. A girl who could take them off the runways and into their imaginations. A girl who could open doors just by the way she moved her hips. A model who could sell organdy and cotton and tweed and twill the way bond traders sold futures. "The new Bardot," *Women's Wear* said; "the next Deneuve," *Vogue* enthused; "an original," *Elle* prophesied.

It wasn't just that she was prettier than any of the other girls. Pretty was everywhere and, as Frederick well knew, what you weren't born with you could buy, including his own magical services. No, it was what was behind the eyes: the trust, the joy, the excitement for living that she gave to everyone around her. True, the tilt of her chin was square and strong, giving her a fearless look, even though she was really very shy. The nose was tinier than a nose should be. The tip pointed up exquisitely and was distinguished by a perfectly placed indentation, as if an angel had marked her for something special. The cheekbones were so high and full, they made her face three-dimensional even in the hands of an inferior photographer. In fact, that was one of the reasons the photographers adored her: Fling made *them* look good! They loved her, too, for her promptness, and the cheerful thank-you notes she took the time to write with her third-grade spelling. Her skin glowed with good health. She never suffered the effects of a cocaine hangover, because she was drug free, and didn't use coke to keep her weight down the way some models did.

Fling was the model for the nineties. Even with her full lips, big breasts, and strong shoulders, she carried herself like the least pretty girl in the class, who compensated by being overly nice and overly friendly. In fact, she'd been considered ugly in grammar school in Corpus Christi—too tall, too big bosomed, with lips so dramatically full she'd grown into them like an older sister's hand-me-downs. The highest point of her voluptuous mouth would have collided with her nose if the tip hadn't pointed up so dramatically. And the legs, legs so ridiculously long and narrowly tapered that if she'd had two more, she could have qualified for the Kentucky Derby. Easily!

Fling pranced over to Frederick and hugged him. "Imagine me, Sue Ellen Montgomery, a good ole Texas girl, signing a one-million-dollar contract for a Carmen ad! For my own fragrance, Fling!" She flung off her towel, fresh from a shower, and stood naked, her exquisite body posed for the Hasselblad of Victor Skrebneski or, now with her hip thrown out and one arm shot up, for the lens of Scavullo.

"I'm going to be a *real* model! I'm even going to be able to pay the rent," she laughed, posing with the bottle in her hand.

"Oh, God." Frederick threw the towel back at her. "And I can say I knew you when. I'm afraid wet hair and no maquillage is not the look we're going for tonight, Miss Fling. Somehow or other, with alchemy from my bag of tricks, you're going to shine in a roomful of stars." As if she needs my help, he thought. He lightly patted her poreless skin with Carmen Cosmetics' No. 1 Very Light Liquid Matte Makeup, and took a swig from the Roederer Cristal champagne bottle lying open amid the clutter of hair sprays and wet makeup sponges.

"Let's call Kingman." She impulsively reached for the phone.

"Not now, luscious. We've got a hundred things to do," he sniffed.

Frederick adored Fling. "The Looker," Rusty the head booker at Ford Models had called her before hitting upon her trade name. Frederick and Fling were like silly sisters together, but he also felt protective of her. She thought everyone was nice and well meaning. She never saw the evil in anyone, as he could. Being uncomplicated was part of her charm, he guessed. And now, at twenty-one, she was under the spell of Wall Street's toughest new takeover titan, *a very married tycoon* who was giving Fling a fragrance the way other rich men might give their girlfriend a bracelet or an apartment. Only, a fragrance was a tax write-off for him as a company expenditure. Or a potential source of profit.

Frederick held the receiver away from her in vain. She grabbed the phone to dial the number Kingman Beddall, the new owner and chairman of the privately held Carmen Corporation, had just installed for her in his cigar drawer. Frederick hated Beddall. Just didn't trust him. He was married to one of the most genteel society women in New York and supposedly had a brassy mistress on the side. What did he want with this beautiful, naive child?

"Straight men." He groaned and reached for a sponge. "We'll call him later."

"Oh, okay."

Fling couldn't believe her luck. Her own fragrance, her own ball, a million-dollar-contract, and now she had her own hot line to power and love. She loudly sang the first few bars from "The Yellow Rose of Texas," at least the parts she could remember—off-key.

"I want to dress for Kingman tonight. Which of these do you think he'll like the best?" The towel was off again and she was heading for the designer dresses, costing upwards of ten thousand dollars, casually strewn around the tiny walk-up apartment. Gowns borrowed from the showrooms of the designers Bill Blass, Bob Mackie, Carolyne Roehm, and Oscar de la Renta, to wear in front of the photographers' lenses tonight. Tonight, when she would walk down the runway alone as the Carmen girl, like a bride walking down the aisle to meet her groom; only *he* would be standing at the end of her walk to meet her for all the world to see. Publicly, it was all right. He was her boss, the owner of Carmen Cosmetics. Privately, he was her lover. When she took her long walk down the runway, with the pop of flashbulbs all around her, in a sea of human faces, she would be walking down a long illuminated aisle only to *him*, seeing only *his* face at the end of a tunnel of people.

Frederick gently folded a terry-cloth robe over the lithe nakedness of the daydreaming young girl. She was no match for Kingman's excessively cultivated charms. "You can undress for him later. Get over here. I've got an idea." Of the two of them, Frederick was the intellectual giant. "Tonight's the main event. This perfume's being launched at a *society* fund-raiser, right?"

Fling was sitting perfectly still as he pulled the damp sponge over the makeup. "Lots of understated elegance, black dresses, old-money ball gowns, inherited jewels, right?"

She could only nod. Now she was all one color, a blank slate, a tabula rasa, on which he could create any persona. Only her eyes, those pale-blue limpid eyes, could shine back at him from the contourless, one-color face he had just painted as if he, the artist, had just primed his empty canvas. He considered himself the Monet of makeup, the De Resnais of the human face.

"The point is for *you* to stand out. This is a major media event: *The New York Times*, *Women's Wear Daily*, *Town & Country*, CNN, and hundreds of other beautiful women."

"Uh huh." Fling gently fingered the card with the now familiar double-*C* logo that had accompanied the giant yellow basket brimming over with hothouse jonquils and new bottles of the fragrance that bore her name. The soon to be unveiled bottles of Fling! perfume, cologne, eau de parfum, and dusting powder. A saffron sash ran around the basket rim, the same saffron yellow that marked the packaging and bottle caps on the less expensive Fling! bath splash.

*"For my darling Fling! Tonight is our night. Love, King."* She read and reread the note as if it held a secret message only she could decipher. She felt a warm rush wash over her. He made love to her with such patience, such sensitivity, never hurrying to his own pleasure, unlike the few teenagers she'd known in Corpus Christi who'd hurried her through like they had only ten minutes before the Tastee Freez closed.

She looked up. Staring back at her in the mirror was the funniest face imaginable. Frederick was highlighting her features with (don't tell Carmen Cosmetics) William Tuttle's creamy cover, which he had streaked across her face with a fine sable brush, down the side of her nose, under her eyes, across the bottom of her cheeks, and used to define the natural lines that marked the small hollow between her nose and lips. In fact, what he was doing was emphasizing and exaggerating her features so that her astonishing beauty, perfect from five feet away, would become dazzling at fifty yards and more visible to a paparazzo's camera. At this point, however, she was just an Apache war bride run amuck.

"If understatement is tonight's theme, why not go against the crowd? It *is* the launch of a revolutionary fragrance. If *you* blend in with the other women, why should the department-store buyers and Mrs. Average America think your fragrance would be different from all the other stuff on the counter?"

Fling was all ears. Somewhere there was a lesson to be learned and, as she was fond of saying about herself, she might be dumb but she wasn't stupid! She watched intently as Frederick dusted a handful of baby powder over her entire face to hold the cool of a matte look over a long hot evening under the lights.

"So," he pronounced as if he had just solved a Charlie Chan murder mystery, "if the fragrance is an extension of you, then you simply must go as an extension of the fragrance!"

What was he telling her? To go as a bottle of perfume? Perhaps like a Las Vegas cigarette girl—a bottle with legs! Or maybe with just a big saffron bow around her neck! No, *everybody* was getting all dressed up. Women had been planning their gowns for weeks. There wasn't an idle hairdresser on the Upper East Side of New York at this very moment. People were desperate to be invited to Carmen's spectacular Fling! Ball tonight. The waiting list was as long as the guest list.

She glanced over at the uncorked magnum of Roederer Cristal champagne Kingman had sent over, which they had been swigging from all afternoon as if it were San Pellegrino water on one of their regular shoots. Maybe Freddie was smashed. Oh God, what would he do to her face? The way he was sculpting her cheekbones with the deep brown powder, Fling thought she was beginning to look like an anorectic chipmunk. A little wrinkle crossed her perfect brow.

"Are you suggesting I wear nothing but me and my fragrance?" She pushed out her lip in a pout as she picked up the phone and dialed 555–1989. Perhaps she should wash her face and start over. Was he going to freak out on her tonight of all nights?

"Kingman!" She waved Frederick and his brushes away. "My beautiful Kingman. I'm so excited about tonight." She blushed right through a quarter inch of pancake makeup in her unbridled enthusiasm. "Frederick wants me to go naked except for a stopper as a hat. What do you think?" She threw back her honey-blond hair and laughed. "Of course, you're right, sweetie." Her voice got softer and huskier. "There *would* be less to take off.

Kingman, I love you . . . not because of this . . . because of *you*."
Her eyes started to fill.

"If you cry and streak your makeup, Fling, I'm gonna kill
you!" Frederick warned.

She covered the mouthpiece of the phone with her hand and
whispered into it, "I can't wait either," and shyly moved away
from Frederick as if he hadn't seen her naked twice today and
wasn't privy to every detail of her intimate relationship with Kingman Beddall, the incidentally very married Kingman Beddall.

She settled back into her chair, laughing, and threw out her
arms. "Okay, darlin', make me to die for!"

"Good. Trust me, luscious. I've got an inspiration." Frederick kicked dresses and shoes aside as he commandeered the
phone.

Cinderella couldn't have had a more creative fairy godmother. Frederick frantically instigated a flurry of activity, turning pumpkins into carriages and making footmen out of mice.
Every jeweler for whom he had styled ads was summoned and
bolts of fabric were hurriedly purloined from the Plaza, where
saffron satin slipcovers were still being made for the chairs and
the tablecloths, heavily swagged and bowed for tonight's dinner.
The Siamese seamstress from downstairs was pressed into service, the expensive designer dresses abandoned and shoved into
a corner.

Fling was content to daydream during all the hubbub, as
people waved their wands at her. For the rest of the afternoon,
every brain cell in her head was concentrated on Kingman Beddall, how they would launch their perfume tonight and how they
would celebrate, alone, afterward. If she closed her eyes, she
could conjure up his own wonderfully masculine smell. She barely
moved as the seamstress hand-sewed the saffron satin directly
onto her, molding and cupping it to her perfect body, leaving her
swan's back as bare as possible to show off her tapered waist. Her

excitement was so great, she didn't even breathe when two armed guards and the manager of Harry Winston brought over something called the Yellow Star of India and fastened it around her neck. She whispered, "Thank you all so much!" and she held her breath as Frederick feathered her eyebrows with a gray pencil, brushed them up, and then set them with gel so that her expression would be framed into an arch of wide-eyed expectation, her trademark. Now she knew what she was anticipating: the love of Kingman Beddall. The look of pride in his eyes that would let her know she had done just fine. Escape from a childhood of poverty. Her own success. Her very own fragrance. She shivered and caught her shimmering reflection in the mirror. The mirror didn't throw back the single small worry line in her forehead. She was escaping the world of uncertainty and unpaid bills for sure, but she hoped he wasn't letting her into his castle just to view the roped-off furniture. She wanted to stay in his world forever. Cinderella at the ball for one night was all right for fairy tales, she told Frederick. "Cinderella" was their favorite story.

"Don't worry, honey. We'll get you a condominium at the castle!" he promised.

Beauty, which since time immemorial has been a passport over social borders, was hurling Fling headlong into the spotlight, into the fast lane, and into the arms of billionaire Kingman Beddall. The illegitimate daughter of a waitress from Corpus Christi was on her way.

Propped up in bed with a pride of Pratesi pillows, Anne Randolph Beddall was hard at work. Strewn over the bed were a dozen seating charts for tonight's gala. Smythson of Bond Street sold the hunter-green leather cases that held round, square, or rectangular charts for the hostess who took her entertaining seriously. They could be found in almost every embassy, where dining was a diplomatic art. The benefit she and her husband,

Kingman, were hosting tonight for the New York Historical Society at the Plaza and which was underwritten by Carmen Cosmetics, was using round tables. She inserted two more cards for her own table. The company PR man had just called to insist The Model be seated with the chairman and his wife, and that meant Anne had to find a suitable extra man ASAP. If her instincts and fears about this girl were correct, then it would be in her best interest to find an attractive eligible bachelor. She closed her dark eyes and involuntarily inhaled the intoxicating male odor of her husband's body on the pillows and sheets enveloping her. The feminine green and white ribbon patterned sheets of the finest cotton held his familiar smell of musk and Cuban cigars. She spun her Rolodex around to "Bachelors," hoping it was up to date. She could always turn to *E* for "Escorts," with its much fatter file, for names of the usual walkers and perennially extra men; but she was looking for someone with a normal sexual appetite. In New York! She let out a ladylike groan. She wished she'd had a file under *W* for "Womanizers," as this baby-faced model was obviously in need of a hormonally straight man so she wouldn't constantly be sniffing around her husband, Kingman. He could be so cold to her, his own wife, sometimes. So, so hurtful. He made Rhett Butler look like . . . oh, well, wasn't the Rhett Butler myth the hero every good Southern girl was brought up on?

What could Kingman have been thinking to cull together people who wouldn't ordinarily give one another shelter from the rain? Store buyers from Brooklyn and models, with Rockefellers, Van Rensselaers, and Randolphs at a ten-thousand-dollar-a-table fund-raiser to launch Carmen's new commercial perfume with the vulgar name of Fling!

She was as jittery as an Abyssinian cat. She nervously reached for the teacup on her breakfast tray, accidentally tipping it over and staining the embroidered monogram of her coverlet.

"Oh, heavens!" She pushed back the tray and glanced at the antique Tiffany clock. It was three o'clock already. She rang for the maid and pulled herself out of bed. She had to be at the Plaza by five-thirty to attend to last-minute details. It looked as if she would just make it from her nightgown to her ball gown . . . again. She sighed. Life was getting ahead of her. She couldn't seem to catch up.

The room was still darkened. The heavy floral chintz draperies hadn't been drawn today. Somehow, she didn't feel like letting the world in just yet. The room was fragrant with fresh jasmine and hyacinth arranged in antique Oriental Lowestoft bowls inherited from her grandmother, Virginia Harrison Byrd.

If you closed your eyes or kept out the view of New York, you could imagine the room was at Boxwood, her mother's home, just outside Richmond, Virginia. Try as she would, she was never able to turn their Sutton Place apartment into a gracious home like those in her beloved South. A genteel, slower-paced South, where men hunted foxes and quail and not one another. A place perfectly suited to her temperament and what Kingman referred to as her "Southern genes." She adjusted the rheostat of the Waterford crystal chandelier to a more flattering glow, gracefully moving to her dressing table, skirted in an elaborate floral chintz, and poured herself a glass of bourbon, neat. How lovely it had been when they first lived at Boxwood, in familiar territory. Dinner at the Richmond Country Club, picnics on the James River Plantation under the dogwood. That was before Kingman had gotten rich, very rich, and New York had become his new stalking ground. He had less time now than ever for her and their daughter, Anne II, whom he had annoyingly dubbed Also. Well, maybe it was time to admit her mother was right: You couldn't turn a sow's ear into a Judith Leiber evening bag.

"And you, Kingman. You, sir, are no gentleman," she said

aloud to his photograph, in which he wore his hunting clothes. For heaven's sake, gentlemen's hunting clothes for fox hunting on Tennessee Walker and Arabian horses, when he had never even mastered sitting on a horse properly. The horses had longer bloodlines than Kingman. Sometimes it crossed her mind that after all these years of marriage, she had never met a real "blood" Beddall other than, well . . .

She dropped the hairbrush from her hand. She couldn't seem to hang on to anything these days. "Why can't those girls remember to polish the little Georgian spoons?" Anne bemoaned, her doe eyes widening. "Isn't life difficult enough without having *little* things to worry about?" She rearranged some of the antique Victorian crystal jars with the silver repoussé lids that held her various cosmetics. The spoons were used to avoid introducing bacteria into the creams. Just because Kingman bought Carmen Cosmetics eleven months ago didn't mean that she had to forego her La Prairie and Elizabeth Arden. She had always removed the creams from their original containers anyway—such cheap, unattractive jars they used. They made a lady's dressing table look like the counter at Macy's. She quickly surveyed the silver monogrammed hairbrushes, Victorian buttonhook, and clothes brushes neatly lined up on her vanity. Everything was in order.

Anne swirled the bourbon in her glass for a moment before she peered closely into the magnifying mirror, the one she'd needed ever since her fortieth birthday so that she could get her mascara on straight.

Between little sips of bourbon and light applications of Carmen's wrinkle tightening cream to the area around her eyes, she fielded phone calls from Joyce, her husband's longtime secretary, as well as from the director of the New York Historical Society, which she now jokingly referred to as the New York *Hysterical* Society. After working on this gala she certainly qualified to belong, she nervously laughed. Half-heartedly, she was trying to handle the peculiar crises that arise when mixing the city's top business moguls with old-guard Invisible Society in some sort of public promotional stunt.

As usual, Kingman had relied on *her* impeccable social credentials to lure descendants of New York's first families to mingle with the retail element, all to pay homage to a low IQ model and help increase the net worth of her husband's coffers.

"What a good egg you are," Anne Randolph Beddall said out loud to the mirror in her most dulcet, aristocratic accent. Reaching for the bottle of Virginia Gentleman under the ruffled skirts of her dressing table, she poured herself a generous refill. She pulled her lustrous auburn hair back into an elegant chignon, smoothing the few stray hairs into place with her fragile fingertips.

With her small-boned frame and flat chest, she was a couturier's dream. If she had been interested in fashion, she possibly could have been an internationally renowned clotheshorse. Her slight figure hadn't altered at all, not even after the birth of their daughter. She could still fit into the dress she had worn when she "came out" at the debutante balls on the Southern social circuit—Richmond, Charlottesville, Atlanta, and Charleston. She'd been asked to debut at the New York Cotillion as well but her mother and grandmother had snubbed the invitation in favor of the International Debutantes' Ball in London. The sweet, snobbish Anglophiles. A slight smile crossed her lips as she remembered. She smoothed her hands down her sleek body. She was one of the few women she knew who had the option of wearing something over twenty years old *and* wearing it well!

The black Galanos, she decided, and reached into her heavily sacheted closet. She would wear the eight-year-old black Galanos with her grandmother's Victorian diamond-and-pearl choker. Ancestors always gave her an air of confidence. Model girls couldn't buy those, she assured herself. She nervously shot a look at the rose jade clock.

Just where was Kingman? If he didn't arrive soon she would have to go alone or with Mother and the chauffeur, and only this morning he'd promised to escort her and stand by her side in the receiving line. "Count on it," he had said. She had an idea: she'd recruit her daughter, she'd be home from school soon; put her in the brown velvet with the lace collar, and seat her at their table— next to The Model. Yes. Kingman and Anne's daughter seated right next to the flibbertigibbet model girl. Anne II couldn't be more than five years younger than Fling, but their life-styles were a universe apart, with at least thirty pounds difference between them. Anne II, bless her heart, had put on such weight at Brearley. If Kingman couldn't get back in time, maybe she would recruit Uncle Byrdie to take them both. Governor Byrd Harrison of Virginia would be seated on her right at dinner, anyway. She picked up the phone on her dressing table and dialed 555–1989, the private line Kingman kept tucked away in his cigar drawer— the one he kept for her calls alone. There was no answer. She sprayed the Galanos-filled antique crystal atomizer over her head, letting just a hint of the luxurious perfumed mist fall over her. Too much fragrance was vulgar, she'd been taught at finishing school. She must stay cool. Appearances were everything. Why did she get so unnerved? Why wasn't she stronger or even New York tough? She was a Southern gentlewoman, that's why. And that was what Kingman admired and expected in her. She sighed and then resumed her traditional St. Catherine's School posture. Thank God she had an appointment with Dr. Corbin tomorrow.

The maid was coming. She could hear her rubber-soled shoes squeaking on the bare oak floor that separated the spaces between the scattered Savonnerie rugs. Anne Randolph Beddall, the former Southern belle, flipped her magnifying mirror over to the normal side and asked the mirror aloud, "If Scarlett O'Hara had reached the age of forty, would she be going to fancy-dress balls by herself?"

The woman tottered down the darkened hallway on her stiletto heels. She was listening for the doorbell to ring any second. He was always prompt. The soft dusky twilight of a New York autumn partially lit her body through the lavender Levolor blinds. She was half hidden in shadow as she opened the door to him after the first ring. He wasn't the kind of man you kept waiting. She shut the door when he stepped in, and stood there in the half light of the hall to catch his mood. Her antennae sensed "tough." Tough and dark and tense. So now she knew. She bent over to adjust the rubber catch of the garter belt holding up her black silken stocking. She guessed his mood and dressed for it. She accidentally snagged a run in her stocking as she caught it on a long frosted fingernail. He watched as the run slowly spread down her thigh. They locked eyes for an instant. His, slate gray and so narrowed they were only small slits under dark bushy brows. Hers were pretty and blue, but slightly darkened with fatigue and etched with fine lines. With her brassy bleached hair, turquoise eyeliner, and inch-long fingernails, she wasn't the kind of woman you'd have to talk to about Mozart's operas or Balanchine's ballets. She was pure sex, and she was very good at it. Their response to each other was Pavlovian. A spontaneous gesture from her could arouse an instant erection in him. She was one of the few people with whom he could actually perform. It had even gotten to the point that when he wanted to make love to another woman—in a normal fashion—he would have to come to her first, both for the arousal and because she took the edge off, exorcised him of his demons. When she expertly sucked the juices out of him, it was as if she sucked some of the malice from him too. At five-fifteen, when other men headed for their sports club with their squash racquets, he often headed uptown to her. She was always ready, always subservient, and always welcomely wet. But that's what women like her were for. There were no emotions, courtesies, nor expectations to deal with. He watched her waiting for him to make the first move, shivering in her black lace bustier partially exposing her large rosy nipples. He grabbed her wrist and pulled her hand onto his zipper.

"Make me come," he ordered. Still in the shadowy hallway, she obediently fell to her knees and touched him with her deft fingers, her tongue darting through the tangle of hair at his crotch. And with the knowing expertise of familiarity, she brought him to the brink of climax. He roughly pushed her head away and walked into the bedroom.

"Sit here." He motioned to the open-slatted chair. The white-lacquered chair was turned away from him. She quickly sat down on it, her back to him. "The other way, facing me. I want to see, white trash."

She knew what he wanted. She always knew what he wanted. Her pouty mouth curled up in a half smile.

"The pants, take off the pants, you whore."

She slipped the pants over her silk stockings and straddled the chair, facing him clad only in her bustier and garters.

"Show me your sex. I want to see. Open wider, you sleazy slut." She opened her legs as wide as possible, slowly thrusting her pelvis toward the bed, where he was lying half naked. She hadn't seen him this aroused in a long time. She lowered her eyelids to half-mast and gently parted her sex with her fingers. She knew she was glistening.

"Show me. Show me everything." He was straining every muscle in his body.

"Okay, okay, trailer trash. Filthy carnival trash!" she

screamed at him. It was her turn now. She knew her part. "You filthy, lying, no-good carny man. Nobody'd want you. Nobody wants Carney Eball, you worthless redneck."

His face was contorted in pain. She had to hurry. "I'll fix you, dumb fuck." Timing was everything. She was on him in a minute, her legs straddling him, clutching him inside of her until he cried out louder and with more anger than any man she'd ever known. When his breathing returned to normal, he brusquely touched her hair and closed his eyes again.

After he was showered and dressed, she helped him arrange his pocket handkerchief into three perfect points. She smoothed his soft curly hair and folded his Hermès tie with the coronets into a Windsor knot with her skillful fingers. He kissed them coldly, the first kiss that had passed between them.

"Thanks, Tandy. I'm running late. Big night tonight. We're launching the new fragrance at the Plaza. Fling!" He grinned. "Plenty of fireworks. We're going to wow all the big mucky-mucks. Got anybody who's anybody coming. You can read about it tomorrow." He winked at her.

"Yeah." She felt an unwanted anger rising. "I can *read* about it in Suki's column."

"All those hotshot bastards who wouldn't have given me the time of day last year, coming to launch *my* perfume Fling!" He *pinged* his finger against a copper pot, a look of boyish mischief crossing his face. As he turned to leave, he felt an unfriendly twinge in his chest. He dismissed it as the recurrence of an old injury he'd incurred during his stint as a lumberjack. Tandy wrinkled her brow in concern but he bolted out the door before she could say anything. He was humming something. *Nobody does it better.*

Nobody can get out a door faster than this man, she thought, switching off the tape recorder.

She picked up the phone a few minutes later on the first ring. Sometimes he called her from the car on the way home. Sometimes she'd like to kill him.

It was Joyce Royce, Kingman Beddall's secretary. "Hello, Tandy. Has the boss left yet?"

"Three minutes ago." She could hear a note of exasperation on the other end.

"This schedule of his is going to kill one of us," Joyce complained good-naturedly.

"Yeah, if one of his women doesn't first."

# 3

If anyone had told Gael Joseph six months ago that her career in the cosmetics industry depended upon the success of a fragrance named after a tall ditz-bunny named Fling, she would have laughed in their face. To Gael, there was nothing remotely humorous, however, about losing her family business to a cold-blooded takeover tycoon. The way he decapitated his cigar with his razor-sharp Dunhill cigar cutter had sent shivers down her spine when she first met the wonder boy of Wall Street in the hall of Carmen Cosmetics, the day after he had won his hostile, junk-bond-financed takeover, nearly a year ago. Gael had been humiliated to find she had been locked out of her office, her possessions unceremoniously dumped in the hall, while the Beddall team stomped through Carl Joseph's building like a mop-up artillery ground team looking for bodies the air division had neglected to strafe bomb. She had lost her company, her pride, and all her money. More important, the name of her father had been sullied in the dirtiest battle over the control of a company that had ever been waged. As dirty as any street brawl. Gael had sworn to herself on the way to the ladies' room, to throw up and have a good cry, that if it was the last thing she would do, she'd get her company back, resume her rightful place, and get even with the mysterious "master of the art of the deal," as Kingman Beddall was now being called. Even if she had to take a job as Carmen's janitor to plot her return.

Revenge had been boiling in her blood that day as she formed a secret pact with herself to keep her emotions in check. She kept a foot in the door, a job with the company, and six frantic months ago she had gotten down to the business of hitting it big-time with a fragrance named after a fling of Kingman's, all in order to save everything that mattered to her. She had to be at the Plaza to launch Fling! fragrance in twenty minutes if she wanted to check and double check all the elaborate details for tonight's big-budget promotion, which had started out so disastrously—was it six months ago? She caught her reflection in the elevator door. She had been so busy since she started her campaign, she hadn't had time to look in a mirror for weeks. A not-unpleasant face with a mask of tension returned her glance. As she descended in the elevator, the memories of the past months whirled before her in little colorful vignettes, like a dying man's life flashing before him in his last few seconds on earth while falling over a cliff.

*NEW YORK*

*SPRING 1989*

"Fling! Schming!" Gael Joseph brusquely shoved aside a crystal flacon of eau de parfum and a shiny black and yellow plastic atomizer of eau de cologne sitting on her beige-and-black-speckled marble conference table.

"Has *he* gone *mad*? What is he thinking with—his dick? Bed-All Beddall!" Smoke was beginning to pour out of her ears. "*Fling!* I can't believe it. Since when does Carmen Cosmetics give away a piece of the action to a piece of ass!" If Gael Joseph hadn't been vice president of new products and the fragrance division of Carmen Cosmetics, she could have made a model Marine sergeant or a fine salty tongued sailor. Her vulgar verbal skills were honed from years of being tutored by tough-talking men whose second language was English and who proudly adopted a low-class street vernacular to show that they had mastered the American dialect and dream.

"We'll be laughingstocks. The trades will tear us apart. *Fling!* my foot! And what kind of budget is this, Arnie? With the launch just six months from now!" Gael was even more desperate than she sounded, sitting in the conference room that used to belong to her swarthily handsome immigrant father, Carl Joseph, a few feet down the hall from the low-tech laboratory where he and his partner and best friend, Max Mendel, used to mix nail polishes late into the night and then deliver the home-brewed colors, with such names as Manhattan Red and Central Park Cerise, to the drugstores along Lexington and Madison avenues and popular beauty shops all over town. Carmen Cosmetics, an acronym for "Carl Joseph and Max Mendel," had grown to enormous proportions. In the sixties and seventies Carmen had been a household name, every bit as famous and ubiquitous as Revlon and Estée

Lauder. While Revlon and Lauder had gone worldwide and poured millions into research and development, Carmen had lost its share of the market in the "widow wars," as Gael called them, as the two shiksa second wives of Carl and Max had battled the company to pieces. Max Mendel, a five-foot-two Orthodox Jew from Kiev, had married a five-foot-eleven impoverished Protestant aristocrat from Tuxedo Park, New York, whose entire dowry had consisted of fourteen memberships in exclusive "restricted" clubs up and down the Eastern Seaboard—none of which ever wanted Max ("Call me Max") Mendel as a guest, let alone a member. Max was entirely gaga for Amanda Whittingham Mendel.

"Class, Carl, class," he would remind his partner daily. "What I'm married to is called *class*," he'd say, propping his little feet up on the partners' desk they shared.

The two associates began the bickering that ultimately broke the back of their company over their second wives. Carl had selected a Pan Am stewardess from Sweden for his second wife, and always felt he had made the better deal. This suspicion was confirmed three years later, when Max Mendel died at the age of fifty-nine after his wife accidentally gave him several Lomotil, when she had meant to give him digitalis, after a severe heart attack. She had taken him high in the Andes to recuperate. The medical attention he had received was found wanting. "Amanda Wanting" was how Carl Joseph referred to her, or "The Black Widow," after the lawsuits had begun. Those lawsuits were continued by Carl's widow, Heidi Joseph, after his premature death from a skiing accident in Aspen, where Heidi was teaching him to ski on Ruthie's Run of Ajax Mountain.

"He's crazy. Goddamned crazy. That's what he is!" Gael Joseph, daughter of Carl, jumped out of the swivel chair behind her terrazzo-topped terrain and addressed the bedraggled group seated or slumped around the table. "He's not taking my company down the drain!" Carmen Cosmetics' vice president was fuming. "The company my father built up from zippo is not going out on a whiff and a whim." She snapped her bitten-to-the-quick fingertips in disgust. "My father made *nail polish* in the *kitchen* with Max, for God's sake, until he almost asphyxiated the whole family! Built it into number one. *This* guy is an ax murderer. That's what!" Her face was almost the color of Carmen's nail enamel Midnight Madness.

"I think you're missing the point here, Gael." Arnie Zeltzer's voice was very soft.

"Shut up!" Gael Joseph shouted. "*What* point? The point that Kingman Beddall thinks my company is worth more dead than alive? That if he sells off each division piece by piece *his* take is higher? Bullshit!" she yelled so loudly that the pit bull lying lazily nearby in Kingman Beddall's luxurious office picked up his head and sprang to attention.

"Bullshit!" By the time she had uttered the last excremental epithet, the sturdy dog was obediently on his way down the hall.

"The point is, Gael," Arnie Zeltzer was the lulling voice of calm, "it isn't *your* company at all. Not anymore. Kingman Beddall owns this company lock, stock, and barrel. And he didn't take you out of Chapter Eleven, my dear, he took you out of Chapter Seven, so he owns *you* as well." He punched and flipped some numbers on his hand-held Wang. "He owns you to the tune of twelve and a half million dollars—twelve and a half million dollars of your personal debt, which he picked up for four million five hundred thousand and twenty million dollars in promissory notes for the rest of Carmen, to be exact. *That* is the point, Miss Joseph."

Arnie Zeltzer infuriated her.

Gael Joseph might have thrown the mock-up bottles of Fling! perfume across the conference table if Pit Bull hadn't charged in at precisely that moment with a highly motivated Joyce Royce in hot pursuit at his heels.

"Here, Pit Bull." Joyce was frantically waving an oversized Yum-Yum dog biscuit behind the cranky animal.

"Get that carnivore outta here!" If Gael Joseph was alarmed, she wasn't about to show it to the splinter group that was all that was left of her impressive executive committee. The rest had been "let go and sent on to new opportunities" by the cost-efficient Arnie Zeltzer—commonly known as Kingman Beddall's number cruncher. As Gael Joseph was being made to realize, her team had been whittled down to a state of ineffectiveness.

The only players remaining were Lynn Babbitt, her executive assistant; Phillipe DuBois, new-product director; The Bob-O, creative director and conceptualist supreme; and Christopher Klutznick, the aging but still most brilliant art director and advertising mind in the beauty business.

The Furies had taken possession of Gael Joseph at birth. She was a colicky baby, thrown out of nursery school for lassoing the other children, and suspended from P.S. 149 in the eighth grade after diagnosing three of her fellow classmates with terminal breast cancer after intense bare-chested examinations, causing hysterics and havoc among her terrified classmates and ire among their parents. The terminal cancer was like the one her mother, Rose, was languishing from at home, lying shrunken and sallow on the immense Victorian bed she shared with her beloved husband, Carl.

Gael learned that tough talk and sharpened insults kept the prissy, pitying neighbors away and at bay—just where she wanted them. She finally gave up most normal schooling and all her friends, except her two best in the world: her father, Carl, and his partner, Max. She, Carl, and Max were a team. She strutted like them, swore like them, and mixed batches of nail polish and vats of perfume with them. In fact, Gael had been in on the launch of Carmen, the perfume. The black frosted crystal bottle was em-

blazoned with the now-famous silhouette of a Carmenesque flamenco dancer holding a rose in her mouth, her castanet-clacking
fingers frozen in an aristocratic Castillian dance, embodying all
the essence of passion, violent obsession, and forbidden love in
one single silhouetted posture. All the passion of the world, as
scored in song by Bizet in his opera *Carmen,* was captured and
frozen in a blend of oils and essences in the perfume Carmen.
Cistus oil from Spain, jasmine absolute from Morocco, musk tinc-
ture from Nepal, and vetiver from Haiti, all combined in the
perfume that eclipsed Chanel No 5 and Revlon's Intimate when
it was introduced in 1959 outside the Metropolitan Opera in New
York, where *Carmen* opened the season. In typical Max and Carl
fashion, the two ballsy partners had brazenly peddled free samples of Carmen at intermission and after Rise Stevens's bravura
performance of *Carmen.* Carmen, the most dangerous obsession,
the most seductive heroine in operatic lore.

Gael, upon graduation from high school, at long last, had
been hustled off to Grasse, in France, to learn to be a "nose,"
someone who is able to sniff out the components of a fragrance
and create aromatically new scents. Carl Joseph told his feisty
daughter she would have to develop Leonard Bernstein's sense of
harmony and combine it with his own bookie's memory because
she'd need to record and distinguish the thousands of ingredients
available to her and then unscramble the myriad different scents
and smells to invent her own perfumes. *Carmen,* the opera, and
Carmen, the perfume, had been a perfect, lucky, blind blend. In
Grasse, she learned what she, Max, and Carl already had hit upon
instinctively: perfumery *is* closely related to music. For simple
fragrances there are simple accords made from two or three raw
ingredients, with two or three notes working like a small chamber
group. When one puts a multiple layering together, it becomes
like a symphonic orchestra. Under the tutelage of the great perfumers of Grasse, Gael learned that harmony was everything in

musical notes and floral perfume notes. Both the ear and the nose responded best to a proper layering of well-balanced notes working in syncopation. If one floral note was too strong, it was like the clashing of cymbals and the bellowing of bassoons intruding upon the sweetness of cellos and woodwinds, resulting in cacophony, or discord and disharmony and, in the case of a fragrance, disaster.

As a perfume city, Grasse has a fragrant historical heritage all its own. Resting like a voluptuous botanical garden at the foot of the Mediterranean Alps, its crowds of cloves and riots of tuberoses and fields of jasmine and lavender grow wild in splendidly large amounts. The climate is ideal for the exotic herbs and spices imported from India, Persia, and Spain to flourish alongside the citrus-fruit trees. These deliciously aromatic trees provide perfumers with neroli oil from the blossoms, bitter orange oil from the fruit's skin, and tangy *petitgrain* oil from the leaves and twigs.

One of the legends told to Gael in Grasse was the story of Catherine de Médicis stopping there on her wedding trip after her marriage to King Henry II in 1533. She shared her secrets of blending scents with the French Court, thereby introducing modern perfumery to France. As the seventeenth-century French were not yet keen on frequent bathing, powders and fragrances were substituted for soap. Grasse flourished as the center of perfume making.

It was in Grasse, amid the fragrant splendor and the air heavy with history, that it came to Gael. In this aromatic aerie, memories of her mother, Rose, suddenly surfaced and combined with the heady atmosphere of Grasse, to ignite her creative juices. Daily, she sat for hours at the perfumers' console, the shelves of which held two thousand little bottles of fragrant substances with which she could experiment. She was almost feverish with the desire to create the perfect aroma. Like a crazy cook, she culled together different ingredients, trying to invent a new recipe from memory. One day, she aggressively dipped a scent strip into the oil from the Bulgarian damascene rose. Of course, this was the scent of her mother, the scent of her mother's heritage. Rose Joseph's grandparents had been peasants in Bulgaria, where for thirty days each year they had also been flower pickers in the valleys of the Balkan Mountains, harvesting the precious treasure locked in the delicate rose whose bloom lasted but a moment in time. Gael remembered her mother's tales of being a little girl in the fields of flowers, furiously picking the pink petals with her mother and sisters and stuffing them into their pouches. As the sun would rise in the fields, the delicate blossoms of the damascene rose would lose their essential oils, so the picking had to be fast and precise. By midday, the fragrant roses they picked were only half as rich in perfume oils as the roses picked at dawn.

Finally Gael had it. She invented the fragrance she had been secretly seeking to pay homage to her mother. The perfect blend of Old World and new; top notes of Mediterranean sensuality, a middle note of warm remembrances, with a bottom note of maternal nurturing. Gael didn't know it, but she had just hit upon what would be Carmen Cosmetics' biggest seller of all times: Rose. It was launched on Mother's Day in May of 1964, the same year that Yves Saint Laurent brought out his fragrance, Y, but for that year and the decade that followed, Rose was a bigger seller than that sassy, sophisticated French scent. Max was elated. This was the crème fraîche on the strawberries, the Beluga caviar on his *blinis*, the four-star Michelin rating on Max's and Carl's cosmetic delicatessen. Carl was proud. They had been overjoyed, and welcomed Gael back as an adult and third partner into the company. She gained their respect but lost her childhood at the same moment.

Funny thing about fragrances: they could whirl you back into the past or rush you into the future. As Kingman Beddall (Pit Bull marching at his heels) came striding down the hall of Carmen Cosmetics, which *he* now owned, Gael Joseph was jolted into the present. Kingman strutted into *her* conference room with a speedy swagger too exaggerated for his short legs. Gael counted them, thirty-six swift steps in twenty-six quick seconds. Kingman waved his right arm in greeting, never stopping, and called out in his customary cheery voice, "Hi-how're-you-doing?-What's-the-budget?-Half-it!" And he was out the conference room's second door, Arnie Zeltzer folding in behind Pit Bull, and that was that.

"Goddamn him!" Gael Joseph's heart jumped. He had just buried her in less than ten words. Half their budget! Cut their budget in *half?* Why, they would barely have enough to launch a nail polish. But, she sadly muttered to herself, reflecting and recouping, "the budget is just enough to sink a ship." Her ship, the fragrance division of Carmen Cosmetics. "Bed-All, Dead-All, screw you!" And that's exactly what he wanted to do. Kill off her division and dump it! The rumors on the street were true. The bastard had even waved his fingers at them over his head as a farewell can't-bother-to-stop salute as he bolted out of the conference room, never even stopping to see the damage his bomb had wreaked on the floundering ship or if there were any survivors. He could get out a door faster than any other man on Madison Avenue, she thought. A pall came over the room. They were sunk and they knew it. Might as well give up and go home. He was going to embarrass Gael Joseph and then sell off her unprofitable division. Max and Carl were surely spinning in their graves.

Cool down, Gael, calm down, a voice inside her said. A good captain doesn't go down with her ship, a good captain gets out the lifeboats and saves the sailors. And these lifeboats had the name Fling written all over them. Fling didn't know it, but she had just made the best friend of her life, the one who was going to push her over the top and fling her into worldwide stardom. Gael would turn the rage and hatred she harbored for Kingman Beddall into her own weapon. She would take the bomb he had casually dropped and toss it right back. If he was going to try to bury her and her father's company with a dizzy cloud called "Fling," then she would take that girl and that fragrance and turn it into something bigger than Carmen perfume and with more worldwide sales than Rose. Damn it, she would turn Fling! into the Charlie of the nineties.

"Let me see the picture of the goddamn girl," she roared at Lynn Babbitt, her assistant. The launch was set for just six months from now.

"How far can we go on half of nothing, Bob-O?

"What can we get for free, Phillipe?" She was spinning in her swivel chair. "Maybe we should launch this fragrance at a charity fund-raiser; *that's* never been done before. Make them pay to attend the launch and smell the juice."

Everyone in the glass-enclosed conference center laughed, breaking the ice, the first sigh of relief since Kingman had stomped through the room in record time, creating the same stunned effect as Sherman's devastating march through Atlanta.

"Okay, a charity launch is a pretty good idea," said Phillipe DuBois, picking up the ball and hesitantly taking it down the court.

"This girl is very fresh," said The Bob-O, holding up Fling's model composite picture. "She has incredible bloom, she's very nineties. Look at those lips and that bosom." He turned the picture on its side. "Why, she'd be a natural for a lot of free editorial."

"Free!" Gael lurched out of her chair. "Give me more *free*!"

"I've heard nothing but great things about her," piped in Lynn Babbitt. "Every designer wants her for the runway. Speaking as the woman on the street, I'd like to look like this girl, let alone smell like her," she said shyly, "and if she has Kingman

Beddall by the balls," she looked up to see how they were receiving her words, "she's got to have something."

Christopher Klutznick broke in, "Let's bottle that! That 'something'!" The old pro knew of which he spoke.

"They have been trying to bottle sex since time immemorial," snapped Gael.

"So why don't *we* bottle it?" said The Bob-O with a twinkle in his eye and a mischievous mouth. "Come on, sex is not what it used to be, it's fresher! Romance is back, isn't it? One-on-one, one significant other . . . woman."

Everyone in the room was on alert when The Bob-O had an idea, for no matter how crazy it sounded, it always worked. The Bob-O took a long drag on his ever-present Newport cigarette, and everybody in the room held their breath until he exhaled his next idea in a cloud of smoke.

"Yeah, let's bottle it. What is it, that thing that makes a man risk everything? Leave his wife, change his life. Puts a kick in his step. Is it a fling? Is it a girl? An affair is too eighties, too tawdry. Nothing vulgar about *this* girl. A fresh fling is what's happening now. A fling is two people mutually attracted . . . catching his eye on the street. Better yet, catching a whiff of her fragrance! Following it. Pursuing it. Romancing it. Having a fling! Who cares if it's consummated! Maybe it's just a flirtation. Flirting makes us sit up and feel good, doesn't it? If construction workers stopped whistling at you, you'd be insulted, wouldn't you?" Lynn nodded enthusiastically. Gael wouldn't know. Nobody had whistled at the forty-five-year-old tough-looking broad in eons.

"I hear she's got the IQ of a slow turtle," Gael snapped.

"So?" The Bob-O snorted. "Who wants to smell like Margaret Mead?"

The room laughed but didn't interrupt him. Not with The Bob-O on a roll.

"It is what everybody needs and what everybody wants;

maybe it is something innocent, maybe devious. Naa," he observed, holding Fling's picture up to the light, "this girl is not an affair. She is too classy. She looks sexy *and* nice—you'd like to be her friend. Ten to one that guy takes a whiff and wants to marry her! Maybe *she's* the one who's having a fling and walks away with the bank." He flashed the grin he hadn't used since he helped Victor Skrebneski "discover" Paulina for the latest Estée Lauder ads, making her the "toppest" model in the world for her moment in the spotlight.

"But we have only six months to bring out this stuff," moaned Phillipe DuBois, checking the calendar.

"So what do we have on the shelf? What's already developed that we can doctor up to make this a smash hit?" demanded Gael.

"I could call Roure. Their scents are very, very sophisticated. I think that's what we need. Opium was *magnifique* and Rive Gauche for Yves Saint Larent was a pretty perfume, yes?" Phillipe rose to his feet as if to catch the Concorde to the Parisian House of Givaudan-Roure, the prominent perfume establishment run by the aristocratic Jean Amic, a man of impeccable taste whose firm created exquisite fragrances befitting a French gentleman whose wife would have been queen of Hungary if the Communists hadn't rearranged her historic lines of succession. The company had anonymously given birth to many of the world's greatest perfumes though its existence with its houseful of noses was rarely acknowledged outside of the industry.

"Nah, I want earthy," Gael puffed out her bosom. "And cheap. This stuff has got to be affordable."

"Don't forget Roure created Obsession for Calvin Klein and Guess for Revlon! If you're looking for a home run, Gael, we better go with the best." Phillipe threw up his shoulders for emphasis.

Gael thought for a minute. Givaudan-Roure had created many of the world's most famous fragrances. Christian Dior's

Poison, Hermès's Amazone, Bijan, even Elizabeth Taylor's Passion had been aromatically invented by the French fragrance firm that had been brewing up special scents using some of the best noses in the world since 1820. Roure would be perfect. But Kingman had just knocked her budget to smithereens.

"Do we have anything in house?" She turned in desperation to her team.

"Well, we have that stuff Max was brewing up for Marilyn Monroe; she wore it privately for years," said Phillipe with disdain.

"If it was good enough for Jack and Bobby Kennedy," added Lynn Babbitt, an avid reader of the *National Enquirer*, "it should be good enough for America's lusty lads." She blushed.

"Well, dust it off and juice it up." Gael was in her element now. Max and Carl were sitting on her shoulder. She'd do it: launch a winning fragrance, win her company back, and get revenge on Kingman Beddall, all with the contents of a single saffron bottle and some dingbat named Fling. *Oy vey*. Hail Mary. And she'd get the word out. She remembered Estée Lauder's formula for selling fragrance . . . *Telephone, telegraph, tell a woman.*


S E P T E M B E R   *1 9 8 9*

S U K I ' S   C O L U M N


Dahlings! New York history just got more social and the New York Historical Society just got a great big ole infusion of Southern dollars—let's hope it's not Confederate money! Although this season, with a fund-raiser every night of the New York week, the Charity Ladies will gladly collect *any* currencies for their cute little causes.

The ever-so-sweet Blaine Trump announced at the Armory Antiques Show on Tuesday night at the super-elegant benefit she and Mario Buatta cochaired for Boys Club, that if someone wanted to underwrite with wampum for next year, their offer would be taken under serious consideration! Oh woe, Gotham! As Suki's friend Cole Porter penned, "Anything Goes!"

Over at the New York Historical Society, which has gobs of relics from the early Dutch New York settlers and chronicles all the best and oldest families in Manhattan—which, if you remember, darlings, was bought with beads and wampum and a very few dollars itself—the Old Guard is changing. Mrs. Kingman Beddall of the very, very, very social Virginian Randolphs has just been made president of the Women's Board and named chairman for this November's New York Historical Society Ball, traditionally the most proper and upper-crusty, if somewhat stuffy, ball in tout New York.

As you may not know, precious ones, since the Randolphs are the kind of people who pay to stay *out* of the papers, Anne Randolph Beddall and her family have lived at the charming, genteel Boxwood Plantation for over two hundred years.

Don't even *bother* going down to visit Boxwood, dears, unless you can sit a horse properly, ride to the hounds, and have ancestors painted by Thomas Sully and John Singleton Copley hanging all over your drawing-room walls. Why, the Randolphs have been in Virginia *soooo* long, little ones, that they think Pilgrims are upstarts and arrivistes! The Randolphs were here evah-so-long before anyone evah heard of Plymouth Rock. Down there they think Plymouth Rock is an inferior brand of bourbon!

The very slender, lovely Anne Randolph Beddall is putting together a *very* social gala committee. Everyone is dying to be on it. Her husband, Kingman Beddall, just gave two million big ones to help pay off the grand old Museum's debt. He's new on the block. He's the fella who just bought Carmen Cosmetics—don't you know. Bet the party favors are bottles of Carmen perfume or Rose perfume—two of Suki's favorite oldies but goodies. Classics in the best sense of the word, like Anne Randolph Beddall.

# 4

Dahlings! SCOOP! I have it on the best authority: next month's *entirely* sold out New York Historical Society Ball—why, the only way you could get in now, you-Johnny-come-latelies, is to come as a waiter—is creating a brand-new parfum for its guests. At $1,000 a person they *should* get something—besides the opportunity to rub elbows with anybody who's somebody in New York. Felicia Rockefeller, Whitney Astor van Straaten, and Princess Piaget Balducci of the party-favors committee say that Carmen Cosmetics, underwriter for the ball (so that *all* the monies raised that night go directly to benefit the Historical Society), has cooked up something *really big* for the party. *A brand-new perfume.* Suki thought we'd be getting those little black-and-white double *C* goody bags with our *old* favorites Carmen and Rose perfumes. Not to worry, judging from these past few months' round of galas chaired by the so-charming and very social Mrs. Kingman Beddall—anything this refined charity queen does is top drawer! Why, everyone on Park Avenue is even trying to affect her softly spoken Southern accent! Tiffany Powerhouse, Governor Cuomo, and Governor Byrd Harrison of Virginia will all be at the ball. Arnold Scaasi has been busier than a Worth Avenue jeweler whipping up creations for his ladies, Amanda Whittingham Mendel Wellington IV, Pat Kluge, and Princess Yasmin Aga Khan. Whew! What a workout of lace and Lesage beading.

The very social Mr. and Mrs. Kingman Beddall have instructed his alchemists over at Carmen Cosmetics to create the most unforgettable party favors yet. And with guests like Barbara Walters, Lady Chesterfield, and Mr. and Mrs. Trevor Cutting Jr., it better be good.

Suki had it put into her ear just seconds ago that Mr. Kingman Beddall is busily watching CBS, and we don't mean the news. Kingman Beddall is watching the stock! And as anybody who is somebody knows, Mr. Beddall was in lumber and media communications *long* before he got his golden nose into Carmen Cosmetics. Maybe the night of his wife's ball he can launch a fragrance *and* buy a network. As for the very social Kingman Beddalls of Boxwood, near Richmond, Virginia, who says the South lost the war? If you're a descendent of Robert E. Lee, honey, stand up and hoot!

\*   \*   \*

Gael Joseph stepped out into the crisp autumnal day onto Central Park South and breathed in the cool, fresh air, fresh by comparison with the incense-laden Rigaud candle scents mixed with kitty-litter smells hanging in the stuffy, overheated rooms of Suki's cavernous apartment. She knew for a fact none of the windows on the first floor of the duplex had been opened for twenty years. They probably couldn't even be pried open. They had always been kept shut and the drapes drawn, as far as she knew, even in her father's day.

"Aunt" Suki and Gael Joseph were the closest thing either one had to a relative. When Gael's mother, Rose, had become terminally ill, Carl Joseph had taken to "calling on" Suki, the attractive divorcée who was just taking over the society column at the New York *Daily Sun*. Carl had befriended the beautiful woman, whose real name was Esther Rosenthal, handled her investments, and since he had been very close to the Wineburgers, who had owned the *Daily Sun* at the time, generally helped her career. Today, she was a rich woman, immensely. She had been Carl Joseph's "closest secret friend" while his wife had lain bedridden for eight years, and had benefited from his business acumen, stock market tips, and generous gifts of too vulgar, but very valuable, jewelry. She had even become close to his problematic and fiercely precocious child, Gael. Over the years, Carl's lady friend and his daughter had bonded, filling the gap in each other's lives. In fact, grown-up Gael had comforted Esther (for Suki was never a real person) after her father had married Heidi, the Pan Am stewardess, on a layover in London. *"C'est la vie! C'est l'amour,"* Suki had sighed. "Say what," Esther cried and immediately lapsed into a depression that sent her to her bed for weeks. When she got up, the devastated Esther was dead and buried and only Suki remained—except for the first Sunday of every month, when Gael Joseph and Esther (Aunt Suki) Rosenthal would faithfully "do" brunch at her relic- and memento-crowded apartment.

Much of Suki's apartment had remained the same as it had been on that day twenty years earlier, like the residence of a latter-day Miss Havisham. Only the dozens of Woburn Abbey Roses and Leron linens were changed daily.

When Gael arrived for their "Sundays," the enormous little woman, as wide as she was high, would be gathered and pulled together in a stained, voluminous, ornamental brocade caftan, her head wrapped in an exotic turban. Suki, unbeknownst to her millions of readers, was entirely bald, the result of an overzealous hair colorist decades earlier, when she was going from brunet to platinum in an effort to wash Carl Joseph right out of her hair.

Gael Joseph cared deeply for Suki. Suki was arguably a surrogate mother of sorts, but now Gael was calling in her chips and any outstanding emotional IOU's.

Anyone who had ever been helped up the ladder by the generous and lovable Carl Joseph and Max Mendel was being called in for paybacks. Gael Joseph wanted her, *their*, company back.

Suki said that Kingman had been planning to divide up Carmen Cosmetics piece by piece, holding on to only one lumber company and the twelve radio stations Carmen owned. Max had bought Eureka Lumber when he thought it would be cheaper to ship their cosmetics in their own crates and boxes. Carl had branched into radio when he got tired of the stations persistently raising the air rates they charged for Carmen's commercials. Both of these divisions had become very profitable.

Let *him* have all that, thought Gael. All I want is to save my company, the company of Max and Carl and Carmen and Rose and now, she smiled to herself, Fling! She threw her tweed-plaid shawl over her shoulder and pointed herself uptown to collect on another old debt. Fling! would be a bloody stinking success. Kingman Bedd-All Dead-All may have broken her budget but he wasn't breaking her spirit. She laughed aloud, remembering

Max's favorite homily: "Fuck me once, take me to lunch. Fuck me twice, fuck you!" Laughing, Gael Joseph hurried to the corner to catch a cab.

*N O V E M B E R   1 9 8 9*

*S U K I ' S   C O L U M N*

Flash! Flash! Scoop! Scoop! Fling! Fling! What?! Have a Fling! folks. Everyone who is somebody in New York is having one. All the right people soon will be wearing the same scent on Thursday night at the Plaza and having a fling doing it. You heard it here first. That divine, *that gorjus*, that unearthly, creature staring back at us from every bus and billboard in Gotham is single, twenty-one, and the new spokesperson for Carmen Cosmetics' newest fragrance, the first new fragrance Carmen has launched in twenty years. Fling! The most divinest girl since Suzy Parker and Marilyn Monroe (Suki's favorites). This one has captured New York's attention (and that isn't easy). Fling, they call her. But which came first, the fragrance or the girl? The very social, very clever Mrs. Kingman Beddall has snared her husband's newest fragrance from Carmen Cosmetics to be launched at her very staid New York Historical Society gala fund-raiser. Can't you just see all those Van Rensselaers, Rockefellers, Loebs, and Biddles tossing off their Chanel No 5, their Jean Patou, and Joy for a fresh whiff of Fling! Suki can hardly wait! The fragrance has been a major, practically CIA-guarded, secret and nobody, absolutely nobody, knows what Fling! smells like except maybe Mr. Kingman Beddall himself.

The Decoration Committee, Jamee Gregory, Mrs. Atwater Hopewell, and Mrs. Burham Bass, even promises fireworks! Can't wait. Kudos to Mrs. Kingman Beddall. She's a dead ringer for Audrey Hepburn and with more class than anyone else on the whole continent. Word is, over $2 million has already been raised by the elegant fund-raiser for the heretofore-bare coffers of the venerable New York Historical Society Museum. And Suki's best friend, photographer Marshall Valeski, promises those gorjus lips and upper measurements on Fling are positively for real—no silicone for this girl. Dahlings! Have a Fling!

This time a happier group of campers was gathered around Gael Joseph's terrazzo-topped terrain. And camping they had been—practically living in Gael's conference room and looking more bedraggled but cheerier by the day. They babbled noisily among themselves, and were so berserk by now—underfinanced, under pressure, underslept, over-the-deep-end—that Gael Joseph, The Bob-O, Christopher Klutznick, Phillipe DuBois, and Lynn Babbitt occasionally hugged one another, cracking up like friendly Bedlam inmates. They were interrupted by periodic hysterical outbursts from Joyce Royce and Carmen's public relations man, visitors to the asylum.

*For free* they had the cover of *Vogue*. And the cover of *Cosmopolitan*, shot by Scavullo! Fling was so sexy and saucy on the cover of *Cosmo* that the 7-Eleven stores had kept the magazine tucked behind the counters, where people had to ask for it, and ask they did. The inside cover caption had noted she was wearing Fling! cologne, even though when the picture was shot no such thing even existed! The cover story of *Cosmo* teased, "How to Make Him Fling Himself into Your Arms," and was followed by a special tear-out insertion, "*Cosmo*'s Guide for Getting Your

Man," listing five very un–Emily Post-like "Rules for Flings in the Afternoon":

1. Carry an extra pair of silk stockings from Fogal's in your purse in case the first pair gets snagged on the chandelier.
2. Wear a lace bustier, preferably Natori, under your business suit; men are suckers for lace in the afternoon.
3. Carry a small atomizer of Fling! cologne in your briefcase and spritz anything that passes for a crevice or cleavage.
4. Invest in a fur-lined trench coat. You can always use it for a blanket.
5. Open a corporate charge account at the Box Tree Restaurant and Inn. There's a room upstairs just like the one in Claude Lelouch's film *A Man and a Woman*.

Inside were twelve spectacularly bright color photos of Fling attired in "Fashions for a Fling," all of which showed a great deal of bosom and a whole lot of lips. There isn't a woman alive who hasn't read one of *Cosmo*'s cover stories at one time or another. Even Anne Randolph Beddall brought the issue home from her hairdresser's, partially tearing off the cover, leaving only the big black *C* and *O* so her maid would think she was reading *Connoisseur* alone at night in bed instead of *Cosmopolitan*.

For free . . .

*Vogue* had sent André Leon Talley to style Fling in grainy black-and-white photos by Patrick Demarchelier, all shot in different bedrooms of the Hotel Lancaster in Paris. Fling in Natori lingerie, a glimpse of a rough-looking naked young man, his shadow, his back, his arm, his three-day-bearded profile, entering and exiting the picture, while she, sensuous, eyelids set at half-mast *a la* Marilyn Monroe, spectacularly arranged in chairs, doorways, and on rumpled beds next to empty wineglasses and full ashtrays . . . since the French still smoke . . . just looked steamy.

For free . . .

*Sassy* magazine's cover line shouted, "16 Years Old and About to Have Your First Fling!" Included was a guide to Rollerblading without bruising your knees and a story on mountain climbing and bringing along just the bare essentials: a rope, a mountain pick, a boy, a thermos of Evian water, a pot of lip gloss, and a bottle of Fling! Splash!

For free.

But Gael Joseph's favorite was *New York* magazine's cover story on "The Seven Most Discreet Places to Have a Fling in New York," written by the brilliant, pithy writer Julie Baumgold. Gael had torn this article out and stuck it in her own purse. Just in case. No telling when a person might need that kind of information. She had torn it out just as millions of women and young girls were tearing out the perforated scent strips that reeked of Fling! cologne in practically every women's magazine—"When was the last time *you* picked up a magazine that didn't smell back at you?" Gael had asked her group, and the deed had been done—along with The Bob-O's piece de résistance, the toll-free number 1-800-U-R-FLING! The Bob-O had arranged this magnificent addition to their efforts on his own—calling in his own chips. They were getting hundreds of calls a day, from forty-year-old women to twelve-year-old girls, asking to order Fling! cologne directly, and the phone companies were in a tizzy because they were being besieged by young girls dialing 411 information to find out how to dial the "!" that followed "Fling" on their touch-button phones.

And who hadn't been awestruck and swept away by *Harper's Bazaar*'s traveling editorial on a wholesome, smartly dressed Fling photographed in Athens (classical Fling), Paris (French Fling), and Scotland (Highland Fling), in each shot reminiscent of a sensual Grace Kelly playing a cool goddess in the movie *High Society*.

Kingman had refused to pay to buy counters and spaces in the big department stores, so Gael had basically eliminated the perfume and gone with the less costly cologne and Fling! Splash! in drugstores, bypassing the big stores until Kingman coughed up or they could generate their own cash. In the meantime, they were launching exclusively with Bloomingdale's in New York. This was a must.

"It's not enough to have the best-smelling perfume in the world," Carl Joseph had always said, "you have to *sell* the product."

And selling she was.

*Telegraph. Telephone. Tell a woman.*

The weeks of trade-offs and negotiating had taken their toll on Gael. She was getting migraines and was convinced she had contracted anosmia—the loss of smell. Buzzy Cohen had sued for that once. The guy he represented testified he couldn't smell the food that had gone rancid in the refrigerator and almost died of food poisoning after a neighbor's flowerpot fell on his head. Couldn't even smell a leaking gas valve. Dangerous. But what Buzzy had gotten the big dollars to his client for was compensation for his loss of pleasure in life: his inability to smell his wife's hair after she shampooed and showered; his loss of olfactory memories from his childhood, when he lost the capability to smell suntan oil or home-baked bread rising in the oven or honey-glazed ham; or new memories that he couldn't even fathom and would never know, like the freshly powdered scent and the sweet milky fragrance of his newborn son. And people thought smell wasn't important. Bullshit! She caught herself from saying the word aloud and inviting Kingman's canine bodyguard to charge prancing into her private domain.

It had been a stroke of genius on her part to involve the wife in the perfume launch. Anne Randolph Beddall had graciously and generously offered to pitch in if it would help her husband—

help her husband to be more attentive, was more like it, Gael mused. Even with the budget cuts, he couldn't deny his wife's big charity drive, the same public relations–motivated philanthropy that came straight from his wallet and was making him increasingly more visible in a moment in New York history consumed with overbearing giving and obsessive spending, all in the floodlight of Watch me, everybody—I'm on fire, rich, getting richer, and I'm in New York. Fortunately, the moment was passing, but this was 1989 and as Suki would later note, the shakily junk-bond-financed moment was still in full swing. And in the case of Carmen Cosmetics, in full Fling!

"Good luck, everybody," an exhausted Gael weakly called out to her zombie-looking staff. "If this launch goes well tonight and we hit gold, face-lifts for everyone. On me!" They all laughed too hard, a little bit out of control. Only The Bob-O seemed buzzed up. Gael grabbed the Donna Karan dress hanging in her office and pulled it over her head.

"Hey, did someone remember to invite John Ledes?" she yelled as her dark hair poked through the yoke of the black jersey.

"Invite?" Lynn Babbitt had one foot out the door. He was the most powerful man in the fragrance industry, the cutish, witty publisher of the cosmetic world's bible, the trade newspaper *Beauty & Fashion*.

"Invite?" Lynn shouted over her shoulder down the hall, which echoed back her words in the empty six P.M. corridor. "He's my date!"

And everybody left for the Plaza to launch Carmen's newest fragrance and Kingman Beddall's newest girlfriend, Fling.

Peals of laughter erupted from chauffeured limousines and gaily carried up the carpeted outdoor stairs of the Plaza Hotel.

Through the revolving brass doors that whisked fluttering debutantes to tea dances, brides to their elaborately catered first weddings, and tourists to their newly renovated Trumped-up rooms, whirled the guests who had paid dearly for their charity supper and the privilege of being the first on earth to inhale the light intoxicating fragrance of Fling! perfume and cologne. The socials were out in force.

Whippet-thin women in slinky satin gowns or Scaasi sensations ballooning over pointed-toe dancing slippers were ushered through the Edwardian elegance of the recently redecorated lobby that now bore a passable resemblance to an eastern European palace. Beneath the gleaming green copper–gabled roof that dominated Fifth Avenue from Fifty-eighth to Fifty-ninth streets, an elite to be reckoned with was gathering. The statue of the lady Abundance centering the Pulitzer Fountain in the Plaza square outside was embarrassedly outshone by ladies sumptuously decked out in ballwear. Their tuxedoed escorts blended in like so many quotation marks.

"Dahling," the statuesque Mrs. Elwood Upman Stratham, elegant octogenarian, raised her signature elongated neck displaying six strands of diamond-punctuated pearls and twiddled her manicured arthritic fingers at Mrs. Astor. The two women lightly kissed the wintry air around one another's earlobes in the traditional tribal greeting *de riguer* for these official nights out on the town. It was Thursday. Gael had calculated correctly. New York's great ladies of conscience and charity hadn't yet left for the weekend in the country and the retail trade was out *en masse*, prizing their saffron and gold invitations to the ball like jeweled Fabergé eggs.

The Plaza was packed.

"Aren't the Beddalls dears to do all this for the Historical Society?" Mrs. Patterson waved a lorgnette at the room ablaze with a thousand tapered candles while Mrs. Guest surveyed the winter's garden that had been created by Renny. Armloads of yellow, white, and saffron roses spilled out from frosted Lalique containers onto the full-skirted tablecloths gathered up with Volkswagen-size bows of black and saffron satin. The Puerto Rican busboys and waiters of Scottish descent passed hors d' ouevres of caviar canapes and champagne flutes among the descendants of Peter Stuyvesant and the other original Dutch settlers as well as those whose relatives had waved to the Statue of Liberty on their way to New York Harbor and eventually to this fund-raising gala at the Plaza Hotel.

"Here Billy, it's yum-yum." Oatsie Warren, perky wife of the chairman of Midland Marine's Bank, pushed a triangle of caviar-topped toast into her husband's gaping mouth. She had caught him mid-speech in a dialogue with a former secretary of state, a man who had passed the Statue of Liberty himself on his way to the New World and the White House. Oatsie didn't trust anyone who hadn't been born in America, unless they were roy-alty or dress designers, and since New York was such a demo-cratic melting pot, she preferred to live in Connecticut. She only accompanied her husband on important business events or for something old-guardy like the Historical Society bash. This par-ticular event was both and as she looked about the room, she observed *everyone* worth knowing was here. The perfume launch was an extra. She was simply delighted to get freebies of fra-grance. What she couldn't use for Christmas stocking stuffers she could always use as favors at her annual Easter Brunch. She had carried a sensible pocketbook-sized evening bag to the Plaza so she wouldn't have to look like a bag lady carting home all her free perfume. She had given away all her silly miniature evening purses to her divorced friends who used them as diaphragm cases.

"I told Felicia a dozen times, only votive candles. Tapers drip wax over everything!" Two of the decoration committee ladies were in heated discussion over the long yellow beeswax candles that were lighting up the room and throwing romantic shadows onto the wall. They were busily changing place cards, altering the seating arrangements at their tables. The guests would be moving into the main ballroom at any moment.

"Well if Anne Randolph Beddall says it's alright, it's purrr-fectly fine with me."

"Oh, there she is now. Isn't she lovely. I love her sad look. It's sooooah aristocratic!"

"Anne dear," Muffy Phipps picked up three yards of skirt and rustled over to the ball chairman. "Isn't Kingman here yet? We should be going into dinner."

"Oh yes," Anne blushed. "Let's do begin. My workaholic husband thinks social occasions are for business. Kingman does his 'gentleman-and-cigars' talking before supper. The sweet dear, he always gets it backwards." She lifted a champagne glass from a passing silver tray as she leaned farther into the shoulder of her uncle, the governor, and smiled wanly, the corners of her mouth twitching up. Her mother raised a concerned eyebrow in Anne's direction and then cast her wise eyes about for her errant son-in-law. The receiving line was just breaking up and she hadn't yet seen him make an appearance. Surely he wouldn't stand up Anne at his own launch! Virginia Randolph, queen of Southern society, needn't have worried. A barrage of flashbulbs preceded his entrance. Virginia Byrd Randolph was appalled. The late arrival was holding a press conference in front of the elevators! Slapping friends on the back, throwing his head in hearty laughter displaying his amazingly white teeth, he charmed everyone in the anteroom, except for his mother-in-law.

"Sorry I'm late, hon," he said to his wife, sporting a boyish grin on his good-looking face and a brand-new tuxedo. He was always forgiven. The dinner chimes sounded and the bejeweled and begowned reluctantly moved to their tables in a wave of anticipation. The conversation and people-watching at cocktails had been so good, how could sitting between only two people be as exciting.

Above the din of charming chatter and beneath the glow of the massive crystal chandeliers, Kingman Beddall pulled out his wife's chair at the head table just off the end of the runway, listening courteously to her slightly slurred chastisements.

"King, where have you been? It is utterly thoughtless of you to expect me to greet every one of your business types when I've never even met them. I swear, Kingman, it's like two entirely different parties. The Old Families on one side and your New People on the other!"

"Yeah," Kingman grinned, his eyes sweeping the ballroom. "Like a high school mixer, with the boys on one side and the girls on the other. Maybe I should spike the punch and get things rolling." His eyes twinkled mischievously. He was clearly delighted at the turnout.

"Oh, Kingman, do sit down and be serious." Anne handed a black napkin to her husband. "By me," she patted the satin slip-covered chair beside her. Everything in the room was black or saffron, the colors of the Fling! packaging.

"Where will Fling be sitting after the introduction?" Kingman was circling the table like a kid searching for his place at a birthday party, stopping to kiss the top of Also's head. His daughter's hair was pulled back off her round little face into a scraggly ponytail.

"Next to me, Daddy. I can't wait to meet her in person. I saw her behind the curtain and she looks like a golden Statue of Liberty."

"Hush Also," her mother softly admonished. "Just be polite. The girl is just business for your father and not a new friend for you."

The photographers bird-dogging Kingman's every move

were ushered to the back of the room, which was cordoned off for them by a Taitinger-colored velvet rope. The Trumps' thirty-million-dollar restorations had rendered the room simultaneously old and new, keeping the elegant old bones but giving the shoddy appointments a face-lift. From their vantage point, the photographers and TV cameramen could capture a sweeping panorama of the very rich and the fashion world dining at leisure. Ladies who had spent the day getting manicured at one of Tandy's Nail Emporiums, coiffed by Monsieur Lupe, and otherwise coddled at Georgette Klinger's cocoon of a skin-care salon were now exquisitely pale and powdered, their violently teased hair stiffly arranged on their heads like protective helmets. The bank vaults had been raided that afternoon for jewels that hadn't seen the light of day for years. The Fling! launch was the epitome of eighties-style existential entertainment. If a tree falls in a forest and no one saw or heard it, did it really fall? If the monied New York society, old and nouveau, had a party and no one took pictures, did it really happen? Rich men and aloof ladies, famous for being stingy with their money and kindnesses, were suddenly generous with their profiles and best photographic angle. *The* party of the high-flying eighties decade where rich people replaced movie stars as celebrities was taking place and would be remembered long after in the annals of socialdom. There was a white-gloved waiter behind every chair and a silver Cartier calendar engraved with the Carmen Cosmetics logo at every place setting with the November date circled. The three silver wine goblets, lined in vermeil and filled to the brim, had been purchased especially for the evening. When the archbishop rose to give thanks for their supper, all denominations bowed their heads in prayer, more grateful for the boom-boom years of outrageous financial gains than for the artfully arranged petite portions of food on their plates.

How long could the *high* be expected to last, they wondered irrespective of their faith. Liza Minnelli shook them out of their reveries in song, and as soon as the last entrée of *foie gras*–stuffed pheasant, linguine, and hazelnut timbales was removed, and before the salad and dessert of *soufflé glâce aux framboises* was served, the drum rolls sounded, Peter Duchin raced his fingers across his piano keys, the chandeliers dimmed, the runway lights switched on, Bobby Short stepped up to a microphone, and on the saffron satin–covered runway an empty spotlight waited. There wasn't a raised fork in the Plaza Ballroom nor an unraised eyebrow as the Golden Girl took her place in the spotlight and then glided down the runway all legs, breasts, and shiny free-swinging hair, her body moving as much from side to side as straight forward, the enormous voluptuous mouth switching from a sensual pout to a dazzling smile as she spied Kingman standing at the other end to welcome her into his world heady with the scent of success. Little knowing looks were exchanged over the tables as the girl's hips swung out in rhythm to Bobby Short's lyrics, "Just Have a Fling with Me." You could have heard a soufflé splatter on the carpet when the customarily cool Kingman embraced the Fling! Girl, the look in his heavily hooded eyes all icy appetite. Fling, who was as elegant as a draped evening column and as saucy as raspberries and chocolate after sex.

Anne Randolph Beddall let out a gasp as her husband kissed the model, a gasp that was indistinguishable from the communal gasp that went up in the room in response to the fifty or so waiters carrying silver trays loaded with bottles of Fling! fragrance as they paraded down the runway and out into the audience. A thousand black and saffron balloons were freed from the ceiling and a screen was lowered into the ballroom showing the rocketing fireworks going off outside in Central Park. The Fourth of July in November. New Year's Eve at Thanksgiving time. Usually patrician people popped open their Fling! perfume and cologne bottles like so many champagne corks and even the most staid New England Yankees and Dutch descendents were out of their seats as a second fifty waiters passed out additional favors of Polaroid cameras already packed with film so the guests could record this moment and each other for posterity, Bob-O's and Gael's "tie-in" to the New York Historical Society that chronicled New York history for the ages. Flashbulbs, fireworks, whiffs of perfume, and dessert distracted most of the diners from the sight of the model and mogul kissing on a suddenly deserted runway.

"Come with me, perfect face. There's an empty reception room across the hall." Kingman Beddall grinned and grabbed his model's slender hand into his own rough, calloused fist and marched her across the crowded parquet dance floor where they had been barely swaying in each other's arms to the sounds of patrician Peter Duchin, conducting his own orchestra from his classy piano. Duchin had played at Anne and Kingman's wedding.

Fling gave out one of her tomboyish, goose-honk laughs and threw back a double mane of honey-gold hair, which kept tumbling into those azure eyes.

"King, wait!" She laughed too loud, causing a ripple, and then a wave, of overcoiffed heads to turn in their direction. "I can't run in high heels. I bet you've never seen anybody run in the marathon with spike heels!" Her feet were killing her after six straight hours of standing in her satin black-and-saffron-striped four-inch heels under heat-producing klieg and camera lights. She was as giddy and high as a World Series winner. She had been hitting home runs all night just by being Fling. The girl was more at home in the spotlight than anyone at Carmen could have imagined, and Gael Joseph was excitedly taking orders for Fling! fragrance from retailers' tables while Anne Beddall and the Randolph clan were being properly mortified—business at a ball!

"How vulgar," clucked Virginia Randolph to her cousin, Cyrus Fleming, someone who could appreciate the heinous social crime that was being committed.

Kingman led Fling from the confusion of the flower-bedecked, media-hyped, society-ball circus and into one of the darkened reception areas just beyond the powder room, closing the door behind him. He took her in his arms, burying his head into her young breasts as ripe as golden apples.

"Take off your shoes," he ordered, bringing her down four inches and closer to his eye level.

"With pleasure." She casually kicked the fifteen-hundred-dollar Manolo Blahnik pumps off to the side. "I would like it put in my contract that I never have to wear high heels ever again." She stretched her arms up like a giant awakening feline and arched her feet, wiggling her toes.

"I'd like it put in your contract that you just stay in the supine position." He put his hands around her waist and pulled her closer.

Fling looked baffled. Kingman knew so many words. "Sew-pine," she repeated. She'd commit it to memory and look it up later.

"Are you happy with me? Did I do okay tonight?" Her face was still fully flushed with excitement. "I was so nervous. I didn't think I could make it down the catwalk, until I saw you there!"

"Let's have a display of approval now." He pushed his fingers into her bare-backed spine and brought her mouth to his.

"Kingman," she whispered, brushing her lips against his own. Part of her was melting into him. "Did I please you?"

"You did phenomenal. New York is nuts about you. Listen to that noise. It's like New Year's Eve out there! I've never been so proud. This tough-to-impress city that's seen it all before has fallen on its knees for you." Kingman was actually gushing.

Fling took his face in her hands and pushed it away to examine it as carefully as her own reflection. She read pride in every craggy line on its handsome weathered surface. She thought she saw a softness in his eyes that she'd never seen before. She knew the look of Kingman's desire. Here now, in her hands, she was holding his look of pleasure and admiration. Beneath the dark bushy brows, which usually shaded his steely slate-gray eyes, were flecks of warmth.

Kingman gently took Fling's fingers and lightly kissed them in a courtly gesture more befitting a Lancelot worshipful of his lady than a tough tycoon seducing his childlike girlfriend.

"Let's have our celebration now, King! We'll go to the apartment and I'll make love to you all night long. I don't want you botherin' to come up for air. I'll just breathe *for* you!" She fluttered her heavy lashes at him.

Kingman hardly knew where to look, whether to take in the astonishing gold-encased curves of her body, the adoration in her eyes, the perfect contours of the Model of the Moment's face, *his* Model of the Moment, or the voluptuous, pouty, bee-stung lips that looked like they had never been intended to speak but created only for his personal carnal pleasure.

The thousand-carat face was all lit up in two-thousand dazzling facets for him. He felt a familiar stirring. He held the mouth to his for a kiss that pulled each of their breath into the other. A kiss so long and all consuming that neither one of them noticed his daughter, Also, quietly opening the door, slipping into the room, and standing shocked and hurt at the sight of her father and the beautiful model. There was the model she had looked forward to sitting next to all night, ready to copy her posture, table manners, even what she ate, in her secret wish to be just like her, and not like the upper-class girls at Brearley. There was her favorite model, until this moment her fantasy role model, now tangled up in a mélange of shoulders and arms with her father, breathing heavily and noisily, totally unaware of her pudgy presence.

"My mother was looking for you, to present the check to the museum," Also, her eyes lowered, said in her best imitation of her grandmother, the strong-willed Virginia Randolph, a habit she would fall back on all her life in times of pain or indecision.

"I'll be right there, Also. Go back to the table, honey." Kingman dismissed his daughter with more annoyance than embarrassment. "I have to finish talking business with Fling."

Fling was undone.

A tear the size of a pearl slowly descended her high cheekbone. King removed his handkerchief and gently wiped the translucent teardrop away, along with all of Frederick's pancake makeup, contouring, and artificial artistry.

"See," Kingman said soothingly, "you're much more beautiful without any of that war paint. There's my pretty girl underneath all that icky gook."

Fling's faucet was on. The tears were falling.

"Oh, King. We can't hurt anyone. I love you. I worship you, but, but I can't sit across a table from your wife. She's so lovely and refined. I kept using the wrong fork with my salad and dessert, and I know she noticed! And now, how can I have the nerve to go back and sit nonchalantly next to your daughter? She must feel terrible. I feel terrible! I'm a secret. I hate secrets. I can't even keep secrets." Her voice was breaking. "I'm just your fifth wheel. We *can't* hurt anyone. Not your wife. Not Also. Not me. Not you, Kingman." She was sobbing now. "I want to go home with you. I want to spend the night with you. Make breakfast for you. Darn your socks. But it's really impossible, isn't it?"

She dropped her head on his shoulder.

"You don't want to darn my socks, honey," he laughed

softly. "See, you get the best of me now. You see only my good side." He tilted her chin toward him. Feelings of sexual arousal, guilt, hurt, and confusion whirled between them in a potpourri of passion.

"Nobody's getting hurt, Fling. Anne and I have an understanding. Maybe even an impending divorce. We haven't shared the same bed, let alone the same bedroom, since Also was born," he lied. Fling brightened. Well, maybe, she thought, if the marriage was already over . . .

"I don't know, King. People shouldn't hurt other people." The words tumbled straight from her heart.

"Listen, Fling, count on me to make sure nobody gets hurt. Anne, Also, especially you."

*She hadn't wanted to enter his world just to view the roped-off furniture and marvel at the untouchable, priceless treasures.* She'd wanted him *and* his world. To share with him. Suddenly, visions of family photographs, Thanksgiving dinners, and private moments that didn't include her swirled in her mind. A frown crossed her beautiful brow. Kingman hated her frowns. It meant she was thinking. He could have picked up a Barnard girl if he'd wanted thinking.

"Fling, buck up. Now trust me to do the right thing at the right moment. With no hurting. You get back in that ballroom." He smiled paternally at her. "Leave off the makeup. You're better without it. Be my good girl and get back to the party. I'll be right behind you."

"You'll take care of everything? No one will get hurt?" She sniffled back her tears and kissed his palm that was holding her face.

"Count on it." And he stuffed the overworked handkerchief, ponderous with Carmen cover-up, Fling! eau de parfum, and Tandy, back into his tuxedo pocket.

It was a promise. "Count on it."

\*     \*     \*

The telephone and alarm clock were going off at the same time. Fling picked up one of the ringing machines and put it to her ear. It was the digital clock. She read off five-thirty A.M. from the illuminated numbers.

"Whoops!"

"What whoops?"

Frederick's cheery voice sounded like he hadn't been to bed yet. Fling was doing *Good Morning America* today. As part of the Carmen promotion, Gael Joseph had arranged the next three hundred and sixty-five hours of Fling's life down to the last nanosecond.

"Rise and dazzle," he chirped over the phone.

She willed her eyes open. Her heavily fringed lashes felt as if they weighed a ton.

"Should I bother to make you up for *Good Morning America* or will you be going to the ladies' room with Kingman again and wiping it all off? Talk about kiss and tell! You might as well have left your dress in the powder room. Couldn't you guys have waited until you got home?"

"Oh, *that* whoops." Fling reached for the bowl of melted ice by her bed and plopped two cold cucumbers onto her eyelids. It wouldn't do to have puffy eyes in front of all *Good Morning America*. People liked their puffed wheat or rice in cereal bowls, not their celebrities puffed on their morning television screens. She had finally cried herself to sleep at three A.M. Fling raised her chin, her milky white skin glowing in the light of the digital clock as she patted the cucumbers. Bright eyes, a pouty mouth, and a luminous complexion were her weapons to conquer the world this morning. She'd have to jolt herself awake. She groped for the ice dish and poured it on her stomach.

"Eeeehhhhaaaah!" She sat up, the round green edibles falling to her breasts.

"Fling, are you alone? Is King there?"

"I'm alone. All alone. Completely alone." She pushed her lower lip out.

"I'll be right over. Sounds like I've got my work cut out." The dial tone sounded unforgivingly loud in Fling's ear. She rousted herself from the bed and into the shower, wondering how Joan Lunden got to work every day at such a crazy hour. She let the water cascade over her, rinsing off everything unpleasant about last night. It was still dark outside and the shower water wasn't yet hot enough in the predawn.

"I'm here! Let me in, star baby. A star was born last night. What an entrance. You laid them out, darling, screaming for more." He imitated her runway walk as he sashayed into the bathroom.

"How'd you get here so fast?"

Frederick and Kingman both had keys to the apartment.

"Called from the corner. Haven't been home yet. Cha, cha, cha."

The unused ball gowns from last night were crazily strewn around her small studio, lying in bright heaps of color, silk sashes and satin ribbons dangling from lamps and doorknobs like drunks the morning after.

"Flingy!" Frederick eyeballed the scene that looked like the inside of Saks's designer dresses department after an earthquake.

Toweled off, she slithered into a butter-yellow sweater dress while Frederick powdered her nose and darkened her lashes.

"Good morning, America!"

"Good morning, Frederick," she said glumly.

"You were such a hit. They loved you, my darling. Texas conquered New York last night. Eat your heart out Jerry Hall. I can't wait to read Suki, Suzy, and Billy Norwich."

She shook her hair out of the dampened ponytail, the shiny

blond tresses falling into place like the Radio City Rockettes kickline.

"Kingman has a wife."

"Well, didn't he always?"

"Yes, I suppose. But I never *met* her, or Also, before."

"What's an Also?"

"His daughter."

"How sweet. I suppose it's better than, 'hey you'!" Frederick smoothed a dab of Brylcreem over her ends, tucking the shiny straight hair into a perfect pageboy. He patted her lips with Vaseline. "Clean and shiny. A very good morning look."

"The wife is nice." Fling was sullen.

"I'm glad you approve."

"She's a lady. I don't want to hurt someone so nice. I wouldn't want to hurt *anyone*, even if they weren't nice."

"Ah, the tragic trilogy. Romance in a triangle. So give him up. I've always told you he's a selfish, no-good, lily-livered egoist. The kind of guy who only lives for two things, his prick and his pocketbook!"

They looked into the mirror at each other. Their faces were almost interchangeable. Only this morning Frederick's eyes were brighter, dancing gaily beneath his naturally high-arched brows. A shank of straight brown hair fell saucily over one chiseled cheek, playing hide-and-seek with his aquamarine eyes. He nonchalantly pushed back the shock of hair, exposing his delicately contoured features. Fling's face was sensual, his haunting. The curves on her body were voluptuous; his frame was lithe and angular. Together they were the Venus and Vinnie de Milo.

"Oh, why don't you go in my place?" Fling threw her hairbrush over her shoulder. "I'm in no mood to tell anyone on television how to have a successful life. How can I possibly give advice to women sitting around their kitchen tables surrounded by their families. What am I going to say? 'Hi, I'm in love with somebody's husband. Here, just use my fragrance and you too can spend New Year's Eve alone with your goldfish!' " Her shoulders shook as she buckled under the pressure of being the center of attention, the vortex of a whirling public relations media blitz, the most beautiful girl in the world who certainly had never had a *problem*, a word that couldn't possibly be in her vocabulary, limited as it was.

"Flingy, it's you they want. This is business. Do a great job, make a success, and you can dial a man. There are fancier financiers than Kingman. Single ones with better manners than that greedy takeover tycoon. He's not doing you any favors either, sweetie. If this fragrance works, Kingman makes *big* bucks. If not, he writes it off. Dumps you *and* the company."

"He wouldn't!" Fling turned on him defensively. "He loves me."

"And maybe he loves his wife, too, and Other."

"Also!" Fling was rising to the occasion. A sparkle was returning to her powder-blue eyes.

"Oh, who cares what they call that little cow. I had a long talk with Bob-O last night, *backstage*. Gael Joseph is the driving force behind this fragrance. She's trying to save her company. Bob-O filled me in on *everything*. Oh Fling, couldn't you tell they loved *you*? You were gorgeous. The store buyers and the magazine editors were going bonkers. This whole kooky thing could work, Fling. But you can't sell product if you're feeling sorry for yourself. Greeeeat, folks. Try her perfume and get depressed!"

Fling giggled. "I love Kingman," she said stubbornly, retrieving her hairbrush and resuming her bright personality. "It's just that this situation is so, so complicated." She brought her head down with such emphasis one of the bright gold earrings that Gael had assembled as part of her Fling! wardrobe tumbled to the floor.

"Is it broken?"

"Which? Your earring or your heart," smirked Frederick. "Both can be fixed."

Fling ran her fingers over the smooth, shiny golden hoop. It was not broken. Maybe things will work out for the best, she thought, taking the unbroken earring for an omen. They usually did. She'd put her faith in Kingman. He just wasn't Frederick's type, that's all. And last night Kingman had promised her nobody would get hurt, hadn't he? He'd take care of everything. She would count on it.

"The ball was enchanting, wasn't it?" she smiled over her shoulder at Frederick. The scientific observer would have seen them as a dimorphism, two separate entities that had derived from the same single source, like two sibling child stars that had broken away from their parent planet. She shouldn't have stayed up all night crying, she thought, peering into the oversized, white-laminated circle mirror. She had probably ruined her looks. She seriously examined herself for wrinkles or sagging chin muscles but there were none. Her face was perfectly intact, there wasn't even a trace of redness or a hint of a puff.

"Enchanting! Flawless! The whole affair was perfection," Frederick enthused. "Of course, I viewed it from the fly on the wall's perspective. The gowns, darling, were dreamy. I counted over twenty Couture gowns, and those babies start at over twenty thousand dollars. There was some heavy-duty clout there last night. And while you all dined on salmon mousse, lobster-filled squash, and stuffed squab, we backstage jockeys got trays of turkey sandwiches and champagne. We did make the right decision, Precious. Your golden saffron dress made the perfect statement. Under the lights, your body looked like Aphrodite after a month's workout at The Vertical Club. Patrick McCarthy from *Women's Wear* even asked who the designer was." Frederick flung an orange wool coat over Fling's broad shoulders. Both of them raced down the cement stairs. Fling would be on most of the country's TV screens in half an hour. The network car was waiting.

"Ooh luxury!" Fling twinkled.

"Oh, yeah. Beats the subway." The first day of success was beginning to smell sweet and the sun wasn't even up. Fling caught the sleeve of Frederick's overcoat.

"Pretty terrible whoops, huh?"

"Not horrible. I'm sure Gael Joseph's PR machine has gone to work on the rumor of The Model and The Mogul disappearing from the ball for half an hour with The Model returning a rumpled mess."

Fling pulled her lips together so tightly, the voluptuous mouth almost entirely disappeared.

"My best advice to you is not to see Kingman publicly—if you have to see him at all. Not unless you're thinking of bringing out a fragrance called Misty Mistress." He shook a finger at her. Frederick who wore Obsession for Men because he liked the way the naked muscled hunks looked in the advertisements, was an unlikely candidate for a lesson on morality. "Misty Mistress," he mused. Had to admit, it had a ring about it.

"No more tears, okay? Fling! is launched with a smile, okay?"

"Okay." Fling nodded, her lips turning up. She always felt better with Frederick by her side.

"*Entertainment Tonight* is running the whole gala launch tonight but their cameras left right after your runway walk and the one thousand balloons cascaded from the ceiling. Suzy doesn't dish up the dirt too much, and Billy's pretty fair." Frederick was giving his best predictions of the society gossip columnists' coverage of the ball. He hoped they would leave out the embarrassing escapade of The Model and The Mogul necking in the john.

"However," Frederick rolled his eyes pushing Fling into the car, "I can't *wait* to read Suki."

## *SUKI'S COLUMN*

Fling! was launched at the Plaza Thursday night. O, Heavenly Scent. Holy Fireworks! Darlings! Anybody who was Everybody was there. And if you weren't, you better pack up and move to Philadelphia, for Lawd's sake, because you're not on the "A" list anymore. Mr. and Mrs. Kingman Beddall (she in vintage Galanos) presided over a sea of saffron silken tables of omygosh Rockefellers, Fishes, Mellons, Stuyvestants, sitting in slip-covered chairs heavily swagged and bowed by Parties Galore. Every chairman of every major corporation in Suki's Gotham was there. It was just like the Roaring Twenties. Champagne flowed, and the Scaasi and Oscar de la Renta ball gowns were *so* big and billowy that the first and second Mrs. Casholds got stuck in the same ballroom elevator and had to be pried apart, as the Lesage beading on their ball gowns had gotten tangled and meshed.

The chairman of Chase Manhattan Bank announced a gift of $1 million to the New York Historical Society, and Mishima Itoyama (who, dears?) of one of the banks of Japan gave $100,000. Since when is *Japan* preserving *our* heritage? Suki can never quite remember who *did* win that war.

Liza Minnelli belted out "New York, New York," and the archbishop of New York said grace. But all this was a prelude, folks, just the warm-up act for the main event. The Girl, The Breathtaking Beauty, The Fling Girl herself, stopped Everybody dead in their society tracks when she floated down the runway under 100 klieg lights, swathed in something saffron, all cheekbones and lips with (Lawd, I thought it was in the

Smithsonian) *the* Yellow Star of India around her neck. That's the one that's bigger and shinier than the Hope Diamond, folks, which *is* in the Smithsonian. O holy blinking blinding Lights of Jewels. While Bobby Short sang "I Want to Have a Fling! with You," Fling the Model waltzed down the silk-saffron-covered runway. Straight into the arms of the chairman of Carmen Cosmetics, Kingman Beddall himself, standing at the end of the runway, which ran the length of the whole ballroom, who presented her with a 10-foot-high bottle of Fling! perfume for all the flashbulbs and photographers and World who weren't invited to see.

The sweet Model Fling kissed the King of Carmen and cried tears—just like Miss America—as the two of them held onto the giant bottle. And when 1,000 saffron and black balloons were released, confetti rained upon the guests, and 50 faces of Fling unfurled from banners, it was breathtaking. O glorious fireworks! And evidently all too much for the delicate Mrs. Kingman Beddall (of the very proper Virginia Randolphs), as she fainted into her uncle Governor Byrd's arms.

Or maybe it was all those heady, sexy bottles of Fling! cologne, carried out on silver trays by fifty white-tailed waiters, being opened all at once and the entire top-drawer social and financial world of New York suddenly caught up in a heavy cloud of Fling! perfume. Everybody in the room smelling just like the beautiful Model Fling. *Wow!* And if you couldn't be there, darlings, because the president needed to consult with you or your malaria flared up, you can experience the whole mad wonderful thing in the Fling! bottles going on sale at Bloomingdale's today! Suki is exhausted and diving into a tubful of Fling! bubble bath!

\* \* \*

By the time Tandy got her hands on one of the most widely read Suki columns of the season, it was smudged and stained with all kinds of Carmen nail enamels. The customers had passed the New York *Daily Sun* around Tandy's Nail Emporium like a hot potato, only, everybody had stopped to read it and then put their own spin and analysis on what Suki was really saying. What everybody in the shop wanted to know, including the six gum-chewing manicurists who worked for Tandy, was the real reason Mrs. Kingman Beddall fainted.

After her last client, Tandy hurriedly turned off her manicurist's light and glanced at her watch. "Well," she said to herself, "I'll hear all about it in half an hour." Kingman was due at her apartment at five-thirty P.M.

# 5

*F*ling draped one elegant elbow over the frayed edge of the yellow taxi's dog-earred vinyl seat and hiked up her hose.

"Frederick, don't take that stuff, it's more than terrible for you!"

"Come on, luscious lips. *You* don't need drugs, *you* don't *take* drugs. But if *I'm* going to escort you to one more 'Hail to the Fling' circus, risking my short but lascivious life in the hands of some Iraqi terrorist trying out for the Indy Five Hundred, *I* need a little Ecstasy." It had been almost two months since the launch of Fling! had swept the nation on a huge aromatic tidal wave.

The E-tablet that Frederick popped into his mouth was as

friendly and familiar as Bayer aspirin, the little round white pill it resembled. This "disco biscuit" guaranteed Frederick the euphoric feeling of floating head-over-heels higher than the nameless throng of pulsating bodies dancing to the beat of some primeval-inspired rhythm. Once the pill fully kicked in an hour from now, he would be oblivious to anything unpleasant, and supernaturally tuned in to anything luscious and beautiful. It was Frederick's small way of surviving a cruel and imperfect world. And when it came time for him to move to the wood-floored center stage of the dance club with his best friend "girl of the moment," model of the month, scent of the decade, and the only other person in New York as extraordinary looking as Frederick, he would have the courage to do so.

An hour from now it wouldn't matter if he were a boy or a girl or a star or the most beautiful androgynous makeup artist in New York. Nothing would matter but Fling and Frederick—the two best girlfriends in the business, dancing, posing, and Vogueing with a bevy of other model girls and boys. Nothing would be seen in his E-tab haze but the spotlight focused on them, erasing, obfuscating, anybody unkind, unpretty, or just plain critical. Frederick liked his little magic pills. No hangover. He didn't drink hard liquor, he rationalized. And these little pills were illicitly made in the laboratory of an Ivy League school, so maybe they were even smart. With Ecstasy, he could see and feel without knowing, and it always eliminated the job of forgetting the night before.

They careened up Tenth Avenue in the taxi, enveloped in its own aroma of old socks and couscous, on their way to Twenty-seventh Street and New York's hottest new model hangout, The Sound Factory.

"Slow down, Hussein, please!" Frederick called out as he and Fling were bounced off their seats bumping over an obstacle course of potholes.

"Call me Ishmael." The driver turned his toothless smile on them, spinning his head around as if he were a possessed character from *The Exorcist.*

"Aren't you the perfume girl?" He breathed a whirl of Arabic spices into the backseat.

"Slow down, Ishmael, the potholes are killing us," Frederick grimaced. Fling giggled as both of them were bounced clear off the backseat, her long legs flying to Frederick's side of the cab.

Tenth Avenue on New York's lower West Side was like war-torn Lebanon with its cracked pavement and filth from the cargo trucks that parked in the industrial garages, which half filled a neighborhood of empty run-down warehouses, deserted parking lots, and eerie silences from abandoned factories. This blighted panorama lined their route to the hip club, only a block away from New York's shipping piers.

Out on the torn-up street stood José, the skeevy downtown doorman who held the power of the celebrity bouncer/doorman as had Mark, who'd guarded the door at Studio 54 in its heyday. It was in José's power to let the pretty girls, pretty boys, and pretty boy-girls into the workmen's warehouse converted into a disco. Some he let in, some he kept out, but when his practiced Cerberean eye caught the willowy silhouette of Fling, the hit of uptown and downtown, and her equally beautiful friend, he lifted the grimy velvet rope to let them enter the pop paradise without the eighteen-dollar-per-head ticket of admission. In this other world, Frederick knew, pretty people never pay.

"Oh, wow! Fling!" José leered, opening the door to the sounds of the disco. The shining couple surveyed the crowd a moment before plunging into it.

Tonight was a big night. It was Fashion Night at The Sound Factory. Almost everyone would be beautiful, except the wannabes loitering around outside.

The sound immediately enveloped the pretty duo. Black Box was belting out "Everybody, Everybody" over the sound system, and almost Everybody was there. In the cavernous dark, the only light shown onto the three-story-high dance floor.

It was impossible to see who was in the bleachers, who was watching whom, and who was on the prowl, ready to pounce on the sexual prey of his or her fancy.

Frederick didn't have to see to know that every eye in the place was on Fling, fresh from her latest cover shoot and still modeling the Christian Francis Roth dress, the "money dress," that was featured on the cover of *W*. Even in the consciousness-raising, environment-nurturing nineties, this money dress had been the hit of the young designer's show. Even though it was designed to look like a single dollar bill, Fling looked more like a million bucks in the chiffoned, see-through, cut-up-to-the-wazoo mini-dress with George Washington and "In God We Trust" emblazoned across her healthy chest.

Frederick swept a protective look over his best friend and made sure that all the other girls gathering around her weren't mauling The Dress. It had to be back at Christian Francis Roth's showroom in the morning for the fashion buyers. He stood patiently by her side, acting as her seeing-eye friend, as the barrage of flashbulbs always blinded her. Now Fling with Christy Turlington and Linda Evangelista, now Fling hugging and cheek-kissing Naomi, the pretty black model who had caught the momentary attention of Sylvester Stallone—all preserved for posterity in the party pictures recorded by the glossy magazines.

A communal gasp of delight swept the crowd. The classical violin strains of the prelude to Madonna's hit song "Vogue" crescendoed out of the booming speakers and into the air. The crowd loved this song—their national anthem. The dancers lifted up their noses and postured like hunting dogs, hearing the thumping bass.

Frederick rolled his eyes back into his head and ran his tongue across his lips as he swayed his hips to the beat.

Fling began to bounce up and down in a schoolgirlish hop-scotch that had none of Frederick's pulsating sexual rhythm. She smiled sweetly as the crowd whooped and cheered at her. What better show could they see in New York tonight than this week's cover of *W*, this month's cover of *Vogue*, for God's sake, dancing and laughing, her head thrown back to the strains of Madonna's "Vogue"? It was as if Madonna herself had entered the dingy club.

The volume rose.

"Strike a pose," Madonna's voice called out, and strike Fling did. All her natural shyness disappeared, as if once again she were where she was most comfortable, in front of the cameras, in front of the lights, being told what to do.

Immediately her eyes brightened, her nostrils flared, her cheekbones rose, and she and her best friend, almost alike, batted their eyelashes and posed and Vogued, whirling and laughing and moving and strutting like the two great beauties they were.

Every eye in the place was on them. What did they care? What did they care.

"Strike a pose, there's nothing to it." The two beautiful children sang along with Madonna and the crowd cheered. Fling clutched her breasts, shot her left arm up, rolling her shoulder forward, ready for the Hasselblad lens of Herb Ritts. In response, Frederick pulled his lips into a pout and threw out his right hip, primed for the camera of Bruce Weber.

The music grew louder. The crowd circled Fling and Frederick, moving all in array, arms weaving and spinning in a staccato roll.

"Vogue, vogue, vogue, vogue!" The crowd clapped and shouted along with Madonna.

Fling in *Vogue*!

The dancing duo were totally unaware and unknowing when a clique of uptown people swept into the club. They were too totally immersed in their own powerful narcissism, preoccupied poses, and their own whirling aura, to see.

They never even sensed the bizarre entourage that moved like a phalanx into the club to silently watch. The very elegant man in the center of this phalanx watched the most intensely, because he was a watcher. He was one of the individuals who never participates, only watches and observes. Safer that way. Everyone in his party had the same cool, aloof expression that people generally put on their faces when they enter these clubs incognito. When they view slumming as a sport.

Baron William Wolfgang von Sturm was wearing his coolness like his custom-cut English suit and intensely watching all the time. His hazel eyes settled on the cool posturing of these two magnificent young creatures moving in an aloof way that reminded him of his collection of Art Deco sculpture. The girl was astonishing, her beauty flawless; but the other one, in the other one there was a vulnerability in the posturing, and a stronger muscled beauty in a leaner body. The legs were covered in black Levi 501 jeans, the shoulders in a silk Armani jacket, the short hair slicked back and, although the open wing-tipped collar was unbuttoned to the waist, it still left the observer unsure whether this was a male or a female. The Baron ran his eyes up Fling's endlessly long legs, around her perfectly contoured face, her slender neck, her expression locked into an orgasmic trance, and down Frederick's feminine features and ambiguously swaying torso.

"How beautiful. How lovely they are. We must know them. We must have them up. We must have them over," the Baron intoned to Cyrielle de Resnais in a whisper, watching.

As no liquor was served in The Sound Factory, the entourage of Baron von Sturm urged him, after half an hour, to take his party uptown to Au Bar, the more civilized private dance club and more to their tastes. This was only one of the places his entourage had taken him while he was in New York to oversee the Von Sturm collection opening on loan to the Metropolitan Museum . . . and maybe to buy Black's Fifth Avenue.

"To Au Bar, where one can drink champagne, dance to Latin rhythms, and sit on cozy leather couches and in the banquettes," said the chairman of Black's into the Baron's ear.

The Baron was hesitant. He was a great collector of beauty and was enchanted by this young couple. Watching them was a good finale to his day. His entourage smiled to see the Baron with the deutsche marks and the dollars in a growing retail recession, smile at the girl in the dollar dress. They would have her up. The famous model must meet the Billionaire Baron.

"Gene Kelly, Fred Astaire, Ginger Rogers dance on air. They had style. They had grace. Rita Hayworth gave good face." Madonna's voice was husky. The crowd on the floor was wild. Frederick was in Ecstasy.

"Dieter, let's have them join us," the Baron semiordered. He was smiling. All the Black's people smiled when Baron von Sturm smiled. Cyrielle de Resnais lit up a Gauloise.

The normally blasé crowd roared and applauded for Fling and Frederick. Frederick had made half the girls there the model stars they were, but Fling was *the* star. This was as good as it got at The Sound Factory. But Fling was anxious to get home now for Kingman's phone call, and Frederick felt an anxiety of his own.

For those familiar with international finance, and the followers of the billions of Eurodollars buying up and infiltrating America in the nineties, there would be no surprise as to why Baron von Sturm, possessor of one of the oldest and greatest fortunes in Europe, was far from his Fifth Avenue and Wall Street lairs.

Anyone who had read the *Financial Times* this morning knew that one of the Baron's companies, WWVS, had been asked to come to the aid of the nearly bankrupt giant retailer, Black's Fifth Avenue. The chairman of the board and the pretty-boy president, who had suddenly developed German ancestors, were spending some of their excessive entertainment budget on the Baron and his entourage, which included Lynn Manulus, one of the visionaries of style, daughter of the immortal, legendary Miss Martha, who was to the fashion world what Estée Lauder was to the cosmetics world. The Baron had come to know Lynn and her mother when he had loaned them his lavish baronial suite at the Ritz during an overbooked collection season in Paris some twenty years ago.

The ever-shrewd Lynn noticed the Baron's eyes lingering in the direction of the girl sporting the star design, the dollar dress, from her latest protégé's collection. She shouted to Von Sturm, trying to drown out the din of the disco beat.

"That's the Christian Francis Roth dress that I was telling you about. Money, the money dress. Perfect, I'll have him make you a deutsche mark dress, if you like." She was screaming so loudly and with such enthusiasm that she feared she might have burst the Baron's eardrum.

In response he blinked his eyes a dozen times, as if in some sort of disco Morse code. She caught the words "meet them" over the deafening beat.

Lynn daintily maneuvered her way through the crush with such a determined dexterity that she was suddenly the only person in Fling's line of vision. She enveloped fashion's new star in her own diminutive arms.

"Come, meet the maybe-next-owner of Black's!" she said, pushing Fling and Frederick through the crowd.

"Baron, I want you to meet The Dress," she said, pointing to Fling, whose glowing cleavage showed a few beads of perspiration glistening after the slight aerobic workout, her full bosom peeking out over George Washington's stern visage.

Frederick watched as this refined, elegant gentleman lifted Fling's hand and grazed the air above her knuckles with his lips. The Baron acknowledged Frederick with a slight nod of his regal head.

"It's so bloody loud in here, I can't even tell if he is clicking his heels in some sort of Teutonic salute," he yelled to Lynn. He couldn't believe it when he saw Fling curtsy. Poor sweet Fling, who had been brought up in the Tastee-Freez school of etiquette, curtsying to some business baron in a suit in some sweaty disco.

Oh, boy, Fling.

The man was older, definitely older, but extremely handsome.

Some sort of robber baron, I bet, thought Frederick. At times like this he felt a wave of jealousy. Sometimes . . .

He felt Fling tugging on his Armani sleeve.

"I've got to get out of here. We've done what we were supposed to have done. It's okay to go home now, isn't it? Everybody has seen The Dress," she shouted as she cupped her hand into a human megaphone directed at Frederick's ear.

"Oh, Fling! How can you do this to me again, just when we're having some fun?" Something else was pulling at Frederick's intuition.

"Come on, Freddie, Kingman's gonna call." Fling turned her Fling charm on. He hated it when she whined. "I can't leave this place alone. You *have* to take me home." She widened her turquoise pools of eyes at him, the ones that Frederick always fell into.

The ever-observant Baron lifted his head, ferreting out something unusual in the air with his high-bridged, aquiline nose. It wasn't just Fling's fragrance. He smiled to himself, thinking that this might be an interesting evening after all. And he had thought all he would be getting out of it was another department store.

Fling blew little kisses into the air and waved good night to all the other pretty girls around her, tossing out her light silvery laughter in her adieus.

Charming, the Baron thought as he watched the dynamic duo wave their good-byes, lingering like the Von Trapp children from *The Sound of Music* leaving the grown-up's party to be shuffled off to bed.

"I have a car outside. May I offer you a lift?"

This time Frederick did swear he could hear those Teutonic heels click. As the Baron led the way out, Frederick linked arms with Fling and whispered into her ear, "I wonder what you call a baron in bed?"

"Probably just Your Bareness," giggled Fling.

"Au Bar, Dieter," the Baron instructed the uniformed driver of his itinerary for the rest of the night. The Cyrielle woman was waving her fist at them from the curb. This was going to be fun: Fling, Frederick, and the Billionaire Robber Baron. Too bad the stores weren't open. Frederick was prepared to outlast this night.

"Oh, no no no no no no." Fling fell into the gray leather doeskin of the backseat and pulled the chinchilla throw up to her chin. "I've got to be home—like twenty minutes ago. Oh, my stars!"

Frederick whirled his eyes around the backseat, feeling a rush of panic commingling chemically with his Ecstasy. He read the precise time from the burled-wood control panel over his head. Everything in the car was a German mechanic's dream.

"She turns into a pumpkin in twenty minutes," he apologized slightly, piqued and annoyed.

Why does she have to shut down the party for all of us so

early? he thought. He was feeling a surge of excitement that could not be attributed to the disco biscuit.

Something wonderful was supposed to happen this evening, and now it wasn't. Frederick slumped into his seat next to Fling, who was tugging on his sleeve and mouthing, "Kingman, Kingman," and crazily signing her hands in some sort of dizzy sign language for the deaf.

Frederick was exasperated. He didn't want to acknowledge Fling's reluctance to continue this evening on into the wee hours of the morning. The Baron, however, was understanding.

"Then home at once, my dears." The Baron's voice was surprisingly soft and good-natured. He rested one slender wrist over the other. It was as if he had been bred not to show disappointment.

What a dumb shit his best friend was! Here was one of the world's richest, most elegant, and handsome men, courting Fling . . . *single*, too! And she was going to ruin it all and rush home to wait by the phone all night in case her married man called. Frederick, whose bloodlines were mixed and mongrelized, somehow resulting in his astonishing good looks, wore his disappointment on both sleeves and all over his excessively chiseled face just like a sorrowful seraphim. She was flinging away the single Billionaire Baron, the one with the castle in Germany, the privileged artworks on his walls, hard cash in a leveraged land of junk money.

All this information Lynn Manulus had managed to bequeath to him while car assignments were being made in front of the club.

Dammit! Fling, the nearsighted, was rushing off to await a call from the very married Beddall. Sometimes Frederick, with his Aryan, poster-perfect features, wished he were a girl and could seize the opportunities as they arose. At least *he* could see an opportunity coming. They could be an incomparable international threesome. He could tag along with the Baron and his Fling from watering holes to museum-quality castles to European society balls. They could spend their winters whirling from Viennese hunt balls to Milanese opera balls. A trio "balling" in Europe! Here they were, sitting in the lap of luxury, and Fling wasn't even interested. Running off from the royal invitation and she probably wouldn't even remember to leave a phone number or her glass slipper! Well, he'd leave it for her.

The Baron's voice interrupted his petulant reverie.

"I hope that the Cinderella time clock is not running out on you too, Frederick. Howard is holding a table at Au Bar."

"By all means, have him hold it." Frederick smirked smugly, crossing his legs. Oh, boy! What were he and the Baron supposed to do? Pick up girls? *Yippie-ay-yey.*

As the silver-gray Daimler pulled up to Fling's walk-up apartment, Frederick jumped out to escort her safely into her doorway. She excitedly pecked him on the cheek under the streetlight.

"You're not sore or anything, are you?" She patted his shoulder with a worried look.

"No, not much."

"Oh, good. Do I look okay for Kingman, really, truly to die for?"

"Yes, yes, luscious lips, he'll drop dead as soon as he sees you." Frederick wished he would.

"Oh, stop, you silly." Fling was always working with a limited vocabulary. But in actuality, Frederick observed, she *was* beautiful beyond words tonight.

"Don't get into trouble at one of your places, you know, tonight," she sighed like an overworked mother. "And don't forget to take your potassium. Those nasty E-tabs eat it all up." Her oversized lips were moving into the enormous Fling mouth, the mouth most men would leave home for just to graze it against their own.

What a looker, he thought. And what a dumb shit. Wasting her time on a married man. Girls like Fling, even as exquisite as she was, had only six good years at best. In this business, you had to make hay while you still sparkled and before the fine lines set in.

The Daimler door was opened to receive Frederick back into the lap of luxury, and the car headed uptown to the world of leather banquettes, and clubs where only bona fide members entered through private portals.

"Au Bar is just getting really good this time of night." Frederick nervously glanced at the clock. "The owner is thinking of opening up a branch in Palm Beach." Suddenly he felt Fling's absence like a missing second hand. Just what do you say to a Baron and, as Lynn Manulis had whispered into Fling's and Frederick's ears as way of introduction, the richest industrialist in Germany? Somebody who, like, was on a list . . . one of those rich lists?

He drummed his fingers on the glossy wooded armrest and looked up, startled to see the Baron answer a ringing phone. An annoyed look flashed momentarily over the, up until now, controlled face of the Baron, and Frederick noticed how handsome he was as a flood of light beamed into the Daimler at a stoplight.

The Baron uttered something that sounded like an expletive in German into the receiver, and then spoke very softly, carefully choosing his words for Frederick as if English were not Frederick's native language.

"If you don't mind," Frederick knew instinctively that what came next would be a disappointment, "we won't be going to Au Bar. There is some person there I'd rather not see."

Damn. I knew it! Fling flees and nobody wants the stepsister. Frederick was crushed, but couldn't quite understand why he was so overwhelmingly disappointed at having an evening with this intriguing man end so soon.

The corners of the Baron's mouth edged slightly upward.

"It's early yet. Perhaps you'd enjoy a brandy at my apartment. I'd love to show off my latest acquisition from Sotheby's. It hasn't even been uncrated yet. I'm quite excited about it."

Frederick was no snob: what was good enough to excite the Baron would probably drive him to ecstasy.

"Yes, sir," piped up Frederick, his spirits miles higher, wondering what the hell did you call a Baron in a darkened Daimler limousine gliding uptown, to share a brandy.

The experience of any great New York apartment, as any *Architectural Digest* editor will tell you, happens once you are safely ensconced within, off the dirty streets and away from the ubiquitous gray walls obfuscating sunlight, moonlight, and twilight; as if you have to crack open the geode to discover the sparkling crystals within. Not so with Baron William Wolfgang von Sturm's New York pied-á-terre. The moment they stepped off the elevator, carefully attended by a uniformed "driver," Frederick knew he was in a connoisseur's paradise. The gems of Manhattan's skyline somehow crowded together to gaudily show themselves off, shimmering and twinkling, through the Baron's twenty-four-foot-high glass wall of window that stood at the end of at least one hundred feet of highly polished onyx marble flooring stretched out in front of them. All of Central Park was framed by a necklace of illuminated skyscrapers.

"Ah, my Disneyland," Von Sturm laughed. "How do you take your brandy?"

"In a glass would be fine." Frederick was overwhelmed. Maybe the Baron preferred golden goblets.

As certain lights in the full-floor duplex were carefully rheostated, Frederick came face to face with Caravaggio's masterpiece, "A Young Boy with a Fruit Basket." The last time he had seen "Ragazzo con Canestro di Frutta" had been in the Metropolitan Museum. Now Frederick had just enough buzz from the

E-tab to wonder if the Baron knew that Caravaggio often slept with the young boy urchins he took off the streets to paint in the guise of saints, and as objects of desire. As Frederick became accustomed to the darkness, the only light being focused on the masterpieces of art, he let his eyes wander around the vast living room with its low-flung burgundy velvet built-in couches, offering seating for fifty, with tasseled Fortuny pillows arranged in military precision. A quartet of massive Art Deco "elephant" chairs, as well as a desk of Macassar ebony and shagreen, were impressive, if uninviting. It was as if Frederick had entered some private museum where the visitor was required to stand and watch, but not allowed to sit down.

Baron von Sturm handed Frederick the fifty-year-aged Hennessey in a Steuben snifter, and suddenly raised his voice in delight.

"Ah, today's trophy! Dieter has already uncrated it." Frederick, at his host's heels, moved closer to inspect the star lot from Sotheby's sale of antiquities. Standing on a stark marble pedestal was a red-figured calyx krater, circa 510 B.C., which was estimated to bring $400,000, and for which the Baron had plunked down $1.76 million, an auction record for a Greek vase. Because the Baron had to have it. And what the Baron had to have . . .

"Come, look here." The Baron patiently pointed out that the krater was signed by Euphronios, the ancient Greek vase painter. He looked up at Frederick, querying politely, "Are you interested?"

"Interested!" Frederick, who worshiped beauty before all else, who noticed shape and form and contour and texture before he even saw color, was in a fool's paradise.

The figures on the vase were male; the piece's major scene depicted Kyknos battling Hercules.

"Look here," the Baron said. "The fragments on the rim and the reverse side are also by the master's hand."

Frederick's eyes were fixed on the two seminaked muscled titans locked in the impassioned embrace of battle.

"If it were not for you Americans going bankrupt, I would not be able to have such a wonderful trove to choose from." He squarely hooked Frederick's dazzled eyes, which threw back his own reflection. Frederick looked away to another spectacular piece of art. He suddenly felt very shy and vulnerable under the cool connoisseur's discerning gaze.

"Nelson Bunker Hunt and his brother were forced to sell these treasures to pay off the Internal Revenue Service. Lucky for us, no?" The Baron moved to refill Frederick's glass.

Frederick, who usually had his legs up over his head for any anonymous muscle boy by this time of night, nervously cast about to focus on another, less-arousing work of art.

"Ah, 'The Mechanic' by Léger. A good painting. Notice how the solid figure, with his huge hands and tattooed cylindrical arms, is removed from the colorful geometric background. Interesting construction, yes?"

To Frederick, the man depicted in the Léger, with the lit cigarette, crossed arms, and heavy black mustache, could have been any guy out cruising on Christopher Street, not the central focus in a work of art from 1920.

The Baron's art-history lecture moved on to a large Constructivist painting of flailing arms and limbs.

"In 1940, Léger was working on his 'Divers' in Marseilles, a painting of maybe five or six men diving. He left for the United States and one day went to a swimming pool there." The Baron pulled a cigar from a leather case. Frederick wondered if he should light it for him.

"There, the divers were no longer five or six, but two hundred at once. Just try to find them for yourself. Whose head is that? Whose leg is that? Léger had not a clue. So he did a fascinating thing. He scattered the limbs in his picture." The

Baron was an animated wizard holding Frederick spellbound with the magic of his voice, opening up Frederick's understanding of the artist, his painting, and where this evening might be leading.

"Léger said, 'I think I was far closer to the truth than Michelangelo was when he studied the details of each limb. I have seen Michelangelo's figures in the Sistine Chapel: they don't fall. They stay put in all the corners of the building. One can distinguish their toenails. I assure you, when those fellows in Marseilles jumped into the water, I had no time to observe the details, and my divers really fall.' "

The Baron threw back his head and laughed. "Can you imagine Léger taking on Michelangelo?"

"Well, I certainly wouldn't have minded taking on Michelangelo. I understand he appreciated male beauty on more than just his murals or stone. It thrills me to think of the flesh and blood 'David' in the arms of his creator, breathing fire into Michelangelo's impassioned soul." Frederick could *more* than imagine.

The Baron looked startled.

"Perhaps breathing fire into cold, hard marble was his genius," the Baron replied hesitantly. He appeared puzzled as he studied the beautiful young boy across from him as if he were one of his priceless possessions.

"So now what?" asked Frederick.

"You might," said the Baron slowly, "you might like to see some of the pieces I keep upstairs."

Frederick was jubilant. The Baron wasn't interested in Fling! The Baron had wanted to meet him! The Baron wanted the wild thing with *him*! But Frederick had no way of knowing that all the Baron had done for the past ten years was collect and observe. He watched many bizarre and erotic performances, but he never participated. Not anymore. Not since his Tadzio . . . that beautiful boy in Brazil.

As they climbed up the staircase, he turned to the boy on the landing behind him. "I hope you don't mind, I'm going to detain you." This was the first time the Baron had said this to anyone in ten years. With a demanding look in his unwavering eyes he added, "I'll keep you here."

Frederick brazenly sighed, "I was meant to be kept." *Now what?*

The figure that met Frederick at the top of the stairs was neither a Michelangelo drawing nor a Caravaggio painting, but the work of a modern photographer, Victor Skrebneski. The larger-than-life, monumental male nude who was emerging from the shadows of Skrebneski's world of light and darkness was meeting Frederick head-on. The man-boy in the photograph was holding a coconut, a bronze ball, a discus—what did it matter?—on his modeled shoulder, carved valleys above a chiseled chest. His washboard stomach was so tightly rippled that even the dirtiest shirt would come clean. As Frederick's eyes followed the natural Grecian line of composition, they rested on the long, inviting cock arched and hung beneath a forest of leafy pubic hair. The boy in the photograph was classically beautiful.

Frederick was beautiful. It was that simple. He felt the Baron's warm breath on his back as the Baron's hands encircled his chest from behind, searching into his open shirt and gliding down the smooth, silky surface of Frederick's hairless body.

His mouth involuntarily gaped open as the Baron's wanting mouth moved hungrily across the nape of his neck. Frederick swooned as the Baron lightly kissed his shoulder, running his surprisingly large and elegant hands up Frederick's perfect torso.

To Frederick, *small* hands meant *small* dick, so he quivered in anticipation at the exceedingly large hands with their long, tapered thick fingers. Only once in Paris had he felt hands this large and this in control, and he had not surfaced for weeks. So what was in store for him now?

It wasn't Fling. It's me! Frederick's own sensualities and desires were awakened by the Baron's fingertips, searching as if the Baron were a blind man reading Frederick's beauty in braille—tracing, finding the contours of his iron-hard stomach, his lean torso, and finally his slim hips and tautly rounded ass.

As the Baron removed his shirt and jacket, Frederick was turned around, his clothes discarded in a silken and woolen pile at his feet. With each caressing and probing kiss, Frederick grew more toned, higher, taller, more beautiful, as if he were changing himself, chameleonlike, to fit the Baron's unearthly expectations. He trembled in an involuntary clench, contracting the exquisiteness of his rib cage and muscled stomach like a blacksmith's bellows. As many times as he had taken the drug, the E-tabs, the Ecstasy pill, he was only now comprehending the *true* meaning of ecstasy. He was just now experiencing the passion that could be realized only between two members of the same sex. He was held in a state of silent suspension where nothing happened. Frederick was feeling intoxicated by the practiced fingers of centuries-bred predilection. The smooth surface of his skin sported goose bumps. The Baron was caressing and licking and tasting the delicious skin from the sweat-soaked body of the beautiful boy.

"Ohh, uhh." Frederick's cheek was bumped by something cold and hard. Had he walked into some sort of sadist's lair, with unfriendly tools and toys? he wondered as his eyes fixed over the bed. There were two Roman bronze lion heads attached to the wall, with round handles running through the lions' open jaws, strong enough for leather tethers.

"My ring," the Baron said flatly. "I never take it off," he explained the cold object, and added distractedly, "I have another one, too."

Another ring, another baronial signet ring that would coolly contour more of his body, a body becoming increasingly pliant and willing with each of the Baron's strokes and licks.

The Baron was tasting him. As one hand played with his left nipple, the Baron's mouth was grazing and pulling on the right nipple, bringing it up and out as if in some sort of royal salute. Only, it was touch and passion and practice and artifice—not reason—that was enlarging Frederick's muscular pecs. Frederick's normally oversized nipples were now the size and hardness of silver dollars.

For Frederick, experienced beyond the wildest realm of good taste, practically a prostitute for pleasure, it was just beginning to dawn on him, clouded in a mist of desire, that he was being made love to.

William Wolfgang von Sturm held Frederick's delicate hand and with his other unbuttoned the five buttons on the 501 Levi's, when all Frederick was aching for was to have his new master rip open his jeans and free his throbbing cock.

Frederick was in ecstatic pain, groaning in pleasure and pain as the pressure in his groin became unbearable. He was jolted back to his fairy-tale experience as the cool-cold signet ring hit his hot pulsating tumescence, the warm large hands gently caressing his balls before the Baron engulfed him completely. Frederick panicked as he felt he was going to come. He couldn't hold back: the E-tab, the ecstasy, the muscled beauty, man to man, the headiness of it all.

"I'm going to come. Can I come now?" He was almost whimpering.

"No, I'll tell you when, my dear."

"Yes, yes," Frederick cried. The pressure was building up so, he had to have relief or he'd burst. He gasped as he felt the heavy probing at his finely contoured buttocks, felt the ringed finger at the opening of his ass. He wanted to wait but couldn't. As if sensing his young beauty's sudden loss of control, the Baron swiftly took his mouth away from the young boy's beautiful cock.

"Not yet, my dear, not quite."

"Yes, yes, whatever you want, my lord." What the fuck did you call a Baron when screwing him? His head was spinning. Any brains he had left were blown clear out of his head when the Baron's lips recircled him, pulling him into his commanding mouth. Frederick arched his graceful back into a position achieved before only by Olympic gold medal gymnasts. He had never been so pliable, so obedient, so hot.

His back grazed the coolness of the marble nightstand, which bruised him lightly as he was led to the Art Deco masterpiece, the Jean Dunand million-dollar love bed with two wood nymphs and two satyrs dancing on the headboards. What did they know of real ecstasy? thought Frederick. What did they know of wanting, needing, of the elegant masculine merging of pain and ecstasy? He could think of nothing except what was between his legs. He was intoxicated with the scent of men, the scent of strength of thousands of years of men who were above and beyond the limited places of women. His body was now perfected by desire into the muscled moldings of Michelangelo's "David"; Michelangelo, who occasionally took a young model, a young boy, for himself.

As the Baron's ringed finger delved deeper into Frederick, the boy, to himself, was only an object of wanting and needing. To the Baron, he was a romantic, Byronesque hero, a beauty so noble he must be claimed and removed from the ordinary, dirty world just as Caravaggio took his dirty street urchins and elevated them into young gods on canvas. In the Jean Dunand mirror, Frederick, the hot, crazy, disco-dancing, fuckable-on-the-first-date Frederick, on the brink of loosing all control, finally caught a quick shadowed silhouette of himself and found a reason to hang on to his depreciated semblance of sense. He saw his beautiful torso, his sculptured ass riding high in the shape of two perfect crystal balls. In the mirror, he could clearly see his own reflection, the demanding desire of the Baron, *his* neediness, and suddenly Frederick could hang on. He could hold back from coming to please the Baron. He must please the Baron! This was not a *Honcho-Torso* pornographic fantasy. He couldn't wait. He could. He closed his eyes and held his breath as the Baron moved him over his own lithe, taut, and surprisingly well-toned body for a man of fifty-some years. He had to please the Baron. He felt he must come with him. He concentrated on any self-control he could muster up. Straddling the Baron, Frederick gasped as he reached down to grasp the Von Sturm cock, larger than he had imagined, to guide him into the private region of man-to-man orgasmic combat. The rush of pain was ameliorated in a few seconds as the enormous weapon turned into a velvet saber and a groaning, mindless, conquered Frederick rode his master like a medieval knight on his mammoth charging stallion into battle to serve his lord.

In the mirror was reflected a curiously choreographed military dance, in which two muscled torsos twisted and turned. In this untamed world, rough riders on white horses herded wild bulls, and a pair of intrepid warriors galloped to the edge of the world!

The obscure and inner glories of man-to-man love, privately known to certain civilizations of ancient Saracens, Greeks, Romans, and Visigoths, were now revealed to Frederick and his baron.

The cool rich man and the pretty boy writhed together in a shocking and unexpected passion. Where moments before reason had prevailed, there were now only two wild things bucking like stags, their locked horns grappling in an artful frenzy, until Frederick rode the Baron over the top, their panting breath coming in short spurts as they shuddered in mutual ecstasy.

"Oh, my God," gasped Frederick, rolling off the Baron and collapsing onto his side.

"Not your god, just your Baron. And keeper." The Baron laughed in exhaustion and relief. "My beautiful boy." He stroked

Frederick's head, the moist strands of hair curling over his forehead, resting on the Baron's chest.

"You were like Nijinsky as the fawn in *L'Apres-Midi d'un Faune*," he said, stroking the sleeping form, "bucking his balletic orgasm so gracefully for all of Paris to see. The ballet, *Afternoon of a Fawn*, was so shocking for Paris in 1912 that it was banned, and just as Nijinsky stunned *le tout monde* of Paris on that night, so will you. Wait until you see what I have in store for you."

Frederick stretched awake and snuggled into the Baron's protective arms and asked, yawning, "So what do I call you, anyway?"

"Wolf, my dear. I will be your Wolfy."

Fling bounced up the stairs to her third-floor walk-up, taking them two at a time. Had to hurry. Her long legs didn't even bother with the in-between steps. She bolted up to her studio apartment, where she would be able to hear her telephone and wait for Kingman's footsteps. At last! Oh, now, what if she'd missed the call? She tumbled into the apartment, her sunny-blond hair flying straight out behind her. This was her third year in New York and second year in this place, which still had an airy, whitewashed, just-moved-in feeling to it. She'd never been able to afford furniture before the Carmen contract, and since then she hadn't been able to organize her time.

"Oh, my gosh." She nervously called her answering service, remembering to say thank-you. He hadn't called yet. She checked the time.

"I'm late, oooh." She wrinkled her nose. "He hates late." She whizzed through the apartment like a pent-up puppy, watering the plants, putting the tea kettle on the stove—the stainless-steel kettle and two unmatched mugs were her only kitchen utensils. Most New York model girls didn't cook much, let alone eat much. The yogurt and honey in the refrigerator were for her homemade skin-moisturizing brew. The only "artwork" hanging in her one room were posters of animals—not model girls and not a single photo of Fling herself.

She practically cried every time she passed the poster of the white baby seal staring back at her with those sweet, moist, innocent eyes. She knew Brigitte Bardot slaved away to save the seals, and she felt a kind of bond with the sixties sex kitten, and not just the fact that they both shared the same oversized, sensual mouth. She checked off her calendar with a red Magic Marker, carefully crossing off "*Vogue* cover shoot," "runway work for Christian Francis Roth," and "promo party for The Dress." She sunnily circled "Kingman" and added a few *X*'s and *O*'s of her own: what Fling lacked in originality, she made up for in enthusiasm. She dragged the phone into the bathroom, where she turned on the "hot" faucet and threw in a capful of Fling! Splash! from its bright-yellow plastic bottle. Unbreakable, she sighed gratefully, as it slipped from her hands and tumbled onto the white tiled floor.

She threw The Dress off and into the corner, then thought better of it and shoved tissue paper into the sleeves—tomorrow The Dress would have a big day—and with her hair piled high on her head, Bardot style, plunged into her steamy, soothing sea of bubbles.

It felt good to lie lazily in the water after working on high heels all day and night. Poor Frederick, he was so disappointed. She hoped he didn't mind going home early—early for *him*. She worried so about her dearest best friend. She wished he'd find somebody like she had. Why, only last week Anthony Clavet, the makeup artist, had died of AIDS.

She shook off an armload of suds and blew a shiny, translucent bubble over her head. She'd think about that stuff later. Frederick was her best friend, and whatever he wanted to be was just fine with her. She'd just look after him, that's all. After all, he'd been her only truly loyal and best friend since she'd arrived in New York from Corpus Christi, tall as Texas and just as naive. Frederick had found her the apartment, loads of jobs, and showed her how to get *everything* in New York for practically free. They would walk down Madison Avenue, hand in hand, at night after work. And when Fling found something especially neat or terrific in the windows, Frederick could usually get a hold of that particular shirt or Azzedine Alaïa dress wholesale or, better yet, he would turn up with the somewhat-soiled sample that had been worn by another runway model. Somehow Frederick was able to get those little things done that she was too shy to do or demand for herself. Poor Frederick. He was so pretty. He was as pretty as any of the other girls, Fling thought, busily building a bubble mountain with her toes. Why, she giggled to herself, only yesterday, during a lull in the photo shoot, the models had turned the tables on Frederick and made *him* up for a change. Later that night, at Iman's birthday party at Nell's, with Frederick lip-lined and powder-cheeked, with subtly mascaraed eyes, he had joined the conga line of model girl duplicates, mixing with the world's beauties as if he had always belonged to this bevy line of pretty feminine faces. And everybody knew that the world's prettiest faces eventually ended up in New York. Fling slowly brought the sea sponge up from her ankle to her thigh. Only, some of the other girls had been jealous because Frederick looked better than them. Boy, most of those girls would kill to have his slim hips and tiny butt.

Now she stopped thinking because she was concentrating on making two bubble mounds around each breast. It was amazing that she was a model at all, with breasts as big as Corpus Christi and those rounded sassy hips that did not fit the model "norm."

She splashed two handfuls of water over her face, musing that if it hadn't been for the Francesco Scavullo portfolio, which

Kingman had paid for as way of apology for practically running her down with his silver Mercedes and slushing her and her entire portfolio of pictures with snow and mud, ruining them beyond repair, she might never be where she was today. She didn't even know who or what a "Kingman Beddall" was that day three years ago, as she had lain crying and freezing, with two bleeding elbows and splattered with dirt, on the sidewalk of Fifty-ninth and Madison. All she could think about at the time was that her first real photographic portfolio, the one that had cost her every penny she had ever managed to save, was destroyed. Still lying in a hurt heap on the sidewalk, crying her eyes out, she had been saved by the very gentleman who had almost killed her with his Mercedes 560 SEL. Concerned about her safety *and* a nasty lawsuit, which Frederick kept insisting was the real reason for his solicitous concern, he'd had her elbows X-rayed at Lenox Hill Hospital, paying for everything, including new pictures for her portfolio by Francesco Scavullo, who shot the covers for *Cosmopolitan*! She'd had to wear her arm in a sling—Frederick redid it in a pink-and-mauve Hermès silk scarf of bits and bridles—but it had been worth almost dying, to meet Kingman Beddall. Look at all the wonderful things that had happened to her since! The receptionist at Ford Models had practically flipped out when this lanky unknown had sauntered in off the street with a portfolio by the great Scavullo himself under her arm—the I-wouldn't-photograph-you-unless-you-were-Cher-or-the-hottest-new-model Scavullo—showing her off to every breathtaking advantage.

Boy, had that been a lucky day: the day Kingman ran into her, literally, she thought, sinking into the suds up to her giraffelike neck.

"I can't stand these steps. They're going to be the death of me," said Kingman, panting at the bathroom door and leaning his full weight from his head to his elbow into its arch.

Whoops! She forgot he had a key.

"Funny, Frederick says the same thing," Fling said, bobbing her head out of the water.

"Stand up, my little one. You're moving up in the world." Kingman grabbed a towel and grinned.

"Oooh, am I moving uptown with you?" squealed Fling.

"No, we are a secret, remember? No one is going to know about us."

"Ooh, I forgot. Okay, then, we'll just whisper. Come closer, honey," she said, tugging on his ear and splashing him with water.

"You're getting me wet." Kingman ducked. "No, not here. I can't stand this place. It is too cramped, just like living in Nicaragua."

Fling immediately stood up in the tub with a puzzled look on her face, trying to figure out exactly where Nicaragua was. Was it uptown or downtown? Wasn't it near TriBeCa?

Kingman shook his head and shrugged. He couldn't stand that puzzled look: it meant she was thinking. He preferred she didn't.

She rose fully up out of the tub like an elegant white whooping crane, her long arms extended behind her like the wings of the bird spread out to take off and flutter in flight.

She knew Kingman was looking at her, and she couldn't help flirting with him. As he lifted her up off her feet, she worried.

"Kingman, your back!"

"My back, smack. If it ain't broke, don't fix it. Plus, I got a whole golf course of doctors, the best orthopedic guys in the city, at my beck and call. So feel free, lean on me."

"And just where is this 'up' that we are going to?" She snuggled her long, willowy model figure close to him, soaking the front of his custom suit with Fling! bubble bath.

"Upstairs," he pointed. "You're moving to the penthouse. The top floor of this dump."

She jumped out of his arms like a slippery salmon, the towel flying off behind her as Fling romped naked up the stairs.

He watched her from behind with a wide grin, amused and relieved that he didn't have to lug 118 pounds of model up two more flights.

"But there is nothing up there," she said as she spun around on the fourth-floor landing. "Nothing there but empty storage space." She pointed to the top floor, directly above her.

"Not if you haven't looked lately. You'll love it. It's like one of those artist lofts. One of the swishy guys from the office just finished it today."

"Ooh, Kingman, I'm so excited."

"Yeah, now we'll have a place where we don't have to make love standing up." He groaned and grinned at the same time.

"But, Kingman," a worried expression crossed her face, "how are you ever going to make it up all the stairs? You hate stairs!"

"The Otis elevator man is coming in the morning."

She jumped up and down, modestly covering both her breasts, forgetting that the rest of her was completely naked.

He was smiling between pants from climbing the five flights of stairs. Who needed racquetball or aerobics when he had his women?

He was only one step behind her.

"Ooh, Kingman, won't the rent be so expensive? A whole floor!"

"We can work it out; I'm the new landlord."

He'd tell her later that he bought the building in her name; no need for Joyce Royce to be poking her nose into *this* extramarital affair. It was enough that she was on his back about Tandy, and it would be one less thing for his wife, Anne, to know about in case she ever decided to call it quits. And in this crummy neighborhood, this pile of rehabilitated brick probably wouldn't be worth much anyway.

Right now, he had other things on his mind.

He silently unlatched the four Medeco locks, necessary accoutrement for New York downtown living. His heart was racing rapidly in his chest, more the result of anticipation than exertion. Fling poked through the enormous space, dragging her towel behind her.

Boy, Fling looked great in the raw. His eyes followed her beautiful body whirling through the sparsely decorated space like a wood nymph gamboling through a sylvan forest.

The decorator from Kingman's office had placed potted trees in such a way that they appeared to be planted, and had added only a minimal amount of white cushion poufs and low *faux* Corinthian columns for tables.

"Look." Kingman beamed at her proudly, pointing to the plants. "Living. All these goddamn trees are alive. Just the way you like!"

"Oh, Kingman," she purred, spinning on her heel in a pirouette, pleased as punch that he remembered her desire to save the rain forest.

"Let's look over here."

"No." His voice was firm, with a hint of husky. "You can look later. When I'm gone."

He crooked a finger at her. "Let's look at you now."

The damn beautiful creature was naked. Hell, she was always naked. Even when she sauntered down the runway modeling one of those god-awful couture jobs, she was naked. You could feel those breasts, her hips, every curve of her body that redefined latitudes, under the bulk of the fabric. You could see the perfect form in the diaphanous chiffons and see-through stuff they were wearing these days. Hell, it was like having an affair with a goddess, thought Kingman.

What a lucky dick he was. This goddess girl ought to be on a pedestal, where other businessmen could see her and only *he* could touch. Then all those poor bastards would envy him.

There was a flicker of mischief in her eyes, which were smiling down at him, her mouth drawing into that sexy, pouty thing he found so adorable. Her smile and upbeat, happy attitude *were* contagious. It always felt good just to be around this girl.

He held her chin in his hand and tilted it toward him. What a looker, he thought. *My* looker.

He took her by the hand and started to the bedroom, almost colliding with the pedestal table in the dimness of the room.

"Where the fuck is the track lighting? I told those guys to have it installed *today!*" Kingman was livid.

"Shhhh." Fling held her forefinger to the famous Fling lips. "Look, King. Moonlight from the skylight!" He grinned again. Got to admit, this girl had a way with him.

She was like a once-woman stress reducer. How could you be serious or upset with this delicious, dizzy looker? Hah, maybe she wasn't so dumb after all. He had put this dump in her name, hadn't he?!

Suddenly he stopped thinking as the luscious lips moved against his, the famous mouth opened to inhale his breath, and her little-girl tongue darted into his own lusty mouth.

He lifted her up into the air and tasted the tips of her breasts, which pointed like quivering arrows. When she came down to rest, it was on the pedestal, where he left her, naked, lit by moonbeams flooding in through the skylight as if even the heavens or demons wanted to have a look at sheer human perfection. Probably she didn't need an apartment at all—just a marble pedestal.

"King, it's cold up here. My feet are freezing." Laughing, she lifted a foot from the pedestal.

"Well, give it to me." And he kissed her elegant arch and warmed her long slim toes in his hands.

She threw back her honey-blond hair, the highlights dancing around her face in the enchanted moonlight, and laughed a laugh that sounded like sleigh bells.

Those guys on Mount Olympus have to be wanting this girl, thought Kingman. Didn't they come down every once in a while and try to screw a wood nymph or something? Yeah, he thought, and remembered the story about some guy-god who spotted this mortal beauty and comes down from the heavens, and some fool girl-goddess saves her by turning her into a tree! A panicky look struck Kingman's face as he saw his own model-goddess standing like a statue of pulchritude, the exquisite curves and valleys of her body bathed in the shadings of moonbeams, in the middle of a forest of fucking trees the swishy decorator had moved in. Hell, he'd have to have the skylight painted over. No telling who could be looking in and spying. Neighbors, there was no trusting neighbors. Later. But now he'd have a look. He'd have a lick of looks.

Fling, who always came alive in the light, the camera light, the strobe light, moving, taking direction, so that she lost her puppylike moves and grew, stretching and turning, even more voluptuous, more desirable, more perfect, now came spectacularly alive in the moonlight. The same enraptured look came over her face—lips parted, hands on her hips, swanlike neck arched dangerously backward—that she had postured a few hours earlier at the dance club with Frederick, where they had Vogued and posed, showing off their well-earned narcissism.

He grasped an ankle from the pedestal on which she stood, seemingly created for her to be perched on. She responded by balancing on the other foot. She posed and played with her delightful body, teasing, arousing him until his hand grasped her toned, trim thigh and moved into the places that weren't muscled or firm but wet and soft and inviting. He could feel her grasp his fingers inside her. Hell, did she have exercised muscles there too? She was all abandon, all mouth, all breasts and legs, and he was having her. She was the best there was—star, a cover girl that every guy in New York could covet—and he was the only man in New York who could have her. He always had the best and, right now, on this continent, in this hemisphere, she was the best.

She kicked out one of her Cyd Charisse legs, the kind they used to call gams, a high-kicker on a pedestal, and let out a small, low moan. She loved the touch of Kingman's fingers, rough and calloused until you got to the smooth, highly buffed, manicured fingernails at the tips. It was like having rough-textured wool rub against your naked skin, arousing a certain sensual response, with a hem of velvet or chiffon grazing you in other, softer places.

Kingman was exploring her in those other places as she writhed and posed upon her pedestal. But he'd take her off that pedestal. Her beauty and unavailability aroused him, but he wasn't some worshipful sap who idolized and worshiped a woman. He wasn't a lovesick fan genuflecting at the shrine of an unattainable goddess, or a young summer-maddened fool consumed with wild expectations of everlasting bliss.

Nah, Kingman knew a woman was more apt to fall for the cad and the playboy deft in the wiles that ensnare women's hearts than for the timid, cautious, solicitous suitor on bended knee. Let the assholes worship her from afar. He'd ravage her in his own time, for his own pleasure. He must protect himself from her allurements. If he fell in love, all was lost. He'd lose her, he reasoned. Kingman long ago learned that women wouldn't love you if you were below them looking up. No, they had to look up to a man to want him. He had learned all this wealth of womanly wants the hard way. Being aboveboard with a woman was tantamount to being thrown overboard in rough seas. Too dangerous, too unpredictable. Losing your heart, falling in too deep. Things to be avoided by the Kingman Beddalls at all costs. Better to give away an apartment than your heart. Less expensive in the long run, he rationalized. Women wanted pieces of you, to run your life and run you ragged. And men like him needed to travel through their busy gray-flanneled lives with no excess baggage, to change partners as new opportunities and better business deals turned up. He loved women, sure, he just didn't want to fall *in love* with any of them. And this one. Boy, this one was tugging away at his heart strings, where he always thought he probably just had a big black lump of coal.

Nah, to Kingman love was a soccer game and the only guy who won was the fella who scored the most goals. So score one for Beddall, scrambling down the field, ball between his legs, kicking it between the posts to make a goal.

In one swift action Kingman moved Fling off the pedestal, out of the starlight, and brought her to earth, pulling her to the downtown floor with him, where he ran his hands expertly over her body, playing a practiced push and pull at the soft tawny muff that was yielding so freely and passionately to him. Off her pedestal, falling into him, she called out his name in a supreme surrendering. Goal one.

He moved over her, under her, with a determination that was more intense than impassioned, until she was dizzy with a riot of joyful shudderings coming crazily one after another. It wasn't until then, until she could stand no more pleasure but this last one, his own, that he determinedly moved in for his own pleasure. With all the finesse of a great matador, El Córdobes moving in for the final plunging of the bull, his eyes and every sinew of his body concentrated on this one single thrust, did he move in for the one goal that really mattered, his own. The score was perfect, six to one, and he had won as the rockets went off.

"Oh, Kingman," Fling sighed as they both fell back to earth. "I love you." Then there was the silence when she always expected him to echo her words but he didn't. She was always disappointed. Barely out of breath, perspiration beads glistening in the crevice of her breasts, she moaned to herself her own after-lovemaking mantra, "He'll say those words to me one day. He'll say them," tears in her azure-blue eyes, as if saying those magic words would make them true. "Clap your hands if you believe in Tinkerbell" might have been more realistic. If she of all people couldn't get the man she loved to say those words to her, what was the *point* of her beauty? She curled the litheness of her body into his, entwining the endless Fling legs into a tangle with his, inhaling the smells of him, the rough masculine scent of him that she loved, that she would gladly give up her own line of Fling! fragrance for.

"Oooh, if only they could put this musky man smell in a bottle," she sighed, happily inhaling the sweat beads on his chest.

"Yeah, eau de stink," he grunted and kissed the tip of her nose.

# 6

There is a pride of people who live among the fragrant azaleas and manicured boxwood along the verdant, gently rolling shores of the James River of Virginia. There are some among them who look upon the Pilgrims as nouveau arrivistes, tattered immigrants evicted from their homeland for harboring disparate thoughts and notions. Virginia Byrd Randolph's ancestors had smooth crossings, landing with royal grants and charters tucked under their belts. Going off to a new world honorably, at the request of their beloved King James I they landed in 1607, a full thirteen years before the Pilgrims set foot on Plymouth Rock. In fact, at Boxwood Plantation, they celebrated a Southern version of Thanksgiving each year, the *real*

Thanksgiving, Founders Day, they called it down here among the magnolias, dogwood, and garden gazebos, and far away from Massachusetts.

Virginia Byrd Randolph was one of those quietly proud and civilized citizens of a privately privileged South who knew which of her ancestors had set sail from London on the *Godspeed* for the New World in December 1606, which forebearers had penned their names to the Declaration of Independence on July 4, 1776, and which relatives had led the charge at the second Bull Run in 1863. Virginia Byrd Randolph's father had been president of the Jamestown Society, and her husband and her son were members of the Society of Cincinnati, the elite club of firstborn sons who were descendants of military officers who had served under George Washington or General Lafayette during the Revolutionary War.

Virginia was a member of the Colonial Dames herself, and a treasured trustee of the Virginia Historical Society. She was one of those grande dames who was so soft-spoken and so pale of complexion that she was presumed to be a fragile Southern flower, when in reality she was as iron wrought as the heavily ornamented gates that guarded her handed-down-from-generation-to-generation properties.

The gravel crunched beneath Virginia's purposeful and pragmatic gait. Wasting no steps, she strode up the seven terraced gardens on the James River side of her beloved Boxwood Plantation. Without a sideways glance she passed through the purple-hued tulip poplars forming a stately *allée* leading up to the back portico of her Georgian mansion.

Between the second and third terraces, Virginia skirted through the small circular formal garden consisting of four pie-shaped plots separated by gravel walks and centered with a gurgling ivy-covered and conch-encrusted fountain. This little garden had been christened The Beauty Spot by her great-grandmother Evelyn Bland, in 1842, and had remained intact even when Boxwood had been used as a hospital during the Civil War. The gardens of Boxwood were considered some of the most beautiful and luxurious in the South.

Ordinarily, Virginia was always renewed by the flash of a cardinal's scarlet wings darting through the foliage, the fuchsia flame of azaleas and dogwood, and the enchantment of graybeard moss bewitching Boxwood's giant ancient trees in the dewy mist of one of her early morning's walk. But none of this mattered now to the aristocratic, genteel matriarch as she single-mindedly climbed the stone garden steps heavily bordered by rose bushes and fragrant bunches of lilacs. Virginia was a woman with a mission. Her daughter, Anne, had to be dealt with. She was still lying in bed weeks after her husband had publicly humiliated her in New York, pulling Virginia into a much ballyhooed tug of war. Not only had the rogue rousted her daughter, he had done so with daily updates in New York's cheap newspapers. Why, taxi drivers and checkout girls had even taken sides in the Kingman Beddall-Anne Randolph Beddall-Fling triangular scandal! The patrician Virginian shuddered and pulled her cashmere sweater around her shoulders. Any kind of publicity was anathema to Virginia Randolph. Equally unacceptable to her was her fragile daughter's inability to cope with her tragedy. This was unworthy behavior for any true Virginian, let alone a Randolph.

Taking a look around her gardens at last, she made a mental note that the hedge of althea needed pruning and then majestically swept into her house.

In the great hall, she placed the overflowing wicker rose basket on a highly polished Georgian end table and paused in front of a dulled Chippendale mirror to pat her silver coif into place, straighten the bow on her paisley-patterned silk morning dress, and carefully smooth away any sign of stressful worry from her brow. Virginia Byrd Randolph never appeared harassed. It was unthinkable to her and unacceptable behavior to any woman in her position. In the Boxwood Bible of Proper Conduct, temper displays and woeful demeanor just didn't exist. She pulled off her garden gloves and quietly surveyed her domain. In the hushed serenity of the perfectly proportioned rooms and furnishings, Virginia could feel the hearty approval of her ancestors haughtily looking down on her from their severely depicted portraits. She loved to feel the vitality of Boxwood's ghosts. Sometimes she could almost hear the festive footsteps of young girls in full-skirted crinolines rustling down the staircase, the hum of long-deceased servants carrying silver trays through the whistling hall, and the *clickity-clack* of horse hooves hitting the circular cobblestone driveway of the carriage entrance. Occasionally she imagined she could hear the distant echoes from the roar of cannons going off, as part of Boxwood's original 12,500-acre tract had been a battlefield after the South had seceded from the Union.

Virginia Randolph always thought that hats should be doffed to the long-dead mistresses of Boxwood, who with deceptive effortlessness had kept this large establishment operating while simultaneously displaying Southern charm and graciousness. Even in the midst of war, turmoil, and carpetbaggers, the Boxwood women had always prevailed, and no Kingman Beddall was going to upset that tradition or insult Boxwood's ghosts. High time for Anne to get out of bed.

"Here, put that rose vase on this tray." Eva the cook bossily directed her husband, Hook, to arrange some of the bountiful variety of red and yellow roses grown at Boxwood in a dainty Waterford crystal bud vase that would brighten up Anne Randolph Beddall's breakfast tray. She covered the tray with a Madeira linen napkin, popped a silver cloche over the toast, and placed the floral porcelain teacup, from the *morning* china cupboard, next to a matching egg cup and a rolled-up copy of the New York *Daily Sun*, delivered daily to Boxwood.

"She won't eat none of this," her husband said slowly, moving out of the cane kitchen chair. "She won't talk none, eat none. The woman has gone and got herself a nervous breakdown, and this house ain't never had one of those before." He moved toward the hallway, added on *recently*, in the 1870s, that connected the kitchen with the main house. When the central house had been built, in 1730, the kitchen had been erected separately so that a kitchen fire wouldn't burn down the entire mansion.

Hook mumbled to himself as he moved through the entrance hall lined with portraits of "family," carrying the breakfast tray through the foyer filled with Randolphs, Byrds, Harrisons, Carters, and Bollings, decorating the walls above the pale-green wooden dado. These were familiar names in Richmond, Virginia, and along the plantations and homes hugging the lazily flowing James River.

"Humph," muttered Hook, climbing the grand staircase, "nothing but dead people around here. Dead people on the walls, dead-acting people in the bedroom, even the dog, Skylar, that old black Lab, hasn't moved in days. Maybe he's dead too."

Also practically steamrollered over the old servant on the second landing. "Hook, don't bother." Also plucked the sterling-silver cover off the breakfast plate, poking her nose inside. "Unless this tea is laced with bourbon, Mama's not going to touch it."

She slid a piece of toast and an egg simultaneously down her throat. "If you can get your teeth into it, Mama doesn't want it," she said with her mouth full.

"Better stop it, Miss Anne," Hook reprimanded her. "You're supposed to be the one on the diet, and your mama's gotta eat . . . and you shouldn't be talkin' that way about your mama, with no respect."

"I respect her, I love her," Also said, still chewing. "But Grandma's on the warpath and on her way up for a talk, and Mother said she needs reinforcements. I have the two empties under my sweater."

Hook groaned. With Also's girth it was impossible to tell where the two bottles were hidden.

"There's a case in the smokehouse, three bottles in the dovecote, and one in the fireplace under the portrait of Robert E. Lee. But better be quick. Miss Virginia is coming up the stairs . . . at a pace!"

Anne scurried to retrieve the bottle of Virginia Gentleman stashed beneath Robert E. Lee's three-quarter profile as Hook gently rapped at Anne Randolph Beddall's bedroom door.

Anne Randolph Beddall was in her four-poster canopy bed, where she was lying as rumpled as the opulent array of ecru antique Italian linens that covered it. She was so thin she looked like a small sparrow lost in a mahogany forest. A fire was burning warmly in the hearth, and the breakfast tray lay cold and untouched at the foot of the bed. As soon as she saw her mother enter the room, Anne nervously reached for the teacup laced with bourbon.

"Good morning, sweetheart, it's the most glorious morning. You would never know it's May. The rose garden thinks it's the Fourth of July!" She pulled back a heavy chintz drapery, inviting a wide beam of light into the corner room, Anne's childhood room that still displayed her dollhouse, an exact replica of Boxwood, on a special table.

Anne rolled her eyes back up into her head. Maybe she could will herself into a coma.

"Today is gazebo day!" Virginia's voice was a medley of drawing-room charms and matriarchal commands. "We are bundling you up and taking you out to the gazebo. The sheep have formed a little reception committee, they are all *baa-baa*ing for you on the bluff."

Anne wondered if her mother had arranged for a sedan chair. She was feeling a bit tipsy this morning.

"Mother, I think that tomorrow will be a better day."

"Don't pull that Scarlett O'Hara melodrama on me, Anne. This is your mother, the wise old owl, speaking to you now. With that kind of attitude, we would never have won at Bull Run."

"But, Mama, the Yankees won the war."

"Nonsense. We still have Boxwood." A look of determination crossed Virginia's face.

"But, Mama, in New York . . ."

"Oh, hush. In New York there is nothing but Puerto Ricans and uppity Negroes rapping on street corners." She shook her silvery head.

"Mama, that's outrageous!"

"Oh, I didn't mean it the way it sounded. I'm no racist. Hook and Eva are like family. But remember how nice it was, dear, when all the waiters at the Jefferson Hotel would be lined up in their livery and white gloves to serve us Sunday brunch and called us by our proper Christian names? I do miss those days."

Anne remembered those days fondly, too, when the lobby of the hotel had been filled with the best Richmond families dressed up in their Sunday church finery. The small children gathered around the foyer fountain to view the live alligator which happily lived there, while the older girls sashayed down the staircase in their Mary Janes, the very same staircase that had been used in the movie *Gone With the Wind*. How Anne loved that hotel, that staircase, those brunches, that childhood. That was where she belonged. It was having to live as an adult in Kingman Beddall's wicked world that had driven her out of her mind.

"Mama, I can't cope, and don't ask me to. All of little Anne's friends at Brearley 'rap' after school, and in New York the Puerto Ricans are very nice." She pulled the coverlet to her chin. "Please let me just stay here in bed. Mama, I'm just not strong, I just can't pretend anymore. He's publicly humiliated me for months. Why, why, some tabloid paid some window washer to take photographs of our bedroom!" she stifled a sob, "and every woman in New York smells exactly like my husband's mistress!"

"Anne, dear, you have just got to try harder when you are in a foreign land," her left eyebrow arched, "and not be so visible. It's not respectable."

"It's useless, Mama, I did everything I was supposed to. I lunched at Le Cirque, I ran all the charities; I even saved the New York Historical Society, and who cares about their history . . . and he had that, *that girl!*" Her concaved chest heaved. "When people invite us for dinner they never know if he's going to show up with me or her. They have *two* sets of place cards!"

"But, darling, every man has a mistress or a horse or a diversion at one time or another. It's just a part of being a man." She patted her daughter's hand.

Anne was sobbing now. "But he *had* a mistress. That white-trash manicurist. Only this one is different. He takes her out in public everywhere, Mother, and all my friends are wearing her perfume!"

Virginia raised her shoulders and looked at the windowsill. Fling! bath splash was the biggest seller in Richmond's department stores. At least her friends, the Colonial Dames, had the good sense not to wear it. Not around her. But it was everywhere else. Why, she even found a bottle of *it* tucked away in Also's drawer.

"I tried. I'm a failure. After nineteen years he's just walking out on me and little Anne. I just want to be left alone." A dark look crossed Anne's face. "And I did what Daddy wanted. The precious homestead is saved; let me go." A mixture of hurt and hatred, Virginia feared it looked like self-hatred, dimmed the already pale light in her daughter's eyes.

Virginia cradled her daughter's hand in her own, gently stroking it. Before long, Anne drifted off to sleep . . . again. Virginia leaned down to kiss her daughter gently on the forehead and quietly tiptoed out of the bedroom, practically tripping over Also, sitting glumly outside her mother's door like a Rubenesque guardian child.

A storm was brewing over Boxwood. The deer were scurrying deeper into the deer park, the rabbits burrowing into their cozy, warm shelters, and the sheep were herding closer together.

A storm was brewing in the great wood-paneled library at Boxwood as well, with its twelve hundred leather-bound volumes and six hundred first editions, many of them from Thomas Jefferson's vast collection, as he had sold them whenever he had been hard-pressed for cash. Virginia's family had *always* had money, horses, tobacco, and lumber, although the amount had varied over the decades. Sometimes they were cash strapped, but they had always been land rich. They had never been forced to open Boxwood to the public to make ends meet, the way the other great houses had done.

Over at Shirley and Berkeley plantations you purchased a ticket, the price of admission, and were shown through the once-private rooms by young people in period costume. But now all that was wrong with Virginia's world had to do with the very public Kingman Beddall. She hadn't even expressed her great worries to her son and her husband, who had both foolishly embraced the out-of-nowhere Kingman Beddall and invited him into their gentlemen's fraternity. Now all was in danger of being lost. Her dumb, handsome men, who had won and collected all the sparkling silver sports trophies prominently displayed around the library, had allowed Kingman's glib charm and ready cash to seduce them, and with all the ethics of the uncouth carpetbagger he really was.

Virginia entwined her fingers in the heirloom double strand of pearls draped around her crepey neck, leaving a red patch where she unconsciously, repeatedly, pulled at it. Maintaining her perfect posture, she leaned over to switch on one of the Chinese-export porcelain lamps with the pineapple finials, the pineapple being the sign of Southern hospitality.

Hmph. If only they had not been so hospitable to the brash young man. To her, he had always looked like a used-vacuum-cleaner salesman. To her husband, James, huntsman of the Richmond Fox Hunt, and her polo-playing son, James II, he had been heaven sent, a modern day "King" Carter.

James II had followed Kingman around like a dazzled puppy when he was courting his sister. And Virginia's husband had been so bamboozled—he had remembered his good manners but completely forgotten any business sense when he had allowed his new son-in-law to heavily invest in the privately held Boxwood Plantation. The silly gooses had ridden to the hounds with the superficially appealing Kingman and, after he had joined them in the private male coterie of sports, horses, and hounds, they had allowed him into their real estate holdings!

Virginia had just learned from her cousin, Cyrus Fleming, who served as her attorney, that the majority interest of Boxwood, including the manor and its garden and lands, was in danger of ending up Beddall land! She had to stop this man. She would go to her grave and take Kingman with her to prevent Boxwood from falling out of the genteel hands of the Randolphs, who had nourished it with their life's blood. She had been mistress of Boxwood since she was seventeen years old. Her children, James II, Anne, and her granddaughter, Anne II, would not be cheated out of their proper inheritance, and *no* counterfeit "King" Beddall and some woman whose name rhymed with *thing* would get their hands on their legacy! Imagine Boxwood with the likes of Kingman Beddall as proprietor: what a wail Boxwood's ghosts would raise. Why, Kingman Beddall wasn't even FFV. (Every true Virginian knew that "FFV" was the insiders' terminology for descendants of First Families of Virginia.)

She reached down to pat Skylar's shaky head. The Labrador had just puddled on the burgundy-and-vermilion Oriental rug. Poor Skylar was getting so old he was losing control of his kidneys. She scooped the ancient dog up onto the floral chintz sofa and thumbed through some of the leather-bound family scrapbooks.

## *1 9 7 1 , I - 9 5 , V I R G I N I A*

The handsome young man with the soft curly hair downshifted his racy red Triumph Spitfire and sped down I-95. He turned up the volume on the convertible's radio. Johnny Cash was lamenting "Folsom Prison Blues." On an impulse, the young man steered off the highway to pull into the roadside Stuckey's, the McDonald's of the South. He felt strangely at home among the pretty but hefty waitresses and, in a burst of nostalgia, ordered up chicken-fried steak with gravy, piping-hot grits, and a Coca-Cola. Everything looked the same, everything tasted familiar, only *he* was different.

When Carney Eball fled Hopewell, Virginia, hopping a freight train in the middle of the night thirteen years earlier, the only thing he had with him was his leather jacket and the twenty dollar bill he had stolen from his mother's, Dreama Sue's, pocketbook. Now he was back with a vengeance. He knew exactly what it was he wanted, and it was much more than grits and chicken-fried steak. Why, the bright wide tie that he was wearing today cost more than twenty dollars. It was almost as if he had driven down I-95 from Canada just to seek revenge on his past.

As the young man finished his grease-fried food, he knew that this was the last bit of his past he would allow to enter into his self-determined golden future. As he pulled out of the restaurant's parking lot, he decided to take a back road, to avoid the main thoroughfare into town—"shunpikin," they had called it down here when he was a fourteen-year-old illegally driving his father's pickup truck, avoiding the superhighways for the pleasure of driving fast and reckless on the back roads. He maneuvered the car as if on autopilot. He knew these roads like the back of his hand, even though he had been away a full thirteen years. Lucky thirteen, he laughed, and floored the car with no thought to the rising needle on the speedometer. Only his eyes betrayed him as he sped past the red-dirt carnival grounds, now vacant, where he had sold batter-dipped hot dogs on sticks, run the Ferris wheel, and counted up the day's divvy for his dad, Big Carney Eball, and his child bride, Dreama Sue, who occasionally doubled as the Fat Lady.

Contrary to every other little boy's dream, he had run *away* from the circus, because he knew full well the dirty reality of transient ties and dirt-poor carnival life. He thought he caught a whiff of the pervasive smells of his childhood: french-fry grease, day-old open beer bottles, the sticky-sweet aroma of sugar and food dye spun into cotton candy, and the stench of donkey dung.

He handily two-wheeled his car, doing seventy-five mph on a curve like a racing cyclist in a veladome defying the laws of gravity. The adrenaline pumped through his system as he shifted his roadster, speeding through the muddy, red-clay-lined back roads leading into Richmond.

He felt a twang of the familiar "I don't belong here. They'll never let me in the front door," from his boyhood as the fancy uniformed black doorman and the overall-clad white boy came charging up to him at the side entrance of the palatial Jefferson

Hotel. Could they see through him? Did they know he was the poor carny boy whose departure hadn't even been noticed for weeks?

"Careful, son. Park that thing carefully now." Carney summoned his courage and called out after the boy, waving a ten dollar bill at him.

"Thank you, sir." The car parker widened his eyes. "I'll keep it in one of the empty hotel rooms, sir!" He ran, sprinting, around to the driver's side of the car.

Big Carney Eball's son broadened the nervous grin on his face. His pocketful of credit cards didn't say Carney Eball!

The trim, handsome man who walked into the marble lobby, with its high, widely spaced columns, was sweating heavily, soaking through the back of his well-cut, store-bought suit. This broad-shouldered, firmly muscled, yet slight man with a swarthy Black Irish complexion, intense green-gray eyes, and dazzling cosmetically arranged smile, bore no resemblance to the blubbery, scraggly toothed, acne-faced boy with the slick-backed Brylcreemed hair and angry attitude. And violent enough to commit murder.

Now Carney Eball was just a name from the long-dead past. Kingman Beddall was home safe.

Eva refilled the Georgian silver montieth herself so she could get a good look at the likes of Mr. Kingman Beddall *himself*, invited to an "at home" dinner at last.

*6 quarts Jamaican rum*
*8 quarts Apolinaris water*
*1 jar maraschino cherries*
*Juice of 1 1/2 lemons*
*1 can sliced pineapple (for hospitality)*
*1 small tumbler raspberry cordial*

This all went into the traditional recipe for Robert E. Lee Punch. Eva had gone into the drawing room to see with her own eyes what all the fuss was about. Why, Kingman Beddall, Kingman Beddall, was all anybody was talking about, backstairs, upstairs, everywhere, in this house for two weeks, and now this name without a face was finally being ushered into the dining room at Boxwood Manor without much enthusiasm on the part of Boxwood's patrician hostess.

Eva almost collided with her son, Rodney, who was home from the University of Virginia's law school for the weekend to help serve, as she bustled back into the kitchen.

"Well, what's going on in there?" she quizzed him the minute he returned from the dining room after serving the fish course, fresh shad crisped in butter and garnished with bacon.

"What's going on, or what do I think is going on?"

"Rodney!" she hollered at her son, who ranked third in his law class.

"Well," he picked up the Meissen sauce dish and the silver ladle, "if I were conducting a voir dire," he drawled this out, "that's picking a jury, Mama, I'd pick every person at the table except for the guest of honor. Why, he's spinning tales faster than the others at the table can swallow them."

"Why, Rodney! Here, Hook, you take in the sauce." She shoved her husband out the swinging door.

"He boasts like a carny hawker, Mama, regaling everybody with his adventures as a Canadian lumberjack. When last I left, he was just escaping death at the hands of a felled tree, a runaway saw, and a horny bear."

"Rodney!" Eva threw one of the oven mitts at him after she pulled the roast beef out of the oven.

"Those teeth, Mama." Rodney shook his head. "Nobody's got teeth that perfect. Was this guy in Hollywood or something?" He knew that this would get his mother sparked.

"What's Mr. Randolph doin'?" Eva gasped.

"Hanging on his every word."

"And James?"

"Hanging around him like an Elvis fan."

"And Miss Anne?"

"Looking down at her fish."

"And Mrs. Randolph?" Eva was beside herself. This was more exciting than *As the World Turns.*

"Looking at him fish-eyed."

"And Mr. Beddall? What he be doin'?" Eva could hardly stand it.

"Staring at Miss Anne like he'd like to buy her at auction!"

"Oh, git on back in there and git them plates, and do some more listenin'," commanded Eva.

"Yes, ma'am." Rodney grinned at his mother.

As soon as he was back with the fish plates, Eva was upon him.

"Well, what's he doin' now?" she questioned.

"Mr. Beddall is offering Mr. Randolph a whole lot of money for the two lumberyards."

"Business at the dinner table? Why, that's unheard of at Boxwood," she gasped.

"More money than they're worth," Rodney stated with authority.

"Oh, my Lawd. What's Mr. Randolph say?"

"Saying it's a deal. Going to take him fox hunting in the morning. Everybody's smiling. Guess you won't have to bring me home for serving anymore. Sounds like there's going to be more money floating free around here. You can hire your own table servants." He poked his mother playfully.

"Now where are you going with that silver platter?" Eva shook her head.

"Going to give it to Mr. Randolph so he can have something proper to offer up his daughter on!"

\*     \*     \*

Virginia watched the rain clouds forming over the bluff out of the beveled-glass-paned library window and stroked faithful old Skylar's floppy ears. She sat there under the John Wooton equestrian painting, a family treasure, remembering how the impertinent Kingman Beddall had weaseled his way into the hearts of her family. But not into hers. She was not so easily seduced by the young lumberjack-turned-lumber tycoon from Canada, who with his father comprised one half of Beddall and Beddall of Calgary.

She watched her vulnerable and physically frail daughter fall under his shady charms along with her husband and her son. Virginia Randolph had always made sure her delicate-featured, fair-skinned, auburn-haired daughter experienced only the best of Southern society and none of the harsh realities of the other world. Maybe she had overprotected her.

Anne was educated close to home, at Foxcroft and St. Catharine's, and intentionally kept pristine and virginal for her debut and some imminent important marriage. Anne Randolph, pianist of average accomplishment, horsewoman of mediocre performance, shy and demure around men, carried with her the soft scents of magnolias, quiet Southern nights, and innocent ambitions. She was no match for the slick determination of a hungry man of the world.

Virginia had looked out this very same window on a cloudless spring night, to spy Anne and Kingman dancing in the garden gazebo under the moonlight, only one month after he had first set foot in her home. Later that evening they had breathlessly run into the library, hand in hand, Anne flushed with excitement while Kingman politely asked to speak privately with her husband. The two men had entered the study and, after scarcely five minutes, reappeared conspiratorially, both of them with cigars in their mouths, happily back-slapping each other. Kingman was going to marry Anne and there was nothing Virginia could do about it. James had not only let Kingman into their family companies, but now James was letting him into the family as well.

She glanced over at the Queen Anne table, her eye stopping at the silver-framed photograph of her family: James and James II in their formal tails, their hands jauntily stuffed into their pockets, standing behind the settee where Virginia was regally seated in black lace and pearls, holding Anne II as a baby in her christening gown. Anne was gracefully arranged on the floor at her mother's feet. Kingman had been in Calgary on business when his daughter had been baptized.

The early years hadn't been that unpleasant. Kingman had prospered enormously in Richmond, acquiring more lumber mills, more radio stations, and more money, expanding his empire to the Carolinas and up the Eastern Shore. Virginia watched as her husband, James, relied more and more on his street-smart, business-wise son-in-law to satisfy the continuously increasing financial demands of running Boxwood.

Kingman occasionally tried to charm his mother-in-law, "the Silver Fox," as he called her behind her back, but she was having none of that. She always knew that eventually he would be no good for the Randolph family and Boxwood. Bad blood always bubbled to the surface in the stew of life.

Cyrus Fleming was due at Boxwood any minute. Virginia had asked him to "look over James's shoulder" a little. Usually she left the financial matters to her husband. With his cousins and old-guard FFV advisors, his one inherited duty in life was to preserve, if not enhance, the family fortunes as the Randolph primogeniture.

But now Virginia instinctively felt it wouldn't hurt to go poking her nose in a bit. She'd want her overbearing, ill-mannered son-in-law out of any deals that James may have let him into, in the event of the unspeakable, a divorce. Life would be simpler for her daughter, for all of them, if they were not all attached financially at the hip. Virginia wouldn't tolerate an enemy as a business partner, and if Kingman divorced Anne, *he* would automatically become *her* enemy.

It had been hinted that James had made several seriously bad investments, and Kingman had eagerly come to his rescue. But what exactly had he taken in return? Virginia sighed and rang for Hook. Cousin Cyrus had implied to her over the telephone this morning, in his guarded lawyery voice, that a "bailing out" had been going on for years!

Cyrus was a coffee drinker. Hook would brew him his preferred blend. She picked up the antique bullet that lay on the coffee table as a reminder. The Yankees had used Boxwood as a hospital near the end of the Civil War and, with anesthesia and even liquor scarce, many of the men had been forced to "bite the bullet" during amputations and other painful surgical procedures. Over the years, more than a hundred of these teeth-marked bullets had been found on the Boxwood grounds.

Bite the bullet was what everyone at Boxwood had always been able to do. She must instill this in Anne, who seemed to have died by inches and years since Kingman had moved her and Anne II, whom he rudely referred to as Also, up North. The anger was silently building in Virginia. Eventually, she would have to retaliate, if only to protect her own.

Hook carried in the coffee on the silver tray, heavy under the weight of the four newspapers she'd begun to read after Kingman moved his family to New York, breaking the hearts of the three separated Southern ladies. She had subscribed to several New York papers just to be familiar with the frenetic world they lived in. Now, as she opened *The New York Times*, she was stunned. There, on page one of the paper, for heaven's sake, was a picture of Kingman Beddall with the prize-winning architect, Philip

Gladstone, and the newish mayor, announcing the city's official approval for the construction of the world's tallest building, the Beddall Building.

At Kingman's side in the inky photograph was the model "Thing"! How dare he! That ruthless publicity seeker. She hoped Anne hadn't seen the papers yet. No, the poor child was probably still sleeping. Virginia had a good mind to share some of her private information on Kingman's shady past. Well, only if her hand were forced. After all, any dirt she dug up on Kingman Beddall would only fall down upon her daughter and granddaughter, who carried his name. Better to let the dirt lie, just now.

Her husband, James, still in his bathrobe, descended the staircase at the very moment Cyrus Fleming entered the library carrying both a briefcase and a rolled-up newspaper.

"No, thank you." Cyrus declined his usual cup of coffee and kissed Virginia good-morning on her proffered cheek as her husband dutifully bussed her other cheek. Her sharp eyes scanned the imprint on the paper Cyrus was waving: the New York *Daily Sun*. That was the one with the appalling "Suki," who chronicled her daughter's life like that of some gaudy film actress! From that column you would have thought the Randolphs had been letting Elizabeth Taylor wildly ride their horses at steeplechases. Virginia felt a vein twitch in her neck.

"Can it be something unpleasant that brings you over so early?" she asked sternly. If there was a problem, her lawyer and her husband should have anticipated it and seen to it! Cyrus had called at the crack of dawn.

"Virginia," Cyrus said brusquely, unfurling the scandal sheet that Anne usually read with her breakfast in bed, "if Kingman is asking Anne for a divorce, we might have some legal difficulties on our hands."

A divorce! thought Virginia. "How vulgar, but if it must be

. . . Of course, a divorce is a legal matter, that's what you're paid for. Quite handsomely, I might add," she said sternly to her first cousin. "Let me see that paper."

James turned crimson and beelined it for the bar.

"James and your son have been branching out in their investments over the past five years. James, I assume you've kept Virginia up to date?" Cyrus asked sarcastically.

Virginia sat down rigidly on the couch and folded her hands, visibly shaken. If anymore bombs were going to fall, she might as well already be sitting down.

"Get to the point, Cyrus."

"Well, those last two Eastern Shore development deals turned sour and Randolph and Son took quite a beating. Lost a bundle," Cyrus stated flatly.

Virginia shot an annoyed look at her husband. If only he'd stay on a horse, where he belonged.

"The bare bones of the matter is that Kingman Beddall bailed them out, substantially!"

"How bad can that be, Cyrus? You can work that out." She pulled Skylar onto her lap, nervously scratching a patch behind his collar until the dog winced and pulled away.

"Kingman took collateral."

James interrupted from the bar, a tomato juice with something else mixed into it in his hand, "We transferred some land over at Warrenton and some other deeds to Kingman."

"You transferred *several* deeds and a *lot* of land over to Kingman." Cyrus paused either to minimize or dramatize his point. "Kingman Beddall *owns* Boxwood!"

Virginia turned as white as one of her Boxwood ghosts. How could one be expected to maintain composure at a moment like this?

Just then, Hook burst into the library. Also, panic stricken, was at his heels. Had they heard the bad news already?

"Miss Anne has just gone and slashed her wrists with a broken bourbon bottle!"

### SUKI'S COLUMN

The South has fallen again. Alas, nothing lasts forever. Suki has it on the best authority that the Bickering Beddalls will soon be riding to the hounds in opposite directions. Kingman Beddall was spied leaving the law offices of Raoul Felder, noted divorce attorney, and he slings mud, dahlings, not hash. Could it be that the very Southern Anne Randolph Beddall, Kingman's wife of 19 years, probably won't make it Sweet 20? She has taken to her bed at Boxwood, her family home in Virginia. I shouldn't wonder what with every maître d' in town paid by Kingman Beddall to make sure his wife and he are never seated in the same restaurant when he's dining with his company's spokesperson-model. Apparently, Carmen Cosmetics' Fling has become Kingman Beddall's Passion! Kingman's current diversion of public appearances with his gorjus Fling will have to be put on hold, as *Town & Country* magazine is planning to photograph the supermodel in Ecuador on the equator. Imagine Fling frolicking in the surf with those friendly sea lions of the Galápagos. Darlings, wonder what will keep the audacious take-over *King*man Beddall amused while his favorite model's away?

With her whorey big tits, raspy voice, overbleached hair, and gutter genes, she was his white trash slut and he couldn't get along without her. The room was dark, but with just enough light to discern shapes but no details.

Alabama alternated with the Judds as the CD player spun out country-and-western rhythm, played good and loud to cover up the yelps and screams. Her black stockings were hitched high to her nude lace garter belt as she worked him over, whacking the weasel in the palm of her black leather glove. While she sucked with a ferocity that encompassed his entire shaft, slurping, tongueing, he let loose.

"White trash women must take semen in the face," he hollered at her as he covered her pretty features with the sticky stuff. Kingman would never have mistaken Tandy for wife material, even on a lazy moonlit night. Even his cock thought with his brain. They worked in conjunction with each other, as if the two primeval organs were linked by a thick bloody artery, bypassing the heart altogether.

Her hungry eyes searched his, wanting something more. She wiped her face with her fist and bit on his thumb, pulling it into her expert mouth. She smiled and half-masted her eyelids in a Marilyn Monroe look, crinkling her lower lids, as she deliberately brought him to full mast . . . again. She put his rough palms on the insides of her satiny thighs, and when he started to hurl white trash insults at her again, she closed his mouth with her lips. Kingman always responded with animal awareness to her well-orchestrated wanton gestures. It was the only time Tandy was ever in control.

While she held him inside, she knew he needed her. She thought she could even *feel* his need. One of the manicurists told her that Marilyn Monroe had confided in her that the reason Marilyn went to bed with so many men was that it was the only time she felt they really liked her. Tandy was like that, only it was just *Kingman's* love she so badly needed. That, she would kill for.

Now he was delving deeper into her like an uncouth forest

animal burrowing its way into its hole, rubbing the pink firm mounds of his white trash woman raw. He would never be able to do this to a *real* lady. A real class act would never hold her legs open like this for him or offer up her ass.

She was the only one who could drive him wild with her amoral sexual animal instincts. She had once jokingly told him that she was sorry she didn't have more orifices to offer up to him. But now she was bringing him to an eruption so intense and so violent, he yelled into her ear at the top of his lungs like a grieving Greek. She lay beneath him as he fell, spent, into her warm cocoon of languorous oblivion.

Tandy lightly stroked his thighs and calves as he made little grunts of pleasure, and no business thoughts at all whirled in his head.

"You blew my brains out, baby," he whispered as his body lay on hers like a lump of molten lava.

"I know, Carney. I saw them fly out your ears." She smoothed his hair while he was still coming down. He still needed her.

"Yeahhh," he groaned. "I'm just a brainless, no good carny man. Right?" He couldn't have removed the smile etched into his face if he tried.

"Hey, you cheap no good." She playfully poked him. "Nobody but your white trash Tandy would want you." At least, not as Carney Eball.

"Tell that to my wife and fiancée." He was half asleep, and not fully alert in his own mind.

Fiancée? The no good wouldn't! He couldn't do that to *her*! She felt the old rage rising. What was she? Just his friendly fuck?

"Kingman Carney Eball! What fiancée?" she demanded.

"Fiancée?" Kingman pulled his fuzzy thoughts together on command. "I must have meant *finance*. You just scrambled my brains. I've just been seduced and am brain dead. Who could get their words right now? Jeez, you take me places nobody's ever been to, honey." He half grinned.

"Well, I've never been to the altar." Tandy's face was aglow with the warm cum of Carney Eball, but she was falling into a fight with the superior obstinateness of Kingman Beddall. She hated the metamorphosis. She thought it was like the finale of a bad werewolf movie. She laughed her big generous laugh, imagining good ole Carney growing hair and teeth and turning into the monster/mogul Kingman . . . millionaire monster.

He was still under the influence of the best sex he'd ever had. That he *always* had with this woman.

"I'd never leave you." He opened an eye. "I always come back, right? And you got no strings on me. See?" He lifted a limp arm. "You got it great!" He was coming to life. "Three of those nail shops . . . Tandy's Nail Emporiums . . . and me! Why, you're a mogulette!" He brushed a blonder-than-blond strand of hair off her shoulder. Kingman loved to take inventory.

"And Fling?" she said boldly, blowing her own hair off her cheek.

"Fling's business. *My* business. Not *your* business." His eyes dropped twenty-five degrees in temperature, turning an icy gray. "And you're my pleasure and my friend. You're the only one that has me and you don't even know it." The cold eyes cut like a laser into her own.

"So, big boy, are you getting divorced?" She ran a finger under his chin.

"No, but I'm getting a hard-on."

"Oh, Kingman, can't we ever have a serious talk?" Tandy threw up her peach-frosted fingernails in exasperation.

"Talk is not what I come here for. Talk is what I do with Gael Joseph, Arnie Zeltzer, and Gordon Solid. Joyce even monitors my talks. Talk is what I do all day, every day. I talk to my crazy wife, Anne, and my mother-in-law. I talk to the accountant and the chauffeur,'' he boomed. She sat up on her knees.

"You!" He lowered his bushy eyebrows and raised his eyes in an effort to be cute. Instead, his eyeballs just disappeared somewhere into his head, creating a mechanical, stuntman effect. "You and Pit Bull," he pointed at her, "are the only ones in the world who I *don't* have to talk to. The only people on this earth who understand me. Talk is cheap." He looked at her over his shoulder. He was giving her his best carny-man sales pitch.

Tandy stared at him, mesmerized. As usual, she bought the whole sideshow.

"Talk is cheap," he reiterated for effect. This much was true. He reached for his shirt.

Someday, someday, she'd like to drop some Diazepam in his orange juice and have him stick around after making love. If they could spend some real time together, he would realize how absolutely ideal they were for each other.

"Well, what about Fling? She's very young, isn't she?" She retrieved his trousers from the hall. "She probably doesn't even have enough birthday candles to fill a cake!"

"She's legal." His face was expressionless, always a warning signal. Kingman was done. He was like a night raccoon sniffing out danger. He had always handled his women's anger with his hat. He simply left the room, left town, went skiing, kayaking, left for New Guinea on the boat, anything. He couldn't stand to argue, when he was always right. Why should you stand and fight when you could usually win by leaving? Let the other guy think with his emotions; Kingman thought with his guts.

"Incidentally, at the salon today, all the talk was that your wife, Anne, tried to kill herself, or at least get your attention." She thought her words would shock him. She hadn't wanted to mention it before and risk upsetting him.

"No, she didn't do it for attention. The cuts were vertical on the wrists, like this, not horizontal." He fastened his cuff link. "Dr. Corbin says that wasn't a cry for help, that was definitely a self-kill. Here, fix my handkerchief like you do, will you?" And he was out the door before Tandy could get in another word.

Tandy felt sorry for Anne. Suddenly she realized poor Anne had never been the competition.

# 7

The perspiration danced on Fling's skin, shining through the neon leotard that barely covered her body. Just twenty-five more sit-ups before she could collapse into an exhausted heap on the mat, she thought. It had been Frederick's idea to tone up her body at the Safety Harbor Spa in Tampa, Florida, before her big swimsuit shoot for *Town & Country*. Fling didn't want to look like Ashley Adams on the cover of *Sports Illustrated*, busting out all over like some gigantic cow.

Frederick reminded her that she could use a week of constant aerobic exercise and beauty pampering before this tremendously important shoot. And it didn't hurt to get the girl out of sight and out of range of the tabloid reporters' cameras. He didn't want Fling to get famous as a home wrecker. That was a sure-fire *career* wrecker. Best not for Fling to be seen with King for a while. She could return to the limelight when things calmed down a little. And hopefully, she'd *forget* about Kingman Beddall.

Fling was being groomed for fourteen glossy color pages and maybe, just maybe, the magazine's cover. Frederick had cheerfully accompanied Fling to this low-key spa, where a lot of the New York models anonymously toned up before shoots, and highly visible, powerful Washington women spent a quiet week doing leg lifts, their hair pulled back into ponytails from their makeup-free faces, out of the political spotlight.

Frederick threw himself into the water aerobics classes with a vengeance. He had his own reasons to tone up his hips! Fling didn't mind paying for her best friend, whom she so rarely saw these days. She'd been so busy with Kingman, or promoting Fling! bath splash in department stores around the country, shooting ads, and working on the Save the Seals campaign with the EPA, that she'd barely seen Frederick. Frederick was busy, too, being royally courted *Nacht und Tag* by the elegant German baron, William Wolfgang von Sturm. Frederick promised Fling a shopping spree at Black's Fifth Avenue if the Baron decided to add it to his many acquisitions. Just imagine the two of them let loose in the famed department store with no limit to their splurging!

"Seventeen, eighteen," panted Fling, "nineteen . . . twenty." She gasped in relief that her abdominal crunching was finally over for the day.

"Lookin' good, luscious lips," Frederick called over from the Nautilus pectoral machine. "When those gloriously perfect pictures that *Town & Country* will take of you come out, you will thank me for this torture."

Fling groaned, wishing Frederick wasn't such a perfectionist. She shuddered to think how he'd respond when she got her first wrinkle. She was reluctantly beginning her second series of squats, to tone and firm her upper thighs and butt, puffing and panting. She suddenly stopped, dropping her hand weights.

"What's wrong, darling?" queried Frederick, moving on to the quadriceps machine to strengthen his own thin legs.

"Oh, Frederick, I just wish that you were going on this shoot with me. I'd feel so much better, it is so far away from . . . everyone." She looked forlorn. "You've *got* to come. You would *love* the Galápagos Islands. They have all of our favorite animals, baby sea lions, turtles," she tempted him.

"But, darling, you know that next week Wolfy has invited me over to his ancestral castle in Bavaria, and what Wolfy wants . . . I don't plan to blow this one!"

"I'm sure that is *exactly* what you are doing," Fling giggled as she thrust her body up from a full deep-knee squat. Back to work. "A model's work is never done," she sighed.

"Well, at least *some* of us are going out with available men." Frederick simultaneously lowered his luxuriously thick lashes and the weights resting on his shins. This program was strenuous for Frederick, too, but he wanted to look his best next week in Germany. Objects of beauty had to stay lovely to look at. In Frederick's world, that was rule number one. Wolfy had seductively hinted to him that he was welcome to stay longer. Bavaria. He'd never been there. Maybe he'd be expected to run around in *Lederhosen* or some Bavarian costume.

"Next time you fall in love, Fling, why don't you try a single man?"

"But, Frederick, if Kingman weren't married," Fling cooed, "than that would mean nobody wanted him." Sometimes Fling made Frederick crazy with her simple yet charming logic. Why, she had even rationalized Beddall's wife's suicide attempt, although it had troubled her greatly. The sweet thing couldn't imagine why any living thing would want to die.

"I'm done for the day; why don't we take a relaxing dip in that ever-so-inviting pool outside?" suggested Frederick, climbing off the steel-and-chrome machine. "And the pool boy is really cute."

"Frederick, you said no more of that. Remember your promise to me?"

"There is no harm in looking. I'm not dead, you know." He was as much the coquette as Fling. "I'm not officially taken, either. But I think Wolfy is getting very serious." And just what could "serious" mean in a relationship like theirs? he wondered to himself. Everlasting dating?

"Oh, Frederick, I want so much happiness for you. I will keep all my fingers and toes crossed!"

"Just wait till we get to the pool before you cross your toes, luscious lips. I would hate to see the most famous face of the nineties falling flat on her nose."

Fling and Frederick hurried hand in hand down the hall like a giant Barbie doll and her perfectly matched Ken playmate. The passageway was decorated with paintings and photo collages by the multitalented Michaele Volbracht, who had moved to Safety Harbor, giving up a glamorous life as one of New York's most famous fashion designers and artists. He had designed Elizabeth Taylor's gown for her when she had opened the inaugural ceremonies for President Bush. *That* had been an evening!

The famous Liz had not wanted, out loud, in no uncertain terms, to spoil her black artichoke hairdo with the required earphones linking her with the television monitors. Volbracht had been dispatched to negotiate the "peace talks." Later, he had come down to Tampa for a quiet holiday to recuperate and hadn't quite left yet . . . several years later. Volbracht was now revamping America's oldest spa. Freshwater mineral springs had been discovered all over the grounds of Safety Harbor, making the spa a popular watering hole for the most hip fashion and beauty people, fleeing New York either to lose weight and tone up or just simply to release their pent-up poisonous frustrations.

Fling and Frederick simultaneously dove into the clear-water outdoor pool, causing quite a splash. Some of the other, less beautiful, guests looked up to watch. After several exhibition laps in the shimmering turquoise water, the beautiful couple bobbed up at the shallow end like a pair of playful porpoises.

"Oh, Frederick, this is so much fun being with you again. Just like old times." She hugged him, a mermaid hugging a merboy. What would she ever do without him?

"Not like *old* times, darling, but like the wonderful new times that shall be our destinies." Frederick was a firm believer in astrology. Patrick Walker's chart had predicted that he and his twin—Frederick was a Gemini—were destined for fabulous riches and royal positions all before the month was over. He was getting ready. As he was fond of quoting, chance favors the prepared mind—and body.

The ever-pesky spa proprietor, making his daily poolside rounds, checked on his special guests. He knelt down to speak to the lovely creatures frolicking in his pool.

"Do you need anything? More towels, diet bread sticks, or Evian water?"

"Yeah, pizzas and ice cream," piped up Fling. "This mad boy is working me to death. He thinks I'm training for a fight, not a photo shoot! Right, Freddie?" She scooped up a handful of water to playfully splash him.

The proprietor shook his head, laughing as he walked away. The two most beautiful bods in America were pumping iron and counting calories *here*, among the pleasantly plump and obviously overweight. Just another day at the fat farm.

"Frederick," Fling asked quietly, snuggling next to him in the blue-tiled pool, "you don't suppose that Mrs. Beddall's 'accident' had anything to do with me? Honestly, I would never see King again if somebody had to get hurt."

"No, my sweet," she was so beautiful in the naked sunlight, "Kingman's wife is a manic-depressive and an alcoholic." It was the first thing that popped into his head, but it had *some* truth to it.

"Oh, okay." Fling bit her lip. "I couldn't live with the thought that my love for King made her try to take her life. That is a cardinal sin, you know. Nothing could be more terrible than that." Tears mixed with chlorine and pool water streamed down her face.

"No, my pet, their marriage has been over for years. Everyone knows that, and she regularly goes into those black moods after one of her bourbon binges." He didn't even bother telling her that there had been a long line of Flings.

"But I definitely think it's a good idea for you to be out of the limelight, like on the equator, for a few weeks . . . no *National Enquirer* reporters or stringers down there in Darwin's paradise."

"Okay, whatever you say." The worries were gone. "Oh, I can't wait to see the giant turtles and the blue-footed boobies, I'm so so excited." She climbed out of the pool, heading for the diving board.

"Look at me!" She bounced on the board, laughing, a mermaid with legs. "I'm head over heels in love with King," and she somersaulted off the board and into the water.

Gael was proudly puffy-chested this morning. The figures were in: Fling! was breaking records. Carmen Cosmetics' newest fragrance had topped the thirty-million-dollar mark in just four months. If Gael's short arms could have reached that far, she would have patted herself on the back. She had done it! She had pulled a rabbit out of the hat, given birth to an elephant, and convinced millions of American women to change their fragrance, in an already saturated market. She swiveled around in her chair and propped up her feet on the same partners desk that Max and Carl had shared. If they had AT&T in heaven, she'd give the guys a call.

"Lynn," she yelled out. She hated the intercom. "Get me my Diet Coke fix!"

In less than three seconds, Lynn Babbitt skidded into the newly redecorated office, bearing the icy-cold can. Gael Joseph was happy.

"Yes, sir! Madame President!"

Gael beamed at her assistant. "Say it again, Babbitt."

"Will you have it in a glass or the can, Madame President?" she said with a flourish, knowing full well Gael always drank out of the can. She turned on her heel and skipped out to juggle the barrage of phone calls. Suddenly, Gael Joseph was one popular lady.

Gael had her old title back, president of Carmen Cosmetics. Kingman Beddall was chairman of the board and CEO . . . for the time being, she mused, and took a swig of Diet Coke. Kingman had been forced to reward her. He had to do it. Who else in the world, she thought, could have taken some dumb cluck with big boobs and long legs and only ten IQ points short of being an imbecile, and turn her into the industry's hottest fragrance since Revlon's Charlie? As she was constantly reminding her staff, she was working under a severe handicap: she'd had to pull the girl out of Beddall's bed to shoot the damn print ads, photographed by the great, thank-you-very-much, Gael, you-hit-a-home-run-on-that-one, Valeski, whom nobody else could have gotten. *The Marshall Valeski whom you had to call months ahead just to get an appointment with his assistant*, she had produced at a moment's notice. Pulling rabbits out of the hat again and pulling old debts out of the drawer.

Lynn poked her head in the doorway. "Christopher Klutznick and The Bob-O want to meet with you. One o'clock okay?"

"Sure. I never lunch when I'm dieting," said Gael smugly.

Lynn Babbitt widened her eyes in delight. Gael dieted only when she was happy, and happy was easier to be around.

At a time when every celebrity who wasn't on a walker was launching their own fragrance—Baryshnikov's Misha, Cher's Uninhibited, Julio Iglesias's Julio, Catherine Deneuve's Deneuve, Herb Alpert's Listen—this no one from nowhere was outdistancing them all. And Gael had done it. With this one big hit she had become a legend in her own hard-as-nails industry. And they hadn't even gone worldwide yet. Only Elizabeth Taylor's Passion had done better. Over thirty-five-million-dollars worth of the little purple bottle offering up dreams of violet eyes, jeweled bosoms, and romantic liaisons was sold within the first four months of its 1987 release. Elizabeth Taylor and her purple passion were leading the pack . . . until now.

Gael sucked in her tummy. She wanted to wear something slinky when she received the perfume industry's version of the Oscar, The Fragrance Foundation Award, and not some sequined mu-mu!

She was happy to be home. She looked around her old office, the one Kingman had taken away and then given back, stuffed with her familiar clutter of memorabilia and current projects: Max's pipe stand, Carl's memoirs, published fifteen years earlier and still in print, and the newest Valeski story boards of Fling!

Lynn Babbitt, Christopher Klutznick, and Phillipe DuBois had all booed when she had authoritatively announced that none of the hot, hip photographer stars of the day would be creating the image for Carmen's youthful new fragrance, Fling! Not Annie

Leibovitz, famous for her eye-stopping American Express portrait campaign—"I've been a card member since"—and her daring portfolios for *Vanity Fair* magazine. Not Bruce Weber, who, in a double dose of genius, created both the bisexual "which is which" bodies for Calvin Klein's Obsession and the polo-playing, croquet-enthusiast, wicket-whacking WASPy world of Polo-Ralph Lauren, in which the clothes were photographed to look like ancestral hand-me-downs. Not even Herb Ritts, who shot Gianni Versace's ads and directed some of Madonna's hottest videos. Not even Patrick Demarchelier, Phillipe's favorite, who had captured Carolyne Roehm's aristocratic life-style for her fashion advertising and who photographed the "new" Ivana Trump for the cover of *Vogue*. And not superhip Matthew Rolston, either, who had photographed Hollywood faces for *Interview*, the latest fashions for *Harper's Bazaar,* and cooked up the Gap ads spotlighting minor celebrities shot in an "everyday Joe" kind of way.

Six months ago, Arnie Zeltzer, number cruncher, had groaned when Gael announced she was flying out to Chicago in an all-out effort to persuade the reclusive Marshall Valeski, almost in his sixties, to design and shoot the Fling! fragrance campaign. Valeski was the Ingres of the camera world. In his cool linear pictures, Apollonian elegance still reigned.

"Are you crazy? He hasn't shot outside his studio in twenty years! He'll never go on location. He won't be able to catch the spirit!" Phillipe DuBois screamed at her all the way to the airport. He had driven Gael out to LaGuardia because the day before, Kingman had canceled all company cars. Getting Zeltzer to pay for the airline ticket had been relatively easy. Getting Valeski to say yes had been almost impossible, even though Carl Joseph and Max Mendel had given the twenty-five-year-old Valeski his first big break, letting a virtual unknown shoot the heavily hyped Central Park Cerise campaign. Who could forget Carmen's model, Dorothy Lee, clad in a red chiffon Mme. Grès, riding in a Cerise carriage driven by a munchkin of a man in a red top hat around the reservoir in Central Park? Who, indeed? Valeski was putting up resistance to Gael, who was trying to collect on another old debt.

"I don't shoot mistresses," Valeski told her in his friendly but aloof manner of speaking. "I don't like mistresses. I didn't even know people still had mistresses." When he didn't want to do something, Valeski spoke entirely in soft repetitions. He held up the photographs Gael had brought with her.

"What are these? These are photographs?" He put on his glasses after insulting the work of a major photographer whose work was included in the young model's portfolio. He shook his head as if he were looking at pictures of Playboy Bunnies.

"I don't like big breasts. They're outré." She matched him step for step as they paced around his stark white, high-tech studio. "Those are lips? They look like purses. Why are they so big?" He handed the pictures back to Gael with two fingers, as if he didn't want to contaminate himself. Clearly Gael had her work cut out for her. But she had come well armed.

"Marshall." Gael gazed at him as if he were a hot fudge sundae and she was a starving woman. She was just one hell of a desperate woman trying to save her father's company.

"Marshall, would you do something for me?"

"Up to a point," he said, knowing full well she was going to haul the old Cerise carriage out again. They were entering the inner sanctum of his studio, where epiphanies were performed.

"I want you to autograph the picture of Brigitte Bardot that you did for *Life*." She held out the famous photo of the French sex kitten that the young Valeski had shot some thirty years before, just after she had starred in Vadim's *And God Created Women*. It was the famous picture of Bardot in a gingham kerchief and sunglasses, all big petulant lips and full bosom. Valeski smiled. Behind it was the one he had done of Bardot on location in France, hair flying, pedaling on her bicycle in Capri pants. His smile grew wider.

"This is what I want," Gael's words burst out of her mouth. "You already did it once. I want it again, only better," she said excitedly.

"Only Marshall Valeski can do Marshall Valeski." He grabbed the pictures from her and started to plan how he could improve on his earlier work. It would be a great challenge. He would be competing against *himself*, his only real competition. And when he finally said yes, Gael danced one of his Japanese assistants around the room, singing "Everything Old Is New Again."

Gael had somehow hit upon the one dominant theme for the nineties . . . nostalgia.


Lynn Babbitt announced Gael's staff one by one as if she were the majordomo at a fancy ball. It was one o'clock.

"Phillipe DuBois! Christopher Klutznick! The Bob-O." They were carrying flowers and story boards and kissed her congratulations on the Fragrance Foundation Award nomination. Gael was all a titter.

"Oh, guys. We're a team. Right? The Carmen Team, crazy but creative. What's all this?" She plunked down the flowers and went right to the boards. Her little team was revved up and ready to go, a far cry from the sorry sight they were a few months ago.

"You know," Phillipe DuBois joked out loud, "the competition's top executives are all out scouting for girlfriends so they, too, can have a hit fragrance."

"Oh," deadpanned Lynn Babbitt, "so that's what Ricky Berkowitz was doing at Rex's at three o'clock in the morning. He was scouting." They all giggled.

"Shut up, you guys," Gael barked, "the fuzz is coming." She spied Arnie Zeltzer coming down the hall.

"Miss Joseph, everyone." Arnie slid into his chair. "These numbers are a little better than I thought. Fling! fragrance has done over thirty million dollars in the first four months and could have done more, but we can't meet the demand. All the department stores are back-ordered, the drugstores are crying for more. Especially," he hesitated, "for Fling! bath splash."

"Well, of course," stated Gael sarcastically, "you only budgeted for eight bottles of perfume in the launch!"

"There are two thousand calls a day coming in on the 1-800-U-R-FLING! number," Arnie continued. "Kingman is reopening and retooling the New Jersey plant, increasing production by three hundred percent."

"Thank you," hallelujahed Gael, raising her hands to the Lord. She had hated the day when Kingman closed the manufacturing facility, the first step in the dismemberment of Carmen Cosmetics.

"Kingman has approved your budget for the Fling! perfume and makeup line launch."

The Bob-O let out a "wolf, wolf" cry, waving his fist around his head.

"Since we did this kind of volume in only four hundred doors," Arnie flipped to the next page of his report, "Kingman feels we can triple our numbers by being in fifteen hundred doors by this time next year."

"Which doors?" Gael asked. "Doors" was the industry's term for department stores and drugstores.

"All the doors Carmen Cosmetics has ever been in, and then some," replied Arnie.

Well, what do you know, thought Gael. Carmen wasn't going out of business after all. She looked up to the heavens to see if Carl and Max had heard. Estée Lauder commanded 36 percent of the four-billion-dollar department store beauty business. Evidently, Kingman Beddall wanted his share of it too.

Arnie stood up to leave. "And Gael?"

"Yes, Arnie?" Her voice was theatrically cheerful.

"Kingman says his plane is available for all of Miss Fling's personal appearances." With that, he exited Gael's office. He was due at another meeting with Beddall Lumber Inc. down the hall.

"Beats flying commercial." Phillipe DuBois winked.

"Does this mean that Kingman will replace me as the hand holder on the tour?" queried Christopher Klutznick. "I was hoping to pick up some frequent-flyer mileage."

One of the top executives always accompanied the celebrity spokesperson on department store personal appearances. There was too much that could go wrong. The cosmetics counters had to be sufficiently stocked, and the sales staff given pep talks and briefed on updated information on selling techniques. Newspaper advertisements had to be coordinated with the arrival of the spokesperson and, in full-blown department store launches, the colors of the perfume packaging were used in decorating the store with banners, streamers, and new carpet runners laid out for the occasion. Close attention had to be paid to the window displays. It was nigh-high impossible to capture the aura of a fragrance. Perfume was not a dress or a set of luggage you could see through a pane of glass from the street. Large factices, dummy bottles with colored alcohol ten times the size of real ones, were displayed to implant a visual identification in the mind of the casual consumer, along with photos and lifelike mannequins of Fling herself. Then there were the ubiquitous sample girls who spritzed the customers entering and exiting the stores. Bloomingdale's girls were particularly aggressive in this area, whereas the more restrained floor girls at Black's Fifth Avenue always asked first. In some cases, you could walk into a store for a pair of socks for your husband and walk out smelling like a French whore.

"So what do you guys think? Do you like these colors?" Gael pointed her finger, which everybody's eyes followed to the mock-ups for Fling's new cosmetics color line.

"Who's got what to say? The Bob-O?"

He held up the story board showing off a black-and-white Valeski head shot of Fling. Gael smiled smugly. She recognized the original. Fling's hair was in a chignon, partially hidden by a gingham kerchief prettily tied under her chin. The Bardot picture. Nothing but lashes, and fingertips resting lightly on her face and lips, "lips as big as purses."

Valeski, you old hypocritical genius, Gael thought with a smirk.

"Wow! Big wow! I'll take whatever it is she is selling," Phillipe DuBois said. "You can almost feel the warm breath on those lips."

Hotsy-totsy, thought Christopher Klutznick, who was always the pragmatist. "But how do you expect to sell a line called *Colors* in black and white?"

"Ah, the beauty of the sytex machine." The Bob-O pulled out the second story board. "Valeski shoots the girl in black and white, we color in the lips and nails and lashes."

The second photo was identical to the first except for the startling addition of a touch of pink to the lips and nails, and a luscious black brushed across the lashes.

"Valeski shot this picture at the end of the first fragrance advertising shoot. It has the exact spirit of a fresh, natural girl having a fling, just the right attitude for the Fling! Colors line. So with a little magic from the world of computer technology, we can save time and money that Kingman will probably renege on anyway, by using this picture. The public already identifies with the girl in black and white; now the emphasis will be on the exact colors that we are trying to sell. None of our competition has ever tried selling lipsticks in black and white, so once again Carmen will be seen as the innovative cosmetics company."

The group nodded collectively. The Bob-O's vision was always right on.

"We will introduce the three basic color groups, the Passionate Pinks, the Ripe Rich Reds, and the Naughty Natural Nudes. These groups all have names associated with seduction. After all, we *are* selling sex."

Gael beamed. They would do it once again. Who could resist the lure of these fresh colors with such provocative names? And the girl? Perfection.

"Fling has insisted that there be no animal testing on these products, and that the packaging be recyclable—for the environment, you know. There is a clause in her contract that stipulates this."

Christopher Klutznick hit his forehead with his hand. "Well, I guess you promise a girl anything if you are trying to get her into the sack."

"Yeah," Gael shot back, "or if you think the fragrance ain't never gonna happen 'cause you're gonna dump the company. Go on."

"Look," The Bob-O was like a gallant knight, "this girl is really easy to work with, and I think we can use this clause to our advantage in the environmentally conscious nineties. All the ecologists will love us. Valeski's nuts about her and he's never liked the healthy, sexy ones."

Over the years, the modern master had photographed his share of girls who could pass for cadavers.

"Face it, the girl's gorgeous, nice, the public loves her, and we've hit the jackpot. If Beddall found this one with his dick as a Geiger counter, we should put it on the payroll."

"Lynn, tell everyone about the success of the Overnight Fling! Tote. This is really great, guys, this is good."

"Because Kingman had cut the promotional budget for the PWP, Purchase with Product, Gael and I went to Hudson's and picked up five hundred seconds of little overnight totes. They're seconds, you know, the stuff that doesn't come out just right, with snags or tears. They practically gave us the stuff for free! We had Fling! printed across them and dumped them in stores. Well, before you knew it, Black's Fifth Avenue was calling for more, everybody using them to go to the Hamptons overnight. Betsy Bloomingdale was photographed boarding the Concorde carrying it, you guys all saw the picture in *WWD,* and it was the only luggage that Cindy Crawford and Richard Gere took to Brazil. Revlon must have loved that!"

Gael took over. "The stores called and asked if we'd put in everything for an all-nighter. These ladies, ages fifteen to fifty, were coming in and asking for the All Night Fling! bags. Like, they thought it was a kit with everything already in it." She counted off the items on her fingers. "The perfume to attract the man, the lipstick, the lingerie, the Fling! bath splash, and con-traceptives, for God's sake!"

"Well," joked The Bob-O, "maybe we can put different-colored contraceptives in the line, perhaps even scent them with Fling!"

"Back to earth, kids." Gael corralled her crazies. Her little geniuses all tended to go overboard on occasion. "Go on, Lynn."

"Look at these reports from the stores. There are secretar-ies, housewives, top executives, women who haven't been laid in years or had dates for months, tearing one another apart at the counters trying to get the Fling! bag. Who would have thought that the girl would become a role model?"

"Let's call in the Wathne sisters and have them design and

manufacture more bags, then, and put them in all our doors," said Phillipe DuBois.

"Question, Gael dear," said Christopher. "Who's got Suki in their pocket? This woman is a one-man sales army!"

"I dunno." Gael smiled under the veil of her secret. "Maybe she tried the stuff and somebody whistled at her."

Suddenly Kingman streaked into her office, with Pit Bull scurrying to keep up.

"I see the A Team's all here." He showed a sharklike flash of white teeth as he whizzed around the table. "How's it going? About that budget . . ." There was dead silence as the five terror-stricken executives all swore they could hear the theme song from *Jaws* playing in the background as they were all jolted back into the déjà vu nightmare of one of Kingman's budget cuts.

Kingman's eyes glittered shrewdly as he circled them. He liked keeping people off balance.

"Gael." He stopped so abruptly that Pit Bull collided into him. "I like what you are doing with the Fling! campaign. Let me know if you need a few more dollars." With that, he marched out of the room so fast that he didn't have time to see the stunned look on their faces.

"That man is going to drive me crazy. He is going to make me nuts," Phillipe DuBois said dramatically, clapping both hands on top of his head.

"No, nuts is what he drove his wife," corrected The Bob-O. "Didn't you hear? She's at that place for rich lunatics!"

"All right, you guys, that's enough. Gossip isn't going to sell product here," Gael scolded her team. Well, maybe that wasn't entirely true, she thought, as they left her office. As Carl Joseph had often told his daughter, fragrance was 10 percent ingredient and 90 percent fantasy. Fling! was being wafted across the country in a storm cloud of gossip. Was she or was she not walking off with one of the country's most *in*eligible men? . . . Only her perfumer knew for sure.


## EDGEMERE

Edgemere was neither a hospital nor a luxury resort, but its guests stayed in its plush thick-carpeted suites for months on end, were pampered by the attentive staff, usually got better, and often made return visits.

Dr. Corbin kept four of these sanitariums for the rich and crazy across the country. Kingman had sent Carmen Cosmetics' *Gulfstream III* to whisk Anne off to the private retreat nestled at the foot of the Blue Ridge Mountains. Virginia had refused the extravagant gesture and she and Anne had driven up in the Lincoln Town Car with Hook.

"Do you still love him?" Dr. Corbin asked his patient.

"Do I still love Kingman Beddall?" Anne parroted his question like a woman still in the grip of madness. She was stretched out on the chintz-covered chaise in her private solarium. Her skin still was so unnaturally pale that it was almost translucent in the broad stream of sunlight pouring into the bright, cheery room. If you held her long slender fingers up to the light, you could practically see through them.

"How can you love something that eats you up?" She dropped her head into her hands. The wrists were still bandaged and painful. It was a month since she had been removed from the life-support systems at the hospital and brought to Edgemere. Kingman was paying Dr. Corbin's bills.

"He calls here daily, you know," Dr. Corbin said, rapping his pipe against the side of a table.

"Probably to see if he's getting his money's worth." Anne clasped her knees to her chest.

"I can't live in his world, you understand. It whirls around me and I can't fit in. I'm like Alice in Wonderland. I have to run very, very fast just to stay in the same place. *His* pace is getting even faster and faster, you know. I keep imagining he's going to whirl himself into a hurricane and wipe out a whole town or destroy the whole coastline, until he blows himself out to sea, just another gusty wind."

"That's an interesting analogy, Anne."

"He just never seems to grow tired or grow up," she continued. "He can't complete a book to the end, you know. He doesn't have the attention span. Joyce Royce will read it and then make some sort of Cliff Notes for him. When he watches television, you can't imagine, he has a console with four screens and he actually watches them all at once. His eyes just flicker from one to the next. He wants everything. He's like the hungriest little boy I've ever known."

"Anne, you realize that since you've regained consciousness, you've spoken of nothing and no one else except Kingman. Aren't you a little curious to know how your daughter is taking all this?"

"Anne II is a young girl. She has a lot of resilience. I haven't." Her speech was surprisingly strong for a woman who had lost half her body's blood and was swimming in a sea of prescription drugs.

"I haven't decided if I want to keep living yet, you know." It was almost as if she were throwing a threat to Dr. Corbin. Even here, Anne could conjure up the errant whiff of an excellent Cuban cigar, the cedarwood humidor he kept by the bed, the tangy, arresting breath of a very fine red Margaux lingering on his lips. In her mind, Kingman Beddall could join the ranks of the more infamous blackguards in history who dallied among the fertile folds of femininity: Bluebeard, the Marquis de Sade, even the Boston Strangler, could be his cousin. For he used trusting women more than other men, which is in itself a sin, she thought wearily. He used them to the point that they self-destructed or imploded or were brought to their knees or simply grew withdrawn and died inside themselves, where no one would ever notice.

"I feel part of me is dead already. It's always a surprise to me that I wake in the morning." Anne's voice was hardly audible.

Dr. Corbin rubbed his elbow patch and fiddled around with his pipe. He was professionally concerned but he still had to see a dozen more patients before he flew back to his New York office tomorrow. Later in the week he would stop in and check on his patients in the three other sanitariums he owned. Besides Edgemere, he now owned "retreats" in Englewood, New Jersey; Lake Forest, Illinois; and the Virgin Islands. Kingman was his financial partner in Edgemere, and in Englewood and the Virgin Islands. Corbin catered to the rich, the famous, and the crazy, and had done so for thirty years. As his patients branched out and traveled, so did he. Kingman had showed him the way to incorporation and millions of dollars. He had been Corbin's silent partner for almost five years now, though the good doctor had treated Anne for at least six. Dr. Corbin thought Kingman Beddall was a financial genius, so what if he was a little bit rough around the edges? and, yes, he was certainly capable of driving anyone crazy.

"Do you love yourself, Anne?"

"Love myself?" she repeated his question. She kept fading in and out. "Love myself? Can you love yourself if no one else does? Is that possible? Or what if you don't have a self? I guess I'm buried somewhere in Kingman's ego."

Corbin frowned for the first time. Buried in Kingman's ego would be a very dangerous place for a fragile woman to be.

"Oh, yes, Anne. You have a very lovely, gifted self." Dr.

Corbin made a note for Dr. Kronsky to drop his sessions down to once a day and supervise a daily walk around the grounds for her. Maybe one of the bird-watching groups might be good for her. His shier patients usually began to feel like they had friends or other caring souls if they had human interaction. Although many of them preferred their privacy, and to pursue their insanity anonymously.

He had treated some pretty impressive "nuts," as he called them, particularly here at Edgemere, which serviced Washington, with its White House–induced nervous breakdowns. Painskill in Englewood, which catered to his New York patients, was a veritable barometer of Wall Street's financial climate, on a par with the Standard & Poor index.

Suicide among the rich vexed him. It was hard to work up sympathy for a person who *wanted* to be dead. And so, he gave them his professionalism but not his sympathy.

"Well, maybe you did the best thing you could do, by signing those divorce papers this morning. You'll be free." He lit his pipe. "Kingman didn't want it, you know."

"He didn't?" Anne was puzzled. Was it only this morning that Uncle Cyrus and some other gentleman had brought her the papers? She looked out the big picture window to a mountain lake with swans gliding on the smooth, cool surface. The sounds of honking geese and the fluttering of wings were very pleasant to hear. Edgemere was a sanctuary for wildlife, as well.

"No." Her voice was ever soft. "I'm sure it's what he wanted. I couldn't do the things he needed," her voice trailed off, "the things he wanted."

"And what do *you* want, Anne?"

"I want to rest," and she stared out into the serenity of the pines, oaks, and soothing colors of the green-and-purple mountains.

\*   \*   \*

In the cruel world of sixteen-year-old adolescents living in the self-contained, gossip-driven environment of an all-girls' boarding school, the new girl who had arrived in the middle of the year was the latest object of rumor and ridicule. Anne "Also" Beddall, daughter of Kingman Beddall, was Miss Porter's latest sideshow. Unfortunately for her, her nickname had followed her to the elite secondary school.

The shy, overweight teenager didn't like any of it one bit. With her father's deep-set stormy gray eyes monopolizing her entire face, sheathed in the poreless pallor of her mother, she appeared a beefy wounded deer poised for flight at any moment.

The skittish, high-strung girl was constantly discussed with concern and worry in the teachers' smoking lounge, viewed as an implement of finance for the new wing of the library in the headmistress's office, and the butt of dining-room pranks and jokes by the snide classmates who read Suki's column. She was also an object of envy and awe on the part of the nicer girls who wanted Fling's autograph and thought there was some family connection to Also! Also wanted to go home.

She had skipped dinner again, pretending fatigue, and was in her room crying her eyes out. Directly across from her, over her roommate Bunny Thaxton's bed, hung an enormous poster of her father's girlfriend. Fling was laughing and dancing in a bright yellow bikini, frolicking and splashing her slim golden legs in the sea.

"I *hate* you! *And* my *father!*" she sobbed at the poster as if it could hear her. This poster was plastered in practically every room of the dorm. The gorgeous model in the Fling! poster that hung in Also's room, at the insistence of her roommate, overpowered the small, oval, enameled Cartier picture frame, in the best of taste, that delicately held an elegant, aloof picture of her mother, Anne. Also furiously pounded her childish fists on the bed, muffling her cries with her pillow.

Also had learned from her first woeful, homesick days that your peers lashed out and became more cruel only if you showed them your fears and unhappiness. She was learning the art of the stiff upper lip, already brilliantly practiced by the Randolph women, the skill of mastering her feelings and perfecting a stand-offish aura of artificial superiority as an impenetrable wall between her and those who wanted to harm her. So she cried in private.

All the meals that she was missing could be made up later. She buried her head into her feather pillow and sobbed and sobbed. By the time Bunny came bouncing back up from the dining hall, tossing her hockey stick across her unmade bed, Also's face was a puffy mess of red blotches.

"Gosh, Also!" Bunny Smithburg Thaxton from Winnetka, Illinois, was deeply horrified.

"Are you having an allergic reaction?" she gasped. "Should I get the nurse?" All five feet eight inches of her was hysterically hovering over her chunky roommate with the swollen face.

Bunny played right wing on the field hockey team and Fling was her idol. Bunny kept their small room blitzed and smoke-bombed with Fling! bath splash and sometimes stood under Fling's poster in her cotton underwear (with her nametag sewn into the waistband), twisting and posing, trying to get Also to notice the vast similarities between the model and the roommate.

"Yes," Also abysmally rubbed her eyes and fibbed, "my father sent me lobster from Lutece. I guess he forgot that I'm allergic to it." She was becoming a practiced liar; she could probably even pass a New York district attorney's lie detector test by now. Not a flicker of emotion showed in her face. She swung her heavy legs straight over her thin mattress and sat bolt upright, her hands folded neatly in her lap, like her grandmother always did in times of crisis.

"Boy, lobster from Lutece! You have the most exciting life in the entire world, you lucky stiff." Bunny tossed her copy of this week's *Time* over to Also, which hit her on the shoulder. The one with Also's father on the cover with his big-deal tallest building in the world. She'd already seen it, it was under her scrunched-up pillow.

"A mother on a plantation or in some ritzy-ditzy sanitarium. It's so Charlotte Brontë! All my mother ever does is take a week at the Golden Door. You're practically best friends with the *most* famous model in the whole entire world, who works for your father, who's on the cover of *Time* magazine, for God's sake." Bunny didn't always get her facts straight, a charming characteristic that men would find appealing all of her adult life.

"A yacht to sail the high seas." She cupped her hand over her eyes as if she were searching the watery horizon. "Boy, the only place *I* get to go is The Onwentsia Club to flirt with the lifeguards and watch my parents play golf with each other!" Bunny threw up her hands in dramatic despair as if she'd announced that both of her parents were on the FBI's most-wanted list. "Talk about deprivation!" She pulled off her lucky lacrosse socks, which she reserved for games, and stuffed them back into her hockey shoes, holding her pretty WASPy nose.

The smells of Edgemere last weekend had been full of country life: fresh-cut grass, the woodsy odors of oaks, willows, and pines commingling after a midspring's rain nudging arbors of wisteria and lilacs to full fragrant bloom. She had taken the train down, as nobody in her astronomically well-to-do family had figured out she might need an allowance. Not Grandma, not Uncle Cyrus, not the lawyers working on the divorce, not the bankers, not Dad, and not Uncle Jamey. Only Joyce Royce had sent her an envelope of traveler's checks. She'd asked Eva's son, Rodney, to meet her at the Amtrak station and drive her up to Edgemere.

Like a real Randolph, she was land rich but cash poor. Bunny, with all of her wily resources, had covered for her absence at school. At least Also had lucked out in pulling a roommate who thought everything in Also's gloomy, neglected life was "romantic" and "madly exciting!" "Mad" was obviously a good adjective for her family. For once, Bunny's romantic notions were correct. She envisioned Boxwood as a Southern *Wuthering Heights*, with the whole mad bunch of them riding to the hounds on the moors. Also's mother had been temporarily declared legally mad, so Virginia could play her daughter's role in the divorce. Her grandfather rode merrily as master of the hunt, decked out in a scarlet flyaway coat trimmed in velvet, like a character from Henry Fielding's *Tom Jones*. Her Uncle Jamey was perpetually fooling around with the stable boys and trying to keep it a secret, while her father—she glared at the cocky grinning face of her handsome father staring back at her from the cover of *Time*—was building the world's tallest building. So tall that special engineering firms were being brought in from Canada to control the strident wind gusts created at street level by the huge mass that blocked the natural air flow, creating little hurricanes at street level! Talk about mad. She wondered if she should just check into Edgemere now and avoid Act II of her own life.

"Oh, this place is not much different from Edgemere," Bunny confidently reassured her after Also had returned to school a devastated blob. "Only, we have homework."

So Also had calmly resigned herself to a life in the best boarding schools, private colleges, country clubs, and probably the most expensive nut houses and drying-out clinics for the insanely rich. It was in the cards.

Also heaved a sigh. She had brought back several cartons of fried chicken, ribs, and cheeseburgers from Stuckey's. She and Rodney, who now worked as an assistant district attorney in New

York but was home visiting his folks, had stopped for lunch before he took her to the station.

"My mother didn't seem to know me at all." Also had been weepy and devastated.

Somehow, sharing it with Rodney and then Bunny put it all in perspective. Somehow her family and her life were like a novel to be picked up sporadically, savored, laughed at, wept over, and reread again, but not taken too seriously. If she did, she'd go mad. If Also had been chosen to live her life in a novel collaborated on by William Faulkner, Ibsen, the Brontë sisters, and Judith Krantz, she had better learn to play her part. She reached for the *Time* cover with Kingman Beddall and Philip Gladstone on it, and tacked it up on her side of the room. Maybe you could redeal the hand that they dealt you.

"Bunny, my father wants me to sail on his boat with him in the Greek islands this summer. Would you like to come, as my friend?"

"*Would I?* Would I like to be marooned in an avalanche with Tom Cruise?" Bunny hugged her new best friend. She'd definitely put in for Also as next year's roommate, and do a better job of protecting her from the bitchy girls, as well. "On the *Pit Bull*, in the glamorous Greek islands, with the gorgeous Kingman Beddall and maybe superstar Fling! Oh, boy!" Bunny would go on a diet immediately. She glanced over at her new best friend, who was crunching up the Stuckey's bags, and decided to put Also on a diet as well! Boy, did she need a make-over.

That day, Also made two conscious decisions of her own. Like one of the heroines in the novel she was supposed to be living in, she vowed to try *not* to go crazy, and she would *never*, no, *never*—there were big tears welling in her eyes as she thought of her mother talking to the ducks, deer, and the flowers at Edgemere but only waving abstractly to her own daughter—she would *never* touch a drop of alcohol.

## SUKI'S COLUMN

### KING AND FLING NIXED BY NYYC

The ever-present and seemingly indestructible Samson of Gotham has just been dealt his first fatal blow. The stuffy uppercrust of the New York Yacht Club have turned down Kingman Beddall's application for membership in the "better" boating club. The *Pit Bull* has been moored next to the *Chelonia*, owned by Henry Clay Frick II, for the past several months. But Kingman always seems to turn bad news to good, spinning straw into gold. Instead of those salty blue bloods viewing his sumptuous 250-foot yacht, the most extravagant seaworthy palace created since Cleopatra's barge, formerly owned by Saudi Prince Khalid Bin Sandar, Kingman has invited Robin Leach and all his viewers to cruise aboard the *Pit Bull* on that glamorous and glitzy show *Lifestyles of the Rich and Famous*. There is even a Carmen Cosmetics sweepstakes with Fling! fragrance, and the glorious grand-prize winner will cruise all around Manhattan with Gotham's most glamorous couple, the new Antony and Cleopatra. You can get the details for the contest at all department store Carmen Cosmetics counters.

"How could they *not* let me into the New York Yacht Club?" Kingman thundered at Joyce Royce. "Who do they think they are? Why, my boat is bigger and better than all of their goddamn canoes put together. Longer, too!" He was slamming doors and carrying on like a five-year-old throwing a temper tantrum. Pit Bull smelled blood in some sort of instinctive animal response. The dog was wearing a crazy, wild look on his already fierce face.

Joyce Royce raced out her pacifying props. She knew it was one of *those* mornings.

"Look, Kingman, I've had it framed. Doesn't it look great!" She held up this week's cover of *Time* magazine in the thick silver double-rolled frame from Bulgari and tossed the dog a Snausage. Pit Bull swallowed the canine pig-in-a-blanket without bothering to chew.

Kingman stopped in the midst of his tirade to admire the color photograph of himself and Philip Gladstone standing with the architectural maquette of the Beddall Building. It looked like a skyscraper from a Flash Gordon movie with its blue-and-silver sparkling spire pointing into the sky. Philip Gladstone, professor of architecture at Yale, first recipient of The Pritzker Prize for Architecture, and veteran of over fifty major structures, had planned the Beddall Building as a modern cathedral—a modern monument to commerce skypointing into the stratosphere.

"Look at me. Don't I look great! Um hmm." He tapped his fingers against the glass. "This is the cover of *Time*, you know, not some bullshit publication. People actually *read* this thing. Even illiterate people look at the pictures!" He nodded knowingly. Joyce nodded along with him. "I'm a cover boy." His eyes brightened. "Just like Fling!" He was clearly delighted. "I don't think Gladstone looks well in this picture. Don't you think I make him look bad? I mean, his baldness next to my full head of hair? Why, he looks a hundred years old." A worried look crossed his face. "He'll live long enough to finish my building, won't he?"

"Of course he will, Kingman. He's in perfect health."

"Hmmm, but it would have been a better cover with just me and my building. This looks like a crowd up here. You know, it's the cover that sells the magazine. They should have cropped him out. Just me, the building, and the date, March seventeenth." A light bulb went on in his head. "I would have been a much better cover. Me alone, a nice Irish boy on Saint Patrick's Day! I bet me and what's-his-name, who runs Heinz, are the two most successful Irishmen in the world."

Joyce had long ago ceased being amazed by Kingman's direct, linear descent. He was a Canadian who had spent time in the South but was a full-blooded Black Irishman.

"Jealousy," he pronounced it as if he were a black-haired, gray-eyed actor playing Hamlet to the hilt, "those assholes at the yacht club are jealous. When's the last time somebody with Dutch ancestors, a Van Rensselaer, was on the cover of *Time* magazine? I'll tell you when: three hundred years ago. Before they lost their money, that's when. Let them hang on to their boat slips. I wouldn't begrudge them that.

"Get Edgemere on the phone. Let's see how Anne is." He strutted around his desk.

"I already placed the call. She's better today."

"What's she doing?"

"Anne is walking with ducks," she read from her notepad.

"Anne's out on a duck walk? My Anne, who keeps the drapes drawn till noon, is up at dawn with ducks? I'm paying for walks with ducks? She's had some weird walkers in New York, but this is absurd. Never a duck." He poked Joyce Royce in the ribs, laughing at his own clever humor.

"Ow!" Joyce was not his sparring partner. Joe Murphy, the trainer, didn't come in until eleven.

"Kingman, Itoyama's call from Tokyo is ready for you."

"Yeah, yeah. Tell him to hang on to his sushi for a minute. Did you send Anne's roses? Those little tea ones she likes?"

Joyce nodded. It was on the list.

"And Also?" He was moving around to his phone console.

"Also's writing a term paper on sperm whales. She sounded kind of down."

"Whales. Call the director of the Museum of Natural History and have him fax her all the stuff she'll need. They owe me. I just paid for the revarnishing of that big fucking blue fish hanging from the ceiling.

"Hello, Ohio, Isao, what do you say? Moshi, moshi." He winked at Joyce and gave her the "okay" sign. He'd gotten his loan.

*"Dōmo Arigatō."* His business voice was one of perfect pitch and control. "I look forward to our meeting in Japan."

When he hung up the phone, he planted a kiss on Joyce's cheek.

"We got the loan, Joyce. And with a full fourteen percent less interest than Citicorp wanted." He was giddy. "The network deal's in the bag! Get Arnie in here, will you, and get the Solid brothers on the phone."

An hour later, Joyce buzzed him on the speaker.

"Kingman, you better pick up."

"Yeah?" His telephone voice was soft as usual.

"Tandy called, and was very upset." How could she be upset? He hadn't even done it yet.

"Upset? Why upset?"

"She's been robbed. Her apartment has been ransacked."

"Get her on the phone for me.

"So," Kingman's voice was disarmingly charming, exuding concern, "I hear you've had burglars."

Tandy sounded hysterical. It wasn't like she kept Rembrandts in the apartment, Kingman thought.

She was crying into the telephone. "Kingman, they trashed my apartment. They went through everything. All my drawers are upside down. The lamps are broken."

"Don't worry. I'll get you new drawers. What'd they get?" He was genuinely concerned.

"They went through all my lingerie. All my personal stuff.

It's like being violated. The police were here. They said it was like somebody was looking for something special." She heaved a sob. Thank God they hadn't gotten her tapes. They were stashed in the plastic tape boxes marked with Barbra Streisand labels.

"All right, all right. They made a mess. A mess we can have cleaned up. Did they take anything of value? Did they take money?" Kingman was still trying to figure out why a burglar would break into a nobody's apartment on Third Avenue.

"That's the odd part: they didn't take any money. They took things."

"What kind of things, honey?"

"Little things." She was almost scared to tell him. "They took the leather handcuffs, the ones *we* play with, and a picture frame."

"Which picture?"

"The one of you that you autographed for me." She started to list a few other personal items. Why had he signed the bloody picture?

"Give me the cops' names." He sounded angry.

"What?"

"The cops' names who came to your apartment."

"Hold on a minute. One of them gave me a card." He held on as she noisily rummaged through the mess.

"Here. Detective Patrick Sullivan, Theft, and wait," she read it out, "Sergeant Buffalo Marchetti, Homicide."

Kingman lurched in his chair. "What did you do? Kill the intruder?"

"No, no, the Buffalo guy," the handsome one, she remembered, "had just been having lunch with the burglary guy."

"Holy shit! I'll call you back. I've got to take this other call." He went to the window. He had to think. The cover of *Time* magazine, and now somebody had stolen *his* picture, signed to Tandy, from her bedside table. Who? Who would want to know about that? He'd better look into it. Just when he was putting in for his loan from Mishima. In Kingman Beddall's world, he well knew there was never such a thing as a coincidence.

He called a friend of his in the police department. They'd have dinner at Patsy's, on West Fifty-sixth Street, tonight.

"Joyce, could you come in here?"

Joyce and her pad appeared in the office as magically as if Mr. Spock had just beamed her in from the *Enterprise*.

"Where's Fling?"

"In the Galápagos Islands for *Town & Country*. They're shooting her in swimsuits and introducing the new Carmen Colors line in the editorial." She knew all this because Fling had taken the time to visit with her last week when Fling was up to see Gael Joseph. Joyce thought Fling was really a very nice girl.

"When's she due back?"

"Two, maybe three weeks."

"Get Rusty on the phone at Ford's and find out *exactly* when she's due back, and better find out exactly *where* she is, too. I want to talk to her."

"But, Kingman, they're on a ship in the Galápagos Islands. It's not like they're at the Hyatt!"

"You can do it." He turned on his heel, heading back to his desk. "How many islands can there be in the Galápagos? Find her.

"And," he rubbed his fingers together, "find out if Dr. Corbin's in town, and book Tandy with him for ten A.M. tomorrow, sharp." He placed his hands together in a prayerful pose. "She's very upset, and she might get upsetter. Book her with Dr. Corbin every day for two, maybe three weeks. Burglaries are upsetting!" He winked at his secretary, amanuensis, confidante, and surrogate mother. Total factotum. No wonder Joyce Royce was the highest-paid secretary in Manhattan.

Now Joyce looked at him as if he were mad. Was he going to

have Tandy walking ducks, too? His eyes were gleaming mischievously.

"Tell Jack to have the plane ready on a moment's notice. We're taking a little trip." He rubbed his palms together in excitement and went over to the phone to dial Ira Sackman's number himself. Ira had once worked in Roy Cohen's law office. He would need a few legal papers drawn up immediately.

"Joyce," he drummed his fingers on the desk, "Tandy is very upset about this burglary. Let's give her a little pick-me-up; it's the least we can do. Tell Gael Joseph that we are adding a new nail polish to the line. Let's call it Tandy something. You tell Gael, but why don't you wait until I'm out of the building? And call Ron, over at Harry Winston. Tell him I'll be over later . . . and I don't want to read about it in Suki!"

# 8

As they descended the steep steel gangplank, the salty, misted wind stung their faces. Always hauling ample bags and suitcases overflowing with bathing suits, beaded gowns, ornate, elaborate headdresses, shells, flippers, and masks, the two editorial assistants, loaded down like pack mules, scurried to meet the five-thirty A.M. departure from the ship. The sky was inky black with just a thin line of pale gray at the horizon. Sunrise was a key time in the Galápagos Islands. It was still too early to discern if today would bring a shining ascent of dazzling sun, creating "magic light," or a low, cloud-clogged morning of pale, flat light. The assistants hoped for option A, knowing that Fling was being photographed as the "Goddess of the Sun." A clear, sparkling sky would automatically guarantee a flashy-face smile from their very tense boss. When the pictures came together, which they usually did with Fling as their model, the entire photography team breathed easily. The weather was the only unpredictable factor. Satisfactory pictures could always be obtained no matter what the weather, but only when the sun shone did Marks, the special projects editor for *Town & Country*, get the kind of picture that was truly memorable. The kind that ended up in hardcover anthologies, built reputations, and inspired one-man shows.

Andrew Phillip Marks Forrester IV, "Marks," as he was called by all who knew him, leaned over his kneeling photographer's shoulder to confirm the Polaroid's angle.

"I think she should be a little to the left, to avoid the gutter," directed Marks, folding the Polaroid to examine Fling's position on what would become a two-page picture in the magazine. "This will be the opening double-page spread, and we can't have Fling in the seam of the magazine."

Fling inched her way slightly to the left. She had learned that Marks was very specific in his requests, and "a little" was just that. She couldn't believe it. Here she was on the most beautiful and bizarre cluster of islands anyone could imagine. The whole fantastic place was an animal lover's Disneyland, more spectacular than the *National Geographic* television show she liked to watch.

Earlier that morning, Fling had spied twenty giant green-backed sea turtles littering the sandy white cove, lying still at the water's edge, exhausted from their night's journey of lumbering onto land to lay their endangered eggs. Fling had been captivated by the clownlike antics of the lone sea lion stretching awake. The blue-footed boobies had called out *wok, wok* and waddled over to Fling. It was love at first sight. The penguins had been an added surprise. She had thought that they lived at the South Pole but, here, floating on their backs, were these little tuxedoed creatures lazily feasting on their early morning catch. All these marvelous animals. Life was so beautiful. The more varieties of life-forms you discovered, the more you learned to appreciate life itself.

This island had everything, and warm water too, Fling thought pleasurably, half submerged in the sea. She hated it when she had to project warmth and a sexy, sunny attitude when the water was freezing, the sky turbulent with clouds, and her nipples hardening in the cold air.

Fling glanced to the shore, to see one of the assistants hurtling through a mountain of swimsuits, searching for the white pearl-yoked one-piece suit that Marks had decided upon. The other "go-fer" was sifting through the large black hat drum that contained headdresses and hats created for Fling in her role as the "Goddess of the Sun." Scattered around them on the woven straw mats were piles of wooden balsa snakes from Peru, carved Indian shields from Malaysia, and banana-leaf painted trays from Bali. These were the props either collected over the years or purchased in New York that Marks always insisted on bringing on location to add the special touch that created his spectacular signature portfolios. Marks was the only magazine editor who brought his own coals to New Castle.

Fling hoped that today's picture might be more simple than the elaborate extravaganza that Marks had staged the day before. She'd been precariously perched in gold high-heeled sandals on the crumbling wall of the Incan sun temple at Ingapirca. The Bob Mackie gold beaded gown had weighed a ton, but not enough to prevent her from blowing away in the blustery winds when the five-foot-high golden Eric Javits headdress was secured to her head. She felt like The Flying Nun. Nobody appreciated how dangerous a model's work could be. First, you exercised your buns off, then they tried to kill you off in some dangerous location; looking seductive while falling off a cliff in a flimsy chiffon gown in a forty mph wind, remembering, of course, to smile.

Yesterday she'd been surrounded by ten young men costumed in Incan loincloths and capes bearing burning tiki torches, while Fling tried not to cough as the theatrical smoke bombs choked her. Marks had nearly lost it, trying to communicate and give directions to the ten authentic Incan Indians he had insisted on hiring, very eager fellows who spoke no English . . . and Marks knew no Incan, or whatever it was they spoke.

The temple had loomed up behind her as Fling had steadied herself, raising her arms in salute to the sun. *Snap*, whirl, *snap*, and it was all over. With that kind of production for just one picture, she hoped that the photo assistants had remembered to load the camera with film.

Garcia called her out of the water to get ready for today's picture. She hoped she would have time to swim with the sea lions. The crew's naturalist guide had warned them not to touch any of the animals, but Fling reasoned it would be okay for the animals to touch her. She had been told that the baby sea lions were particularly curious and adventuresome, and would often nip at your fins while swimming. She wouldn't mind that. Her only worry was that she might harm them with her size ten flippers. The sea lions were really cute, but not as cute as Kingman, Fling thought. She really missed him.

"Wake up, Fling. Planet Earth calling. Earth to Fling." It was Garcia, snapping his fingers in front of her face. Garcia, who was considered one of the greatest makeup men on the planet, had quickly befriended the face of the nineties. She liked her new friend and loved the work he did, but she missed Frederick, who would always be number one to her. Here she was on the most exciting adventure of her life without Frederick or King-man. Even the blue-footed boobies had mates. She didn't even have a date!

"Fling, did you remember to put on your heavy sun block this morning? You are already burning. We cannot have you peeling in a cover close-up."

"But, Garcia," she stroked his mondo-man mustache, "if I'm supposed to be the Sun Goddess, then I'm supposed to be bronzed." She gave him her most bewitching smile.

"Bronze or not, put on some more sun block. Peeling is not pretty." Nevertheless, he rummaged through his makeup bag for a slightly darker foundation. He only worried that she'd get progressively darker in each shot, ruining the continuity of the spread. Garcia took off his own straw hat and placed it on her head, shielding her from the harsh rays. Garcia had serious work to do. He had to match her eyelids to the azure blue of the sea.

"Garcia," she asked in her most earnest of voices, "don't you think that Kingman Beddall is the handsomest man?"

He mixed some Ultima II aqua eyeshadow with some gold Revlon powder and brushed it over her lids. He had forgotten the Carmen Colors kit on the ship. No one would know the difference from a distance in a full-length shot, and Marks would credit Carmen Cosmetics, anyway.

"I mean, like movie-star handsome." Her eyes were focused on the enormous rock fifty yards away jutting out of the sea.

"Yes, I think about him all the time." Garcia started to feather her eyebrows up in her trademark expression of simultaneous innocence and sexual expectation.

"So do I. He's all I ever think about."

Garcia couldn't believe it! How could this gorgeous creature be so gaga over a midget mogul? Why, the girl could eat soup off the top of his head. It had been Garcia's experience that the more beautiful the model, the worse her taste in men. Why couldn't she go out with a rock star like all the other girls? He patted a mascara smudge with a Q-Tip.

"You know my motto, 'love ain't nothing but sex misspelled'!"

"Oh, Garcia!" Fling let loose a goose-honk laugh, setting off an echo of loud warbling whistles from the boastful frigate birds puffing out their bright red throat sacks.

"Now look what you've made me do. I've set off all the birds."

"Just the boy birds, and you do that to the males of *any* species!"

Fling flared her perfect little nostrils and lowered her eyes to her haughty cheekbones. She was like a walking pheromone. Garcia could swear that every animal on this lovers' island was gravitating to Fling. It was as if the entire animal world loved beauty and goodness as much as the human species did.

Garcia combed her hair back into a wet chignon.

"You have two minutes to be on set," yelled Marks. "Set" meant back in the water, knee deep.

"We'll be ready, Marks," assured Garcia, applying the finishing touches. She was a masterpiece. To die for, he assured her. He handed Fling the white pearl-yoked Gottex bathing suit and held up a towel to give her privacy as she slipped it on. This was not a suit for swimming, this was a suit for fantasy, with six strings of pearls dripping down from its halter neck. This was definitely not an Olympic racing suit, but pure fashion. The only place you would wear this suit was around the pool in Palm Springs, Beverly Hills, or Acapulco.

Marks approached, bearing a necklace from David Webb. Suspended from his hands, the clasp open. He fastened the three-strand South Seas pearl choker with a rock-crystal center stone around her willowy neck, his not-so-subtle salute to the rocky moonscape jagging out of the sea behind her. Garcia dusted a sprinkling of gold powder over the high points of her cheeks and shoulder blades in order for them to better catch the light of the sun.

As Marks placed the eight-pronged pearl crown upon her head, Fling took the gold Ecuadorian mirror in her right hand and assumed the position of the Stature of Liberty, gone south. The clouds broke, the sun burst, and the model was transformed into the Sun Goddess, emerging from the sea in the middle of the equator, exuding all the warmth and mystery of the center of the earth.

"Magic time!" shouted Marks. They had all just witnessed a metamorphosis, and had made another great shot.

The entire time Fling was before the camera's lens, she imagined she was back in her apartment, on the pedestal, posing for her darling Kingman.

"This shot is so good," twinkled Garcia. "I can't wait to go home and raise my rates."

"Change time, everybody," announced Marks.

"Did you say *lunchtime*, Marks?" pouted Fling. "Some of us are really hungry."

"You know the rules, Fling. No food allowed on the islands."

The naturalist guide had informed this merry band of Manhattanites that they could not touch the animals, bring any food with them, smoke, stray off the paths, or remove anything from the islands. The only thing they were allowed to leave on Batalome Island were their footprints in the sand.

"But my stomach is growling," moaned Fling.

"Good. I want your stomach concave for this next shot. Where's the aqua metallic bikini?"

"Have to be a seal to get anything to eat around here," one of the hungry assistants grumbled as she rooted through the pile for the bikini. Right now the endangered turtle eggs were looking pretty good to the exhausted, starved group.

"Come on, team. One more easy picture and we can go back to the ship for lunch. Fling, you will love this shot. All you have to do is lie on the sand at the water's edge and let the baby sea lions nip at your toes."

Fling wrapped her arms around herself and threw back her head and squealed, "Ooh, happiness!"

"And, Garcia, I want Fling a little paler in this shot."

"Oh. No problem, man. Easy," Garcia said, shaking his head. He glanced at the exquisite earth creature cavorting in the water with the playful sea lions, under the harsh rays of the midday sun on the equator. Even at this distance he could see her getting darker by the minute. "Sure, Marks . . . paler." He gingerly stepped into the sea, full of trepidation, to retrieve the fearless girl swimming in circles with two sea lions under her spell. The guide had told him that there were over fifty thousand of these creatures, and Garcia could swear that half that number were moving en masse to play with the pretty nature lover. It was as if they were spreading the news by sea-mammal word of mouth.

Garcia was scared to death when a bull sea lion streaked past him like a jet fighter on a bombing run. He, who had been raised in the Hispanic jungles of Manhattan, was worried he might get bumped to death by an overzealous sea lion. The last time he had seen so many animals gathered together was in Alfred Hitchcock's *The Birds*, and everyone knew how horrible it was when Tippi Hedren was practically pecked to death. *Womp!* He felt something hitting against his leg, and hauled Fling out of the sea with amazing speed.

"Oh, phooey, Garcia. That was really fun. They were barking at me in the nicest way."

"Yeah? Well Marks will be barking at me if you even get a *shade* darker!" He dropped the wide-brimmed straw hat back on her head and popped open an umbrella to shield her from the sun as they marched across the sand like a modern-day Robinson Crusoe and her man Friday. The image that came into Garcia's head was the famous picture ingrained in every photo buff's mind, of Pablo Picasso, bald-headed and tan, walking on the beach with a big black umbrella behind a taller Françoise Gilot, shielding his mistress and mother of Paloma from the *hot* Mediterranean sun.

It would be another perfect picture; in fact, it would end up being the cover! Fling in three-quarter profile, her hair caught back in a Grace Kelly knot, her chiseled features kissed by the sun, her eyelids semiclosed, with streaks of Ultima II aqua-blue eye color mixed with Revlon, was stretched out in a one-armed aqua bikini that caught and reflected back the verisimilitude of the sea blues. Marks couldn't have *planned* this picture. How do you command four shiny black baby sea lions to come strutting and wiggling onto the beach to sniff at Fling's toes and lie down at her elbows, striking a similar pose showing off their sleek profile. It was all Marks could do to restrain himself from draping jewels on their sleek bodies; it would be like displaying pearls on jeweler's black velvet, Marks thought. Fling showcasing four million dollars' worth of rubies and South Seas pearls lavished at her throat, on both wrists and earlobes, the sea lions similarly decked out; would be a photo editor's dream come true. Marks had two mottoes where jewelry was concerned: A real lady always wore earrings, even at the beach, and the more jewelry shown on the editorial pages, the more jewelry advertising the magazine was likely to get.

As for making Fling shimmer, by now, Marks had gotten

wise to the secret word that would bring seductive mystery to the model's eyes.

"Kingman, honey, think of Kingman," he commanded. Fling's eyes lit up like fireworks; their heat practically bore holes into the camera's lens every time she concentrated on Kingman Beddall.

In all the Galápagos, there is no more startling color than that of the intense bright blue feet of the blue-footed booby. To Fling's delight, these birds brazenly performed their courtship dance in broad daylight, paying no heed to their human audience. The courtship ritual began with the male bird throwing his head back and pointing his beak upward in a show-off maneuver, called "skypointing," to attract the female. Then he and the girl bird did a slow high-stepping dance that reminded Fling of Vogueing at The Sound Factory. Just like a disco couple, the girl bird fell into the rhythm of the boy bird and they skypointed together, their wings cocked behind their heads, not to the strains of Madonna but to the sounds of the male's whistles and the female's honks. Since blue-footed boobies don't actually make nests, their scurrying to gather twigs and sticks was more like a prenuptial ritual than really building a home together. Fling watched as they repeated this ceremony several times, before the happy boobies culminated their courtship dance by mating.

Suddenly she was very homesick for Kingman. It had been three whole weeks since she had seen him. She closed her eyes to conjure up the image of her lover. There was no mistaking the rich aroma of his expensive cologne and cigars. She swore she could smell him now. She opened her eyes and turned her head around, skypointing her nose into the air.

"Is this a private party or can anybody join in?" Kingman Beddall's voice was soft and husky.

"Oh, Kingman! I can't believe you are here! Is it really you? I was just wishing you were here!"

"Yeah, it's really me. Cop a feel." He looked past her to the birds. "What are *they* doing?" he pointed.

Fling lowered her eyes and giggled. She wanted to rush into his arms, but she thought she'd try a little coyness. He hadn't flown halfway around the world to check on a photo shoot!

She raised herself to her full height and batted her lashes at him. "Well, the boy bird was trying to show off and impress the girl bird. They call it skypointing."

"Yeah, so I'm building a skyscraper on Fifth Avenue."

She shook her honey-blond hair free from Garcia's carefully coiffed chignon.

"The boy bird asked the girl bird to dance, and they cooed and necked," she continued.

"So you want to dance?" He ran his eyes up and down her bikini-clad body. She had gotten even better looking.

"Well, I don't know. He built her a house, and then they got engaged and made love."

He moved closer to her. "So, do you want to get engaged?"

"No." A look of mischief crossed her face. She could feel her heart beating wildly in her chest.

"I want to get married." She almost fainted. Marks had not let her eat all day.

"The boobies got married and then they made love."

"I'm no boob, let's make love first, then get married."

Fling let out a squeal and threw her endless arms around him.

"Kingman, I love you! You are the most wonderful man in the whole world. I'm so excited!"

"Let's put some of that excitement to good use. I'm a little aroused myself." He grabbed the hand of the hottest girl on the equator and led her back to his *panga*, which whizzed them back to the *Pit Bull*, where they consummated their marriage a little bit before the ceremony.

It had taken ten full days for the *Pit Bull* and its crew of twenty-eight to sail to the Galápagos from Miami. It was well worth the trip. Any great luxury ship is always described in the feminine gender; *she* was yar. *Her* lines were elegant and graceful as *she* sleeked through the water. Kingman Beddall had purchased the *Xanadu*, which he renamed the *Pit Bull*, from a Saudi prince. He was a man who loved to possess other men's treasures. The opulent 260-foot Jon Bannenberg–designed yacht carried two hundred telephones, a satellite communications system worthy of a battleship, a Bell Jet Ranger helicopter, two cigarette speed boats, a skeet-shooting range, and a saltwater swimming pool. The *Pit Bull* also boasted a screening room with a library of two thousand films, a hospital with an operating theater for emergency surgeries at sea, and a high-tech office complete with computers, faxes, and photocopying machines. Its fourteen tanks held enough fuel to carry it once across the Pacific or twice across the Atlantic Ocean without a pit stop.

Kingman had flown down to meet the world's showiest private yacht, which was now being festooned with balloons and streamers by its Greek crew, directed by Marks in an effort to create yet another spectacular extravaganza. Garlands of bougainvillea in fuchsia, tangerine, and white were looped through the ship's brass railings. Marks had created an altar worthy of an Eastern European cathedral from the island's velvety daisies and Darwin's asters.

"Candles, where are the candles?" Marks boomed at the bewildered ship's crew. "This is the marriage of the most beautiful girl in the world to the richest man in New York! Hop to it! This is not a weekend regatta, but a shipboard wedding fit for a king."

Marks stood back and fixed his fingers into a viewfinder, the way he ordinarily did when he set up one of the pictures for his editorial spreads. The effect was terrific. The twinkling white Tivoli lights were strung from fore to aft across the sleek lines of the yacht. The sun was an orange fireball sinking into the sea. This was the moment before the equatorial sun totally disappeared beneath the horizon line in an eerie, enchanted flash of illuminated neon-green lightning. The whole image was good enough for a cover, thought Marks.

The bride-to-be was sequestered in her stateroom. Garcia was weaving garlands of bougainvillea into her honeyed tresses, and draping her in a white Grecian gown. Luckily they had brought along Norma Kamali's classically designed toga. The golden girl, bronzed by the sun, gold bracelet cuffs on her wrists, bare-necked and barefooted, with the most ethereal expression Garcia had ever seen, had become the Goddess of the Sun incarnate. They had been trying to capture the spirit of the Sun Goddess during the entire two weeks. This was the first time they had *really* gotten it right.

Marks was going to give the bride away, and the ship's captain would marry the couple. Garcia would be best man. He hurried up to the main salon steps to retrieve the ring from Kingman.

"She looks incredible, Mr. Beddall. Simply gorgeous!" Garcia fluttered and flapped his hands about.

"Garcia, my man, it is Garcia, isn't it?"

Garcia nodded enthusiastically, as if he had just been inducted into a privileged fraternity.

"Call me Kingman." He dumped a cigar ash on Garcia's sandal. "I just wanted you to know how much I appreciate everything you've done for Fling and Carmen Cosmetics on this little shoot of yours." His voice was as soft as the night breeze. Always a danger signal. "But if you ever, ever, use any cosmetics other than Carmen's on my wife's face again, I'll have your balls fried in oil and you'll be looking at the biggest fucking lawsuit you ever saw."

Garcia recoiled in horror as if struck by a venomous snake. How could Beddall have known that he had used a mélange of cosmetics because he had left the Carmen Colors back on their cruise ship?

"It was a mistake, Mr. Beddall. It will never happen again. From now on, I will carry only Carmen Cosmetics in my makeup bag." He involuntarily twitched his mondo-man mustache.

"Good." Kingman slapped him on the back. "That's what I wanted to hear. You always gotta cover your flanks. The competition is always trying to screw you." Garcia nodded in unison with Kingman. It seemed like the practical thing to do.

"Here's the ring, my boy. You're the best man, aren't you?" He examined Garcia as if he were under a microscope.

"Oh, I am honored, Mr. Beddall." Garcia took the ring, the Harry Winston diamond as big as a golf ball, and nervously asked, "Is there a wedding band too, Mr. Beddall?"

"Naw, she can pick out one of those do-hickeys when we get home. This is what she will really like." Actually, the ring was more to Kingman's liking, big and flashy. Fling would have preferred simple and quiet.

When Fling marched down the makeshift aisle on the deck of the *Pit Bull* on Marks's arm, the entire ship gasped at her breathtaking beauty. One of the young Greek sailors even crossed himself and muttered a prayer, struck by wonder at this heaven-sent creature. As she stood before Kingman, more radiant than she had ever been in her life, even he was overwhelmed. Suddenly he felt just like Carney Eball with his nose pressed up against the window, eyeballing something he could never have.

"Do you, Kingman Beddall, take this woman to be your lawfully wedded wife?"

"Yeah." His eyes narrowed beneath the bushy brows.

"And do you, Sue Ellen Montgomery, 'Fling,' take this man to be your lawfully wedded husband?"

"Of course I do." She let loose with one of her best goose-honk laughs.

Before the captain could pronounce them husband and wife, they were locked in a passionate embrace that would have embarrassed even the blue-footed boobies.

When they finally came up for air, it was as if they didn't even see the well-wishers around them.

"Oooh, my Kingman, you make such a handsome groom." She adoringly patted his mane of dark curly hair into place.

"You think so?" He grinned with one side of his mouth. "But you're the beautiful one. Beautiful like nothin' nobody's seen." She could swear he was almost blushing.

"Oh, Kingman, you do love me a little bit, you do!" She gleefully clapped her hands. "This isn't just a business thing." The worried words just tumbled out of her mouth.

"Of course I do. You're so . . . so good *and* beautiful. Who wouldn't love you?" he stammered.

"Oh, Kingman!" She threw her long arms around his neck. "I'd do anything for you."

As soon as the *I do*'s were said, Marks signaled the captain to fire off the gun flares from the upper deck, which streaked bright red lights across the dark equatorial sky. As if the heavens heard Marks's command, a thousand stars twinkled overhead, one of them falling into the sea, leaving a fiery white trail in its wake. Nature's own pyrotechnics. The steward let loose with the fog-horn, exciting the barking sea lions, which mistakenly took the nasal honk for a mating call. The blue-footed boobies *wok-wok*ed back from shore, while a flock of flamingos, roused from a night's rest, fluttered like a ballet troupe across the lantern-lit aft. The

*Pit Bull*'s searchlights swept back and forth across the sea, spot-lighting leaping porpoises celebrating the marriage of Fling to her King.

Since there were no bands for hire or musicians to be found in the Galápagos, the wedding party shimmied and shaked on the teak-and-holly decks to a makeshift, make-do musical ensemble of a harmonica-playing Greek sailor, a guitar-strumming Span-iard, and the ship's chef banging away on a baby grand piano. The sounds of clinking champagne glasses and merry laughter made this simple pirate party more festive than the Fling! fra-grance launch at the Plaza.

Marks stood in the glare of the spotlighted Bell Jet Ranger helicopter and offered up his glass in a toast. His voice rang out over the three top levels of the ship.

"Ladies and gentlemen, please hoist your glasses in honor of this memorable occasion. No royal wedding has ever been more glamorous than this splendid union of our Fling and her King in nature's own cathedral."

A roar of applause erupted from the crew and the *Town & Country* staff. In excitement, Kingman raised Fling's left arm straight up in the air, showing off her rock of an engagement ring, just like the fight manager waving Rocky Balboa's fist after he had won the World Heavyweight Championship. This was the picture that the *Town & Country* photographer snapped, the one he would sell to *People* magazine, the London *Times*, and *News-week*, all for six figures. This would be the shot seen around the world.

Marks gave the signal for the shower of rice to rain upon the newlyweds. As the happy couple ducked the barrage of Uncle Ben's, the captain led the way to the aluminum steps that would take the small gang of guests to their *pangas,* the small motorized boats that would whisk them back to their cruise ship. Fling and King leaned over the railing of the *Pit Bull*, bidding farewell to their guests. Fling waved royally to her makeup man, stylist, photographer, and magazine editor just like Princess Diana waving to her royal subjects from her wedding carriage.

She suddenly felt very shy. As many times as Kingman had made love to Fling, she knew that on their wedding night, their coming together should be special. Before tonight, she had been a girlfriend, only a thread in the rich fabric of his life. Now they had just promised to love each other forever.

She blushed. She was his wife. Now there were no others. She brushed a loose strand of hair off her sun-kissed face. Frederick had flippantly remarked to her that when a man marries his mistress, he leaves a job vacancy. Not in this case. She was determined to be both his wife and his mistress. She would make him so happy, she would drive any thoughts of other women out of his head. She'd make Kingman Beddall her career. If he didn't dream of her at night and wake up with her name on his lips, it wouldn't be for lack of trying.

Kingman took her hand as he led her through the mega-yacht's grand salon, with its plush custom carpeting and white lacquered walls. The ceiling mosaic of marble and mirror threw back their reflections, moving around the semicircle clusters of ecru down-filled silk couches. Kingman was barreling ahead full throttle to the ship's master suite. He wasn't about to anchor at any other ports of call along the way. He had his destination in mind.

They passed the ornate wall screens with scenes from *The Thousand and One Nights* and descended the gold-bannistered circular staircase. The original owner, Prince Sandar, had rationalized that the time saved not polishing brass was worth the extra expense of gold fittings. They scurried through the sixty-two-foot-long corridor lined in padded goatskin, arriving at the double Moroccan doors inlaid with ebony, gold, and mother-of-pearl as breathless as Dorothy standing in front of the gates of Oz. For some reason, they both felt apprehensive stepping into the opulent master suite, worthy of a sultan's lair. They gasped, overwhelmed at the enchanted vision before them. Marks had taken it upon himself to put the honeymooners into the proper spirit. Luigi Sturcchio, the world's most talented yacht interior designer, had given the room its masculine, sexual overtones, with wide splashes of onyx, suede, rich earthy marbles, gold-plated fixtures, and smoky mirrors. Marks had rendered it mind-boggling. He had set the romantic mood. A hundred scented candles lit the room, reflecting off the lacquered and mirrored ceiling. Fling's favorite CD's were already playing, and a chinchilla throw lay across the extra-large bed, covered with fragrant blossoms. Even the golden rams guarding the bed shimmered in the light of the flickering candles.

*"You make me feel shiny and new. Like a virgin. Touched for the very first time."* Madonna's strong sensual vibrato, accompanied by a rythmic drumbeat, rang out from wall speakers. Fling smiled at the words, the candles, the effect. The chinchilla, she would throw overboard in the morning. For now, she would indulge herself. Marks always put her in the mood for their shoots; now he was putting her in the mood for her wedding night.

As Kingman, standing in the glow of lights, brought her closer to him, Fling suddenly shed her shyness as she always did in the familiar wash of the spotlight. A model girl in the model lights becoming anything you wanted her to be. She grew more graceful and bold under the spell of the mood.

Her neck arched, her nostrils flared, as Kingman gently slipped his fingers over her sculpted shoulders.

"My goddess," he whispered as he wrapped her in his arms and slowly danced her around the shimmering stateroom, then began softly singing into her ear. She felt her breasts growing fuller with every touch, her heart beating faster, as he traced the lines of her dazzlingly beautiful face. She lay her head on his shoulder, more like a child seeking comfort than a sea siren seducing a sailor.

She hoped he wouldn't move too fast. This was her wedding night, the only one that she'd ever want or have. She didn't care if they danced until dawn. To her, it was the first time they were making love.

*"Like a virgin. Touched for the very first time."* In her mind, this *was* the first time.

She stretched up, catching their image in the mirror: one body with two heads and four arms. Lovely, she thought, smiling, as she closed her eyes. A swaying, sexy sea monster. An octopus from the ocean's depths, gyrating to Madonna's music. She felt Kingman's lips brush the nape of her neck, inhaled the smells of Cuban cigars and Moroccan musk, buried her nose into his curly hair before she brought her full rich lips to his. They had all the time in the world. They kissed a passionate kiss for their new life, the blissful life that they would share together. Nothing would ever come between them, she thought as she watched him slip the single strap off her shoulder, causing the silken toga to fall into a puddle of fabric at her bare feet leaving her naked. Goddesses didn't bother with underwear and neither did she. She shivered as she felt his fingers curl into her spine, drawing her closer. Her head fell forward, the perfumed hair cascading over his shoulder as he traced his fingertips across the sleek lines of her back, down her thighs, leaving a wake of goose bumps to show where his hands had been. She found the movements of his hands mesmerizing, his smell spellbinding.

As he worshiped her, kissing and caressing the secrets of her body, she realized it was the first time she had really ever felt beautiful. He picked her up, sweeping her off her feet, carefully finding his way through a maze of candles, surmounting a hundred obstacles to carry her to their bridal bed. He laid her down upon the startling softness of the chinchilla bed throw. Her naked skin, more sensitive after days of salt water and sun, was enveloped by the silver feathery plushiness she was sinking into. He leaned over her, cupping her breasts in his hands. He teased her nipples with his tongue, circling the tips, lightly tugging with his teeth until they pointed directly into the mirrored and tortoiseshell mosaic over their heads. She uttered a little moan of pleasure, which served only to excite Kingman more. She was aching for him to enter her so they could possess each other, but she wanted him to wait, to draw out the moments of their lovemaking, the first one that really mattered to her.

*For the very first time.* She felt him slip a finger into her wetness, both of them surprised at her ardor.

"Why, Fling," King murmured into her mouth, "I think you like your husband."

She felt her own involuntary contractions as she clutched his fingers with her feminine muscle. She moaned again and reached down to remove his hand, to bring it to her lips, tasting her own scent of desire. It was through Kingman that she learned the perfume of her own body, the perfume of pleasure that didn't come in any bottle.

He touched her in different places, lightly, with a certain expertise, playing her curvaceous body like a Stradivarius, tightening one string, easing another, plucking two together until she moaned out in the song of surrender, his favorite melody. He licked the beads of moisture between her breasts, showering her with an inexhaustible caress of kisses, his mannish lips fluttering over the valley of her soft belly. He swirled his tongue around the creases of her navel; she lifted her pelvis in response. He parted her legs, she letting them fall open easily as he thrust his fingers deeper inside her. Just as she opened her mouth to cry out, he kissed her, pushing his warm tongue into her open mouth until their twisting tongues whirled in wetness. Fling's muscled legs folded like melted butter. She wanted him to taste her. He moved his mouth down her body, traveling at his own pace, her pace, until he pushed his tongue into the most mysterious spot of a woman's body, the secret place of her power. She closed her eyes, letting a moan escape her pouty mouth, and closed her thighs around his shoulders, clutching him with her strength. Tossing her head back on the chinchilla throw, she finally let go, shuddering into him, the man who loved the taste of power.

Kingman moved over her to study her face, the most beautiful face in the world, as no photographer had ever captured it. No camera lens had caught the look in those innocent eyes, so sexy after she had just come at Kingman's prodding direction.

As his body moved over hers, she could feel the coarse texture of his shirt against her chafed nipples. She rose up from her waist to help him unbutton his shirt, lightly kissing his chest, which held just a patch of hair between his collarbone and his flat stomach.

"Kingman," she focused all her smoldering gaze at him, "I'm your wife, it's okay to get naked."

"Yeah, but your naked is better than mine," he said almost shyly to his goddess.

"Oh, my lovely baby," Fling cooed, "you are more beautiful than anyone!" She picked up a corner of the chinchilla throw, softly brushing it against his cheek and chest. She unfastened his belt, widening her eyes as she watched him unzip his trousers and throw them over one of the golden rams. She listened to the words of the songs and the pulsating rhythms surrounding them. Now he was naked, too.

"Do you want to dance, Mrs. Beddall?" King asked seductively.

"I thought you'd never ask," she laughed, moving off the bed with him and into his arms. They swayed to the music, sinking into the plush carpet.

"This is our wedding dance, King," she trilled.

"Yeah," King whispered in his husky voice. "Let's hope nobody cuts in."

"Look, King. Look in the mirror. We're dancing. Look at us." Her voice was as radiant as her face.

"Put me in," he whispered, "but only as far as you like."

He put his large erection into her hand like a wedding gift.

"Yes," she said silkily. "I like it as far as it can go." Gently, she held him in her hand, urging him, until he slipped into her, deeper than he'd ever gone before. Pleasure mixed with pain until she opened entirely for him. She gasped. He had never been so large. Surely, if he looked into her moaning mouth, he could see himself up inside her, she thought in a delicious whirl of semiconsciousness.

"Can you feel me?" He narrowed his eyes at her and grinned. They were dancing, moving to the music. In the mirror it wasn't a man or a woman, but a special sea creature joined at the hip. *Octopussy.*

She groaned and he moaned along with her. When they were connected they made the same single sound. They were one entity.

"I love the way we make love," she whispered. "I love it when you take your time." Her voice was low and breathless.

As he pushed farther inside her, she moved one leg up around his waist, like a flexible flamingo. Accommodating him.

Her eyes locked into a passionate embrace with his own. Their lips met, molding into one mouth. She felt his hunger and desire as he pushed into her. Reaching higher, he grew harder and larger inside her. Astonishing her. Her long arms dangled down his back as they swayed, locked into each other's body. Finally she brought both legs up around him. He cupped her firm bottom in his hands, lifting her higher, delving deeper. He carried her to the bed, gently letting her down, still inside her, bringing her knees farther up to her chest so that her face, her breasts, and her power were all in the same place. He pushed, she pulled, in a motion that gently matched the waves lapping against the sleek vessel's hull. Kingman, sensing her need, picked up his speed like the powerful engines that propelled his ship, pumping pistons moving in well-lubricated strokes.

"Yes, Kingman," she moaned, digging her fingers into his back as her pelvis matched each powerful thrust. Their sleek bodies slapped against each other in the oldest rhythm of all, their breath coming faster and faster in shorter pants until, like a sudden sea goddess, strong, she rose, turning him around, placing herself over him, tightening her muscled thighs around his torso, gripping him, controlling his erection. She was feeling his pulse beating inside her. She gripped his shoulders, raising and lowering her hips, pulling him with her in every magnificent motion. She watched his eyes roll back, his mouth fall open, as she sensuously impaled herself on all his splendor. They rode the same wave, swept away in a crest of passion so fierce she couldn't remember the color of his eyes, but only the warm color of their love.

As he dozed, their bodies in a tangle, Kingman still resting inside her, she watched over him like a lioness. She would protect him. She would take care of him. All he had to do was love her. She'd never let anyone or anything come between them. She wanted to possess him so completely, to prevent him from breathing without her, of thinking of anyone but her. She would give everything she had to him; in return, all she wanted was his love.

"Kingman, I love you," she recited her mantra, waiting for the expected silence.

"I love you, too, Fling," he said softly. *For the very first time,* Madonna's voice trilled.

Tears of love and joy streamed down Fling's face. Somewhere Tinkerbell was alive and flying high in the heavens.

Later that night, Fling wired an excited telegram to Frederick. Kingman sent one off to Also, but Garcia sent, by far and away, the longest message to Suki.

That week in New York, Dr. Corbin asked each of the interested parties who were his patients what they thought about the marriage.

Also Beddall had answered, "I don't need a stepmother."

Anne Randolph Beddall had quietly said, "Some women will do anything for money," and cried.

Tandy had been so angry, she had hurled an ashtray across the room and needed four sessions before she could sputter out, "that no good, low-down, white trash son of a bitch carny barker's son! Watch, he'll call me, mark my words! Soon as he gets home, he'll want to see *me* again!"

Millions of women who didn't go to Dr. Corbin had plenty to say about the Millionaire marrying the Model, too, but for the most part, millions of women just rushed right out to buy Fling! perfume and Fling! bath splash. Maybe there was something, some aphrodisiac, who knows? some special ingredient, in the fragrance that would help make *them* more desirable. Maybe if they used a dab of Fling! behind their ears or in the crevice of their bosoms, some zillionaire would come sailing out to sea in his yacht, whisk them off to an island, and marry them. If it happened once, who could tell? Millions of American women sprayed Fling! fragrance on their pillows at night after they heard on the news that the New York business tycoon had made Fling, the model, his wife on a love boat at the equator, in the center of the earth! The most romantic love story to come down the pike in years!

## STURMHOF

The bride stretched awake like a rare pedigree feline in the enormous burgundy damask-draped bed. Sunlight peeked through the twenty-foot-high heavily curtained windows, creating little patches of dappled light on the Oriental carpet in the dark, richly regal room. One single beam of morning light fell directly upon a bronze statuette of a laughing faun. The bride hoped that this was not a premonition of what was to come. The night before, a scandalous wedding had taken place that surely would shock most of civilized society.

The bride silently slipped out of the rumpled burgundy satin sheets and into a robe of the smoothest China silk. Not wanting to wake her deeply slumbering husband, the bride tiptoed to the bathroom to assess the consummated wedding night's damage to her delicate facial skin, and to freshen up for the next go-around with the permanently aroused, oversexed husband.

With a flick of the light switch, the bathroom was a quarry of color. Smoky gilt mirrors reflected walls of bronzed onyx, a lapis lazuli blue sink with gold filigree fish fixtures, and the deep malachite-green sunken bathtub, large enough to be considered a small swimming pool. The bride thought that this kind of luxury wouldn't be hard to get used to. Why, there was everything a girl could want or dream of. Hot and cold running servants, houses with the decor of museums, jewelry so plentiful and large that it bordered on the brink of bad taste, more money than was imaginable, and a loving, devoted husband. Yes, the bride was one lucky woman; only, the Baroness Fredericka von Sturm wasn't a woman at all. Fredericka, formerly Fred of TriBeCa, was Frederick, the most artful makeup man in New York, who had captured the fancy of Germany's industrial billionaire baron.

Frederick had been transformed into Fredericka at the insistence of the Baron William Wolfgang von Sturm. What Wolfy wanted . . . Wolfy got, and Wolfy needed a wife and a child, to adhere to the clauses in his ancestral trust. Frederick didn't mind dressing up as a woman in Paris's finest couture from Christian Lacroix, Claude Montana, and Karl Lagerfeld. He had always been so androgynously handsome that with a dab of eyeshadow, a touch of mascara, and hit of lip gloss, Frederick could become the beautiful Baroness. Frederick had never shaved a day in his life. His chromosomal structure had been forced upon him at birth, and not by any aberrant conscious decision arrived at later in life. He was what he was supposed to be.

Frederick knew that it wouldn't always be easy to be the Baroness, but he would have all his dreams come true. His Prince Charming had rescued him from a life of nameless sex partners and dangerous dragons. In the AIDS age of death and disease, wearing a dress to keep Wolfy happy was a small price to pay. Why, he was Cinderfella at the Castle! And if the high-heeled shoe fit, who was he to argue with a closetful of Charles Jourdan glass slippers?

Sturmhof—or Stormhouse as Frederick referred to it—perched like an eagle's lair high in the Bavarian Alps. With its turrets, watch towers, ramparts, and dungeons, the Von Sturm ancestral seat looming over a precipice on the top of a peak deep within the forest was the reality of a fairy-tale castle.

When the Baron and Frederick had first driven up the long twisting mountain road to Sturmhof Castle, south of Stuttgart, the enchanted home to generations of Von Sturm barons and princes since 1781, Frederick had immediately felt strangely at home and among the familiar. Of course to him the castle resembled Disney's Magic Kingdom! He had almost been surprised when arrogant footmen and servants in loden-green livery had been lined up on the castle's steps to greet them, instead of Mickey Mouse, Cinderella's fairy godmother, and Goofy gaily waving an oversized welcome. And if anyone tried to awaken him now or ever from his enchantment and turn his Daimler into a pumpkin, he'd blow them to smithereens.

Frederick shivered in the morning cold. The onyx marble floor beneath his feet was freezing. He padded back to the baronial bridal suite he had shared with Wolfy the night before. Even Frederick, the unshockable, had been rendered thunderstruck at the suggestion by Wolfy that they be legally married—by a man of the cloth, no less—in Sturmhof Chapel. And good intentions aside, there was no way in a millennium that the two handsome men could create a child to fulfill the requirements of Wolfy's multibillion-dollar trust, the largest of its kind in Europe. No matter how many dresses he wore or how many people he fooled, there simply was no fooling Mother Nature. He was beginning to get cold feet, and not from the pervasive chill in the castle. He wished Wolfy would wake up.

He wondered why the Cinderella saga always *ended* just as she married the Prince. What was the morning *after* like! Had she awakened, frightened, out of her element in the Prince's bedroom, where she was suddenly alone and feeling out of place? Had she sent for a broom and some kitchen mice to make her feel more at home? Frederick had a wild craving for an E-tab. What did you do, ring for a servant to bring you up some designer drugs? He didn't even speak German. *Gesundheit* was the only word he knew. This whole scheme was as crazy as those hatched by Wolfy's distant ancestor mad King Ludwig II of Bavaria, who had a private stage erected in one of his underground grottoes for Wagnerian operas to be performed for his sole amusement while he floated in his subterranean lake at Linderhof in a baroque barge surrounded by swans.

Frederick gracefully moved to the window, as poised and swift as the Blue Point Siamese cat the Baron always compared him to. This analogy doubly alarmed him, as he hesitated to open the great doors leading to the castle's myriad halls and labyrinthian passageways, where the two Dobermans, Hermann and Hesse, patrolled the tapestry-hung halls and cavernous Great Rooms. Yesterday Wolfy had laughingly showed him the "Dogs Room," where an eighteenth-century artist had painted trompe l'oeil kennels, between the real ones, against which hunting dogs were known to have broken their noses. Such mock realism and deceit, excluded from art, were rustic amusements for the Von Sturm royalty two hundred years ago. Frederick hoped he himself wasn't some sort of decadent Teutonic-aristocracy joke.

If only Wolfy would wake up! Frederick stared at his high-arched patrician profile and weathered face, which proudly displayed the cragginess of autumns spent hunting stags in his own forests, and fine sun lines from summers on the Costa del Sol. Frederick gazed adoringly at the face of his enigmatic baron. He had saved Frederick, protected him, and made love to him as if he were one of his treasured works of art. But Frederick did not want to be one of the Baron's trophies, such as the hundreds of stags' horns mounted on the castle walls or the gold and silver jewel-encrusted chalices that were encased in glass vitrines. Over the chapel entrance, the Von Sturm family motto, "Our follies of pleasure are justified by our bodies offered in death for commerce and deeds of right," was etched in stone. Yesterday, at the ceremony in the chapel, with its stained glass windows and the colorfully depicted religious scenes of its eighteen-century ceiling frescoes, Frederick had stood as the boys' choir from the town of Sturmbach, which served as a modern fiefdom to Sturmhof Castle and was owned by the Baron, sang chants from Carl Orff's *Carmina Burana* a cappella, except for the periodic blasts of a heraldic trumpet.

He had worn a simple suit by Karl Lagerfeld, who designed for the House of Chanel, in gray, with loden-green velvet lapels; the platinum Von Sturm Eagle, its spread wings shot with diamonds, its body composed of the flawless Von Sturm emerald;

and a simple black picture hat covered with a sheer voile veil. No rings had been exchanged, only promises. And he had thought he might have to dress up in *Lederhosen* or some Bavarian costume to please the Baron. This was big-time dress-up! There was no ring. How could you give a wedding band to another man?

As the morning light shoved its way into the room with greater intensity, it focused upon a wrapped parcel that hadn't been there the night before. Frederick gingerly moved over to the green box with the gold ribbon and peeked at the card scented with the Baron's cologne of rich Oriental spices: *For my darling Freddie on our wedding night, Wolfy.* Frederick tore the box open and found two smaller boxes inside. One was velvet and frayed, an antique jeweler's box, and the other was wrapped in plain shiny gray paper with a gray ribbon that had the Von Sturm crest stamped on it. Which first? He grabbed for the bigger box. Inside was a fine leather-bound folder trimmed with a fine fourteen-karat-gold edge, in which an aged page from a book was housed. The gold-lettered engraving on the leather encasing read, To Freddie from Wolfy on our wedding night. On the back was stamped "First edition, B. R. Redman; Introduction to *The Arabian Nights Entertainments*, 1932." He read to himself:

> "It is a world in which all the senses feast riotously upon
> sights and sounds and perfumes; upon fruit and flowers
> and jewels; upon wines and sweets; upon yielding flesh,
> both male and female, whose beauty is incomparable. It
> is a world of heroic amorous encounters. . . . Romance
> lurks behind every shuttered window; every veiled
> glance begets an intrigue; and in every servant's hand
> nestles a scented note granting a speedy rendez-
> vous. . . . It's a world in which no aspiration is so mad
> as to be unrealizable, and no day proof of what the next
> day may be. A world in which apes may rival men, and

a butcher may win the hand of a king's daughter; a world in which palaces are made of diamonds, and thrones cut from single rubies. It's a world in which all the distressingly ineluctable rules of daily living are gloriously suspended; from which individual responsibility is delightfully absent. It is the world of a legendary Damascus, a legendary Cairo, and a legendary Constantinople. . . . In short, it is the world of an eternal fairy tale—and there is no resisting its enchantment."

—B. R. Redman, Introduction to
*The Arabian Nights Entertainments (1932)*

Frederick's eyes misted over. The Baron *did* understand the irony and magic of their fairy tale! The Baron knew. Frederick was overcome with passion and emotion as he opened the velvet jeweler's box. Inside was a heavy gold signet ring engraved with the Baron's coat of arms. A man's ring. A man's gift to another man! He slipped the ring onto his finger, his mind ablaze with gratitude, love, and desire, tears resting on his unnaturally high cheekbones. Frederick kissed the Baron on his eyelids, slipped his body into the baronial bed beside him, and he resumed his place in their fairy tale together. There would be no more second thoughts. He would coax the Baron awake with his caresses and then keep their fairy tale alive forever.

The Baron smiled as he awakened. He had a *geschmaltzt* look on his face.

"Ah, *mein Liebling,*" he said to his beautiful boy.

"Ah," Frederick sighed, *"Gesundheit!"*

# 9

ingman Beddall was sitting on top of the world,
literally, in his new office atop the tallest building
in the world, able to look down upon the Chrysler
Building, the World Trade Center, the Empire State Building,
and the Trump Tower with a single glance. Manhattan, Queens,
Brooklyn, the two other boroughs, part of New Jersey, and a
corner of Connecticut lay at his feet. Perched as he was in his own
private eagle's nest on the 125th floor of the Beddall Building, he
liked watching the airplanes taking off below him from La
Guardia. Particularly those with *KingAir* emblazoned on their
shiny silver tails. Supermogul! Kingman had purchased bankrupt
TransAir Lines for a little cash, a lot of promises, a deal with the

unions, and three hundred million dollars of debt. The paint on the KingAir imprints and logo was still wet, and the ink on the contracts barely dry. But Kingman Beddall, who never had been able to afford a toy airplane as a boy, now had an entire fleet of them. Three hundred shiny airplanes with his name on the tail, the way other, less ambitious men put their names on cocktail napkins or golf balls to impress their colleagues. Kingman wasn't entirely sure where he was going but, to the rest of the world, it looked like he had arrived.

The Nikkei was up. Tokyo stocks had risen 209.56 points to 26,607.52 since he had gotten out of bed. The dollar was down, way down, and he was shorting the oil stocks and utilities. He had picked up twenty-five small television companies in the past two years and was negotiating to go halves with the British entrepreneur Robert Castell to start up a news network in Europe and Asia to compete with CNN. The Japanese loan he had managed to get was a full two points below prime rate. Much better than Chemical had come up with.

A smug Kingman drew a long proud puff on his Cuban cigar. He'd had lunch with Fidel Castro a few days ago in Havana, to discuss starting up a baseball franchise. Cuban communism was as dead as a dodo, and the old guerrilla was trying to drum up tourism in the aging Latin Lady, which now resembled Miami Beach twenty years after an Iraqi invasion. Castro had promised KingAir Ways the exclusive route from Miami to Havana if he'd only finance the baseball franchise. Kingman had daydreamed about his "Havana Hurricanes" and how he'd own their air rights all over Latin America, which was carumba-crazy about baseball, and how he'd turn it into a vehicle for promoting world peace and, at the same time, high ratings for his fledgling network, World Network News and Entertainment—NNE. But the Enemies Act, which prohibited Americans from doing business in Cuba, Vietnam, and Cambodia, was still on the books. And it wasn't State Department dictum, either. It was Treasury Department ment stuff! And no self-respecting tightrope-walking business tycoon wanted to mess with Treasury and the IRS!

He'd write Castro a thank-you note for the Monte Cristos and forget about the rinky-dink team. Castro's doctors wouldn't even let the poor old guy smoke cigars anymore. Kingman grinned to himself, patting his flat stomach and dumping some cigar ashes into an antique sterling silver spittoon. Sitting in his high-altitude office, he blew perfectly round circles of cigar smoke into the air. Nice idea, but not worth dicking around with the IRS.

Wednesday, he'd fly down to Washington on the KingAir Shuttle to have lunch with his buddy, Charlie McBane, deputy secretary of state, just to check on the rules. He'd just as soon be seen doing business with Noriega rather than get into it with the Treasury! No way, Jose! Mañana, Fidel. He swung his feet off the desk and checked on the weekly agenda that Joyce always prepared for him.

Somehow Fling had talked him into building and subsidizing the Beddall Home for the Aged, which would take care of indigent homeless and old folks and would be run by the nuns. Being old and defenseless and cared for by nuns—ugh! Kingman's idea of purgatory. These were the kinds of things Fling worried about. The Aged. The Homeless. The Endangered. The Planet. The Beddall Home dedication ceremonies were set for Friday. King had seen the date circled on Fling's big Snoopy calendar in red Magic Marker and highlighted with her signature *X*'s and *O*'s. The girl was so sweet and so damn beautiful, he sometimes anxiously obsessed that she might just be on loan to him. Who was he to have it so good? Almost two years of marriage and everything was swell. What a lucky prick he was and, now, Kingman Beddall was a pretty important prick too!

Kingman had mastered the business warrior's discipline,

prided himself on his punctuality, and had deciphered the New York social etiquette. He had finessed the double kiss on the cheek for the trophy wives who affected the manners of European duchesses, and fine-tuned his ability to point his cigar like a Geiger counter or a truffle-seeking pig in the direction of other big boys doing other big deals. Like Winston Churchill and Edward Bennett Williams, he practiced his extemporaneous anecdotes. Joyce kept a file of prepared witticisms in his office for him. He was learning that powerful men had to be able to hold an audience as well as cultivate the friendship of bankers, politicians, investors, and other insiders. Likability was part of the package.

He had mastered the game. He followed the rules. The social code, he had down pat. No affairs ever with any of the other players' wives—not that they were desirable in the least to a man of Kingman's lusty nature. Those men that had climbed the corporate ladder assisted by their first wives, often relying on their wives' talents and sometimes their bank accounts, were usually accompanied to the prerequisite business-social events by sporting-type women with short gray hair, thickened thighs, and an air of constant, ready alert they had acquired during the leaner years. Good sports, good gals, they knew how to pack light, wear a Burberry trench coat over everything, and smoke and drink like one of the guys, which many of them had become over the years—like Gordo's wife, Biddy. These were tough old birds, hanging on through stock crashes, money acquisition trail drives, flush years, and low times.

They always looked a little apologetic and a lot out of place at King's business dinner parties in the company of the second wives, those appurtenances acquired during the successful years, when the New Age Milken money barons could acquire the best junk bonds money could buy. Women with long, long legs, often six or seven inches taller than their husbands, and who were consistently compulsive doers. Usually childless, they were trophy wives.

These in particular Kingman found very unappealing and aggressively ambitious. No, he felt he had done it right, he had done it better. Anne had helped him achieve a certain status, rubbed the Hopewell, Virginia, red clay off his feet, and offered him an entry into New York as a Virginian gentleman and not just another hungry, aggressive nobody come for the kill in the Big Apple.

Fling was the perfect second wife. She outtrophied all the other trophy wives. And she wasn't even trying. Shy, she seized control of any New York room she entered, simply with her vitality and sheer physical perfection. Fling! fragrance had grossed over seventy million dollars in its second year! The Fling! Colors line was doing bang-up big business in the teen market, her exercise video was right behind Jane Fonda's in worldwide sales, and Fling's endangered species calendar was more popular than Cindy Crawford's and Garfield the Cat's put together. Supposedly not too smart, she was outgrossing all the other supposedly successful working-girl second wives, who were constantly needing financial bailouts.

One poor son of a bitch, Bernie Balsam, had to shovel over thirteen million dollars into a Broadway bomb so his shapely second wife could become a "producer" and acquire some status of her own outside her husband's billions. Bernie had been obliged to continue forking fistfuls of dollars into his wife's play, a musical interpretation of *Gone with the Wind*, even after Frank Rich, the theater critic of *The New York Times*, and John Simon of *New York* magazine, had both dumped on it. The determined Mrs. Balsam had trucked on, pouring more and more of Mr. Balsam's money into the soggy production, which featured an entire third act of rain pouring down over a ruined plantation to symbolize somehow the dampened glory of Scarlett O'Hara's beloved South. "Singin' in the Rain at Tara," the *Daily Sun* critique had begun, and went on to condemn the racism of "the tap-dancing slaves singing away in rain-soaked costumes," and the lightning and thunder, which was supposed to be the big mechanical stunt that audiences so presumably loved, like the helicopter hovering in *Miss Saigon,* and the chandelier dropping amid the smoky subterranean canals and dungeons in *Phantom of the Opera.* King and Fling had gotten drenched sitting in the front row opening night. When the show closed six days and seven million dollars later, the orchestra pit and the first six rows of the theater had to be entirely gutted and refurbished. All this so Bernie's ever socially ambitious second wife would have something to say at a dinner party when the gentleman on her left turned to her and asked, "And what do you do?" Kingman chuckled out loud at his friend's expensive mishap. Mrs. Balsam retired from the theater and resumed her career of spa-hopping and shopping, infinitely less expensive hobbies.

Fling, on the other hand, was a gold mine. The sexy, beautiful girl was making a fortune every day she got out of bed. Nobody ever would have to turn to her and ask, "And what do you do?" They knew. His golden girl was giving Carmen Cosmetics a whole new image and making millions for Kingman as well, millions that were oiling the rest of his growing empire. When he made presentations for the financial analysts, Fling was hauled in to explain the new product lines in progress at Carmen's laboratories—as if anybody listened to her memorized ditties. All of the Brooks Brothers suits were content just to gaze upon the face plastered on the cover of a million magazines in person. Fling was also hauled in for important loan-request meetings, particularly those with the Japanese bankers and financial syndicates. The sun-streaked blonde had become something of a cult heroine in Japan. She even had a line of Fling! Wear that was selling like sushi hotcakes in Tokyo.

Kingman's trophy wife was a winner. He smacked his lips, not so much at his own good luck but at his confreres' misfortunes. When they had bad luck, it made his fortune look even better. He loved leading the pack of all the guys he was riding around with on the financial merry-go-round.

Kingman was one lucky prick indeed!

"King, pick up." It was Joyce Royce on the intercom.

"Yeah."

"There's a Sergeant Buffalo Marchetti out here. Homicide, King. He'd like to see you."

Buffalo Marchetti. The name had a familiar ring to it. Kingman frowned.

"Get Ryan over at NYPD on the phone for me and show Sergeant Buffalo in."

Buffalo, Buffalo. Something was beginning to click. It couldn't be Canada. The statute of limitations had to have run out years ago. Even for murder. That was over thirty years ago. Ancient skeletons.

"Nice place, Mr. Beddall." Sergeant Buffalo Marchetti filled the arched doorway to Kingman's office like a method actor doing an impersonation of a young James Dean and Bruce Willis all rolled into one. He was a kid. A sloppy one, although good looking, just the same. Faded blue jeans, Nike tennis shoes, a black T-shirt stretched taut across his muscled chest, and a revolver bobbing up and down in its leather holster, slung low under his arm, threateningly peeking out through the guy's motorcycle jacket. Rumpled. This was supposed to be an undercover cop? Jeez, wonder what he wears in a really fancy neighborhood, King thought. Well, Hercules Poirot he wasn't, obviously. Kingman noticed this good-looking homicide cop wasn't wearing any socks. To dress this down, maybe the undapper dick had to make up for his lack of sartorial taste with brains.

Maybe Kingman was staring straight at a smart cop, even though the kid was dressed like a downtown artist.

"How do you do." Kingman held out his hand, displaying one of his gold monogrammed cuff links. Whenever he felt unsure or uncomfortable, Kingman always resorted to very proper manners. They shook hands.

"You look awfully young to be in Homicide." He cautiously grinned.

"Anybody's too young to be in Homicide. Look at this." The Buffalo cop thrust a gory photo of a butchered young woman under Kingman's nose. So, the guy relied on shock tactics.

"Not a pretty sight." Kingman looked concerned but didn't flinch. The female corpse was grotesque.

"Should I know her? Is she an employee of mine?" Concerned but not overanxious.

"She worked at Tandy's Nail Emporium on Fifty-seventh Street." Shock treatment number two. This guy was pretty good. Not even all the wizards of Wall Street knew that Carmen Cosmetics held a 60 percent stake in Tandy's Nail Emporiums, of which there were now twenty-one scattered across Manhattan. Tandy's Nail Emporiums used only Carmen Cosmetics nail products, and were open seven days a week, practically dawn till dusk. Who would have thought that when he put up the money— "guilt gelt," he called it—that with a little help from Carmen's marketing magic, these boutiques would become the hottest fast-beauty-service salons, rivaling the cometlike success of Mrs. Field's Cookies? The Beddall Midas touch. So far, so good.

"How can I help you? Cigar?" Kingman sat on the corner of his desk with his proffered humidor of illegal Monte Cristos.

"Not my brand." Sergeant Buffalo's cool gaze fixed on the cigar box and then on the oversized photograph of Fling monopolizing the wall behind Kingman's giant expanse of desk.

"Close, but no cigar, right?" Kingman joked. He obviously wasn't a suspect and he felt no compunction to feign grief over a corpse he'd never laid eyes on before.

"How well do you know Tandy?"

"Very well," Kingman said, short and to the point. With Kingman, if you just set the rules, he could play along.

"How very well?"

"She's one of the first people I met in New York when I moved here. She used to be the manicurist at the St. Regis barber shop. She's from the South, like me. The nail emporiums are a good advertisement for Carmen nail polishes. The customer gets used to the product and buys more." Kingman gave out this drill with a polite grin. The truth, but the guarded truth. If Buffalo was doing a cursory investigation, it would be enough. What'd he think? Tandy knocked off one of her employees? Maybe for giving a lousy pedicure?

"Are you having an affair with Tandy?"

"That's none of your business." He snapped his gold-plated guillotine cigar cutter from Dunhill, decapitating a fresh Havana. All joviality faded from Kingman's face. Nosy cop. He'd check his credentials right now!

"Have a seat, Marchetti, I'll be right back." Don't have a Cuban cigar, jerk. Get him, Pit Bull.

Over the phone, Kingman's friend, Police Commissioner Ryan, hailed the young Detective Buffalo Marchetti as the wunderkind of the homicide squad, the Serpico of the street, a stickler for the truth. Tough, smart, and incorruptible, Buffalo was enrolled in a master's program at Columbia. Nobody you'd ever lie to. Ryan bragged that Marchetti usually knew half the answers before he asked the questions, but the kid was too much of a loner for the powers that be. Just as Kingman had surmised instinctively. So the kid was a one-man battalion, a hip maverick who worked sideways and zigzag and didn't even let his left hand, let alone the force, know what he was doing with the right. The guy was the best the force had, he was told. But what, Commissioner of Police Pat Ryan asked, embarrassed, was he doing in Kingman's office? He was sorry for any inconvenience it might have caused him. He'd reprimand the guy immediately. His buddy Kingman owning a stake in almost two dozen salons, one in which a violent, wacko murder had taken place, was *too* far a stretch for even their young crack murder cop, who played far afield of the rules. Kingman told the commissioner not to worry, he'd help out the young cop all he could and he'd see the commissioner tomorrow for racquetball.

When Kingman charged back into his office, Sergeant Buffalo Marchetti was standing at one of the two solid walls of windows looking out over Kingman's personal New York. The stubborn prick still hadn't sat down. In this light, King could see he was Italian handsome, real tough-guy good looking as he surveyed the skyline and Kingman's airplanes taking off and landing, unobserved in his casual, downtown getup.

So Sergeant Buffalo Marchetti—what a name—wasn't the kind of guy you'd lie to. The piercing blue eyes betrayed a steel-trap organized mind that the sloppy wardrobe was supposed to camouflage. If it was a gimmick, Kingman had plenty of his own. He was the king of gimmick.

Kingman was a *practiced* liar. As far as he was concerned, there was no truth. There were certain facts and then you put your own spin and interpretation on them. He had always done these adjustments on the truth . . . fine-tunings on the intangible. Truth was just an abstract, anyway. He took some matches from the "21" Club off the wide windowsill and relit his cigar.

"Sergeant Marchetti, I've just gotten off the phone with Police Commissioner Ryan, who doesn't understand just what it is you're doing here and, frankly, neither do I! If this is a fishing expedition, Sergeant Hot Shot, the fish in this particular creek aren't biting. And your line's just been snagged!" He blew a wide circle of cigar smoke over the big brass Brancusi. He defiantly planted his short legs firmly in the thick, plush rug, the bottom of his cuffed trousers covering his tasteful argyle socks.

Buffalo Marchetti took it all in and smirked. "Obviously you're an important man, Mr. Beddall. I'm sorry my questions offended you and I'm sure the commissioner will ream me out later. But I've got a mutilated girl's corpse down in the morgue in what looks like a professional kill. A violent crime with no passion. A sadistic murder with no sex. A mutilation worthy of a mob kill *after* the girl was dead; no money stolen, though a safe was broken into. The first few employees on the scene thought it was Tandy herself lying on the floor of the salon."

Kingman sat down and motioned the detective to do the same.

"Five minutes, Marchetti. Lemme see that picture." It was hard to place anyone with her head twisted around backward and her eyes bulging from her skull.

"And this one." Sergeant Buffalo Marchetti handed him a New York beautician's license with the image of a youthful but hardened brassy blonde who could have been Tandy ten years earlier. Kingman was visibly taken aback.

"Her name was Kelly Kroll, twenty-seven years old. Been a manicurist at Tandy's for two years. She was the manager of the Fifty-seventh Street store. The one Tandy is usually at." Sergeant Buffalo's entire delivery was like rapid Gatling gunfire. "She was garroted to death—strangled with a thin piece of steel wire and then all her fingernails were ripped off and neatly lined up on the manicure table. Some strange order, but precise—look here." Kingman looked, then pushed the picture back to the cop's side of the desk. Not the kind Valeski shot for his Carmen ads.

"So you're thinking *Tandy* killed this girl?" Kingman was fishing now.

Sergeant Buffalo's answer was dead-serious silence. Both of them gave out information on a need-to-know basis.

"So this isn't a crime of passion?"

"Yeah, that's the strange part. It's brutal and vicious with absolutely no emotion."

Kingman gave a nervous chortle. The only kind of crime Tandy could commit *would* be a crime of passion. Like, she could kill *me,* he thought. He flashed a mischievous look at the young cop. As far as premeditated, she'd never thought before she acted in all the years he'd known her. He almost laughed. Kingman had heard enough. *He* was in no danger.

"Lookit, my boy, no hard feelings, but I don't see how any of this concerns me." Kingman was on his feet, his eyes narrowing to slits under the full bushy brows. "I own chunks of over seventy businesses and I'm sure there have been deaths or accidents before, but nobody's ever bothered coming to me." So softly spoken Buffalo had to lean forward. So condescending even the tough cop was immediately as intimidated as if he'd just run into a "wilding" gang in Central Park. There was something very, very dangerous about Kingman Beddall.

"Mr. Beddall, I think it does concern you. This was a professional hit, which could have been a warning for somebody. Or an act of revenge. Or maybe somebody was just looking for something." Under the illuminating wash of the skylight, the irises of Buffalo's eyes brightened to a Paul Newman blue. "It's my opinion they got the wrong woman. I think Tandy was the intended hit. This other girl has *nothing* in her past I see so far that warrants a Mafia-like murder, and Tandy herself told us she was there that evening until nine P.M., when she left for dinner with six other girls from the nail shop, leaving the look-alike, sound-alike Kelly Kroll to finish the books and closeup. No robbery, no cash stolen, no rape, Mr. Beddall; this girl was strangled from behind in the dark." He acted out the scene in a method actor's pantomime. "A dispassionate, premeditated murder. I wouldn't even have bothered you, but I remembered two years ago, when Tandy's apartment was broken into, the only thing missing was a photograph of you. Autographed and everything." The left side of his lip curled up.

Goddamn Tandy, thought Kingman. She was trouble. Unadulterated trouble. She was nothing but trouble and sex and always had been. Hell, he'd helped expand her dumb little business after he'd married Fling, just out of the goodness of his heart, and now it was bringing him police investigations. *Trouble!*

"I've questioned Tandy," Buffalo Marchetti continued in his calm, mumbly, rapid delivery, "and she doesn't know of anyone either personally or professionally who would want her dead. Do you know of anyone who'd want her dead?" Wild fishing. Kingman decided the wop cop didn't know anything.

Kingman was standing in a gesture of dismissal. Pit Bull jumped to alert. The meeting was over. He slapped his arm around Sergeant Buffalo Marchetti's shoulder. "Look, Sergeant, this is New York. All you gotta do is pick up the New York *Post* or the *Sun* any morning and read about eight wacko, sicko murders that have nothing to do with warnings or ulterior motives. It's why I don't let my wife go out alone at night and why I keep two bodyguards . . . here." Kingman waved an arm around the inner sanctum of his enormous office. "I'll tell you what," Kingman was walking him to the door, over which hung a Gothic icon of the Virgin Mother, "New York is a sick place. You're in a sick business. Not your fault." He shrugged his shoulders and raised his hands in a Garment District gesture, as if he were bargaining for a better price on fabric.

"I'll tell the commissioner to go easy on you and your Columbo tactics. I always liked that show myself." Kingman flashed his dazzling jacketed teeth. "If you have anymore suspicions about some maniac bothering Tandy's girls—Carmen does have a vested interest here—we can hire some more Carmen security guards." Kingman had Buffalo just where he wanted him. The King was pitching him popcorn, day-old beer, and hot dog sticks at the carnival and was as smooth and slick as the carny man impresario from his childhood. He opened the door for Sergeant Buffalo Marchetti.

"Nice to meet you, Sergeant Marchetti. Good luck getting another nut off the street."

Buffalo Marchetti, put down and brushed off, nonetheless moved down the long carpeted corridor of the Beddall Building like a cocky kid in his Air Jordan Nikes. He mused to himself what a slick prick Kingman Beddall was, and how quickly he'd digested and then dismissed Buffalo's theory about the "Manicure Murder," as it would be called in tomorrow's tabloids. He didn't have a clue yet, but somehow Kingman Beddall was going to be the key. Buffalo felt it in his gut. Maybe business guys played tough. The safe was cracked open but Tandy had counted the cash and said it was all there. This was as professional a hit as a Gambino Mafia murder. Only, some of the details were wrong. It was as if the mob had watched too many Bruce Lee movies. But a hit it was, no wacko, psycho accident here. And he'd bet his Harley-Davidson that it was nobody gunning for Kelly Kroll. All signs pointed to Tandy Love. Yep, that was her real name. He had double-checked that one. That was her given name. Tandy Love. *Mío Dio.* Manicure queen, mistress, former sometimes hooker, with some sort of power hold over the powerful King Beddall.

Buffalo Marchetti knew for sure that Beddall was somehow involved. Even up here from his giant ivory tower. After all, two years ago, when he'd accompanied Detective Sullivan to check on a break-in and burglary in Tandy's little-girl-decorated apartment, they had both stood there stunned as this real-life aging-but-still-pretty Barbie doll had hysterically carried on about how the intruders had taken some of her Frederick's of Hollywood undies, a few sex toys—leather handcuffs and whips—and a personalized, autographed picture of *il capo* of the financial pages, Kingman Beddall. Who could forget *that*? Obviously the billionaire was boffing the manicurist, but as far as he knew, that wasn't a crime. Maybe Beddall was still playing Lothario to Tandy. Maybe not. Maybe she had become trouble for Mr. Kingman Beddall. Maybe she'd become demanding and was blackmailing him, a visibly married man and highly respected member of the financial and social establishment, and he had hired a ninja assassin to murder her. Maybe Kingman had reneged on a loan and Chase Manhattan had given him a warning. Oh, come on, Buffalo, Marchetti said to himself, this is the world of business, not the world of organized crime! Maybe Kingman was totally uninvolved in this whole thing. But of one thing Marchetti was absolutely certain: the guy on the 125th floor was guilty of *something*. Years of crime solving had honed his instincts.

Kingman Beddall was a slick, dirty player. With his connections all the way to the top, even to the police commissioner, he could probably get away with murder, or at least think he could.

If a man had a Fling at home, why would he still need a Tandy, although neither woman was to Buffalo's personal taste. He liked a more cerebral woman, preferred a more delicate lady, more introspective, like himself. Like some of the pale, intense women he encountered in his classes at Columbia, where he was picking up a master's in Art History at his own expense. He had decided he didn't still want to be a homicide cop when he was forty years old, and he wasn't bucking for police commissioner down the road. Too political. No. For a New Age philosopher, independent thinker, someone whose favorite book was *Zen and the Art of Motorcycle Maintenance*, an international art cop might be just the ticket. Stolen pictures were prettier to look at than dead bodies.

You could look at only so many bug-eyed, strangled twenty-seven-year-old corpses with detached fingernails and incisions, and eyeball all the world in suspicion, for so long before you went homicidal yourself. He had an appointment in half an hour with some ethnologist who was an expert on murders with national idiosyncrasies. The way the manicurist had been garroted had an Oriental flavor about it. Just a hunch. That night he had a French Impressionist class at Columbia. Nice balance. Interesting day. Downtown cop on the uptown beat.

He punched an overzealous fist into the oversized brass elevator button and practically collided with a frail young bird of a woman, thin as a rail, hurrying out of the elevator. She wore no makeup, and looked up at him, startled, with a pair of the saddest doelike eyes he'd ever encountered. As the girl moved tentatively and gracefully down the long hall to Kingman Beddall's office, he held the elevator door open a full two minutes and just stared after her.

"Joyce, beef up our security. I want as much as the president of the United States. Better yet, get me some of the president's men."

"Cabinet officers, King?"

"No, Secret Service guys who guard the president. Big guys." He held his hand high over his head. "Guys with walkie-talkies and guns. Get the best. Find out what the president is paying them and double it. But don't get me anybody who was with Reagan when he got shot."

Joyce rolled her eyes as she took notes, but she knew that if Kingman was this concerned, he had good reason to want protection. Had the police sergeant told King about some death threat? He *had* been in the news almost every day, what with the

Beddall Building, KingAir Ways, and Carmen Cosmetics all making headlines. His constant speeches to the security analysts and pension-fund managers to raise capital continuously in an increasingly dry financial well for his extravagant deals kept him a fixture on the financial pages. The highly visible Mrs. Beddall, Fling, was probably the most photographed woman in the world. Her perfect features were splashed over *every* periodical on the newsstands. Maybe there'd been a terrorist threat. Or a kidnapping attempt. Joyce bit her lip, writing at breakneck speed on her dictation pad. She'd get on it right away. Nobody would hurt her King and his Fling. Nobody.

"I want guys all through the building. At home!" Kingman was pacing up and down. "And I want someone for Fling all the time. Even when she jogs through the park. She'll hate that, so we'll tell her it's a personal trainer. Make a list of everybody we owe money to. Creditors, not banks—you know, the private guys."

"Hi, Dad." Also kissed her father on the top of his head.

"Hi, honey. You're too thin."

"You used to say I was too fat." Also put a bunch of papers on his desk and playfully nudged her father. She was working in Gael's office this summer, before her sophomore year at Vassar.

"Put some security on Tandy, too." Kingman waved his unlit cigar around his cathedrallike office while Also examined his latest collectibles in their pristine vitrines, a load of religious icons he had picked up at Sotheby's. She peered through the green beveled glass at his newest acquisitions.

"Get that sleaze McCarthy to follow Tandy around, and keep me posted. I want a confidential report of every coming, going, around the clock—all hours—who she sees, what she does. Unedited, on my desk every morning . . . starting *now!*"

"Right, King. Should I let Tandy know?"

"No, she shouldn't know!" He bellowed. "*I* should know.

But tell her we're giving her security. And make sure she gives this girl a nice funeral. And tell Tandy to be careful. One wacko murder is enough. It's not like they caught the guy or anything, and tell her *not* to discuss me with Sergeant Sausage Dick or any other Dick, for that matter!"

"Have you diversified into Murders Inc., Dad? Or is this a drill?" Also used her sarcasm like a shield. Willowing so she wouldn't break. Her face expressionless so she couldn't register disappointment. Her straight hair short so she didn't waste time, her face free of all makeup so she wouldn't have to be an ad for Carmen Cosmetics or even noticed. Bone thin because she'd just lost her enthusiasm for food and put only natural products into her body because this was 1992 and she was nineteen years old.

"Hello, Dad, anybody home?" She finally cracked a smile. Her teeth were large and perfect. Joyce had supervised her childhood prophylactic dental treatments. Also didn't have even one cavity.

Kingman was deep in thought, staring out his window, which was now viewless because a front of storm clouds was moving in.

What a pompous, overbearing asshole, thought Marchetti, elbowing his way through the noon throng of hungry high-level executives on their way to the Four Seasons, and deli boys delivering bags of tuna fish sandwiches on whole wheat bread. Marchetti sidestepped one of these dangerously speedy delivery boys in a Day-Glo cap. He figured the guy in the big office upstairs deserved some razzing. If not a thorough investigation, then a laparoscopy of sorts of his inner workings, a CAT scan of his brain.

As Marchetti left the Beddall Building, the award-winning monumental ode to money, through the cathedrallike marble-and-granite lobby with its flying buttresses and high-altitude arches designed to humble and awe the people hurrying to and from the elevator banks, he mumbled aloud to himself, "There's something bad about *this* guy. I just know it."

A couple of passersby stared at him. Only deranged street people mumbled aloud to themselves in public spaces, and usually they were hustled out of the better buildings on Fifth Avenue along with the garbage. But with his day-old stubble exaggerating his ruffian good looks, Marchetti usually got away with it. Buffalo Marchetti *was* eccentric. He loped along the Beddall Plaza thinking of how Kingman presented himself with such self-assurance, in a manner almost magisterial. He wondered if it weren't some kind of show.

Buffalo looked up into the sky at the Beddall Building, the tallest building in the world, its sky needle poking into the stratosphere. With the welding together of brass-colored corten and green glass, the edifice resembled a futuristic rocket ship. Only its stone gargoyles gone berserk and its terraces jutting out in unbalanced rhythms kept Flash Gordon's spaceship firmly entrenched on Fifth Avenue. The Tower of Babel. Beddall's Babylonian building. One critic for the *Times* had called it a noble building but geographically misplaced. It would have fit in better in Miami than among the stately "gray flannel" buildings standing smartly shoulder to shoulder up and down Fifth Avenue.

"Ego-ugly architecture, a frigging phallic symbol," Buffalo said aloud to himself. He craned his neck back as far as he could, to see New York's brand-new top tourist attraction. What a hell of a suicide leap that would be. Nobody would use the Brooklyn Bridge anymore, not when they could jump off the Beddall Building! Buffalo slowly walked backward, his neck bent into an elliptical arch, until the compact cop banged right into the base of the Meisian white and green marbled fountain, twenty feet deep at its center, shooting water over three stories high. Marchetti watched as tourists threw coins into the fountain with a wish.

"Boy, oh boy, what a hell of a kamikaze leap that would

make," he said. And then one of Sergeant Buffalo Marchetti's light bulbs went on in his head. Something was clicking.

The surface of Kingman Beddall's life needed attention. The debts, the loans even the recession—these were the usual business problems, but the ex-mistress, who was always dangerous, was stupidly embroiling his world into a police investigation and threatening to expose Kingman's thinly disguised past. The *big* picture was perfect. Kingman always saw himself as a young god striding into a golden cathedral awash in worldly riches and immediate rewards. It was just worrisome that his mythological heritage would be under the scrutiny of someone as smart and perspicacious as Sergeant Buffalo Marchetti. His self-creation could stand all the scrutiny of the press and his biographers— there were PR agents and doctored documents galore to establish his new identity—but something about Marchetti was signaling his alarm button to go off. He picked up the phone to instigate damage control.

"Well, hello." He was using his very soft, whispery "I've been naughty but I'll test the waters" voice.

"Hello, yourself." He could tell she was lighting a cigarette with the phone cradled on her shoulder. Old memories, but not too old. He still knew her. Something familiar and something sexual in him began to stir.

"I was just going through the Rolodex and . . ."

"Rooster shit, Kingman." He could tell Tandy was smiling.

"And I was just calling to see how you were. That was quite an incident at the nail emporium. Are you all right?"

"Scared the shit outta me. She was a nice girl, King. I feel real responsible. I don't understand that Chinese torture stuff, King." He could tell she was blowing cigarette smoke by the way she breathed. He had totally memorized her body years ago.

"I just don't get it, King. I've got security alarms, ADT. The

guy got past everything. We're all a little jittery around here. Poor
Kelly. And now it's cops and robbers." Their conversation left
out the obvious recriminations . . . *Where have you been for the past
two years? I wanted to marry you, you bastard. Business is great!*

"Tandy?"

"Yes?"

"I think we should talk about something."

"Shoot."

"In person. I'm worried."

"How soon, King?" Her voice was emanating the customary
lusty tones that still aroused him.

"Five-fifteen—your place, if that's all right?"

"I still live alone—that's all right." She placed the receiver
down and finished drying her nails. She'd put on the red garter
belt. What the hell. Maybe Kingman was coming home.

"King, Mr. Kurosawa's just entered the lobby. He's on his
way to your private elevator. I suggest you meet him at the
elevator, King. The Japanese, you know."

"Yeah, yeah, Joyce. Get out the geisha girls. I'm coming."
He turned to his daughter. "Let me introduce you to this top
business gook."

"Dad!" For all her erratic upbringing, Also was an intellectual, totally unmaterialistic and sensitive to international insults.
"*Gook* is a bigoted slang word!"

Kingman grinned at her. Slimmed down to runway-model
size—due in no small measure to Fling's friendship—from the
days of her overwhelmingly overweight childhood, she was lovely
in a pre-Raphaelite sort of way. Pale, finely featured, delicate,
she was beautiful to the connoisseur's eye. Pulchritude with problems. She was a Victorian poet's dream. You could sense the
troubled spirit beneath the aristocratically arranged features.
There were a lot of contradictory feelings wrestling inside her,

which had been throwing one another around on the mat since childhood. These internal conflicts gave her an air of breathlessness and fragility, when in reality she was self-determined and strongly motivated. Her presence always created a contradiction. An illusion of severity came from the sharply pointed nose, while a sense of softness was evoked by the oversized expressive eyes, which cried out, "Help me, I'm lost." This was counteracted by a jutting chin that warned, "Stay away, buster."

Gael Joseph joked to The Bob-O that if they ever got into an intellectual line of beauty products—say, the Jane Austen line—Also would be the perfect model.

With her father's slick, overwhelming charm, her mother's delicately sculptured beauty, and all the money in the world, you might have expected something else from Anne Randolph Beddall II. What you got was a fine minimalist sort of artwork that had to be studied and looked at again just to be properly comprehended.

Now, as she accompanied her father down the richly carpeted burgundy hall of their very own Beddall Building, she, lightly gliding on her crepe-soled shoes, side by side with the noisiest deal maker of the decade, left no footmarks, made no sound at all.

"How's your mother, kiddo?" Kingman swung an arm around his daughter's slim shoulder.

"Fine. I'm going down to Edgemere right after the Beddall Home dedication on Friday, and then to Boxwood for the weekend. Grandma's having a Southern soiree." She smiled. The smile was wonderful because it always came as a surprise, if it came at all.

"Fine. Fine. Give your grandfather my best. And Uncle James?"

"Steeplechasing."

"And Virginia?"

"Kingman bashing."

"Boxwood?"

"Thriving."

"Good. If Virginia acts up, tell her I'm selling Boxwood to the Japanese for some petty cash. That'll stick it to her." He grinned malevolently.

"Dad, two things you mustn't mess with: Mother Nature and Grandma Virginia." Also's voice had the melody and lilt of old-line Virginia and proper Poughkeepsie.

"How's it working for Gael the Dragon Lady?"

Also brushed a stray wisp of her short, sleek hair off her alabaster skin. Actually, she was enjoying spending her summer working for Gael Joseph.

"She's a wonderful teacher. She's passionate about her work. I admire that. And she listens to all of us on her team. I respect her for that." Her expression was painfully serious.

"Well, she's a thorn in my side. Always undermining me." They were at Kingman's private elevator now. "She's got, like, that Japanese work ethic thing. You know, *aisha seishin*—'in business'—total devotion to the company. Only, Gael still thinks Carmen is *her* company."

"Dad, profits are zooming. Isn't it one of your most successful ventures?" She searched his craggy face for an answer.

"No thanks to you, kiddo. It's embarrassing to be a cosmetics tycoon and have your own daughter refuse to wear even lip gloss!"

"I like it natural, King. Here's your newest investor," and they both bowed to Toshiki Kurosawa, the treasurer for Mishima Itoyama's bank, who was suddenly bowing back from the open door of the burgundy upholstered elevator studded with brass buttons, framing an oversized portrait of the world famous Fling, shot by the internationally renowned Valeski.

Toshiki Kurosawa had been one of the first to examine the

numbers on Rockefeller Center when it was quietly being put on the block. Now he was holding hands with Kingman Beddall, but sending out industry spies to scare up any secrets, professional or personal, that might be useful to the unconventional lending institution he represented.

"He looks like a guy who's never had jock itch," King whispered to Joyce when they were alone. "He wants to play golf. Find a club that will let me take out a membership. Gooks love golf. Order me some Pings and see where we can play on Sunday." He marched back into his office, where Kurosawa was admiring Fling's portrait.

"How lovely," Mishima Itoyama's leg man observed.

"My wife," Kingman boasted.

"You are a most very luck man."

"So, do you think we have a deal?"

*"Hai, hai."* Kurosawa nodded his head twice in quick succession.

Yes, yes, they had a deal. But not in writing.


"As Sun Tzu says, 'Know your enemies.' " The irony of a naked money lord quoting an ancient Chinese warlord a few minutes after coitus was somehow lost on Tandy. Its message was *not*.

"It's not like I'm asking you to do anything you haven't done before. It *is* what you're best at." Kingman crossed one bare leg over the other and folded his arms behind his neck.

"I'm determined to get to the bottom of this. If someone *is* trying to send me a message, I want to know about it. I'm entitled to know. All I'm asking you to do is sleep with this Buffalo cop kid. He's great looking, and those Italian sausage dicks are supposed to be numero uno in the sack. Just find out everything he knows. Pillow talk." He winked at her.

Tears were welling in Tandy's eyes, and a rage so deep she

knew she'd never be able to quell it surged up from her belly to her bosom. She heaved an anguished sigh, which Kingman chose not to hear. She rubbed her wrists where he had roughly tied the silken cords and then run them around her thighs and between her legs. Suddenly it hurt very much.

A cry came out of her.

"Tandy." He looked startled and annoyed.

She brought out the animal in him. Always had. Maybe he had gone a little overboard this time. It just had been such a physical relief to see her after almost two years. He noticed a welt swelling on her left cheek, which he must have put there. He hadn't meant to hit her so hard.

"Ice. I'll get you some ice." He padded off barefoot to the small kitchen, opened the refrigerator, where there were a dozen or so Carmen bottles of nail polish on the rack—refrigeration prolonged their shelf life—and shook out the ice tray. He hurriedly bundled a pink gingham kitchen towel around some ice cubes.

"Here, Tandy, hold this to your face." He surveyed the damage and thought she suddenly looked very old and worn in this light. He had been in bed with her for over four hours after an absence of two years, and all of his brutality and sexual rage had escaped from him. He felt cleansed. He couldn't wait to get out of here and go home to the effervescence of Fling. He'd shower, beat it out of here, and hurry to the girl with the hair the color of champagne, Taittinger, and the glowing complexion of the Mediterranean—she who wrapped her strong long legs around his at night and held him in her grip until morning. This adoring goddess who worshiped *him*, sometimes keeping his erection alert by sleeping with him in her mouth until he stirred in the early premorning hours, when his lust was greatest. He had the best, the hottest, girl in the world. Everybody's fantasy! Why did he always have such an unnerving craving for the trashy expertise of Tandy? Surely he was above *that*, he smugly thought.

Tandy sat slumped on the bed, furiously pulling the tangle of silken cords off her body and holding the ice to her swelling face. Poor Tandy, no man had ever married her. Kingman might have—years ago. But he was beyond her now.

He was becoming refined, he told himself. He was becoming a world-class financier. He was even becoming an art collector. One day he'd be as rich as Gordon Solid.

He jumped into the shower. As he was lathering up with one of Carmen's sandalwood-scented soaps, he ran some numbers through his head. Things were going unbelievably well. He just needed a little more capital if he wanted to accomplish the really big, colossal projects. He thought of himself, and so did the last issue of *Entrepreneur,* as "The Cecil B. De Mille of the financial world. Everything in 'King' Beddall's vision has to be bigger and grander than anything that's been done before. He has a cash trove unparalleled and apparently bottomless, and has taken the Wall Street world by storm, razzling, dazzling, sometimes paying top dollar, or too much, but always winning, getting the trophy properties, and the trophy prizes." Why, the magazine had even run a glamorous picture of Fling on a full page, calling her the "Ultimate Trophy Wife" and "Carmen's Greatest Asset"!

As he reached for the pink towel, he was startled to see Tandy standing naked in the glare of the bathroom fluorescent lighting, staring at him with a wild look in her eyes. In utter silence. Suddenly he sensed danger. She *smelled* dangerous. That was what had always attracted him to her. She excited him more than any woman he'd ever known. Drove him over the edge. He was able to be his darkest self with her. Exorcising his demons. Now, standing naked and bruised, a strange, frightened, almost mad, look in her eyes, she looked very dangerous. Too dangerous for a respected businessman courting foreign investors and with a nosy cop poking around in his historical itinerary. He gathered up his clothes. She was holding something behind her back. Kingman shoved her aside and walked out.

He wouldn't come again.

After Kingman left, she soaked for an hour in a tub full of Fling! bath splash, drank four Stolichnayas, and went over the past seven years with Kingman Beddall—most of which were on tape—in her head. Tandy felt terrible. She felt as much the victim as poor Kelly Kroll, left dead and mutilated in Tandy's Nail Emporium. Kelly wasn't the only victim. Tandy was a victim, too. Just like the boy in Canada. She sat shaking in the hot tub, a scared and whipped woman, tears rolling down her swollen, blotched cheeks. Bruised, abused, and beaten, she thought, sipping another Stoli. Over the years he had manipulated her, taking all the good from her, so there was nothing left but hatred and rage.

She carefully touched a sea sponge to the darkening bruises on her face, from where he had hit her hard in his unnaturally violent lovemaking. She hated him. She hated anything to do with him. She emptied the tub and poured the contents of her Fling! bath splash down the drain. She'd throw her KingAir Mileage Plus card into the trash. She wanted to empty a loaded .22 Magnum into the body of Kingman Beddall. She closed her eyes. She could almost feel her fingers squeezing the trigger of the gun, envisioned an exploding bullet traveling in slow motion until it hit its target, the smirking Kingman Beddall wearing an I-dare-you-to-shoot look on his self-confident face. She could almost hear the bullet explode upon impact, sending Kingman's entrails and organs (of course there wouldn't be a heart) splattering in a thousand directions, bloodying the walls and ceiling. She gasped in relief at the mere thought of it. As she wrapped her pink terry-cloth robe snugly around herself and peered closely into the mirror, she wondered if they let you touch up your roots in women's prison.

Maybe she should just call up Suki and tell her Kingman Beddall was a lousy fraud. Or a lousy lay. He was Carney Eball, just a low-class con man who had pulled the wool over everyone's unseeing eyes. If she damaged his reputation, maybe he'd lose his high-flying notions and fancy friends. If she damaged him enough so that he lost everything, he'd have no place to go but back to her. She looked into the mirror. Her bruised left eye was swollen shut.

What would New York society think if they knew Kingman Beddall was a killer?

# 10

Commodore Vanderbilt, still smarting after an unsuccessful skirmish with Wall Street's nineteenth-century bad boy Jay Gould, admonished, "Never kick a skunk." Sergeant Buffalo Marchetti kicked a skunk when he challenged Kingman Beddall, and was wallowing in the stink of it for the next few days. He had been taken to task by his superiors, severely warned that the Beddall Building, the Beddall home, and Mr. Kingman Beddall were entirely off limits to him, and threatened with a transfer to Queens. The department wouldn't dare take him off the case yet, not with every newspaper and cabbie in New York screaming about the "Manicure Murder." The way the town was carrying on, you would have thought that Charles

Manson and Son of Sam both had escaped and been sighted in the men's section at Bloomingdale's. The force needed their best cop on this case. Pissed off, Marchetti spent two days boning up on business tycoon Kingman Beddall and his world of fast money and giant risks.

Curiously, from what Marchetti had culled from *Fortune* and *Entrepreneur,* part of Kingman's strategy required private deal making and a low profile. Yet part of his personality needed a giant building named for himself, his name in lights, his craggy visage festooning a myriad of magazine covers, and a gorgeous "envy me, look who I'm fucking" wife. Where was the Beddall father, the grandfather? Where did it all come from? Marchetti knew instinctively that the mangled corpse of Kelly Kroll, lying dead and eerily damaged in the Manhattan morgue, had *something* to do with the lively body blowing cigar smoke rings on the top floor of the Beddall Building.

Buffalo Marchetti, who never went anyplace with socks, who hated the rich, and had never read a society column in his life, was now standing outside an aged ruddy, buffed brick and terra-cotta building on Central Park South, the home of the most widely read society gossip columnist in America. He shook his head and braced himself as he walked into the pre–World War II co-op. It was noon. He was punctual for his appointment with Suki. Emily Post would have loved it. The sickeningly pale, high-strung assistant who greeted him at the door silently showed him in to the "sun parlor," a room heavily hung with dark green damask, tightly drawn velvet drapes, and overflowing with orchid plants. The only light in the room came from a cluster of scented candles crowding a round skirted table that displayed twenty silver frames holding photographs of famous dead people. Standing there on the marble mosaic tiles beneath wooden cherubs, rosettes, and foliate arrangements carved into the mahogany moldings, and overcome by the heady aroma of crowded bou-

quets of "Forever Yours" roses, he felt as if he were waiting in
the anteroom of a very fancy mausoleum. He half expected Suki
to float in like a long-deceased apparition in chiffon and shrouds.
By the time the second wan and thin assistant drifted in to say
Suki's arrival was imminent, he was ready to chuck the whole
dumb thing. Just what did a hot homicide cop expect to learn
from a society gossip columnist who had been around since the
days of Walter Winchell? Plenty. The manicurists he'd inter-
viewed at Tandy's Nail Emporium, and Tandy herself, had all
constantly referred to Suki as if she were Kingman Beddall's
personal biographer and social historian, Beddall's Boswell. The
lady's name just kept cropping up. But now, standing in this eerie
chamber of memorabilia, he decided the whole visit was probably
just a waste of time, probably a dead end. Maybe he should just
be as polite as possible and get out.

He was totally unprepared for the bright butterball, no more
than five feet tall, sporting a yellow floral mu-mu and matching
turban, who came sweeping into the darkened sun parlor like the
Queen of England. She extended her diminutive hand in his
direction, displaying a gaudy ice-cube-sized emerald. He wasn't
sure whether to kiss it or count the karats. Sergeant Marchetti
decided to jump right in.

"Are you Japanese?"

"Pardon me?"

"Suki, the name Suki, isn't that Japanese?"

"I should say not! Are you Native American?"

"Huh?"

"Buffalo, isn't that an Indian name? 'Stands with Fist,'
'Dances with Wolves,' 'Hunts with Buffalos.' I presume that's an
Indian name."

"Oh, no, I'm Italian. *Buffalo* comes from the curly black
hair, see? Neighborhood name, just stuck." A whiff of garlic and
fresh basil accosted her surgically reconstructed nostrils as he

shook his tousled tumble of thick wavy hair at her. "The real name's Joe." The cop grinned widely at the gossip columnist.

"Oh, *Joe*. Well, Buffalo does have a certain animal quality about it." She eyed him appreciatively. "Buffalo suits you." She gave him a smile that was coquettish forty years earlier, but still had a certain charm to it.

"And just what is it that the New York Police Department wants from Suki?" She motioned for him to sit down on something brocade and fringed.

"Well, actually, I'm investigating the murder of a manicurist at Tandy's."

Suki held her own nails up as if for cross-examination. "I get mine done at Arden's."

"You know that Kingman Beddall owns a major interest in Tandy's."

"Of course he does, darling. She was his mistress before he married the current Mrs. Beddall, Fling. Any run-of-the-mill gossip columnist knows *that*!" She adjusted her turban over her left ear.

"Does Mr. Beddall have any enemies?"

Suki laughed out loud and arranged herself over an entire ottoman.

"Enemies? Why, a man like Kingman Beddall has nothing *but* enemies. Social enemies, business enemies, envy enemies, ex-wife enemies. The Kingman Beddalls of this world hardly have any friends at all."

"Where did he come from?"

She smiled like a Cheshire cat. The billion-dollar question. "He came from Richmond, Virginia. Riding on the coattails of the Randolphs, the very *social* Randolphs."

Buffalo Marchetti tried to nod as knowingly as possible.

"When he was married to Anne Randolph, a lovely girl before her crack up, Also's mother—you're keeping up, aren't you—

*she* was supposed to come out last year but wouldn't. Hardly any of the right people come out anymore."

Buffalo Marchetti didn't know what the hell this woman was talking about.

"The whole time Kingman was married to Anne Randolph, he used all her old family connections like mad. The Randolphs live at Boxwood, down in Virginia. Got as rich as he could down there, and then came up here to play with the big boys."

She popped a pistachio into her mouth. "Oh," she laughed, "I don't mean *those* kind of big boys. In your world that probably means something sinister. Mafia, doesn't it?" She narrowed her cosmetically altered eyes at him. "Did anyone ever tell you that you have eyes like Paul Newman?"

Buffalo squinted back at her. He had a feeling that if he could muster up just a little patience, Suki might have a few answers for him.

"Of course, with her impeccable social credentials and his no-big-deal-but-it-will-do bank account, they started to appear in my column. He got here at just the right time, darling, when everybody was getting so rich. You know, that whole nouvelle society thing. Why, we even had to invent a nouvelle cuisine for all the nouvelle people to eat. All the really old rich people have never given up rack of lamb and boiled potatoes, you know." Suki used her Elizabeth Arden manicured nails to crack open another pistachio nut. "Anne went on the boards of the New York Historical Society and the public library. Top drawer— Jackie O. and Brooke Astor are on the board of the library, you know."

Buffalo nodded his head agreeably as if this were the same kind of conversation he and the other cops had down at the precinct all the time.

"Everybody liked sweet Anne, but it was obvious that she would rather stay home than go out every night. *He* was the social cyclone of that family. I think Tandy was the manicurist at the St. Regis barber shop in those days." She offered him a nut.

"Am I boring you?"

"No, please, go on."

"Then, of course, he got a hold of some of that bottomless Milken money. A whole group of them did, and he started buying trophies. Small TV stations; radio stations; the big prize, Carmen Cosmetics; and his latest, KingAir Ways." At this point in her soliloquy she turned and gazed lovingly at a large ancient photograph of Carl Joseph, the cofounder of Carmen Cosmetics.

"Dear old Carl," she sighed. Carl had given her the very expensive but not very tasteful rock she was wearing on her finger.

It was up to Buffalo to snap her out of it.

"Miss Suki, Miss Suki."

"Oh, Mr. Buffalo . . . what a couple of names we have. If Ed were still alive we could do an act on the *Ed Sullivan Show*. Suki and Buffalo." She let out a little girlish chuckle. "Is there anything you're really good at?"

"I solve murders."

"Oh, we'd make a wonderful Sunday night entertainment. I'd give clues and you'd solve murders." They both laughed, sort of.

"Now, where was I? Oh, yes, Carmen Cosmetics. Carl Joseph and Max Mendel were the best in the business. What a pair of boys. Carmen and Rose—there were never fragrances like those before nor since. Their widows ran it into the ground, of course. The two wicked witches." Suki shuddered. "The daughter did a wonderful job trying to save it. But there was just too much debt, so . . ." she plunged her arm down like a nosediving jet bomber, "Kingman Beddall swooped in and bought up the grandma of them all, Carmen Cosmetics, for practically nothing. And bought himself national business fame, as well as social entrée. He took Carmen private, you know, so no one knows what he is doing except, of course, what his public relations firms spin out for the unsuspecting and the unknowing. Of course, Suki knows, Suki always knows."

"And what does Suki know?"

She crinkled her eyes at him.

"Suki knows Carmen Cosmetics is doing great business, just like in the old days. Brilliant strategy for King to marry Fling. Suki knows Kingman owns Boxwood, and the Randolphs are desperate to get it back. Suki knows that Anne, the first wife, tried to commit suicide when he publicly humiliated her, while he was going gaga over Fling. The poor dear spends most of her time at Edgemere these days. Kingman owns part of the place, don't you know. Suki knows the rest of the Beddall empire is very shaky, very debt ridden. The economy, you know." She rotated her index finger in the air toward the general direction of Wall Street. "Suki knows that if Kingman can't settle with the pilots' unions, he could lose his little boy's toy, KingAir Ways, and maybe his shirt. Their airplanes bring them all down in the end, don't you know. Suki knows that in Canada, Kingman supposedly killed a man. Suki knows Kingman stopped seeing Tandy *that* way after he married Fling on the equator. You probably read about it in my column."

Kingman. Canada. Murder. *Bingo!* Suki probably thought that Buffalo and his cop buddies sat around headquarters or parked in their squad cars religiously reading her column. Well, maybe they should.

"Miss Suki, who is he supposed to have killed in Canada?"

"Oh, Buffalo eyes," Suki cooed at him, "Suki knows so much, she couldn't possibly tell you everything in only half an hour." Rising to her full height, she was barely taller than the potted orchid plant behind her. Her assistants simultaneously appeared at the door.

"Oh, it is time for Suki's lunch and then Suki has a column to get out. The Beddalls are going to Germany for the Von Sturm christening." She was talking over her shoulder as her two wan assistants escorted her from the "sun parlor" to the dining room. "Shocking, those Von Sturms, wonderfully shocking, but my readers adore them. The Baron could buy and sell Kingman Beddall on a Sunday, you know. Without banks—with loose change, darling. Come again, Buffalo, only, next time we *trade* secrets. Give me the Manicure Murder scoop and I'll give you more Kingman Beddall secrets." One of her altered eyes either twitched or winked at him.

"Nothing is for free, darling. Call me, Buffalo. Ta-ta." She waved good-bye to him over her shoulder. "Read my column."

He bounced out of the dark room, down the dimly lit elevator, and into the bright of a late spring day. The park was yellow with forsythia. He felt like he had just been in the holding room on the first floor of Bellevue. But somehow he trusted this woman, who reminded him of his gossipy Aunt Lucia and who had just given him his next set of clues. He'd have to see her again. He liked her. The midday traffic on Central Park South was jammed. He decided to jog back to the precinct.

## SUKI'S COLUMN

Dahlings! If you ever had thoughts of reincarnation, you really should come back as Baby William Frederick von Sturm, the privileged son of the Baron and Baroness William Wolfgang von Sturm. The Baroness, "Freddie," as she is called by all her friends, is Europe's reigning fashion queen and renowned for her ever-so-gay dinner parties, at which she hosts royal swells *and* Kings of Commerce. The Baroque Bash to christen the dear child next week at Castle Sturmhof will be so outrageously extravagant that even the little tot's ancestor, mad King Ludwig, would have been proud.

This Wagnerian drama is *the* social event of the international season, gathering some of the oldest titles of Europe, who will be mingling with big-business financiers. Anybody who is anybody is going: Princess Diana, the Gianni Agnellis, the Vicompte de Ribes, the Duchess of Alba, Crown Prince Felipe of Spain, the Rainer princesses of Monaco, the Rothschilds, that darling Sultan of Brunei, the exchequer of London, all of Lazard Freres, and the presidents of Germany, France, and Black's Fifth Avenue, are all on the list. The Samuel Casholds, the William Warrens III, and Gotham's own royal couple, the King and Fling Beddall, will represent New York.

Whew! Wonder who'll get the table by the kitchen? Comtesse Cyrielle de Resnais of the Impressionist paintings De Resnais, and Mrs. Kingman Beddall, as in Carmen Cosmetics' Fling!, will be Little Willy's godmothers. Cyrielle, an *old* friend of the Baron, is said to be giving the baby the priceless masterpiece "Boy in Blue" from her private collection of her grandfather Henri de Resnais's paintings. Only a little less expensive than Van Gogh's "Sunflowers." Wonder if Fling, who is an old friend of the Baroness, will give the baby Baron his own line of children's fragrances? *Sniff. Sniff.*

Oh, darlings. Suki can hardly wait to tell you *all* about it. After the little christening service for 400 in the Von Sturms' private chapel, the guests will gather in Castle Sturmhof's exquisite gardens. Philippe Model of Rue du Faubourg St-Honoré; Philip Treacy of London, who designs those one-of-a-kind wacky hats for Karl

Lagerfeld's Chanel shows; and Queen Elizabeth's royal haberdasher, are all going mad as hatters designing *everyone* a different picture hat for the garden party. How festive. How gay! A baby! Who'd have thunk it? Those Mad Bavarians.

## THE BEDDALL BUILDING

"Hook, Hook! Joyce, where's Hook?" bellowed Kingman.

"He is getting into that Pullman porter's outfit that you bought for him."

"Oh, that's good. I think he looks great in it. Don't you?" Kingman showed off most of his teeth.

"No, King, I think he looks like a house slave from the antebellum South."

"Nah, he doesn't." He knocked one of his elbows into Joyce Royce's ribs.

"Hook adds class to this joint."

Joyce groaned. Thank God Fling was coming in today. He was on one of his ego junkets.

Kingman had brought Hook up from Boxwood to butler in his office, fetch tea and biscuits and beverages for his business guests. Nothing like having an old family retainer to underscore a note of financial stability. Just like the House of Morgan. No matter if it was his first wife's family's retainer and not *his* family retainer. He had done it just to stick it to Virginia initially—a little reminder to the Randolphs that *he* owned Boxwood—but he had grown fond of and accustomed to the kind old man, of always throwing his arm around Hook's shoulder in front of his guests, his fingers pushing against Hook's tight silver curls. Hook, who always smelled like shoe-leather polish and fresh twists of lime and who never failed to impress Kingman's visitors with his air of "old family" and old-world charm in the cold, futuristic Beddall business offices. Somehow it worked.

Hook didn't mind at all. His son, Rodney, had moved up to New York, where he was working in the DA's office. Rodney had turned out pretty terrific, and Hook relished the extra time with him. He enjoyed the little vacation from bossy Eva and kind of liked the action around Kingman's office. Sometimes, when no one else was around, they even discussed business or politics. Decked out in either a tuxedo or a starched white linen jacket with the shoulder braid of a four-star general, he added the extra ingredient Kingman was seeking . . . respectable family ties and old-guard stability. Kingman was absolutely nuts about him.

"Hook reminds me of my roots." He winked at Joyce. They were standing in the vast sun-drenched expanse of Kingman's office atop the Beddall Building.

"You know, Joyce," he waved this morning's *Wall Street Journal* at her, which had a 50-percent-positive profile about him and KingAir Ways on the left-hand side of the front page, accompanied by a 100-hundred-percent handsome illustrated drawing of him, "I'd rather be respected than loved. I don't want love. There is nothing concrete in it. I want *their confidence,* and that's what I've got in my hand, their confidence, Joyce." The *Journal* had speculated on the front page on whether the Wizard of Wall Street could indeed put his name on the tails of an ailing airline fleet and make it fly. An airline with only thirty routes, bad gates, and a mountain of debt, not to mention a disgruntled pilots' union. The article had ventured to wonder whether even the magician of money, who had levitated dead companies, turned around dinosaurs, and sawed cumbersome companies in half and then put them together again, better than ever, could pull this rabbit out of his hat. It would be a tough and dirty grind, but if anybody could turn the trick, it would be tough and dirty Kingman Beddall.

Kingman shook the *Journal* at his personal panorama of New York's skyline beneath his thirty-five-foot-high vaulted ceiling. "Respect you have to earn. Love you can buy," he waxed poetic. "Tell Hook to serve the British gin to Sir Reynolds when he comes up. Sir Reynolds likes Boodles." Kingman took out a chamois cloth and wiped a smudge off the amboyna wood million-dollar Ruhlmann desk. The Japanese were certainly the most visible, but the English and the Dutch held more property in the United States than any other foreign group of investors. And now the British were coming. To Kingman.

"Look at this, Joyce. A smudge. You have to find better cleaning help."

Joyce scribbled all this down.

"And tell Hook only domestic beer and soft drinks for the pension-fund guys. These public-pension managers will never lend us a dime if they think we throw money away on high-priced liquor. Remember that!"

Joyce said she would. She looked at her watch. She'd hoped the lightness of Fling would come prancing in at any minute. She was a good influence on King. The girl was an angel.

Kingman had been dealing with the pension funds of America for about five years. These funds controlled about two and a half trillion dollars of America's cash, and were the nation's largest source of institutional money. Some of the public-pension managers, who would be the audience today for Kingman's presentation, this morning's *Wall Street Journal* story, and the recipients of Hook's bartending skills, represented about one hundred billion dollars of capital. Utah alone had a state pension fund of four billion dollars. The Utah guys would be here today at two-thirty. Oregon, with its twelve-and-a-half-billion-dollar pension fund, was coming tomorrow. Over the past few years these funds, overseen by not particularly sophisticated trustees free of legal restraints on high-risk investments such as Kingman's, had provided him a cash trove that had made him virtually unstoppable. Every time he overextended himself, they had always come to the rescue. Like truck drivers on white horses. Now his competitors had jumped on the pension-fund wagon and the pension guys themselves were becoming more hard-nosed, more sophisticated, and were looking for softer safety nets. Good timing on the *Journal* piece. His public relations machine was rolling right along.

"Hi, Fling!" Kingman lit up like a star-struck kid.

"Hiiiii!" Fling glowed back at him. The sun from the skylight torched her golden hair and lightly kissed her features. A goddess, though she was wearing her daily uniform of tight-fitting Escada jeans, one of Kingman's white Sulka shirts, a pair of up-to-the-knee leather riding boots from M & J Knoud on Madison Avenue, and a cotton blazer with galloping lions and gazelles from her *own* line of Fling! sportswear. The Fling! line of shirts, jeans, and jackets with animal motifs was popping up on teenagers all over the country. She had just walked down Fifth Avenue from the Central Park Zoo, where she was a docent, working with the baby sea lions. Fling was looking forward to private time with Kingman. Finally. They hadn't even been able to get to the house in East Hampton for weeks. Business, business.

"King, we got a problem. Right now. We gotta talk." Arnie Zeltzer was poking his head in the side door of King's office. Kingman pulled his eyes away from his dazzling wife to the blandness of Arnie Zeltzer. It wasn't even a contest. He turned back to his wife.

"King. The pilots are just about to call a strike!"

Arnie had his full attention.

"When?"

"Any minute."

Joyce buzzed in on the intercom. "King, Itoyama's on the

phone, Lord Reynolds is in the conference room, and Oregon wants to know if they can come today instead of tomorrow."

"King, honey, don't forget we're leaving for Europe tomorrow night. A week in Paris and then the Von Sturm christening, and then a second honeymoon on the *Pit Bull,* cruising the Mediterranean." Fling plopped down on the floor to scratch Pit Bull's tummy and fluttered her eyelashes. "I'm supposed to get you all to myself." She beamed up at him.

"Baby," he kissed the tip of Fling's nose, "you go on without me and play with your fruit friend. I'll get there for the christening. But first, go say hello to Sir Reynolds and stick around for Utah. Utah's great. They love you in Utah." He marched out to Joyce's office. "I'll take Itoyama on Arnie's phone," he said. "Invite Oregon to the office for dinner and see if anybody in this fucking office knows how to fly a plane." He hurried down the hall, Pit Bull folding in behind him.


### PARIS


With their noses pointed in the air and their sprocket-hipped runway model's gait in overdrive, Fling and Fredericka strutted out of the Ritz onto the Rue du Faubourg St-Honoré. Individually these two striking six-foot Amazons stood out in a crowd, but together they stopped traffic, literally. Whistles, cat calls, and indecent French propositions followed the two best friends, oblivious to their surroundings, reveling in their private, girlish cocoon of giggles and gossip.

Old times in new places.

"Oh, Freddie, I'm so happy, this is just like the old days, when we would go window-shopping together on Madison Avenue." Her joy at being with her best friend again obfuscated the fact that Frederick was now decked out in Manolo Blahnik suede mules, a royal-purple Gianni Versace satin-lapel suit and thigh-high skirt cut on the diagonal, and a triple string of priceless pearls that rivaled the Duchess of Windsor's.

"Only now, luscious lips, we can afford to buy, not just look. Marrying well has its rewards." They linked arms and marched on, laughing and turning heads. Fling was festooned in an Isaac Mizrahi marigold-and-saffron backless sundress that barely hit the top of her thighs. Dozens of gold bracelets jingled on her endless arms as her bright yellow high-heeled Charles Jourdan sandals clicked on the pavement. Springtime in Paris.

"Freddie, we had fun even when we were poor." She tugged at the Baroness's purple sleeve.

"Poor is never fun. Don't reminisce. To the future!" He pointed them in the direction of Hermès. They had just enough time before their fittings at Christian Lacroix to pick up a few *petis cadeaux* for their husbands.

"Kingman never wears anything I buy for him." Little lines crossed Fling's perfect brow. "Maybe he doesn't like my taste."

"Well, darling, he likes the *way* you taste, and that's enough." They both laughed. Fredericka peered over her enormous Christian Dior cheetah-spotted sunglasses. "And with a no-taste dresser like Kingman, you can't go wrong with an Hermès tie."

"Now, Freddie, you promised you'd try to be friends with Kingman. You know that he means the world to me. He is my whole, entire universe."

"Sorry, darling. I just have never liked the man, never have trusted him. There is something hidden and sinister about him. When you were serving up Tastee Freezes in Texas, *I* was getting street smarts in New York, and Kingman has always smelled slimy to me." Fredericka back-lifted a long leg to adjust her left high heel.

"No, Freddie, you completely misunderstand Kingman. Why, only last week we dedicated the Beddall Home for the Aged. You should have seen him with all the nuns and those sweet old people. It was so touching." Fling's bee-stung mouth moved into its enormous pout. "I love the two of you more than anything else in the whole world. I just wish you'd try to like each other. Promise me you'll bury the hatchet."

"Only in his skull, my dear. Only in his skull," Frederick muttered, holding open the brass polished door at 24, Fauborg St-Honoré to France's premiere establishment since 1837 for silk scarves, leather goods, and equestrian wear.

The entire store stopped to watch the voluptuous Fling seductively sashay over the creamy mosaic-tiled floor to the colorful rows of tie racks. She squealed in wide-eyed delight to discover such a large selection of silk ties decorated with whimsical animals: racing horses, lounging leopards, bouncing rabbits, funny frogs, trumpeting elephants, and hopping kangaroos, a veritable zoo on fine French silk. She wanted one of each but, not being extravagant by nature, called Fredericka over to help her choose.

"Freddie, which one should I take?"

"All of them! We are not poor anymore, *ma chérie*, remember? My hero, the Duchess of Windsor, always said, 'I always thought diamonds in the daytime were vulgar until *I* had them.' " Fredericka turned to the arrogant vendeuse. "We'll take them all. We know lots of men." Fling let out one of her goose honks. "I wish you'd do something about that laugh. We're in European society now." Fredericka arched an eyebrow.

Boy, Fling thought, European high society had to be a lot different from New York society to allow Frederick to dress up like a woman, marry the Baron, *and* pretend to have a baby! Here, evidently, nobody thought anything was odd about it! Or at least they pretended not to. As much as Fling loved Frederick, she thought this charade was really weird. Why, if he had tried this stunt in New York, he would be treated like the main attraction in a P. T. Barnum freak show. A guy dressed up in women's couture, a baron*ess*, no less, and now a mother! It made Fling's head spin. She stood in the midst of silk ascots with coronets, and animals dancing on cravats, totally mystified.

Fredericka dragged Fling away from the racks of ties and over to the ladies section. "Enough for the men."

This time she spoke directly to the saleswoman. "Please show Mrs. Beddall the Kelly bags."

"*Avec plaisir,* Madame Baroness."

The snooty little salesgirl had suddenly become a woman of Gaulish charm. The manager of the store had whispered in her ear that she was waiting on the imperious Baroness von Sturm and the world-famous model Fling.

Ooh, goody, thought Fredericka. Now they know who I am. This is going to be fun. Shopping was ever so much more entertaining with people hopping around at your every command.

"Fling, you must have this bag. Now don't frown because you think it is dowdy." Frederick had developed an international accent that still slightly confused Fling.

"This bag is pure, simple elegance. A subtle status symbol, not that either of you ladies needs that." The salesgirl spoke perfect English. She dramatically presented the Hermès pocketbooks, the kind that Grace Kelly had made famous as the young Princess of Monaco, which were now selling for upwards of ten thousand dollars to status-seeking Stateside socialites. This matronly looking satchel, which resembled a small suitcase, came in luxurious alligator, crocodile, or simple leather. Fredericka ordered one of each. In every color. Fling just added an oversized silk scarf printed with bits and bridles to the ties she had bought for Kingman to her burnt-orange signature Hermès shopping bag. She liked to use the scarves as belts, casually looped through her jeans.

"May I show you the baby gifts?"

Frederick/Fredericka stiffened. Anything to do with babies bored her. The manager of the store was leaning over the counter, casting a shadow over her day.

"Oh, yes! Let's see." Fling clapped her hands together. "Do you have baby saddles?"

"Very well," the Baroness was imperious, "we'll have a look but we haven't all day." Frederick/Fredericka sniffed, simultaneously inhaling the lovely exotic aromas of Hermès Amazone parfum for women and Équipage, the scent for men. The two separate gender scents commingled in perfect harmony in Freddie von Sturm's head.

## NEW YORK

"The pilots' union won't walk if we raise salaries twenty percent, offer stock options, and jack up their pension plans." Arnie Zeltzer calmly punched the numbers into his Wang computer.

"You mean our Vietnam aces will get in their cockpits and fuckin' *fly* if we give in to highway robbery on an airline that's already crippled. Why, I've seen people in the Beddall Home for the Aged in better shape than KingAir Ways. This whole airline is on crutches. *I'm* trying to save it!" Kingman dropped his head onto his knuckles and ran his fingers through his dark curly hair. "It's extortion! These guys are fuckin' anti-American. Fellas," he turned seductively to his army of lawyers, not a single one of them over five feet eight inches tall, "you got to make these fly boys understand that if I'm going to save their airplanes, I gotta shave their salaries and cut the frills. I can do it but I've *got* to have their cooperation. I can't send Carmen Cosmetics' executives up there to fly the friggin' airplanes! Not unless we're interested in selling only one-way tickets—no return flights." He laughed aloud and his legion of lawyers laughed in unison along with him.

"I'm putting *my* name on the line. *I* resurrected TransAir and put *my* blood into it. It's *my* money and *my* name on the tails."

Kingman's cathedrallike office was as smoke filled as a crowded Las Vegas crap table. Everybody in the room was smoking one of Fidel Castro's Monte Cristos, even the nonsmokers.

"So, let's meet with this Peter Szabo, the union guy, and find out what's up." Kingman was in shirtsleeves like the other twenty guys in his office. The skylights in his sky-high office poured in heat as well as sunshine, putting a drain on the Beddall Building's overabused air-conditioning system and a pull on the city's already overtaxed electric power. Something Philip Gladstone had overlooked. On this particularly unseasonably steamy day in late May, circuits were blowing out all over town.

Kingman curled his mouth upward into a crocodile smile. He was giving them a pep talk. It was noon and they had been there since noon yesterday. High noon. In the skylight swelter.

"I don't want a Mexican standoff, fellas. I'm a friendly guy. I'm like one of the pilots. But I'll fight these guys and bury them up to their balls in quicksand if they try to cross me now." He chopped a table with his fist for emphasis. "For chrissakes, make them understand I can have KingAir Ways showing a profit in five years." He was almost pleading. "We can turn this company around. I just gotta have their cooperation." There were sweat rings around his Turnbull & Assered armpits. He wiped his brow with the back of his coronet-emblazoned Hermès tie.

The smoke cleared enough by eight that night for Pit Bull to venture safely back into his master's office, sniffing his way to his doggy decorated Ferragamo pillow that Fling had found and purchased for him. Kingman balled up his perspiration-soaked shirt at the dog's feet and dropped his trousers at the entrance of his private bathroom. Joyce was busily spritzing Glade air freshener some forty feet down at the other end of the office. Arnie and his

Wang were right behind Kingman as he stripped and stepped into the shower.

"King," Arnie had to shout over the nine shower heads spurting water, "the best thing to do now is dump the airline." He punched more figures into his computer. "If you get out tomorrow, we can sell the airline to the unions. The pilots' union and Peter Szabo have got some reliable financing from Izzy Davis to do an ESOP. They're willing to forego salary hikes for equity and ownership. Good for them. Good for you." The employee buyout of KingAir could actually put millions into Kingman's pockets and be used to pay off debt on Carmen and the global network deal.

Kingman reached for a bar of Carmen's sandalwood soap, his favorite, in the cerulean-blue grotto of his twenty-foot-high Philip Gladstone–designed shower.

"Then," Arnie kept punching, "we sell off the European gates to American and," Arnie beamed to himself, "we keep the small Virginia service plant that repairs military aircraft. *That* we take and run with to our government friends and make a kill . . . about two hundred million a year within ten years if we get the right government contracts. You've *got* to take the money and run, Kingman—you'll come out way ahead. You can get rich by losing!" Arnie looked as happy as Arnie could look.

"Don't tell me 'got to,' you asshole! *I* make all the decisions around here. You and all your numbers can go to hell on United." Kingman bellowed in the shower the way some men sang.

He swung open the door, all nine water spouts on high, drenching Arnie just like the first six rows of the theater where Mrs. Balsam's soggy Broadway production of *Gone with the Wind* had been performed.

King grabbed Arnie by his shirt. "I never even had a toy airplane, not even one." He shook himself off all over Arnie like a wet dog. "I got my own airline now. My own shuttle. My own sign at La Guardia! I got an exit sign that says KINGAIR SHUTTLE on the Grand Central Parkway! Just off the friggin' Triborough! I should give *that* up?" He looked violent. "I'll kill anybody who tries to take it away from me."

"King, be reasonable. This airline thing could bring you down." He hated to use the word. The airline could send Kingman Beddall and his empire into a tailspin. Airlines and entrepreneurs just didn't go together. Carl Icahn, Frank Lorenzo, even Gordon Solid, had problems with their airlines. Even Daedalus and Icarus had problems trying to fly too close to the sun. "Call Gordon Solid," Arnie Zeltzer, the undeterred voice of reason, advised his boss. "Let him tell you about it."

Kingman dropped Arnie Zeltzer's wringing-wet shirt collar and moved naked to his bathroom phone. Good idea. He'd give Gordon Solid a call. It was an hour earlier in Chicago; Gordo might still be at the office. He was always in the office. Who wouldn't be, with a wife like Biddy Solid at home.

"Gordo, King here. How are you?"

"Good, Kingman."

"Gordo, how would you and your brother like to pick up some of my airline debt in exchange for some of the empire?"

"I don't like cosmetics, Kingman, and I don't like New York real estate. How's the wife?"

"More beautiful than ever." Kingman liked to stick it to him.

"How you doing with the pilots' union?" Gordo stuck it back. His voice was a mélange of warm brandy and clarified butter with a tinge of perpetual laryngitis. "When I had my airlines, I used to sit up in the cockpits with the boys." To Gordo, anyone under a hundred was still a boy. "I used to schmooze with them. All they wanted to talk about was condominium developments and tax shelters. The airlines could be a great business,

King, if somebody could invent a way to fly the planes on auto-pilot and contain the human element."

Gordon Solid sat quietly on eight billion dollars. He was totally liquid. He made all his business decisions based on numbers, never on emotions. It was one of the rules he religiously adhered to, and one of the reasons he was the third-richest man in America, although on the *Forbes* annual list of the richest people in the world he was usually listed as fifteen or sixteen. Nobody could ever quite figure out the expansive extent of his holdings, herded together as they were under some fifteen hundred interwoven companies and complicated family trusts.

Gordon Solid would have preferred *not* to be on the *Forbes* list. He had badgered Malcolm about it for years, while Forbes was still alive.

Solid despised attention, notoriety, treasury and governmental interference, although everything he did was legal and utterly moral. To Gordo Solid, if it wasn't moral, it wasn't a kosher deal.

Very private, he kept a very low profile. When he did venture out he moved like an active verb down Wall Street, looking down on a rabble of adverbs and prepositions and other insignificant parts of speech. Powerful as he was, Gordo was a mensch. Everyone in the financial fraternity looked up to him, especially Kingman. He worshiped the guy. Gordo had been good to Kingman, loaning him big dollars when nobody else would give him the time of day. He still bailed him out from time to time in Kingman's wild quest for his "expansive empire." Of course, Gordo took as well. Gordo already owned 40 percent of the Beddall Building and 60 percent of Beddall Lumber.

"Gordo, I want you to finance this airline deal. It's really big."

"Sounds like a great big ego trip. Might be fun for you, but in my experience it's not worth the aggravation. I'd just sell off and settle some debt right now." His voice was soft and smooth.

"Gordo, I really want an airline. It's like a personal thing with me."

"Aw, Kingman, why don't you sell back to the unions, and you can buy four 727s for your personal use. Or better yet, order a G-V and you can have the first one on the block. Should be ready by 1995. Of course, I fly coach myself when somebody in the family is using the G-III. The private plane's just a timesaving thing with me. Otherwise, I wouldn't even have one."

Gordon Solid, one of the richest men in America, drove himself, in a middle-of-the-line Chevy—no driver, no limo. On the seat next to him he kept a gym bag, a gift from Kingman, one of the free sample bags that had the name Fling! emblazoned all over it. Gordo used it to carry his squash racquet, white shorts and shirts, and dirty gym socks back and forth to the "Y." Either his wife, the Chinese laundress, or his girlfriend, Tanya, washed the same socks for him every night.

Kingman played on the fringes of the really big deals and financial empires—the outer fringes. Old Gordo was the nucleus. From his bustling office in the sleek anonymous building in Chicago in which he rented space, he controlled a healthy portion of international finance. Kingman didn't even know how lucky he was to have Gordon Solid as his mentor. Kingman's hubris was so large, it was hard for him to see that he was just a comma in one of Gordo's daily paragraphs. Gordo liked talking to Kingman. Gordo enjoyed King's extravagance vicariously. Gordo's small office was covered with drawings by his grandchildren and posters of important Impressionist paintings he owned, but which were on loan to the Art Institute of Chicago. He particularly liked Pissarro and De Resnais. Pissarro was a Jew, and most of his oeuvre had been destroyed by the Nazis. Gordo and his father had saved what they could.

Gordo's empire was in order. Much of Kingman's was built on loose promises, shaky foundations, and press releases. Gordon

Solid, his brothers, and his sons paid big dollars to keep their names *out* of the press, and cemented their deals with firm hand-shakes and solid, never-broken promises. He liked Kingman but he couldn't understand why he needed to set his name in lights, why he had to put himself in striking distance of the general public. Gordo had seen dozens of the flashy ego guys rise and fall—fall hard—in his day. And a lot of the Milken people had just dropped off the face of the earth. Poor Mike Milken, who hadn't taken Gordo's advice, had been carted off to prison for his white-collar crime—without his toupee: no telling what danger-ous weaponry a highly educated bald financier might conceal under the synthetic fibers—a pick ax, an unassembled rifle. Milken, the mathematical big guy who liked to play basketball although he stood under six feet tall, had been warned by Gordo not to get too greedy and to remember to dot the *i*'s and cross the *t*'s on the legal stuff. Gordo had liked Milken until he had crossed him—once. Gordo liked talking to Kingman. He was fun. And he had a pretty wife. Gordo's wife, Biddy, had been around since World War II.

"Gordo, this means the world to me. I want an airline."

"Airlines are treacherous business. I'll give you a no now. But send me the numbers. I'll take a look for you. And feel free to have Peter Szabo call me. He killed my airline deal, but we left on good terms." When Gordo wasn't going to do a deal King knew, he gave out free advice. "See if you can get Von Sturm on board. He's the largest shareholder in Air Deutschland. There's your guy."

"Von Sturm! That fruitcake's married to my wife's makeup man!" King was exasperated.

"Can you believe this crazy christening? Gotta envy the guy for his balls, though. Does as he pleases." Gordo chuckled softly and good-naturedly.

"I'd love to go to the big wingding but Biddy won't hear of

it. Thinks it's immoral." Gordo warmly laughed. "You guys with prenuptials have all the fun. Gotta go." Tanya would be turning the key in the apartment they shared on Astor Street. And then he'd hurry on to one of Biddy's civic projects. "Good luck on this airline business, King. It's a real ball buster." Kingman knew he didn't have a deal with Gordon Solid, just from the tone of his deceptively avunculor voice. He'd have to get the money somewhere else. But where? No one in the country took as many calculated risks as Gordon Solid. And if it was too risky for Gordo . . .

### C A N A D A

Buffalo Marchetti ran his index finger down the *B* pages of the Calgary telephone directory. It was cool in this part of Canada, a welcome relief from the sweltering heat he had just left behind a few hours earlier in New York. August in May, the Manhattan weathermen were calling it. Air-cooling units were blowing out all over town, leaving the city a garbage-littered steambath. Murders always went up in this kind of heat, he knew. The precinct would be as busy and as hot as hell. Marchetti was glad to be out of it. Up here in Canada, the cool snow-tipped mountains of Calgary, the green lushness of the valleys, and the clean, crisp air were like a soothing tonic for his soul. Why would anyone leave a spot on God's earth like this?

The trip was bound to be pleasurable, but fruitless. He'd probably find Mr. and Mrs. Parents of Kingman Beddall at home, sitting in their stately stone house on matching armchairs in a room crammed with stuffed fish they'd caught on Lake Louise, with a scrapbook of their successful son's clippings in the den, a taxidermist's daydream, hung with elk horns, moose heads, and bear rugs.

*Beddall, Kingman*—no such listing. In fact, there was no residence listed for any Beddall. Probably all these rich folks were unlisted, even up here in arcadian paradise. There was a listing in the business pages for the firm of Beddall and Beddall. He'd start there.

He dropped some change into the pay phone, one urban, jaundiced eye on the natural beauty around him, and dialed.

A taped message, one of those voice mails—even up here!—greeted him like a rustic robot. The dry, aloof voice asked him to leave a message or to call back at one P.M. Marchetti checked his watch: ten minutes to one. He jotted down the address and decided to walk over there. It would be a chance to breathe some of the clean air into his lungs. He picked up his stride.

He wondered aloud which one of the tall oil-boomtown buildings was Beddall and Beddall. None of them quite resembled the younger Beddall's flashy Babylonian Tower on Fifth Avenue. Well, maybe the old man had better taste.

He double-checked the street number from his notepad as he stood in front of a six-story red brick converted warehouse two blocks away from the fashionable business section of town. The huge freightlike elevator took forever. There was only a small-lettered "Beddall and Beddall" painted on an old-fashioned frosted-glass door bordered with wood. Inside was a small waiting room decorated with a matching set of green leather couches and chairs and, aha! all those stuffed fish he just knew would belong to Mr. Beddall Sr. A few logger's pictures, drawings of lumber mills, and, on the empty desk, one of those old round silver bells, the kind they used to have on hotel clerks' desks fifty years ago. Buffalo sauntered over on his Air Jordans and punched the bell. What the hell. After a few minutes an officious-looking man, not more than thirty, prematurely balding, entered from one of the inner doors.

"Yes?" His manner was overbearing, like a librarian in charge of first editions. Buffalo decided to martial the troops. He flashed his badge and let his gun poke out of his shoulder holster.

"I'd like to see Mr. Beddall Sr."

"I see." The young man looked efficient, if somewhat unnerved. "You sure you don't mean Kingman Beddall, sir?"

The man twirled a pencil.

"No, I *know* Kingman Beddall." Marchetti leaned across the chest-high wooden desk. "I just want to *see* his father."

"Oh, I see. Background material, right? The family history?" He rummaged through his desk for a printed press release on Beddall and Beddall.

"No, fella. I want to see for myself."

"All right." The office man was in no hurry. The Canadian Beddalls weren't on New York double time like Kingman. "Right this way."

The small and bald ushered the pistol-packing and handsome into a plain high-ceilinged, book-lined room with green window shades. If this was an office, it was the neatest office Buffalo Marchetti had ever seen. The desk was as clean and uncluttered as that in the study of Henry Clay Frick in the Frick mansion, now a museum on Fifth Avenue, where Buffalo studied the Turners and Whistlers for his art history class. But of course Mr. Frick, industrialist, art collector, and philanthropist, had not used his desk since 1919, when he had died. The big brass chime clock on Beddall Sr.'s green leather-topped desk was broken, just as the fancy eighteenth-century French annular mantel clock was stopped in Mr. Frick's elaborately wood paneled library, because time had stopped for him and his singularly sumptuous possessions.

"Should I stay with you, Sergeant, or would you rather pay your respects alone?"

Marchetti looked puzzled. What was this, some sort of Beddall Canadian caper? He stared at the looming life-sized portrait of a tall, rugged, white-haired outdoorsman hanging a few feet behind the oversized desk chair. No Whistler by a long shot.

"This is Mr. Roy Beddall, founder of Beddall and Beddall. That's Mrs. Beddall on the other wall," said the shiny-headed office man, turning and pointing. "Of course, their ashes are in the columbarium."

"You mean he's dead?" Finesse was never Marchetti's strong point.

"I should say so." Short and bald was used to Beddall and Beddall being accused of a lot of things, but burying living people in mausoleums wasn't one of them.

"How long has he been dead?" Buffalo asked, as if he had been late for an appointment with the old guy.

"About twenty years. Strokes. They both had strokes. Mary Clarke Beddall died first and, about a year later, Roy Beddall collapsed at the lumber mill. Doctors said it was a stroke," the office manager rattled off like a museum curator in a dusty old gallery.

"And the son?" Marchetti played a hunch.

"The son, Roy Jr., died in 1962 in a tragic accident at the mill." He moved aside to reveal a color photograph of a tall, sandy-haired, muscle-bound youth who was the spitting image of Roy Beddall Sr.

"What kind of accident?" Buffalo narrowed his eyes, downtown cop at work.

"I wouldn't know. I've only been here for three years. I never knew the family. Most of the Beddall and Beddall business is done out at the lumber mill. I think Kingman Beddall really only keeps these offices for sentimental reasons."

Sergeant Buffalo Marchetti carefully scrutinized the portraits of the parents and the photograph of the son, his eyes darting from one to the other, as only a suspicious New York street cop and a student of Art History and Portraiture could do. How in the hell could three Nordic-looking, straight-haired giant Vikings be related to a small, curly haired, steely-eyed Irishman?

"And when was Kingman Beddall adopted?"

"I don't know about that. I never actually met Mr. *Kingman* Beddall. I suggest you take your questions that aren't answered on the printed press release to the New York corporate headquarters."

Like hell, he would. He'd take that question out to the lumber mill, where *most of the business was done.* Maybe he'd get lucky and find an old-timer who remembered the past but wasn't a part of Kingman Beddall's well-oiled public relations machine.

Sergeant Buffalo Marchetti at work. Street cop playing a hunch.

### PARIS

Fling's world-famous hourglass figure was softly encased in a hot-pink chiffon skirt only just sweeping her thighs, a black bolero jacket dotted with signature gold Chanel buttons, and two or three strings of Chanel's costume pearls casually tossed around her swan's neck. She stretched a long shapely leg over one side of the moped and hung onto Frederick for dear life as the Baroness zoomed off from the stone courtyard of the Ritz as if the flag had just dropped in the Grand Prix de Monte Carlo.

"Freddie, I don't want to die! I'm too young! *Eeeack!*" Fling's goose-honk laugh blew away soundlessly behind her in the wind.

Frederick/Fredericka was coutured up in the matching other-side-of-the-mirror's reflection of Fling's casually correct ensemble for lunch among the French aristocracy: a black linen sundress topped with Chanel's signature long boxy jacket in pink, decorated with bands of bright woven braid reaching almost to the bottom of the skirt's high-hitched hem.

Fling's long honeyed hair, arranged only hours earlier into a perfect page boy at Carita, whipped around her cheekbones, while Freddie's short, boyish coif blew in place. They were chic twins rushing into innocent trouble, weaving in and out of Parisian midday traffic, so full of life that pedestrians and motorists turned around to smile and gawk at the two startling beauties. Freddie gunned the moped like gangbusters around the Place de la Concorde, past L'Orangerie on the Quai des Tuileries, until they roared over the Pont Marie and onto the Ile St-Louis and the home of the La Comtesse Helene de Resnais.

"Freddie." Fling jumped off the bike, brushing off some stray chestnut blossoms that clung to her Chanel.

"Yes, luscious lips?"

"Tell it to me again. The baby thing. I still don't quite understand the whole 'how' of it."

Freddie flicked two slender fingers through his short wind-tousled hair, which immediately fell into place, and then haughtily handed the mini-motorcycle over to the Comtesse's startled majordomo. Freddie pulled Fling aside to a shaded bench in front of one of Paris's most ancient and grand private houses in the fourth arrondissement, L' Hôtel de Resnais.

"Flingy, it's *so* simple." Freddy linked arms with her. "Wolfy is, like, richer than you or I could ever imagine. Richer than anybody else in Europe. Richer than the Rockefellers. Richer than Gordon Solid." Fling looked blank. Freddie wasn't getting through. "Richer than Oscar de la Renta!" Fling nodded. "Now, according to the inheritance laws set up by Wolfy's family several hundred years ago, the title of baron, the estates, and many of the holdings, which are now great banks in Europe and *all* the collections of Old Masters paintings—you know, the Raphaels and the Rembrandts—*everything*, gets handed down from *son* to *son*. Primogeniture. The firstborn son inherits everything. Without a legal heir, everything goes to the German government. I'm not even a legal heir. Wolfy can't break the family line, which has been around since the thirteen hundreds. And try as I may, luscious, there's no way I could give Wolfy a child! I'm a guy, remember?" Frederick snapped his pearls, real pearls, in his fingers.

Fling nodded. This she understood.

"So," Frederick continued, "the royal ruse. It's been done before with infertile couples who had to produce heirs. Did it all the time in medieval days. The husband impregnates someone else who's willing to be the wet nurse, the nanny, live in the castle, have financial security, and be a silent, 'second' mother to the inheriting *enfant*! See?"

Fling saw. But how?

"Well, Wolfy didn't want to actually *do it* with that buxom country girl, who's like one of his serfs or something. Her father and grandfathers and so on have been Von Sturm gamekeepers for centuries. So we went to modern science. The petri dish." Frederick pulled out a Carmen compact to check his makeup. He puffed on a touch of *poudre*. "The little egg gets fertilized in a sterile laboratory by a white-gloved technician and then surgically reimplanted in the surrogate mother. Very precise, entirely scientific, totally German, efficient. Wonderful modern science, isn't it?"

Fling wrinkled her nose at the thought.

"*I* want a baby, too. *I* want to give Kingman a son!" Fling stood up and announced, her fists at her side, frightening a congregation of pigeons and sending them shooting up into the Gaulish sky. "But how in the world do you make sure it's a boy?"

"Ah, *mein Liebling,* the missing X chromosome. I shall teach you the magic of the petri dish." Fling had strange visions of the Baron's sperm floating on their backs in the laboratory receptacle while the doctors readied the poor peasant girl and as Frederick, dressed in Christian Lacroix, held her hand.

"*I* haven't gotten pregnant yet because King needs me to model for Carmen. He really does. He says I'm his best advertisement and he doesn't want me potbellied and lumbering around." Fling smiled broadly, imagining she'd get pregnant the old-fashioned way.

"Yeah, Kingman the father," smirked Freddie the mother. "He'd probably call your son 'Other' to go with 'Also'."

"Being so tall and naturally thin," Fling drawled this out in her Texas twang, the one everyone in Paris found so charming, "I'd hardly show. Why, when Mama had me, back in Corpus, she worked until the last week and nobody at the Tastee Freez even knew she was pregnant until I squeezed out." She unlatched her new Kelly bag, a gift from Freddie, and produced her measured, cyclical container of birth control pills. "I'd just love to throw these silly things away and start on my little family. Kingman won't be getting any younger, you know," Fling said with authority.

Frederick threw up his heavily charm braceleted wrists in surrender. Once Fling had an idea rattling around in her brain . . .

"So, darling, when is the best time for you to get pregnant?"

"Like next week at the christening." She lit up. Day fourteen! She had marked it on her Snoopy calendar at home. "It's our anniversary!"

"Well, toss away these pills," Frederick snatched the little rose-colored plastic case from Fling's hands, "and let's turn our thoughts to seduction." Frederick was always an eager accomplice to elaborately planned seductions. The birth control case and its contents were now floating in Helene de Resnais's Louis XIV fountain in the fourth arrondissement on the Isle St-Louis in Paris.

"Seduction!" Fling giggled and they strode into the Resnais house, their pelvises thrust forward, shoulders thrown back, and their chins pointed in the air: the universal runway-model swagger.

"Comtesse." Frederick bussed the air around Helene de Resnais's jeweled ears. *"Quels bels boucles d'oreilles."* Frederick treated the French socials like the insecure models he knew: compliments, compliments.

*"Merci*, Baroness." Helene air-kissed Frederick's well-powdered cheeks, smiling.

"May I present my dear friend, Fling," Frederick intoned, using his high-pitched, theatrical voice. Frederick stepped back to watch as the first procession of aristocratic ladies from France's great families, usually so blasé, crowded around Fling to ogle and share beauty secrets. No different from what the housewives in the mall in Cleveland had done when Fling and Frederick had been on the road together promoting her new fragrance.

Fling and Frederick stood out, two Chanel-coutured divas, in the midst of the warren of women wearing the best of the houses of Dior, Saint Laurent, and Givenchy. Even the great French beauty Isabelle de Brante visibly gushed and gawked as Fling was ushered through the oval vestibule Louis Le Vau had designed as the entrance for L' Hôtel de Resnais. Nudged by the Baroness, Fling *ooh*ed and *aah*ed at the impressive collection of French masters: Monets, Van Goghs, and, of course, the overwhelming collection of De Resnaises hanging in a variety of interior spaces throughout the exquisitely decorated *hôtel particulier*, once the home of Henri de Resnais himself. Comtesse Helene de Resnais graciously led her guests up a dark and narrow flight of stairs to a wide bright landing that commanded a panorama of an extensive vista of the Seine. Here hung De Resnais's astonishing Post-Impressionist painting "Seine at Dusk." The small viewing audience *aah*ed as they received the maximum impact of the picture, theatrically presented in a backlit arched recess overlooking the Seine itself, the real-life setting every bit as romantic as the Impressionist rendering.

Clucking like French hens, the ladies descended the main staircase, dramatically designed to double back on itself. As she turned the corner, Fling was startled to see a haughty beauty coldly staring up at her. Baroness von Sturm recoiled and pushed Fling along. Frederick despised Cyrielle de Resnais.

"Bitch, she is an absolute bitch!" Frederick whispered to Fling, nostrils flaring, when they were out of earshot of the others. "Dangerous creature; she is the only woman Wolfy ever slept with. She even tried to marry him. I would be amazed if that one had a soul." Frederick shuddered as if he were shaking a spider off his shoulder. "That tramp actually thought she was going to marry my Wolfy. Her morals are so loose, she's probably slept with half the sailors on the bateaux-mouches."

"But, Freddie, she's the baby's other godmother, isn't she?" Fling craned her long neck to get a better look at the cool, slender, feline creature sporting a style and aura that carried no French designer's signature look, but only her own.

"No, Fling, you're *my* godmother for the baby. She's *Wolfy's* godmother for William Frederick!"

They were interrupted when their hostess took them by their arms and led them into the green moiré-silk-walled dining room, dominated by a crystal and silver Louis XV chandelier. The Comtesse seated her two guests of honor at separate round tables draped in rich green satin puddling rivulets of fabric on the Polish rug, woven with silk and silver. Luncheon was served.

Fling was terribly uncomfortable when she realized she was the object of Cyrielle de Resnais's unrelenting gaze in the bronze *dore* mirror behind her. The young French noblewoman had an unnerving air about her. She was one of the breed of European young women that Marshall Valeski would describe as "not pretty, but interesting," or whom the French termed *jolie-laide*. Girls with perfect carriage and more-than-prominent profiles. She was strikingly pale, with flawless skin. Her dark hair was pulled off her face and piled and twisted into a French roll, which only accentuated the dark, almost pitch-black eyes with no demarcation between the pupils and irises; like molten lava, they had melded together. Her bright red lips were the only color on a face untouched by powder or rouge. The jaunty tilt of her head gave her features a flamboyance that seemed to match her flamboyant name: Cyrielle de Resnais.

Fling learned at the table that Cyrielle, a guest in her Aunt Helene de Resnais's home for the first time in years, was a comtesse herself, the single trustee of the De Resnais estate and as much a roué as any male French rogue. Fling, who saw no evil in anyone, suddenly felt more frightened by this elegant thoroughbred than any competitive runway model in New York who had ever put out a slender foot to trip her.

# 11

*NEW YORK*

Arnie Zeltzer's small swivel hips pounded Gael's voluptuous torso like a woodpecker thrashing a redwood tree.

"Oh, God! Faster! Faster!" shrieked Gael, simultaneously beating her arms on the bed and clutching Arnie's small jackhammering buttocks. Gael was amazed that such a calm, meek, number-crunching accountant could make love with a ferocity that rivaled her favorite vibrator.

What started out as a battle over budget cuts and staff reductions had turned into a clandestine passion, scheduled regularly for Tuesdays and Thursdays at two-thirty in Arnie's condominium above Carnegie Hall.

"Oh, harder, Arnie, lower, Arnie, more to the left." Gael was directing him like a traffic cop to her G spot. *"Ooh, aah!!"*

"I've got it, Gael, I've got it!" Arnie took instruction beautifully.

"I'm almost there, you little love machine, don't stop now!" yelled Gael, wrapping her knees around his neck. Arnie was hanging onto Gael's enormous breasts for support as his legs and ass flew up and down, doing their best impersonation of a pneumatic drill. Arnie looked panic stricken. He didn't know how much longer he could hang on. Gael's white pillowy girth and volcanic screams excited him beyond any numbers he had ever crunched.

Her legs shot out in forty-five-degree angles as they rocked the bed and shook the very foundations of the concert hall below them. Gael was coming. "Arnie, you are a dream!" wailed Gael. "Your turn, *go!*" Arnie grit his teeth, threw caution to the wind, and let his systolic and diastolic blood pressure rates fly right off the charts. He loved it when they came together. Hatred turned to passion was obviously the ultimate aphrodisiac.

"Arnie, you're magnificent. Kingman Beddall couldn't do what you just did if his life depended on it."

"Naw, I'm just a number-two guy." His face was as blank as his Wang computer, turned off.

"You shouldn't settle for number two, Arnie. You're a number-one kind of guy."

Arnie beamed at her. He had seen Kingman on numerous occasions in his shower and knew that he, Arnie Zeltzer, was twice as endowed as the Wall Street titan. Arnie bit his lip and looked down at his navel.

"What's the matter, big guy?" Gael questioned.

"Well, it's this crazy airline deal Kingman has gotten us involved with. It's almost irrational," Arnie said.

"How so, Arnie? Is Carmen in jeopardy?"

"This airline deal could take down the entire empire, including Carmen." Arnie sighed. Gael was wildly attentive.

"Carmen is now just a piece of Kingman's empire, a profitable piece, but still just a part of the whole. Kingman had to borrow money against all of his assets and holdings to come up with the money to buy TransAir, which was already three hundred million dollars in the hole. The airline had been losing a fortune for years. Kingman bought it, slapped his name on the tails, and now people want to fly KingAir and business has turned around a little bit. It's just that Kingman Beddall magic, but KingAir is still almost a billion in debt, which we inherited when we bought the crippled company," Arnie lamented.

"So, in other words, Kingman's healthy companies are being asked to get an old drunk up on its feet." She snapped open a can of Diet Coke.

"Yeah, exactly. Only the old drunk owes everybody in town. So now we pick up all his IOU's."

"Well, that's a lousy deal," Gael said.

"Not so lousy. In fact, it's kind of brilliant." Arnie rolled over and took a swig of Gael's caramel-colored soft drink. He always felt important when he talked business with Gael after sex. "King has such an incredible track record. Everybody in the country knows his name. Kingman Beddall is synonymous with success. So now everybody wants to fly KingAir. We show a little paper profit and pretty soon we can sell off little pieces of a giant loser for big profits. Easy!"

"So what's the problem?"

"The problem is, King's dragging his feet on the resale, and problem number two is that the pilots have just walked out on strike."

Gael's ears perked up.

"Compounded by the fact that the airline is into the banks for three hundred million, on which a huge interest payment is due this month. Big bucks. Even if Kingman sold you off," Gael knew this meant Carmen Cosmetics, "and some of his other holdings, he still wouldn't be able to make the payments," Arnie continued.

"So can't the banks bend a little? Kingman bought this company to save it; it's turning around, right? He didn't accumulate this debt. Right?" questioned Gael.

Arnie looked at her with pride. She always caught on. The voice of reason had met his match.

"Yeah, in order for the banks to bend a little, Kingman has to take a partner or get some financing from someone who could pay a billion dollars of debt if he had to. If you have it, the banks don't necessarily need you to pay it."

"Yeah." Gael remembered her experience, trying to save Carmen by herself. If you don't need the money, the banks were happy to lend it to you.

Arnie pulled on his boxer shorts with the little dollar bill signs on them, a gift from Gael.

"So who can King get that will pay three hundred million dollars?" Gael asked.

"Gordon Solid sits on at least eight billion in cash; one of the Japanese investment groups; maybe Baron von Sturm. An alliance with any one of those guys would buy him time to try and put Humpty Dumpty airlines back together again," Arnie answered.

"What about King's pension funds?"

"Too risky for the fellas running the funds. This is a private game for high rollers. Only a few guys have stakes big enough to play at this table, and with no stockholders to answer to. The really smart money would do what I advised Kingman to do. By selling it off in pieces, he can make a hundred million, pay off his debt on Carmen and the network deal, and pocket the change." Arnie threw up his hands. "Simple."

"Arnie, you've got to make him listen to you. You can't let him jeopardize Carmen with this kamikaze airplane stunt. It would be murder." She shook his shoulders violently, exciting him again. "If he just took a little money and put it back into Carmen, we could expand our European business and launch our environmentally safe products properly. We are working on a two-year-old budget, Arnie! How can he expect us to meet our projections with no budget?" Gael shrilled.

"I know, I know, I know. I've tried to make him see, but he is letting some personal fixation get in the way of business. I just rearranged the numbers for Lazard Freres and Bear Stearns, to make him look much more solvent than he is, and I'm not sure that is entirely ethical." Arnie looked at Gael wistfully, his new-found heartthrob. She caught his drift and reached for Carmen's musk balm to massage into his worried shoulders.

"It will turn out fine in the end," Arnie insisted. "Kingman has never made a bad numbers decision in his life. He'd mow down his own mother if he had one, if it would be good for business." Arnie closed his eyes as Gael massaged the top of his shiny bald head.

"Well," Gael huffed, "he never let sentiment or emotion get in the way of a good deal before."

"He can save everything and make a bundle if he'd just sell the airlines. I think he'll see the light. He's got to, he is too smart," Arnie assured her.

"The guy doesn't have an emotion in his body! He *only* thinks with numbers. Remember me? I was there!" Gael was livid every time she remembered how Kingman stole Carmen Cosmetics out from under her.

"Yeah, but he is like a moth to the flame with this airline."

"I've heard him on the subject. I don't know what the attraction is," Gael sighed.

Arnie thought for a minute. "He keeps harping on this deprivation thing, that he never had a toy airplane as a kid."

"*Oy vey*, what is this? He comes from Beddall Lumber money, right? I thought he grew up in Canada. What? F.A.O. Schwarz doesn't deliver there?"

"I guess you're right." Arnie shrugged. "I don't understand it, either. Then there is this business of the nightmares."

"*Nightmares*? What nightmares?" Gael loved true confessions.

"Sometimes he'll take a nap on the plane or in the office and wake up in a deep sweat, really agitated. Once, he was really frightened! Sweat just pouring off him. He told me he had dreamt about some little kid in a carnival selling beer, and tickets to knock the milk bottles off the shelf or shoot the wooden ducks as they went around the wheel. In the dream, Kingman shoots all the ducks and when he goes to collect his prizes, all the creepy characters from the carnival pick up rifles and gun him down!"

"Weird. That is so weird! Maybe he's cracking up! Geniuses crack up all the time. Are there any other symptoms of madness?" Gael asked.

"It's only a dream, Gael. I can't *interpret* his dreams, for God's sake. I'm not Freud!"

"Corbin. You should make him see Dr. Corbin. Arnie, isn't he the doctor who treats all his wives and girlfriends? Isn't King partners with Corbin in all those sanitariums?" She leaned on her elbow and shamelessly grinned. "Maybe Kingman Beddall is nuts. Maybe we should have him committed to Edgemere, and then I can be left alone to run Carmen without interference." She licked Arnie's earlobe, his most erogenous zone.

## EDGEMERE

The puffy-eyed blonde slumped on the stone bench overlooking a small mountain lake and studied the swans gliding across its glassy surface. She watched one of them waddle up on the shore, losing all its grace when it wandered out of its element.

"Like me," she said. "Everybody loves me in bed, my natural habitat. No man, particularly *him*, ever felt I was good enough in the real world." She pounded her thigh with her fist. Her anger totally consumed her. She had asked Dr. Corbin to let her cool down for a while. He had made reservations for her at Painskill, his sanitarium in Englewood, New Jersey, but she had shown up here at this place instead, unannounced. Corbin ran this institution as well, didn't he? Too many familiar faces and voices at Painskill. It was too close to New York. She had clients there, for God's sake. Too many gossipy ladies with French manicures to remind her of what she was trying to forget. Nobody would know her at this place. Edgemere. She liked the way it sounded. There was something dangerous and tranquil to it all at once. A place to go over the edge. Find your *mère*, your mother, by the soothing sea, *le mer*. She laughed a hysterical laugh. She had been vacillating between violent daydreams and homicidal nightmares for weeks. She knew she needed help or she would probably carry out one of her fantasies, one of her murderous fantasies.

"Edgemere, soothe my violent side," she shouted to the picturesque lake.

"I beg your pardon." The lady in the gardening hat and gloves looked up from her roses.

"I was just shouting to myself, don't mind me. I'm nuts. That's why I'm here." Tandy sat on the bench rocking back and forth. The gardening lady went back to her work.

"I'm here because the one thing I think about, day and night, is murder, I want to murder this man, get even with him.

He's a terrible human being, the world would be better off without him. I just have this uncontrollable rage. Have you ever felt like that?"

The gardening lady just went on about her work.

"Dr. Corbin says I still love the fella, but I want revenge because he's hurt me. Are you a patient? Whadya in for?" Tandy asked.

The gardening lady stopped tending her roses, pulled off a thick canvas gardening glove, the kind that prevented her from being stuck by rosebush thorns, and stared for a moment at the gabby crazy lady. She unconsciously rubbed her wrist and then resumed her work. Garden-variety nuisances eventually went away, like leaf-eating aphids.

"I suppose I'll get assigned a job down here, too, won't I? They're sure to find something that I can do better than anyone else that they'll need me for." Tandy's voice grew more high pitched and desperate. She knew if she stopped talking, she'd start thinking; and just what could she do? Would her therapy be her private purgatory? She'd have to give manicures to crazy people and listen to their ravings or, worse, their silences. She felt sick.

"Did they teach you to grow flowers like that here, or did you know all about horticulture before you signed up? I had a little garden once, when I was a little girl, down in West Virginia. It wasn't much—petunias, pansies, daisies, black-eyed Susans— but it was my own. I used the most interesting fertilizers; manure mostly. Necessity is the mother of invention." Tandy's chatty prattle was in part due to her mental state and in part her required manicurist's dialogue; occupational hazard.

Everyone else at Edgemere knew better than to bother Anne Randolph Beddall. She came and went as she pleased. She had her own gardens. She was free to go home for a few months, and then come back to Edgemere. The staff and the other guests showed her the utmost deference and respect. Nobody engaged her in idle, gossipy conversation. Anne was momentarily amused by this flashy woman who distracted her from one of her self-imposed silences. She finished tending her garden and stood up to appraise her work. Very nice, very nice, indeed. Every bit as lovely and fragrant as her mother's gardens at Boxwood. She'd want that trellis moved, though, and a small brick path laid to her bed of roses.

"That's a beautiful garden. I've never seen roses that full and voluptuous. Are those really natural colors? They look like nail polish colors. I've never seen roses that shade of cerise or a pink that pale, and such a warm peach. You're really good. I'd love to know their names."

Anne looked over at the fidgety woman and thanked her coolly. Probably one of the breakdowns, Anne thought. She had that damaged air about her. Anne collected her gardening tools and started up the path to her suite of rooms, freshly painted and refurbished in a bright floral chintz especially for her. She almost didn't stop when the bleached blonde suddenly burst into hysterical sobs, rocking back and forth, pulling her knees to her chin.

Anne Randolph Beddall walked on, ignoring her. She stopped at the toolshed to put away her implements and tried to block out the sound of the weeping woman. She had no business interfering. She was damaged too. Let the professionals take care of it. Then Anne remembered this was Sunday. Dr. Corbin wasn't due until Tuesday, and only a skeleton staff was on duty on Sundays. On an impulse, she turned and walked back to the sobbing lady. Anne noticed she was pretty, in a crude sort of way. Sort of like one of Also's old Barbie dolls, which were still in her playroom at Boxwood. A blubbering Barbie doll. Barbie at forty, having a breakdown.

Anne hesitantly put her hand on the shoulder of the frightfully woeful woman. It was just a gesture. The woman cried with such an avalanche of heartfelt tears, it was clear even to Anne, who blocked out all emotion and moved around in a comfortable comatose cocoon of her own, that this woman was very deeply damaged.

She felt a lump rise in her own throat. She lightly put a hand on the woman's other heaving shoulder and suddenly found herself holding this stranger in a maternal embrace. This childlike woman just cried her eyes out.

Anne, who had never been a crier, somehow envied this wretched woman whose agonies and emotions were bursting forth like a broken dam, finding her blouse and Anne's gardening clothes with a torrent of human tears.

"He used me. He never loved me. He never even liked me!" She sobbed out the words. "I tried to be his friend, make him proud of me. I built up a big business. He didn't care. He owns my company. My friend was murdered and he doesn't care, and I'm scared. I'm alone, and every time I pick up the paper, his face is smiling back at me! He hates me because I know his secrets, and secrets are dangerous!" Her words and tears tumbled out of her pouty mouth, which now was just a puffy opening on her swollen face. She held onto her so fiercely, Anne felt every violent spasm and tremor reverberate in her own frail frame. She tightened her arms around this pitiful creature, who was quaking and gasping, her features so distorted, trembling so violently, Anne feared she might be having an epileptic seizure. She even thought about rushing to the gardening shed for a trowel to prevent her from swallowing her tongue.

Tandy wept continuously for fifteen more minutes while Anne rocked her in her arms, tears streaming down her own pale cheeks. At last she freed the woman from her grip and removed her sunglasses and hat, wiping her tears away with the sleeve of her summer shirt. Anne searched for the monogrammed handkerchief in her skirt pocket and handed it to the woman, whose eyes were now red blurry slits, but somehow still held more life and passion than Anne's own troubled eyes. The blonde gratefully looked up at her, dabbing at her tears.

"Thank you, sweet angel lady. Oh, thank you." She held her angel lady's hand and was startled to find ugly sutured and scarred wrists on this kind woman. Suicide wrists. Tandy closely examined the woman's face and the monogram and fell, stunned, to the side of the bench.

"Oh, my God! You're Anne Randolph Beddall. Kingman's Anne. Oh, Mrs. Beddall, I'm so sorry. Please forgive me!" The sobs were suddenly replaced by shock. "I'm Tandy."

Anne recoiled in horror. Tandy. It was Kingman's little manicurist.

"Oh, I didn't know it was you. I don't know what to say." Tandy grasped her hands together. Anne just stood there, frozen.

Anne wore the look of one of those ladies who lunched at Le Cirque who, upon ordering grilled sea bass, was mortified to find a platter full of snails swimming in butter when the waiter removed the cloche from her plate with a flourish.

"Oh, go on! Hate me. I'm used to having people look at me like I'm a worm or worse!" Tandy shouted defensively.

Anne stepped back two paces, expressionless, and scrutinized Tandy as if she were an insect under a microscope.

"It's Kingman I wanted to kill, Mrs. Beddall. But it's wrong. He's not worth it. You should be looking at *him* that way, not me. I'm not such a bad person." She grabbed one of Anne's paper-thin, heavily scarred wrists. "Look. Suicide! That's a form of revenge too, you know. 'If I kill myself, he'll feel real sorry.' Was it like that, Mrs. Beddall? Dr. Corbin says suicide is a sort of inverted murder, in which anger meant for another is turned inward on yourself. Maybe we both hate him. I'm so very sorry that I might have hurt *you* in any way."

Anne raised her lusterless eyes, leaving her wrists in Tandy's capable manicurist hands. "Secrets. What kind of secrets do you know about Kingman?" Anne's voice seemed to come from across the lake.

## NEW YORK

"Are you fuckin' nuts? Are you out of your blasted mind? My ex-wife and my ex-mistress *bonding* together, for chrissake, at Edgemere? I've made your fortune for you, you Freudian ass-hole, and look what you do, slip up! Fuck up! What are you doing? Group therapy to see who hates me the most!" Kingman was fuming. "A suicidal manic-depressive society drunk and a homicidal middle-aged Playboy Bunny! Oh, whatta pair. Why don't you just give them rifles and let them loose on a shooting spree? Thelma and Louise. They could hold up Carmen, shoot me and Pit Bull, sink my yacht! You've got to keep them apart. Give them electric shock treatment. Lobotomize them!"

Dr. Corbin held the phone three inches away from his ear in his den of tranquility at Edgemere. Outside in the garden, the ex-wife and the ex-mistress were busily trading secrets and pruning roses with gardening shears. Over the telephone wires on the 125th floor of the Beddall Building, Kingman Beddall was going apeshit.

"Kingman, please, get a handle on yourself. These are two mentally fragile and damaged women. They're no threat to anyone. Least of all yourself. They both love you. They're not women with violent streaks. If they hurt anyone, it's always themselves. Please, Kingman."

"You did this, you little psycho! *You* set the whole thing up. Joyce! Joyce! Where are my bodyguards?"

"Kingman. Please. I had no idea Tandy was coming to Edgemere. She was supposed to be treated at Painskill, and Anne was supposed to be with her family at Boxwood. None of this could have been foreseen." He nervously tapped his pipe on his desk. "Tandy is really in much worse shape than I initially diagnosed. I'd like to keep her here for a few weeks. She needs professional care, rest, and supervision. She'd be dangerous only if I were to send her back to New York prematurely, and then only to herself. Take my best professional advice, Kingman. I know wherefore I speak."

"Sure, Dr. Asshole." Already Virginia Randolph had called the office ten times today, *boo-hoo*ing about the accountants and surveyors tracking through her beloved Boxwood. So what if he wanted to sell the old family plantation? What if he wanted to sell them *all* to a white slavery ring? *He* owned Boxwood, didn't he? Fair and square. It wasn't *his* fault if James Randolph and his father were too stupid to play in his league.

"They hate me. They'll bond together and plot and come for me!"

Dr. Corbin shook his gray head. He really must do something about Kingman's persecution complex.

"Kingman, I've explained it to you a hundred times." Corbin had published a study on suicide as an act of inverted murder, in which anger meant for another is turned inward on the self. He had written another article, for *Modern Psychology*, that touted suicide as the ultimate act of revenge. In it he chronicled the case of the mother who killed herself with a cake knife at her daughter's wedding reception after her daughter had taken her nuptial vows with a man the mother despised. That daughter would carry the guilt of her mother's death with her all her life, just as the mother intended.

He noted the famous case of the Bronxville woman who had lain herself across the tracks, in a cocktail dress, in front of the six-thirty commuter train from Grand Central on which she knew her husband always returned home, so he would feel responsible for her death. She was getting even with him for all the wrong she felt he had done her. Revenge.

Another one of the case studies he used in his article was the Fourth of July episode in which a Connecticut man, depressed over his girlfriend leaving him for another lover, left a note for her on a lamppost, stuck a powerful firecracker in his mouth, lit it, and blew himself up on the front porch of her home—thereby burdening her with the explosion of his death and wreaking revenge.

No, these two women who had been seriously wounded by Kingman Beddall were not homicidal, they were suicidal. True, they should have been stronger in their own rights, but Kingman usually surrounded himself with emotionally lightweight, dependent women on purpose. These two were very much alike, although socially and education-wise they were stations apart. They were both shy, insecure, but capable of a single great, all-consuming love for which they would sacrifice everything, even themselves. Both Anne and Tandy had been used and manipulated by Kingman Beddall. In Dr. Corbin's best medical opinion, they were incapable of anything but sadness and self-destruction. Certainly not murder.

He contained Kingman's fears and endured his wrath for a full half hour before Kingman let him have it between the eyes: He was seriously considering securing a loan by putting *his* share, majority interests in Edgemere, Painskill, King's Cove, and Fieldmore, up for collateral. Dr. Corbin could lose his cushy "camps for the crazies," as Kingman referred to these institutions for the psychologically ailing.

"Fuck you, Dr. Screwup!" And Kingman slammed down the phone.

A private dinner with Gordon Solid was a big event. Dinner with Gordon Solid and his wife, Biddy, was a hurried-through nonevent. A private supper with Gordon Solid and his girlfriend, Tanya, meant you were in the loop. You could be trusted.

Kingman booked a table at Elio's, away from the door, near the back, just where Gordon would like it. Ordinarily Kingman would make reservations at Le Cirque, La Grenouille, Le Bernardin, some place French and visible, when he was dining with someone of Gordo's stature. But Gordo liked Italian and invisible; he preferred it that way. You left the limo at home and took a cab or hiked up from the Carlyle on Seventy-sixth to Elio's at Eighty-fourth. Gordo was big on walking. He was the kind of guy who turned the lights out when he left a room. And he was sitting on over eight billion dollars. Cash.

Kingman peered over the bottle of Fiuggi water sitting on the crisp white tablecloth. Gordo and Tanya didn't drink.

"Do yourself a favor, Kingman," Gordo whispered, twirling a twig-sized bread stick, "bail out. Nobody's going to say you didn't do your best. The unions are unbeatable and TransAir is a dog. Always has been. Call it KingAir or Emperor'sAir, it's an unworkable situation. I looked at the numbers, and by selling off the parts piece by piece you give yourself a healthy bonus. The food service company, Bernie Balsam can buy and neatly fold into his operation. Global will buy the gates. I'll even take Bilco, the military air-repair plants, off your hands." Gordon smiled at King. Tanya smiled at Gordon. The waiter smiled at them all and passed out menus.

Even Kingman's most adamant advisors were telling him to hang on to Bilco. Gordon knew it was a license to print money. He'd seen the numbers.

"Sell off everything and I'll go sixty-forty with you on Bilco. We could have fun." Gordon's idea of fun was doing a great deal and sitting with Tanya twisted around him like a pretzel. Tanya's grandfather and Gordon's father had been business partners. She spoke seven languages, skied like a Swede, and had written a romantic history of Henri de Resnais and his oeuvre, which was currently on the best-seller list. Gordon didn't like mediocre.

When Tanya went to the ladies' room, Gordon Solid leaned over the table and lectured Kingman in his soft, raspy voice. "I hear you've been talking to Mishima and that Japanese group." Gordo shook his head and clucked his tongue. "You don't want to get involved with those guys." He did something that looked like origami to his napkin. "Avram Isaac in Geneva had a very unpleasant experience with Mishima and his loan house. *Very* unpleasant." Gordo turned his napkin into something suggesting an airplane or a bird. "His youngest son was in a terrible automobile accident on the corniche outside Monte Carlo. Lost his sight and both hands. Tragic, just tragic." Kingman could swear Gordo had tears in his cool calculator eyes. Gordo loved his sons.

"Avram is convinced Mishima is behind what he alleges was *not* an accident!"

Kingman was riveted to Gordo's weather-beaten face and the telling.

"Gordon, these guys are legitimate bankers. They own shares of IBM, for chrissakes. Mishima has loaned money to Citigroup and the president's brother!"

"I'm not one to carry tales," he whispered over his plate of pasta, with fresh basil and tomato sauce, no oil. Gordon was going to live to be a hundred. He watched his cholesterol. "Mishima and his network are yakuza." Gordo twirled some pasta on his fork. "You know, King, organized-crime rings. And he never loaned to the president's brother's interests. From my understanding, Mishima loaned to Susumu House and two other legitimate loan houses, which then established ties with the presidential sibling. It's all a wash. Avram is convinced his son was mutilated because he couldn't make a loan payment."

"Huh?" Kingman was stunned. Gordon Solid was given to

understatement and never gossiped. If you heard it from Gordo, it had to be the kosher gospel.

"I feel terrible. If Avram's telling the whole truth, I feel responsible. He asked me for a loan and I turned him down. Some cockamamy crazy deal." Gordon waved the cockamamy deal and the blind boy with no hands away with his fork. His eyes were cool again. "He went to Mishima for the capital, instead. There are other stories. Worse. More skeletons in the closet and bodies on the slabs." Gordon was very animated, though his voice was barely audible. "Stay away from Mishima."

Kingman was leaning so far over the table and into Gordo's pasta that the steam from the hot dish warmed his face.

"You've got to be kidding?"

"Why would I kid about Avram's son?" Gordo was suddenly cranky. His eyes cast about the restaurant for Tanya. Her dinner was getting cold. Kingman had never seen Tanya put a forkful of anything into her mouth, ever. She was very thin, like Gordo. Maybe they never ate. Kingman had lost his appetite.

"Don't do the airline deal. Sell it off and I'll buy Bilco with you. I've got the perfect guy to run it. Ex-Pentagon man and a day-to-day manager from Defense. Have Arnie call Joel and we'll take a stab at it."

Slim Tanya ignored her dinner and her chair, slipping into Gordon's chair as he made room for her. In the restaurant! They tangled up like pretzels again. Her arm linked through his as she reached for his water glass. The frugal billionaire and his million-aire girlfriend really needed only one chair, one entrée, and one fork.

Kingman couldn't touch either his spumoni or espresso. Not with pictures of Avram Isaac's blind son with no hands and the Mishima bank loan officers dressed as ninjas whirling in his head. Mishima bank officers he had already borrowed a billion from. With interest loans due this month.

"But, Gordon, I'm already committed to this deal. I've borrowed for it."

"Well, then sell the airline, do Bilco with me, and pay back the loan. Are you sleepy yet, Tanya?" They smiled into each other's eyes.

"Gordo, I want to keep this airline deal. I can't believe there are business ninjas running around!"

"Well, I've been burned twice at the flame. No more airlines for me." He softly laughed. His left hand was somehow on Tanya's right thigh. "Get Von Sturm into the airline, then. He's your boy. With Von Sturm on board, you can keep your airline and your ass! Oh, excuse me, Tanya." Gordon was very careful with his language around her. They both stood up together, attached at the hip, until they walked out of the restaurant, with Gordo maneuvering Kingman between them as if they had never seen each other before. When Tanya and Gordo thanked Kingman for dinner and put him in a cab, Gordo shook his hand vigorously and told him, "Von Sturm. That's your savior. Yep. He's your last hope if you want to keep flying. Von Sturm!"

# 12

"Okay, Freddie, make me to die for!" Fling threw out her arms and laughed. "I don't know what all the fuss is about this De Renais. You're the best artist there is!"

As well I *should* be, thought Frederick. He had been making himself up as the Baroness von Sturm, the madcap toast of European society, very successfully. So successfully that the May issue of French *Vogue* lying on the eighteenth-century Joubert-designed makeup table had a full-page color photo montage of the two international beauties on parade at the spring Paris couture collections. Sitting front row center at the fashion shows were Fredericka and Fling, side by side; dining in cafés with the designers, rock stars, and Europe's aristocrats; even making an occasional sashay down the runways for Chanel and Versace as "guest star" models. The life of pretty rich people.

"Paint, baby, paint."

"Quiet, genius at work." Frederick rummaged through the rubble of cosmetic paints and brushes littering the priceless antique *table de toilette*, which now resembled a cluttered Impressionist painter's worktable.

Fling leaned forward like a long-necked giraffe to the oval mirror, with naked satyrs and nymphs gleefully dancing around its gilded edge. For all of its three hundred years of reflecting, the mirror had never thrown back two such perfect faces.

"*Eeek*, a line! Look it, look at this! My career is over. I'm done, I'm through!" They giggled, imitating the model girls being made up before a runway show. "Get Cher's plastic surgeon on the line. ASAP!" The two of them pulled the skin up around their eyes, so they resembled Oriental exotics.

"Instant face-lifts. Get the embalmers' balm." Some of the girls used embalmers' ointments to firm up their skin before their close-ups.

"Freddie, what can I do that's really different, that will drive Kingman mad with desire?" Fling pushed her thumb into her mouth.

"Hmm . . . a mustache!" Frederick pulled one of Fling's long honeyed tresses over her upper lip. "Maybe he's a closet queen."

Fling turned around wide-eyed with her blond mustache in place. "I don't think so, my good man. Not Kingman Beddall. You're barking up the wrong lamppost."

"God, Fling, I wish you'd get your metaphors straight."

"Well, I've got a straight husband and we're going to make a baby without your fancy petri dish."

"But not without 'Frederick's Guide to Seduction.' "

"This black lace nightie, don't you think?" She held up the

short lacy, baby-doll, see-through nightgown decorated with two enormous black satin bows.

Frederick turned up his nose. "Black. Everybody wears black. Day help wears black." Frederick had become a born-again snob in only two years.

"Let me guess, I *should* go as an extension of myself. A perfume bottle with legs. And a stopper on my head."

Frederick plopped a bottle of Chanel No 5 on her head.

"Yes, yes, I am woman, I am seduction. I am touch and smell." Fling gave her best imitation of a Chanel No 5 ad back to the mirror.

"See, I'm ice. Smell me, but don't touch me. I'm Catherine Deneuve."

"Which reminds me," Frederick raised his finger, "let's change your scent for the night. Everybody in New York smells like Fling! Get into any crowded elevator downtown and it stinks of it. How is that going to excite him?"

"Very interesting." Fling fluttered her eyelashes. "And what do you suggest?"

"Ah," Frederick used his best German accent, "something from the Baroness's private stock." Frederick produced a rectangular basket of a dozen or so numbered glass vials from Annick Fourel, the custom fragrance maker in Paris.

Fling stretched her long arm to pull out a bottle.

"Ahh . . . Madame selects number Sixty-nine, the Baroness's personal favorite."

*"Eeek!"* Fling dropped the expensive little vial and giggled.

"Perhaps Madame prefers something more missionary?"

"Yes, double missionary. Thank you." She flicked back her hair.

"Well, what exactly does Madame want to smell like?"

"I want to smell like warm honey from the hive, golden sunrises in the Bahamas, wild, passionate sex, and motherhood nine months later." She produced a pussycat purr from deep in her throat.

"Hell, that's not asking for much. Here, take the whole basket."

"How about number thirteen? That's my lucky number."

Together they uncorked number thirteen and unleashed smells of patchouli from Sumatra, sandalwood from India, and clary sage from North Carolina, tinged with a trace of violets.

"Mmmm. I'm feeling sexy already." Fling splashed a few drops behind hers and Frederick's ears.

"Careful, luscious lips. This is the real stuff. Pure parfum, none of that watered-down stuff Carmen sells. Just a dab will do you."

"Okay," Fling nodded.

"Now for the music. For this night of seduction I have selected 'Composition for the Guitar' by Manuel de Falla, redolent of endless Spanish nights of romance." Frederick pushed one of the CD's into the battery-operated player; there were hardly enough electric sockets for lighting fixtures in the immense castle. Immediately, the soft sounds of classical guitar, sultry lovers, and swarthy castanet-clicking dancers filled the gilded baroque bedroom, which was to be the scene for Fling's seduction of her business-busy husband.

Fling and Frederick spontaneously launched into an impromptu slow flamenco dance, taking turns playing the swivel-hipped, swashbuckling male dancer and the heel-stomping, skirt-swishing female dancer. Olé, Carmen!

They fell onto the floor rocking with laughter while the ethereal strains of the classical guitar floated out the window and into the garden, seducing the flowers to bloom brighter.

"No more. No more. I'm all seduced out." Fling placed a limp wrist across her forehead in imitation of Frederick.

"But, luscious, we haven't even gotten to the lesson on blow jobs."

"Oh, the lengths to which I will go to get pregnant, Freddie! But I really think I have that procedure down. I'm not entirely without my guiles."

"Yes, dear, but I've been tutored by masters. Let me share, it's all in the jaw. Here," he tossed her a banana, then took one for himself. "Now sit down and watch.

"You hold the banana thus." Frederick was grabbing the banana at its base. "You place your other hand here and move it in a continuous up-and-down motion. At first you slowly insert the said organ into your mouth, licking your lips for lubrication, gradually pulling and blowing until with each gentle tug, you slowly bring it in farther and farther until you are able to touch it with your tonsils and, finally, slide it down your throat." Frederick turned around to see how his pupil was progressing. "Damn it, Fling, you've eaten your banana! You've just castrated Kingman. I don't know what I'm going to do with you!"

"I'm sorry, I was hungry." She casually flung the banana peel onto the priceless dresser. "Let's flamenco again. Olé!"

## CALGARY

Buffalo had a hunch. He was on his way to an assignation in the backwoods of Canada with a guy that had no telephone and hadn't been heard from in years, except by a traveling tinker that sold him the occasional pot or pan. All on a hunch.

Buffalo hiked the whole way, using his Zeiss compass to avoid getting lost. He could do without the hazards of getting into it with the bears and wolves in the dark. Muggers and tough guys he could handle; animals at night in the woods were too much of an opponent for a street cop armed with a Baretta and a badge. Lucky Strike cigarettes, beer, and girlie magazines were in his knapsack.

"Limitations, fella, know your limitations." Buffalo always talked to himself for company.

The cabin was a primitive but comfortable shack deep in the woods, about twenty miles up from the Beddall lumber mill. Logs were corduroyed together with dry mud, and smoke bellowed upward from a tin chimney. At least his "hunch" was home. He hiked up the rest of the hill yelling, "Hello!" and waving his arms. Hermits usually didn't like trespassing strangers or surprise visitors.

He waited outside the cabin, the smoke billowing over his head and into the snowcapped mountains in God's country, until the gnarled old man with a weathered face like rocky terrain decided to acknowledge his visitor.

Sergeant Buffalo Marchetti laid the carton of cigarettes on a tree stump and pulled his collar up against the evening chill.

"Do you remember how Roy Beddall Jr. was murdered?" he asked the old logger.

The trip was worth it. He did.

## AN AIRPORT NEAR MUNICH, GERMANY

The wheels screeched down on the tarmac, jolting Kingman out of his deep but troubled sleep. That bloody nightmare again! He looked down at his Charvet shirt. It was wringing wet. In the familiar frightening dream he was the same conniving little boy, hawking in his eight-year-old's brassy carnival voice.

"Cold beer! Hot dogs! Shoot the ducks! Win the prize!" It was always the same: his baseball cap turned up rakishly at the brim, his too-short chinos, pulled together at the waist with broken reins left from the pony rides, showing off unmatched socks with holes in them, and his father's catsup-stained T-shirt, which was yards too long. This was the outfit the little boy in the dream wore day in and day out; the same one young Carney Eball had worn.

"Tickets, get your tickets to shoot the ducks. Win your toy airplane." Kingman knew the words by heart.

All the faces in the dream seemed to be escapees from reflections in the distorted mirrors of the fun house. Only, on this particular night, all the duck shooters in his dream were Japanese and held Instamatic cameras. When the little boy in the dream, young Carney Eball, had tried to turn around to see the ducks going down one by one, he was able to move only in slow motion, turning inches in what seemed like hours. Finally he rotated full face, to see that the Japanese carnival-goers, holding toy rifles, weren't shooting ducks at all. They were shooting at Avram Isaac's son's eyes and hacking off his hands with beautifully jeweled swords.

Kingman tore open his shirt without bothering to unfasten the buttons. He tossed it in the corner of the empty 747 KingAir Ways jet that he had just commandeered for his personal use. "Just as Onassis did when he owned Olympic Airways," Kingman had explained to a horrified Arnie in the office yesterday.

Last night's dinner with Gordon Solid was obviously weighing on his mind. Gordon's sinister warning had terrified him, but he wasn't going to give up the airline because of childish nightmares or tragic coincidences. Even in this economy. In fact, he reasoned, lousy economic times were ideal for bargain hunting. Vultures had better pickings when people were in trouble. The airline would have been impossible to purchase in flusher times. He had gotten his Mishima loans alright. Now he just had to figure out how to make the interest payments. Avram's son's misfortunes were someone else's coincidences.

Nobody nor nothing could scare him out of his own fleet of silver birds with *KingAir* printed on their shiny tails. Nothing would interfere with his dream of a great global empire connected by his own fleet of sleek airplanes taking off and landing in all the world's capitals of commerce. He was Citizen Kane and KingAir was his Rosebud. So what if he had to dance with the Devil for a few more rounds. He had danced that jig before and nightmares, he firmly believed, were caused by indigestion. Kingman belched. There was a logical solution to every problem.

He buttoned up a fresh shirt, one that wasn't ringed with sweat, stepped-off his plane, and jumped into the backseat of the loden-green Mercedes, which would drive him the rest of the way to Castle Sturmhof.

## STURMHOF

The chapel was a separate edifice standing several hundred yards from the main castle of Sturmhof. Light flooded in through two tiers of broad-arched Diocletian windows running the length of the highly ornate, baroque church. In contrast to the delicate white-ribbon-worked stucco on clustered pilasters and wall columns were the vividly colored ceiling frescoes depicting "Vision of the Nativity" according to Saint Bernard, the familiar scenes of the Virgin birth, spanning three bays of the nave. In 1720, Cosmos Damian Asam had created these extremely rich hued illusions of the Christ child's birth for the only truly religious Von Sturm family member. The artist had succeeded in not intruding into the secular space of the casual churchgoer, instead creating an autonomous religious otherworld above the worshiper's head, for him to enter at will. Billowy clouds and angels on high swept him into the chiaroscuro world of the Baby Jesus, the Virgin Mary, the unobtrusive carpenter, and the euphoric-looking barnyard animals.

These colorful frescoes were bordered by heavy gold frames upon which chubby golden angels rested, playfully bouncing sunlight off themselves as the late-morning light streamed into the chapel. Smaller angels and *putti* in white marble poked out from golden grottoes or hung suspended from golden stucco tassels at the tops of tall marble columns supporting a single broad arched passageway, which led to the apse, permitting an unobstructed view of an ornate rococo crucifix.

Kingman Beddall sat in the fourth wood-carved pew, with an unobstructed view of the backs of three outlandishly baroque hats. Baroness William Wolfgang von Sturm sported a stovepipe chimney-sweep's monstrosity that could only have come from the pages of an imaginative Dr. Seuss book. The tall hat was as gold as any of the heavily gilted angels hanging over the Baroness's head. Its base was wrapped and rewrapped with an enormous white tulle bow, elaborately tied at the back, which hung to the ground like a royal wedding veil. Clustered on the brim were the little baron's first toys: miniature silver airplanes, sailboats, and Corgi cars. Some of the cars hung suspended like Calder mobiles from the back of the brim. Fling more demurely wore an enormous cartwheel of a hat, made of bright orange straw, which measured three feet in diameter. It was happily festooned with clusters of fresh edelweiss and pale pink New Dawn roses, which only accentuated her perfect profile. The most haughty of the three figures, Cyrielle de Resnais, dangerously balanced on her head a Philippe Model chapeau constructed of several feet of lattice work and magenta organza accented with violent combinations of brightly colored maribou feathers. Her hat almost reached to the frescoed ceiling of the chapel.

Neither the couture-chapeaued mother nor either of the two godmothers was holding young William Frederick von Sturm in her arms at his christening. Instead, a strapping young German girl with bright red cheeks and a delightful demeanor, wearing a simple band of snow-in-summer flowers braided into her hair, was clasping the baronial baby to her bulging breast. The nurse. The wet nurse and, as Fling now knew, the mother of the Baron's petri dish son. The young baby Baron was splendid in his white cotton pique christening gown, with a reembroidered lace collar and hem and heavy silk ribbon sleeves, which generations of Von Sturms had worn before him. The emerald Byzantine cross that the baby wore around his neck had been hung around the small neck of every male Von Sturm christened in this same chapel since 1790. The exquisite several-hundred-dollar christening gown that Fling had purchased at Au Chat Botte on Madison Avenue still lay untouched in tissue paper in its box among the other christening gifts in the castle. The Beddalls hadn't understood the importance of tradition to the German aristocracy, especially to the eccentric but still fanatically family revering Wolfgang von Sturm.

"Isn't it a scandal? Have you *ever*? Do you believe we're all to sing a hymn now to *condone* all this?" Oatsie Warren was whispering into Kingman's ear. Which scandal was she referring to? The scandal of The Hats? The amusing scandal of attending the christening of the inheriting baronial baby of two gay men? The scandal of KingAir's pilots out on strike while Kingman sat in the fourth pew of a private chapel in Swabia at a tea party for mad hatters? Oh, which scandal, Oatsie? The scandal of Avram Isaac's son blinded and handless, maybe by a cruel act of the very money lenders that Kingman was now in debt to? With the first interest installment on a striking airline due in a few weeks!

"What scandal, Oatsie?" Kingman turned to face her. Oatsie was a first wife. She was good friends with Biddy Solid and married to Bill Warren, super-WASP and chairman of Marine Midland Morgan, the second-largest bank in New York and one of many that had voted not to bail out KingAir Ways. Too risky for the crusty old bank.

"Kingman! Really!" Oatsie was hatless. She already sported a heavy summer tan. "Fling looks like a dream, though." Oatsie cocked her head to see better over the first three pews, which held the remaining crowned heads of Europe, a sultan, the presidents and prime ministers of several European countries, and most of Europe's industry moguls. "You have to be here, don't you? Fling being a godmother and such." Oatsie's eyes bulged as if she had Graves' disease. "We're here because the Baron just parked two billion in Billy's bank and Billy says if the Baron was keeping company with a mountain goat and they somehow produced a goat boy, we'd still have to be here!"

Kingman politely nodded to Billy over Oatsie's head.

"And of course I promised Suki I'd call her after each scheduled event. What do you think of Cyrielle de Resnais and the court decision? Oh, look, it's the Sultan. Isn't he adorable?"

"Which one is Cyrielle de Resnais?" King asked absently.

"Why, she's the one in the hat who looks like Big Bird, of course! She's an absolute scandal. Cyrielle was engaged to the Baron before this, um, marriage. She just won a big lawsuit, which has been in the courts for decades, naming her the sole executor of the De Resnais estate. You know, Van Gogh, Monet, De Resnais! She must have two hundred of those paintings but not a single cent. She'll be glad to sell a few. I can just imagine. She's borrowed heavily from Billy's bank using her paintings as collateral, you know. I think with the lawsuit settled, she's allowed to sell off half a dozen pictures a year. But what a scandal!" The priest sprinkled holy water onto the forehead of the baby, who began to wail. Oatsie was still rattling on in King's ear. "The last big De Resnais that was at auction, you remember, some Jap bought. Fifty-two million dollars." Kingman remembered. "And now Cyrielle's inherited the whole collection. Gobs of master-pieces. The museum directors are practically camping outside her door. And from what I hear, it's pretty revolving!" Oatsie had a high moral character. "Billy doesn't want her to pay back the loan. He'd rather have a De Resnais for the bank!" Kingman remembered the auction well. A middleman for Mishima had bought the Resnais. He had seen it among Mishima's prize treasures in Tokyo.

Fling turned around to wave her fingers shyly at Kingman. Underneath her wide-brimmed christening hat, her face was more dazzling and radiant than it had been even a week ago, when he had last seen her. He felt a familiar friendly stirring. She looked delectable.

"Kingman, you are married to the most beautiful child I've ever seen." Oatsie had observed their shy greeting. "If Brigitte Bardot and Alain Delon would have had a baby, it would have been Fling!" Oatsie clapped her hands together in a Praise the Lord gesture just as the All Boys Vienna Choir burst into a charming chant from Carl Orff's *Carmina Burana.*

Kingman only had to get through the garden lunch, persuade the Baron to come on board for the airline deal at a seven o'clock meeting Fling had arranged, attend the ball, and then he could have Fling all to himself. He and Oatsie hummed along with the choir. Hallelujah.

The Baron's rich, verdant gardens were so ordered and man-icured, they obviously required endless hours of maintenance: clipping, shearing, mowing, and raking. It was as if the German tendency toward precision had prevailed in the Von Sturms' desire and ability to control and dominate nature. The garden was ordered on a geometric plan, consisting of meticulously mani-cured terraces, sculpted niches, parterres, precisely sculpted per-golas of topiary, gurgling fountains, and pebbled paths, all balanced along a precise central axis. In the middle of a high maze of manicured yews, a secret *Lusthaus* was situated; the place, Freddie teased her guests, where the baby had been conceived.

The exotically hatted receiving line was noisily queuing up at the base of a massive stone fountain cascading streams of water over a stone pack of hunting dogs tearing at a sculpted wild stag's throat. The stone fountain was so lifelike, one half expected to see rivulets of blood flowing into the calm lower tier, where the water trickled quietly.

Kingman grabbed Fling from the receiving line and led her down the sun-dappled *allée* of identically bent birch trees in search of the infamous *Lusthaus*, or lover's nest. He was in such a rush, he caused her to loose her big crazy cartwheel of a hat.

"My hat!" She turned, laughing, as the circle of straw blew away behind her.

"Fuck your hat."

"No, I've got a better idea," she pouted playfully.

"Come into my parlor, then." He jerked her behind a giant topiary wall of rich-green yews and evergreens.

"Said the spider to the fly," she fluttered her innocent eyes at him.

"Take off your shoes. You're taller than me in those things."

"I'll get lost in here." The yew was only the first wall in the labyrinth of sculpted hedges.

"I got a better idea. Let's get lost in each other."

"Heavens!" Fling laughed. "My too-busy-for-anything-but-business husband has turned into a horny toad."

"I've had a hard-on ever since you left New York. Cop a feel."

"Ooh, there is something beating down there."

"My heart; that's where I keep it." He wrestled her to the lush dewy grass, spoiling her party dress. She happily threw both her arms around his neck as he ran his hands down her endless legs. He pushed his eager tongue into her mouth, where she welcomed it. She might not need the elaborate seduction scene after all. Their mouths tasted each other hungrily as he ground his pelvis into hers, naked skin separated only by silk chiffon and pinstriped gabardine. King reached into the bodice of her filmy dress, releasing her breasts, moving his mouth greedily over her fully ripe nipples. Licking and tonguing her rosy aureoles he murmured, "God, you taste delicious."

He pushed aside her moist panties, delving into her with his searing fingers. She clutched them in such a way that he knew she was ready for all of him.

"Oh, Kingman," she moaned.

"I'm right here."

She heard him unzipping his trousers. She was panting in fast little gasps of anticipation.

"Oh, Kingman," she purred, "you feel so good." She wrapped her hand around his, helping him release himself from his trousers. "Take me in your beautiful mouth," he ordered.

"But just as an appetizer, my darling; I want to feel you everywhere." I want to have your baby, she thought. She parted her lips and let her mouth fall open, whispering, "Kingman, we are going to get arrested." She kissed the swollen tip of his cock.

"By what? The Nazi fuck police?" Her giggles were stifled as she pulled him all the way into her mouth. She felt him growing larger and harder as she devoured him according to Frederick's instructions. She laced her fingers around the base of his shaft, gently tugging him deeper into her throat, making little swirls with her tongue as she sucked on him. She was sure Frederick would give her an *A* plus. She sensuously kneaded his testicles with an exaggerated stroking as he pulled his fingers through her hair. Both of them were so deeply concentrating on his pleasure that they wouldn't have been able to hear a tree crashing down in the deep forest around them.

"Oh, Fling. It's too good. I can't hold back."

That's all right, my darling husband, she thought, we have all the time in the world later tonight. And she swallowed the sweet salty taste of the man she adored. The man whose child she would conceive tonight.

## NEW YORK

Sergeant Buffalo Marchetti scrambled up three flights of stairs to his friend's apartment on West Eighty-second Street between Amsterdam and Columbus and across the street from the police station. Rodney and his girlfriend, Linda, were expecting him for dinner an hour ago. He had his ducks in order but he didn't want to show his hard-earned evidence to Rodney in the district attorney's office. This was strictly off the record.

From nine to five Rodney was a meticulously educated assistant district attorney who lived by the letter of the law. In the evenings he was a blue-jeaned galloping gourmet, a whiz in his copper-panned kitchen, where the lithe Linda acted as sous chef.

Rodney opened the door, holding a bottle of Brunello di Montalcino, while the smells of sun-dried tomatoes, garlic, fresh mushrooms, mozzarella, and fettucine wafted out from the kitchen behind him.

"You're almost on time." Rodney grinned. "More murders in Gotham?"

"Yeah, a great one, except the corpse is thirty years old."

"That's the way I like them. That's when they're at their best. Thirty and under."

"No, you courtroom jockey. The murder took place over thirty years ago."

"Well, then, it's dead and buried. I couldn't be less interested." Rodney uncorked the bottle, releasing the scents and flavors of smoky flint and ripe grapes from Tuscany. Marchetti followed him into the kitchen.

"Well, this may be a long-dead corpse but the killer is very much alive." Marchetti shook a fresh salami wrapped in white butcher's paper at the cocky DA until the resourceful Linda retrieved it and began slicing it for the antipasto.

"Well, unless this guy commits a murder every thirty years, I couldn't be less interested. My docket's full. Here, Linda." Rodney handed the pretty girl, with skin the color of cappuccino and eyes shaped like almonds, a balloon glass of red wine.

"Whatever happened to your 'Manicure Murder'? The press was going crazy with that one."

"Well, I think it's kinda, like, tangled up together with this other crime."

"Good. Hard facts to get a conviction on." Rodney tossed some fresh basil into a simmering pan of mushrooms and shallots.

"Listen to this scenario. A guy comes out of nowhere, just walks out of the woods, and goes to work as a lumberjack. Gets pretty good with an ax. Becomes best buddies with the son of the wealthy lumber mill owner. Suddenly they are inseparable, living up at the house with the family or sharing a rustic log cabin in the backwoods. Like brothers. The kid with no past talks his way into the family; he is really slick. One day there's an accident. Nobody sees nothing, he thinks. The owner's son gets sawed in half and the best friend gets an ax wound 'trying to save him.' " Buffalo made quotation marks in the air. "Nobody can figure out how it happened, nobody tries. The grieving parents, Christian Scientists, adopt the wounded stranger, who is like a son to them anyway, and all is forgiven. They send him to college, give him a chunk of the lumber business."

"Oh, campfire stories from Paul Bunyan." Rodney salted the sauce.

Buffalo ignored him. "Turns out the real son of the lumber

owner kept a diary. The last entry, dated the day before the kid's accident, has the real son in a teenager's 'dear diary' dilemma. He discovers his best friend has been stealing from his father, big-time. And if he snitches on him, his father will expel his best friend from the camp, his house, and their lives. But this is a pious family, lives by the honor system. He decides to confront his friend with the evidence. Next day he is buzz-sawed in half down at the mill. The logger who found the body now says it wasn't an accident; almost a quarter of a century later. Says the other kid's wound was self-inflicted.''

"How come he never told the story before?"

"Nobody asked."

"So how come no one found the diary before?"

"The old logger, who couldn't read, discovered it when he moved into the boys' cabin. He kept it as a secret souvenir after he found it jammed into a crack in one of the cabin's corners. He never knew what was in it. I'm telling you, this was a God-fearing family living in the woods in Canada. They wouldn't even think murder!"

"So where was this incriminating diary all this time?"

"I told you. Out in one of the logging camps, deep in the woods, where the old rowdy logger kept his *Playboy* magazines."

"And just how did you get hold of it, this smashing piece of current evidence?"

"I traded him two *Hustler*s."

"Very funny, Buffalo. Very funny. Sit down, pasta's on.

"So what's this got to do with the NYPD?"

"There's this guy who comes charging out of the woods of Canada, no history before his adoption papers." Buffalo twirled a forkful of fettucine. "He's a lumber mill tycoon and suddenly he marries into landed gentry, down South. Rough, but very slick. He picks up some manners, some social graces, and charges into New York like Jay Gould in the eighteen-fifties. No scruples, no ethics: it's the middle of the nineteen-eighties. Of course, he goes straight to the top of the heap. Has his own skyscraper." Buffalo slurped some pasta. All of this was beginning to sound vaguely familiar to Rodney.

"Sounds like a modern Cinderella story to me," Linda said.

"Honey, I forgot the garlic bread, would you mind?"

"Not at all. I do food and life-style at the magazine, you know." Linda was an editor at *Essence*. She winked and loped off into the kitchen.

"Buffalo, where are you going with this? Off the record."

"I'm going to the top of the Beddall Building and I need the DA's help all the way."

Rodney put his fork down hard, tumbling over a glass of Montalcino.

"You're crazy, Buffalo. And I can't hear this unless you're building a case. And no thirty-year-old crime with no witnesses and no mourning relatives is going to get the attention of the law. Especially when it's leveled at one of the richest, most famous tycoons in New York, surrounded by an army of lawyers who went to better law schools than anybody else in America! You're absolutely crazy. The only way you ever get big guys like Kingman Beddall is taxes, buddy. That's what we use RICO for! Kingman Beddall!" Rodney shook his head. "Ax murderer? Sawing bodies in half? You *are* nuts!"

"Yeah, well, I got even more interesting coincidences."

"I don't want to hear anymore. I can't see that stuff officially." Rodney shoved aside a big manila envelope that Buffalo was holding out to him.

"Look," he whispered over to Buffalo, "I know Kingman Beddall."

"What, you work on the sly for Beddall?" Marchetti practically had his gun drawn.

"No, my father does."

"Your father's an investment banker?"

"No, my father is Kingman Beddall's houseman. I was raised on his first wife's plantation." The word stuck in his throat.

Buffalo was speechless. He hit his palm against his forehead and fell back into his chair.

"Does this mean you won't be staying for spumoni?" Rodney shot back. In the courtroom, Rodney was the master of the quick comeback. "Look, Buffalo, I don't mean to offend you, but I had to grow up somewhere."

"I'm recovered. I'll stay, it's just such a shock to think I'm making it my life's mission to nail this guy. I still haven't figured out why, and your father is his manservant Rochester who probably knows all his secrets."

"Let's get one thing straight." Rodney looked Buffalo square in the eye. "My dad doesn't know secrets, my dad doesn't gossip. My dad doesn't work for the DA's office. He really works for the Randolphs, the Randolphs of Richmond. Kingman's ex–in-laws." He reached across the table for the manila envelope. "Let me take a look at this, off the record."

"*Mi piacere.*" Buffalo was delighted.

Rodney spent a few quiet minutes studying Buffalo's unofficial file on Kingman Beddall. Suddenly he threw back his head and roared, "I knew it, damn this for being unofficial and me for being so ethical. I'd love to tell my mother." Eva and her son had been the only two of the Boxwood bunch to suspect that Kingman was red-clay Virginian, not some Canadian émigré.

"This guy is a native Virginian!"

"How so?"

"Look here on the adoption papers." Rodney pulled out some photostats of legal documents. "King Carter becomes Kingman Beddall."

Buffalo was nodding in expectant anticipation for the lightning to strike him. He didn't get it.

"I don't get it."

"Of course you don't get it. You're not from Virginia. If you were from the moon you wouldn't have grown up with pictures of George Washington in the classroom, would you? That's the whole point." Rodney laughed aloud. "Stonewall Jackson, Jefferson Davis, Robert E. Lee, King Carter, these are your heroes when you're a little white kid growing up around Richmond. King Carter's portraits are as familiar as Sly Stallone posters where you come from."

Buffalo was all ears.

"Jackson, Davis, and Lee were all famous for being great soldiers and leaders of men. Robert 'King' Carter was famous for being rich. So *he* was Beddall's role model!"

"What'd he do?"

"He got rich. They started to call Carter 'King' when he got richer in Virginia than King James back in England. He had to divide his wealth among his children so he wouldn't be richer than the *King of England*. Shirley Plantation, right next door to Boxwood, was settled by the Carters, like, in 1613. Every school kid in the area has been on a tour of Shirley Plantation and seen the portrait and knows the saga of rich King Carter. What a hoot! King Beddall. I wonder who he really is."

So did Buffalo. But Buffalo would do more than wonder.

## THE BALL, CASTLE STURMHOF

Baroness Fredericka von Sturm had bleached her hair platinum blond between the christening ceremony and the grand ball held that same night at Castle Sturmhof. The guests were summoned for supper promptly at nine. It was precisely nine-thirty, according to the four hundred priceless antique clocks, which ticked in military unison, tended as they were by two full-time Swiss clock masters. Baron and Baroness von Sturm were making their grand entrance down the great staircase in the main hall, where the guests were already seated at forty tables of ten. Four hundred heads turned in unison, as four hundred clocks noisily chimed the half hour, to witness the descent of their hosts down the sweeping stone and marble steps. The Von Sturms paused for a vainglorious moment on the landing, its torchieres and candelabra lighting their way and illuminating their presence.

The Baroness stood on a carpeted juncture two steps below her self-assured and dignified husband, silently watching his guests and his wife, as was his want. Freddie, the toast of Europe, was gracefully leaning into him from her lower place, her back arched like a blond swan's, her long satin-gloved arm resting on the gold-leafed balustrade. Her small chest, swathed in a periwinkle-blue strapless gown of delicate duchess satin, lightly grazed her husband's sashes and medals. The Valentino ball gown was a slim-fitting sheath that billowed out in the back into a bustled balloon of luxurious satin, to which was attached a gathered and tucked train. Freddie paused and posed for the photographers to capture her in silhouette and half profile gazing adoringly at her Billionaire Baron, conveniently standing two stairs up to make him appear taller. Surely this was the picture *Paris Match*, *W*, and *Hola* would run to chronicle the wacky Baroness's transformation from brunette to blonde between lunch and dinner. The European press called her madcap, elegant, mysterious, but most of all, *séduisant*. The white-wigged servants holding lighted candelabra at every few steps could overhear the Baron's ventriloquist's whisper, "Do blondes have more fun, *mein Liebling?*"

And Freddie's bold reply, "Ask me in the morning, *mein* darling."

An audible appreciative murmur rose from the guests, echoing off the three enormous crystal-balled chandeliers hung between the gilded arches of the vast hall.

"The necklace, *mon Dieu!* He's given her the Queen's necklace." Cyrielle furiously smashed out her Gauloises cigarette into her plate. The appetizer course of Beluga caviar brimming over gold-dyed poached eggs nestled in filigree swans was sitting on swirled blue plates of lapis lazuli, to simulate a pair of swans gliding on a cool Bavarian lake.

Kingman turned, startled, to his left to watch this atrocious display of bad manners. He was already annoyed at the disappointing way his meeting had gone with the Baron. He was anxious to get out of this decadent dinner, unless he could find some other white knight here among all the international financial and political superheavies sitting on cornflower-blue satin-covered chairs swagged in gold braid with football-sized tassels.

The meeting had not gone well. The Baron stubbornly refused to appreciate Kingman's adept manipulation of the numbers. He wasn't coming on board. KingAir was in a nosedive.

"I'm the only other person who's ever been allowed to wear that necklace since the Queen!" Cyrielle lit another cigarette, dropping the match onto her Wagnerian lake plate.

"Princess Alexandra of Schleswig-Holstein-Sonderburg-Glücksburg owned that necklace before she became the Queen of England. Sometime in the eighteen nineties, Wolfy's grandfather acquired it. He loved jewelry. It was his passion. He even wore some of the great pieces himself." Cyrielle turned a devilish smile upon him.

All Kingman could think was, Are any of the Schleswig-Holstein-Sonderburg-Glücksburgs here tonight and if so, are any of them interested in financing an insolvent airline?

King studied the Baron, the Baroness, and the necklace as they promenaded into the room. The necklace was a crown jewel ornament, to be sure. It had 118 large perfect pearls and two thousand diamonds, Cyrielle told the table. A king's ransom in a Byzantine-style setting. Garlands of pearls lacily interwoven with important diamonds festooned with giant golden medallions, each encrusted with seed pearls and centered by another substantial diamond. All looped in such a way that the skin around Fredericka's long neck became a part of the airy heirloom as well. The two large pear-shaped pendant pearls on either side were so valuable that they were insured separately from the elaborate neck piece, which reached all the way to Fredericka's nonexistent cleavage and dropped into the hollows of her shoulders.

Kingman couldn't turn to his right for consolation, because the royal would-have-been—she would have been Queen of France if Marie Antoinette hadn't been beheaded etc., etc., and if Napoleon hadn't been born, etc., etc.—was fluent in French, Russian, Italian, Portuguese, German, and Hindi, but spoke only cocktail-party English. So Kingman was stuck for conversation with the petulant and angry Cyrielle de Resnais.

"How could Wolfy marry such a thing?" Cyrielle would have put out her cigarette, her third in five minutes, on Kingman's plate if he hadn't put his hand around her wrist to stop her. This bit of drama was taken in by Oatsie Warren, eyebrow arched, from her seat across the table; for later development in Suki's column, no doubt.

"The Baroness is a fraud!" One of the Monegasque princesses, the French film star, and the Italian auto magnet seated at the table turned but paid little heed to the ravings of the jilted Cyrielle.

"I don't care much for the Baroness myself. Frederick and I have never gotten along," King truthfully remarked. Cyrielle turned to Kingman, delighted, candlelight dancing in her dark pupils.

"You know, these place cards are a mockery of me and my

gift. The Baroness has insulted my grandfather," she hissed in a rather charming French accent. Cyrielle held a miniature painting, a copy of De Resnais's "Boy in Blue," standing on an ornate easel, with her name hand-scripted across the bronze plate usually reserved for the artist's name. On the easel was the date, "Castle Sturmhof," and the name of baby William Frederick. There were four hundred of these identical favors used as place cards and tangible remembrances of the occasion, mocking or mimicking the original masterpiece "Boy in Blue," which Cyrielle had presented as a gift to Wolfy's baby.

"It's a joke, a cruel, disgusting, despicable joke, you know. Otto Ubelhor painted every one, every single one of these forgeries. It slaps my face." In her red clawlike nails, Cyrielle held a lit match to her original Ubelhor forgery of "Boy in Blue." "Imagine copies of a De Resnais masterpiece for place cards!" She set hers on fire.

Kingman was desperate to change the subject. "Red Revenge."

Cyrielle looked at him suspiciously, clutching her *minaudière*, fashioned in the shape of a reclining Buddha from hammered gold and encrusted with *faux* jewels.

"You are wearing Carmen's nail enamel, Red Revenge, right?" He touched her slender wrist for the second time.

"Why, yes," she gave him her best impression of a Cheshire cat, "how did you know?"

"I own Carmen Cosmetics. It's one of the things we make. Nail polish."

Robust Wagnerian notes drifted over their heads from the musician's stand on the second tier of the great staircase. Cyrielle's body at once assumed a seductive posture.

"How clever of you," she purred. "I wear it on my toes too."

"Here." Kingman flipped his forged De Resnais place card souvenir onto its side and pushed his Cartier Pasha pen in her direction. "Write your name and address and I'll send you a crate of Red Revenge. I'm just expanding my business over here. It must be hard for you to get it in Germany."

Cyrielle threw back her head, exposing her long slender neck, and laughed heartily. "I don't live in Germany, but you can send me nail polish in Paris or Beaulieu-sur-Mer. I like you, Kingman. You know just how to treat a forgery: with no respect. Let's make *le* graffiti on all of them." When she laughed, her Chanel chandelier earrings, dropping to the tops of her narrow shoulders, jingled like wind chimes in a storm.

The French called her look *racé;* a German would have described her as *reinrassig;* the American equivalent was *thoroughbred,* referring with equal abandon to horses, hounds, and humans. High-strung and haughty, her undiluted bloodlines were so aristocratic, she could casually toss good manners and middle-class notions of good taste and fashion right out the window. Kingman was beginning to find her very attractive. There was something exciting about sitting next to a simmering scandal.

Kingman was impressed as the white-wigged, ruffle-shirted, satin-waistcoated waiter removed the first course from the right, while another, similarly attired waiter presented him with a large silver plate topped by a gold cloche from the left. When all the plates at the table were in position, ten white-gloved waiters dramatically and simultaneously unveiled the second course. Epicurean precision. A single summer squash filled with piping-hot risotto and topped with flamboyant shavings of black truffles, in a circle of Gorgonzola cheeses, pompously sat on the silver plate. Kingman paused to see which fork Cyrielle would be using, then thought better of it. This blue blood was such a rebel, she probably ate foie gras with her fingers. He'd just use the next fork in line, starting from the left like they did at Boxwood. As he expected, she found the second course boring, poked at it, and then slid a rich truffle into her mouth with her fingers.

"What an uninteresting menu. How very like Fredericka." She pulled Kingman into her confidence with her prominent chin. "*Regardez*, the place-card forger is dining with the guests. He is just at the next table. I would happily become a cannibal to have him on my plate." She smacked her lips. Kingman suspected she meant it.

"What did Otto what's-his-name do to you?"

"Not to me." She crossed two Red Revenge fingernails over a cigarette. In New York it was very rude to smoke between courses. He wondered what would happen if he lit up one of his cigars. He didn't much feel like eating rice out of a pumpkin.

"To the world he is a fraud. He is nothing but a copy. To copy another man's ideas, another man's palette, is the worst sin of all. Even a murderer just takes a life, but a forgerer takes the soul." Cyrielle clasped her hand to her breast, where her heart should be. "Otto Ubelhor only just got out of prison. Surely you must have heard how he forged six De Resnaises and some Renoirs and Van Goghs. Two of them ended up at the Metropolitan Museum, and the rest turned up in important collections all over the world. The new collecting barbarians couldn't even tell the difference." She turned around in her chair and gave Otto Ubelhor the finger.

"He must have been pretty good to fool the experts. I mean, the Met! Surely the scholars and curators would be able to tell the difference between a masterpiece and a fake." Kingman was fascinated. He had an appreciation for good fakes ever since he had re-created himself.

Cyrielle looked at Kingman as if he were an imbecile.

"He is the greatest forgerer in the world. When he painted like Renoir, he used the same pigments that Renoir used. Otto mixed his own oils so they would have the exact hue of the oils Renoir used in the eighteen-eighties. He only used canvases that had been stretched in the eighteen-eighties by inferior artists, and then he painted over them so that even the canvas would be authentic. You know, of the correct historical period. He is the worst kind of fake. It is no accident with him. He does not do the imitations out of love—he does them out of profit!"

"If he is so good, why doesn't he just paint in his own style?" Kingman was intrigued.

"Because he has no thoughts of his own. Because to be a great artist, you must be a great philosopher and a great craftsman. Because *he* is only a craftsman like a fine carpenter."

Kingman turned around to steal a look at Otto Ubelhor. "He must have gotten a lot of money." His own desperate financial situation was gnawing at him.

Cyrielle was impatient with him.

"None. The forger never gets much money. The man who sells the fake makes all the bundle. The faker makes only this little." Cyrielle held two of her Red Revenge fingernails half an inch apart.

Kingman calculated some numbers in his head. Mishima had paid fifty-two million dollars for a very small De Resnais, his favorite artist. If he could just sell Mishima ten fake De Resnais originals, painted by Otto Ubelhor, that would be half a billion dollars, and KingAir would be flying in friendly skies. He wondered if Otto Ubelhor was listed in the phone book. Kingman had a sudden urge to kiss Cyrielle de Resnais.

She picked up her fish fork to dig into the third course, the only one she found appealing: cold eel arranged in the shape of a bow, tied around a bed of oysters. When Cyrielle finished her portion with brio, Kingman offered her his own.

All the gentlemen at the table suddenly rose to their feet as the Baroness and Fling approached. Fling was a delectable golden vision in form-fitting gold guipure lace with a pouf of bronze-satin taffeta.

Fredericka felt she had to greet all of her guests in person, to show off her new platinum-blond hair. As the Baron wasn't in the mood for table hopping, the Baroness dragged her best friend, Fling, around with her. Fredericka had seated no husbands and wives at the same table, a custom Fling found even temporarily unbearable. Freddie had seated his two least favorite people, Kingman and Cyrielle, together, hoping they would both be miserable.

"This is so much fun, I'm going to have a baby every year." Fredericka waved her arms like a stork as Fling gave out one of her goose-honk laughs. All the ladies' eyes at the table were riveted to Fredericka's neck, with its luxurious loops of diamonds and pearls, while the gentlemen's gazes gravitated to Fling's voluptuous cleavage.

"Oh, Cyrielle dear, I'm so happy you liked the eel. I'm sure it just slithered down your throat."

Cyrielle smiled without showing any teeth. "That's a nice necklace; is it a copy like the place cards?"

Fredericka's initial reaction was to pick up the floral pyramid centerpiece of delicate Duchess of Windsor roses arranged with fist-sized Madame de Pompadour roses and bring it crashing down on Cyrielle's snooty nose. But she didn't want to embarrass the Baron in front of all his business associates and the other important political leaders of Europe. Frederick would be the better woman.

"I'm so happy the court decided you can sell some De Resnaises; maybe you'll be able to finally afford some real earrings." Fredericka tugged at one of the colored glass chandeliers hanging from Cyrielle's earlobe.

"Ooh, the kitty cats are out this evening," Fling whispered into her husband's ear as she embraced him. "I have surprises for you tonight, my darling. I can't wait until this is over and I can have you all to myself." Fling kissed Kingman childishly on his cheek, while he became the object of the other men's envy.

"Count on it." He tilted her chin up with his fingers.

"Come, Flingy, there's more tables." The Baroness grabbed Fling's elbow and the two giant superbeauties were off.

Across the table, Oatsie was trying to stay sober so she could get all the facts straight for Suki. The last glass of German Reisling wine had nearly done her in.

"The wife." Kingman sheepishly shrugged to the table and slipped into his chair just in time for the main course of rack of lamb, and a pair of plumed partridges, with fresh purple grapes stuffed into their beaks, gazing over baby pigeon breasts coated with white *chaud-froid* sauce and decorated in aspic with the Von Sturm coat of arms. All this garnished with baby potatoes and dwarf carrots from the castle's summer vegetable garden.

"Your wife is quite lovely in an American sort of way, but she has terrible taste in friends." Cyrielle knew when to charge and just when to back off. She bit off the top of her carrot.

"Yeah, Fling and Frederick are thick as thieves."

"You seem to have such fine taste. Are you an art collector?" Cyrielle's voice was suddenly as soft as baby William Frederick's bottom.

"Yes. Actually I collect modern sculpture and religious icons."

"Of course, you are *new* money."

"But I have a friend who is passionate about your grandfather's work."

"Maybe your friend will be able to buy a painting soon."

Kingman already knew from Oatsie that the French courts had just made Cyrielle the sole trustee of her grandfather's estate, after a lengthy court battle among cousins, aunts, and heirs of illegitimate birth. The woman next to him was sitting on potentially two billion dollars' worth of paintings.

"You know, we have never been allowed to sell any paintings from my grandfather's estate." She fumbled around for a match in her reclining-Buddha evening bag.

Kingman whipped out his lighter, in the shape of the Beddall Building, and lit her Gauloises for her. What the hell, he'd light his Monte Cristo too.

Oatsie Warren was falling into her plate. They had already been served four kinds of wine, and the Laurent-Perrier Cuvée Grand Siècle was on its way.

"All of the De Resnaises in the museums and private collections were sold during my grandfather's lifetime. There hasn't been a new De Resnais sold at auction for sixty years."

"How exciting. Fresh paintings that the world has never seen before. And you decide which ones are to be sold and to whom?"

*"Exactement."* She pulled on her cigarette and blew smoke through her fine aquiline nose. "But it will be so hard to part with these beautiful treasures. I'm living in my grandfather's house now, in the South of France, surrounded by the most beautiful paintings you can imagine. The children's series, such as the 'Boy in Blue,' which I gave to the Baron's son, which this Fredericka turned into such a joke and had this Otto Ubelhor turn into cheap party favors, are all there. Ah, you should see the garden pictures he did. I have one of the 'Tranquility' series over my bed."

Kingman twisted his chair around so he directly faced Cyrielle.

"God, the insurance must be a killer. Those paintings must be worth a fucking fortune."

*"Oui.* They tell me 'Les Jardins' are very valuable. The last one that came up for auction sold for fifty million dollars. Of course, my 'Jardins' are much bigger and of better quality. So I expect they'll bring much more."

Kingman was imagining Cyrielle with gold bullion hanging

from her ears. A plan was forming in his mind. A Post-Impressionist garden for an airline. Mishima.

"I'd love to see your paintings." Kingman leaned over to her. She studied his face and flicked an ash into the chocolate *sucre* torte in the shape of Castle Sturmhof.

"Well," Cyrielle quizzed him, "how did you get here?" She blew smoke into his face.

"I flew here in a KingAir jet," he said proudly. "I just bought my own airline."

"Well, Mr. King Airlines, why don't you fly me to France tonight and I'll show you my paintings." Cyrielle directed her cool gaze boldly at him. Her eyes were pitch-black pools, her irises melding into the pupils. Kingman had never peered into such intense eyes. They were at once disturbing, unnatural, and sensual, with a slightly wicked gleam. He felt a friendly stirring.

"I'll call the pilots and get the plane ready."

"Good." She smoothed the back of her high chignon. "I don't like this place anymore." Cyrielle laughed. "If you are *very* good, I'll show you my etchings." She leaned over to brush his ear with her mouth. *"Alors, Monsieur Le Roi,"* she purred. *"Etonne-moi."*

Kingman did not have to understand French to know that Cyrielle de Resnais had just invited him to astonish her.

Fling happily splashed a soupçon of lucky number thirteen behind each ear and lit the long black tapered candles. She slid Manuel de Falla's *Nights in a Spanish Garden* compact disk into the portable player and rushed over to the baroque mirror for one last look.

Fling adjusted the spaghetti strap a quarter of an inch on her white silk Josie Natori seduction gown. Perfect. She dove into the slippery black satin sheets on the richly brocaded canopy bed and waited like a shining lighthouse on a smooth black sea.

When the four hundred clocks struck three o'clock in the morning, she was still waiting. The top note of number thirteen had long since evaporated. She rustled around in the sheets with only the smell of violets, a lonely white lighthouse in a black rumpled sea. She was sitting straight up, one slim ankle crossed over the other, watching the door.

At five-thirty A.M., Fling silently padded out of the chamber, her bare feet cold on the marble floor. Perhaps some late-night ball revelers were still up and about. No, even the servants had retired and gone to bed.

Fling felt like she had been kicked in the head. Her temples were throbbing. She didn't want to cry tears. Kingman hated tears. The romantic strain of De Falla's *Nights in a Spanish Garden* was still playing but she couldn't hear music anymore. All she could hear was her heart pounding. Had she done something wrong? Had she blown it in the garden? The room was spinning around her, an unfriendly swirl of rams' heads and lions' paws jumping off the furniture to frighten her. She should never have allowed Frederick to separate them at dinner. Didn't King realize how much she loved him? She didn't even know how to breathe without him.

At seven-thirty A.M., as the summer sunlight poked into the room, dulling the dying light of the burned-out black candles, she heard a cry of pain and anguish so deep and hurtful she shuddered in sympathy . . . until she realized the wounded cry of agony had escaped her own throat.

Fling threw herself on the bed, weeping and sobbing, pulling her knees up to her chin and holding herself to keep from shaking. Kingman wasn't coming. She was alone in the seduction suite with only the faint traces of the lingering bottom note of petitgrain oil from the bitter orange tree. With a trace of violets.

# 13

"Joyce, we're saved. Mishima's flying with us. It's in the bag. We're in the air." Kingman danced a little jig around his secretary on the stone terrace of The Hôtel du Cap as way of welcome. "You should have seen Mishima when I told him I could get him a couple of De Resnaises!"

Joyce smiled. She was his best audience.

"His ears cocked forward, his dick stood straight up." King re-created the scene for her. "Jeez, it did me old heart good to get such a response from old Buddha face." King twirled his personal assistant, who had joined him at the deluxe hotel in Cap d' Antibes, to draw up new documents. It wasn't in Kingman's nature to trust this deal to faxes, Federal Express, or somebody else's secretary.

Joyce was still wearing her Manhattan business suit amid the preseason guests lunching languidly on the terrace in Capri pants and sun hats, or lounging in bikinis and tennis whites around the sea-surrounded pool jutting out of the black rock. She marveled at King's acting skills. He re-created the mannerisms of the Japanese money lender, who usually possessed the enthusiasm of a day-old mackerel, down to the last subtle nuance. Kingman was a superb mimic and an astute study. Formal education had been a complete waste of time for him, she thought. He learned by copying the men from history or the present whom he wanted to become. Just as he had imitated the soft, husky voice of powerful Gordon Solid, affected the cigar of Revlon's Ron Perelman—the day after Kingman had bought Carmen Cosmetics—and displayed the rationalized ruthlessness of J. P. Morgan with the drama of Donald Trump, now he casually crawled into the skin of Mishima Itoyama and became him as proficiently as Laurence Olivier became Heathcliff, Hamlet, or good Prince Hal.

"It's good business to court the Japanese," King lectured his secretary-assistant, who had arrived at the hotel exactly twenty-seven minutes ago. They made an odd couple as they sat down at a terrace table overlooking the glistening Mediterranean. She was wearing a navy business suit piped in gray, a strand of pearls, her neat page-boy-styled hair gray streaked under Clairol's Mink Brown rinse, while he sported a tan worthy of Othello and the superior air of a man who has started his holiday early. His trim, muscled body was dressed in resort clothes: a blue-and-white-striped shirt by Ralph Lauren, creased chinos, and well-worn topsiders. The *Pit Bull* was anchored comfortably in the harbor at Cannes. King's mesmerizing eyes were shielded behind dark glasses reflecting the strong French sunlight off the sea. They were arguing.

"The Japanese bankers are the only ones willing to take calculated risks just now, Joyce."

"The Japanese, yes, King, but not the Ginza's Al Capone. There are other money sources. . . ."

"Look to the visible signs, Joyce, and you'll see who's in power. Everybody's driving Japanese cars, right? Look with your eyes. Remember that! Microchips? Made in Japan. Creative financing? Out of the Orient!"

"King," she lowered her voice and leaned over her menu, "Itoyama has a very cloudy reputation. He's supposed to have yakuza connections and you're so visible and spotlighted . . ."

King knew all the rumors about Itoyama's thuggy Mafia associations, even Gordon Solid's frightful tale of Avram Isaac's tragedy. Avram had a villa a couple of miles from here on a bluff overlooking Monte Carlo. He should give him a call. Later. Business first. He should give Fling a call. She had been on his mind.

"I'm really just a numbers guy," he convinced himself and Joyce, "and Mishima's numbers are worth a risk." He shrugged. He was a daring finance dynamo. King had first walked the high wire as a daredevil attraction in his father's carnival when he was eight years old. He had been straddling it ever since. He couldn't be choosy. He was desperate to save his empire, determined to keep his airline. Who would have thought the recession would have hit so hard?

"I'm plenty tough myself. I'd match the skeletons rattling around in my closet against his, any day." He ran both hands through his curly sea-tossed hair as way of tidying up.

"King, about Fling . . ."

"Here comes Cyrielle. Be nice." He stood to pull out a chair for Cyrielle de Resnais, her dark hair loose in a leonine mane, her face as white as ivory. A crew T-shirt with "The *Bullshit*" emblazoned in bold letters across her boyish chest was tucked into her skintight velvet Pucci patterned pants. Mishima Itoyama was on her arm, wearing a white suit and a straw panama. The two of them looked positively Felliniesque: Cyrielle moving dramatically up the terrace stairs to make sure everyone's eyes were upon her; Mishima looking suspiciously to his left and right, his two enormous sumo wrestler bodyguards standing in the shadows behind him.

Joyce watched King and Cyrielle as they lightly kissed each other's cheeks in the French manner, but with more drama than passion, she thought to herself.

"Mishima, you look happier than I've ever seen! Let me guess, you've just acquired the Metropolitan Museum's Impressionist collection." Kingman took off his sunglasses and grinned boyishly at his banker.

"Oh, my dear King, Mishi was beside himself with joy. I have just showed him the secrets of Villa des Jardins." Cyrielle's demeanor was reminiscent of both a black panther and a well-bred house cat.

"The opportunity to view Villa des Jardins has been a highlight of my life." Mishima's sallow skin yellowed in the bright sunlight. "I am so honored. I am in your debt." Mishima was visibly moved. He acted like a man who had just had a religious experience, seen his god up close.

Monet had his Giverny, the country home of his later years, where he painted most of his "Water Lilies." Picasso had his villa La Californie, his famous cluttered studio home in Cannes, and later his Château de Vauvenargues. Henri de Resnais had his famous Villa des Jardins, where Cézanne and Matisse had painted in the lush gardens alongside him, and the most beautiful women of his day had frolicked with the elderly master. One of these unions had produced de Resnais's only legitimate heir, Cyrielle's father. He had finally taken a wife at sixty-seven, living and painting well into his nineties, and fathering many more illegitimate children.

"It must have been very moving to see where your favorite artist lived," Joyce observed.

"I could not take in this experience all at once. It was very much like a visit to a personal shrine." Mishima Itoyama was clearly overwhelmed. He had paid over fifty million dollars for a single "Garden Scene" by Henri de Resnais a few years earlier, the only one on the market, and now he had just spent the morning in the artist's fragrant private sanctuary, viewing hundreds of the great painter's masterworks that no one besides family had ever been allowed to see. De Resnais had been so prolific that he had even "painted" the bathrooms and the bedroom ceilings. Last week, Kingman had lain awake an entire night in Cyrielle's grandfather's bed, with her sleeping beside him, studying the great "Garden Scene" mural over their heads, wondering how he could remove the ceiling without Cyrielle's knowledge, and finance his debt on KingAir Ways.

"I want so much that I have seen today, my dear lady. I will be in your service because I know you alone decide which paintings to sell and when. I shall guard your life with my own." Suddenly, Cyrielle felt very safe. "I hope you will soon let me purchase the 'Tranquility' series. Business is my vice. Collecting is my passion." Mishima made a joke. Kingman believed him.

"You have such an expensive passion, Mishi! King, will you order me escargots. I have worked up such an appetite in the gardens, in the house, up and down the stairs. *Thees* one," she pointed to Itoyama, "studied every painting like a connoisseur." She tore at some bread with her Carmen-lacquered nails, colored Naughty Nude, from the Fling! line, her concession to the casual manner of Beaulieu-sur-Mer.

"I must have 'Tranquility.' Mishima took Cyrielle's hand.

"I must have lunch. I am so starved." Cyrielle laughed, reclaiming her hand. "You know, most honorable Monsieur Itoyama, I am allowed to sell only a half dozen pictures a year and many of them are already promised to museums. I must protect my *grandpère*'s good name. I should offer some up at auction to see what they would fetch." Her expression was very serious. "But you are such a good friend to my King, I shall see what I can do." She gave Kingman a dazzling wide smile. *"Déjeuner, mes amis?"*

Joyce couldn't eat a bite of lunch. She pushed her *salade niçoise* around her plate and picked at her *loup*, the local sea bass, with her fish fork. Sitting across the table from Cyrielle de Resnais was unappetizing.

Standing at the edge of the balcony after their midday meal, the two men eyed each other warily.

"I would do almost anything to possess the 'Garden Scene' that hangs in Villa Des Jardins' master bedroom." Mishima Itoyama sounded almost plaintive. "I would give four fingers for the 'Tranquility' series. But Comtesse de Resnais does not wish to part with them."

"Mishi," Kingman put an arm buddy-buddy style around the banker's shoulder, "keep your fingers. Let's do this little deal instead. In exchange for the big interest payment due next week on the airline loan, I'll swap you a Resnais 'Tranquility' picture."

Mishima's slanted eyes widened as much as they could. Greed danced in them like desire.

They both knew Cyrielle was unreasonably stubborn and peculiarly ethical about protecting the reputation of her grandfather's oeuvre. She had a methodical plan to place his masterpieces in the world's greatest museums, have several new books published, and then turn some of the paintings over to the auction houses to command phenomenal prices in a sluggish art market, in which only the finest works still brought staggering prices. Mishima was not a patient man, King knew. This plan would not help Kingman's cause.

"Look, Mishi," Kingman's voice was soft and just-between-us-boys, the way he modulated it when he was closing in for the kill, "Cyrielle's a little gaga over her role as guardian of the De Resnais reputation. She'll sell only to museums right now. Seems dumb to you and dumb to me." Kingman shrugged. The two men were huddled so close together there was no space between them. "But maybe not so dumb. It only enhances the artist's reputation in the long run. In the meantime," Kingman hugged him like a brother, "we've got our deal. I'll let her in on the fact a little bit later and she'll be thrilled. It is an honor for Resnais to be in your private collection. Right now, it's just between us. Since Cyrielle has enlisted me as the collection's chief trustee, it shouldn't be too difficult. As a matter of fact, I can get you a 'Garden Scene' right now. The companion piece to the one you have." Kingman smiled and Mishima showed more enthusiasm than Kingman had ever observed.

"Later you can pick out another one. Just tell me the *exact* painting you want. I'll have it delivered. Two weeks, max. Maybe a little cleaning; anything you want." Kingman Beddall had crawled into con man Carney Eball's skin as if it were an old shoe. Hawking beer and pony rides. "But this must be our private deal until Cyrielle becomes more sophisticated in these matters. We can keep it between us for now, can't we?" Kingman intently watched Mishima's face. It was a face that kept a lot of secrets.

"My possessions are my only real pleasure." Mishima seemed to be making a confession. He obviously wasn't such a bad guy. "What would be your greatest possession?" he asked, an afterthought.

"I guess Fling is my prize possession." The answer surprised even Kingman. "Someday, I'll let her know." As suddenly as the romantic notion had stirred him, it vanished. "Nah, my airline is my greatest prize and I'll decorate your whole house with De

Resnais pictures as long as I'm in business. Count on it." Kingman grinned his winning smile to the stony-faced money lender.

Joyce Royce put down her pen. She had been taking dictation all afternoon on board the *Pit Bull*. The smells of olive oil and suntan lotion wafted across the teakwood deck. "King," she stared straight into his mirrored sunglasses casting her own reflection back at her, "you can't finance this deal on something you can't deliver."

"I'll find a way to deliver . . . even if I have to paint those fuckin' garden scenes myself!"

"King, I don't think . . ."

"Then don't. You're not paid to think." In a way, she was glad he was wearing his sunglasses. She couldn't have withstood the searing laser beams of Kingman Beddall's demonic eyes directed at her. When he was cornered or angered, his devilish side came to the surface.

The artist's studio on Paris's Left Bank had more in common with a scientist's hi-tech laboratory than an Impressionist painter's workshop. Otto Ubelhor chemically treated his canvases to give them the proper age. The smells of oil paints, turpentine, wet rags, and strong chemicals permeated the studio. He had meticulously prepared the canvas, frame, and pigments for months when he had forged the "Water Lilies" that hung in The National Gallery of Art as a masterpiece by Monet, until it had been discredited through a blunder in its phony provenance and Otto had been bundled off to prison.

In the case of De Resnais, it was easy. He actually possessed a dozen stretched canvases that belonged to the prolific artist. Otto was well acquainted with the colors and pigments available to De Resnais between 1890 and 1919, when he was painting his "Garden" series. "Les Jardins" had been painted with enormous speed outside *en plein air* to catch the temporal light of the Mediterranean sun. Resnais had often done a single "Jardin" in three days, just as Otto was doing. The speed of the thick brush streaking across the canvas with its heavy impasto was one of the artist's distinguishing trademarks. Waiting in the corner to be neatly crated were three of the "Garden" series that he had done twenty years ago. All they were missing was the De Resnais estate seal, which was required on any picture sold after the artist's death. The seal was in the hands of Cyrielle de Resnais, who guarded her grandfather's works like they were the Dead Sea scrolls. Kingman Beddall was bringing the seal to his studio today. He could stamp his forgeries, rendering them "real." Authenticity was everything in creating museum-quality fakes.

Otto Ubelhor's works usually passed intensive scrutiny under the dealer's black light, which revealed underpainting, or added brush strokes. IFAR, the art agency in New York that could determine the age of a painting the way geologists could ascertain the age of a fossilized tree, had already sanctioned some of his best works. In the De Resnais series, he had worked on untouched canvases that had actually belonged to the randy old goat, so that the X-radiograph would not reveal any additional images. And with the De Resnais seal stamped on the back of the canvas, the only person in the world who would know the painting was forged was the pompous Cyrielle de Resnais, who had helped send Otto to prison. She knew her grandfather's oeuvre like the back of her hand and had every picture cataloged and accounted for.

Revenge and monetary reward at the same time. It was almost too much for the talented craftsman with neither ideas of his own nor morals. The De Resnais stamp! As the buzzer rang, Otto anxiously looked through the peephole. It was Kingman Beddall, alone. And, Otto hoped, clapping his hands, with the stolen stamp of authenticity.

## NEW YORK

The plain brown wrapped package addressed to Buffalo Marchetti arrived at his uptown precinct. He immediately opened the Magic Marker–addressed packet postmarked from Edgemere. The unusual always attracted him. He was disappointed to find no note or letter enclosed, but only a Barbra Streisand tape. Not his favorite singer. If it had been a Bon Jovi cassette, he might have listened to it right away. He was on his motorcycle, weaving in and out of rush hour traffic on lower Broadway, when it dawned on him: Tandy kept Barbra Streisand tapes! He remembered how relieved she had been when they were undisturbed after her apartment had been burglarized, and that they were the first things she collected from her safe after Kelly Kroll's murder at the nail emporium.

He maneuvered the motorcycle into a U-turn, hurried back to the precinct, and popped the tape into one of the other cop's boom box. Instead of Streisand belting out "Happy Days Are Here Again," or "Don't Rain on My Parade," animalistic sounds of grunts, groans, moans, and anatomically explicit directions bellowed out of the speakers. Some of the other cops in the precinct gathered around to hear Buffalo's X-rated entertainment.

Kingman was on the tape for sure. But he twice referred to himself as Carney Eball. Later, Buffalo heard him mention Hopewell, Virginia, as the home base for the carnival.

What carnival? Buffalo wondered. Who Eball? On side two of the tape, after some of the raunchiest sex talk Buffalo had ever heard—even from this bunch of guys in the precinct—Kingman sadly recounted for Tandy how he had killed Roy Beddall Jr., his best friend, with the mill's buzz saw. Kingman had nightmares about it and wanted to share his guilt. He evidently wanted Tandy's sympathy. On the tape, she gave it to him.

Buffalo was becoming Kingman Beddall's official biographer.

He hopped a plane to Richmond. In Hopewell, Virginia, he learned that, despite his adversaries' assumption, Kingman Beddall had not sprung full grown from the depths of hell, the son of Mephistopheles. Instead he had been born in the ordinary way, to Big Carney and Dreama Sue Eball. Tandy's hysterical intimate disclosures had led him to an untidy cement-blocked trailer home off Interstate 95 in Hopewell, Virginia. When Buffalo had asked Dreama Sue how many children she had, she lazily answered "about seven," as if she were used to losing one now and again. Dreama Sue thought her son Carney was dead. Buffalo thought that was probably right: Kingman had left him behind in Hopewell. Carney hadn't been born evil, Buffalo learned from Tandy's tapes. It wasn't until much later that he played with Pluto and the Underworld. At about age eighteen, he committed his first cardinal sin: he took another life. Roy Beddall Jr. was dead as a result of Kingman / Carney's unbridled greed and a manic enthusiasm to be embraced by others, then raised high and mighty above them. The tapes, the lumberjack, even Rodney's anecdotes, were revealing a very ugly life history.


## NEW YORK


"Oh boy, oh no." Joyce Royce was sitting at her desk reading Suki's column. She was just back from the South of France. "Oh, no!"

Arnie Zeltzer was reading over her shoulder.

"Better not let Fling see this."

"Why is he doing this to her?" the faithful secretary asked.

"Well, whatever he's doing, let him keep doing it." Arnie Zeltzer was the voice of reason. He shook his head. "The guy's a genius. He's amazing. He pulled a rabbit out of a hat. KingAir is solvent, made its loan payments, and is in the air!" Arnie put out his little arms and was buzzing around the room like a bald human 747.

"Sometimes I wonder if he *is* human." Joyce Royce threw the newspaper on her desk in disgust.

"He's a fucking genius, that's what. Who *cares* if he's human?"

Arnie punched some numbers into his Wang computer. "Geniuses aren't supposed to have hearts, they're supposed to have financing. Kingman offered the unions an awfully sweet deal. Peter Szabo was actually *civil* this morning."

"Suki says King and Cyrielle de Resnais had dinner with the president of The Banque Nationale de France. It says here he is Cyrielle's cousin." Joyce was still poking her way through Suki's column.

"King met all the union's demands, except now he controls all the equity," Arnie grinned. "The pilots at American and Global are threatening to walk out if they don't get a pay hike like KingAir's employees."

"Suki says that King and Cyrielle have now been back and forth between London and Paris over six times."

"Has Hook uncrated the latest package from France?"

"Not yet. I'll buzz for him."

"Hi, gang." Fling sauntered into the anteroom of Kingman's office. She was tightly gripping Pit Bull's leash.

"Oh, Fling," they said in unison. She was wearing a pair of form-fitting jeans and a T-shirt that read, "Missing in Action." Pure Fling. Sadness with a sense of humor.

"Any word from the front?" Fling's eyebrows were arched in an expression of hopeful expectation.

"Not today, dear," Joyce Royce said compassionately.

"It's been over a month since I've seen him. Doesn't he say when he is coming home?" The lips pursed and the eyebrows fell.

Joyce stood up and walked over to Fling to comfort her. "I can assure you, my dear, that everything he is doing over in Europe and the Orient is strictly business. He sends his regards." Joyce was embarrassed.

"Yes," Fling said softly, "but when is he going to call *me*?" She unsuccessfully fought back tears.

Joyce didn't know what to say. "Hook is uncrating the last package from France now."

Fling and Pit Bull dragged into King's office. They both missed him. There were puffy little shadows under her eyes.

"Gael needs to see you about the new fragrance when you're ready, honey." Joyce followed her into the office. She was concerned.

"Hi, Hook." Fling smiled as casually as possible. "What's in the crate?"

"So far a lot of Styrofoam balls and shredded paper." Hook and one of the office boys struggled to pull out an enormous impressionist canvas of dappled mauves, pointillist dabs of gray accented by light clusters of irises, and brilliant strokes of rich greens and reds. A "Garden Scene" by De Resnais, at least seven feet long, was being carefully uncrated. She watched in horror as the painting was placed in the space where Valeski's portrait of Fling had hung the day before.

Fling fell back in shock, holding onto the Brancusi sculpture for support. She felt faint. The bronze Brancusi, spiraling in space, almost toppled as she clutched at it, the waves of pointillist, dappled mauves and clusters of irises sweeping over her.

"How could he! How could he buy a De Resnais, of all things!" What was he going to do, take down all of her photos and hang De Resnais on every wall? she thought hysterically before she burst into tears and ran out of the room.

\*     \*     \*

Arnie Zeltzer made a note to himself to ask Kingman who Otto Ubelhor was when Kingman called him from London at one P.M. There was a five-hour difference between New York and London. A check made out on KingAir's account and personally signed by Kingman for four million dollars had just cleared. Who the hell was Otto Ubelhor?

Kingman's call came in at exactly one-thirteen, according to Arnie's stainless-steel Rolex. He sounded on top of the world even though he was only in London, telephoning from a bedroom suite he was sharing with Cyrielle de Resnais at Claridge's, the superb hotel where attendant staff unpacked their bags, drew their baths, and ironed Cyrielle's silk stockings.

"King, I'll fax you the final draft of the pilots' union agreement. It looks pretty good. I can't believe you pulled it off!"

"Yeah, I'm pretty fuckin' amazing." Cyrielle was pulling off the black silk cords from her wrists and pulling on her red kimono, a gift from Mishima, that matched her Carmen Revenge Red lips, fingernails, and toes. Kingman observed her intently, the phone cradled on his shoulder. This girl had so much arrogance, she thought bondage was a means of manipulating him! Ha! Him. The master manipulator.

Anne had given him class and easy entrée into the world of business and society. Fling had given him flash and financing and worldwide name recognition, turning Carmen around from a flea-bitten dog into a golden global cosmetics conglomerate, and now Cyrielle, a sleek international whippet of a woman, had given him the key, the De Resnais collection, to unwittingly use as collateral to wipe out his debt. Mishima loved garden paintings by De Resnais better than he loved the Old Emperor. King's airline and global news network were assured. The European banks were opening their vaults to him like femmes fatales invitingly opening their legs. Kingman was doing business at continental dinners, with a fascinating woman open sesameing the heretofore closed doors.

"Europe is the eighties for the nineties," he told Arnie, and Cyrielle was his well-connected latchkey. Old times in new places, Kingman enthused. A first wife for class, a second for flash, and maybe a third for a kingdom. He couldn't afford to be sentimental.

"But, King, the eighties are dead. Boom-boom stocks and go-go-get-'em deals are gone. Milken's in jail. It's the nineties. We gotta save the trees; our box company is considered the enemy. We're up to our eyeballs in environmental 'protective' lawsuits at the lumber mills. No more animal testing at Carmen." His list was merciless. "Fling wants to give up modeling and have babies! Carmen needs her. We've all got to move cautiously over here! Money is tight," Arnie had inserted somewhere in the transatlantic call.

"Bullshit!" boomed Kingman. "The eighties are alive and well and living in Europe. Does Pit Bull miss me?" Kingman hadn't wanted to discuss Otto Ubelhor. "Don't even mention his name in public. I don't know the guy, see. Cyrielle and I are now going to Mark's Club to have dinner with her uncle. He's the head of the exchequer, you know. Then I gotta go to Tokyo, alone, to see Mishima in the morning. I'll call you from The Imperial Hotel."

"He'll call you when he's not feeling guilty. When he's done with this deal, he'll come to his senses." Also, slim as a willowy reed, was holding Fling, the giant Aphrodite, in her birdlike arms in the gallery of the Beddall Park Avenue apartment. The apartment was as immense as it was eclectic. There was no particular style that could be associated with the cavernous rooms, as a series of *au courant* decorators had trudged through the place imprinting their own version of haute interior design on the spacious, labyrinthian apartment, which had once belonged to J. P. Getty. Mongardino had done the library like the bibliotheca of a Borghese palace. Fling never went into this room, hung with burgundy velvet drapes trimmed with golden satin tassels, and winged brocade armchairs wide enough for two. The elegant decorator had selected the volumes for the bookshelves, most of which had never been cracked open. Bruce Gregga had done the sleek living room in four shades of beige marbles, and faded Flemish tapestries. Mario Buatta had finished their bedroom like a setting from an English country house, in floral chintzes, over-stuffed sofas, and sunny curtain poufs. Fling had finished off four rooms herself, with whitewashed walls hung with animal posters, naturally bleached floors, crowds of plants, and occasional wicker furniture.

Fling and her stepdaughter were sitting cross-legged in the "save the seals room."

"I know my father, Fling. He's not a monster. He's just very selfish. He's so full of himself and saving his shaky empire right now that he'll bury all thoughts of you deep in his brain. If he calls you, he'll have to think about you, so he won't call. Not until he straightens out his financial mess."

Fling was crying without making any noise. She loved Also like a sister. How many times had Fling taken charge and led Also out of the rabble of her life and into a sunny place?

"Oh, Also, you just have the best attitude." Fling sunk into a gloomy pile on the parquet floor. "I've been feeling like taking a leap from the balcony. I've been so miserable. I miss him so much. I love him." She looked bereft. "I'm not even angry at him."

"Well, you should be! He's behaving like a selfish seven-year-old. You should be furious. God. Don't get suicidal on me, Fling. I couldn't stand it again. Why do women think that killing themselves will make the man feel bad? Like it's revenge to take your own life and make him suffer? They suffer, all right: for ten full minutes! And then they find something else to think about."

Also was reliving every moment of her mother's retreat from the real world into her own never-never land. It made her crazy to think her father could manipulate two women so cruelly, the two women she loved and protected even though she was the daughter *and* the stepdaughter.

"For God's sake, Fling. If you're angry, be angry. If you want to make him hurt, get your revenge. Steam the labels off his wine bottles! Launch a new fragrance and take it to the top. Be your own person. Be the center of your own universe. Don't be one of his starry-eyed satellites. He doesn't appreciate it, Fling. I know."

Also threw off her blazer. It was warm in the enormous Park Avenue apartment and she was fuming. Fling stared at her in wonder.

"Look, Dad didn't even notice me until I started to survive, until I became self-sufficient. Once," she twirled the single strand of pearls around her neck, a gift from her grandmother, "once he didn't call me for six months. I put on sixty pounds waiting for him to call, and then one day he just showed up at school, unannounced, to endow the library with you on his arm, and you know what he said to me? After six months?" She lowered her head and spoke in a low voice to imitate her father. "He said, 'Also, you're fat.' That's all. Not, 'Also, you've eaten yourself into a tragic state out of my selfish neglect. Come live with me and I'll fix everything.' Just, 'Also, you're fat.' Or like when mother just couldn't take it anymore. I know she's not strong and she's such a gentle creature, but I really believe she wanted him to feel sorry for her. And you know what Dad said when he heard that mother had slashed her wrists?" Fling just shook her head like she had never heard this scary story before.

"He said to me, 'Your mother is not a very happy camper.'

He said those words to me!" Also's eyes flashed like her father's when she was angry, even though she had inherited the round, gentle, nearsighted doe eyes of the Randolph women.

Fling was stupefied. "That's not very sympathetic." She crinkled her nose as if someone had just put a plate of smelly sardines in front of her.

"*Sympathetic!* Dad is anything but sympathetic. He's brilliant, tenacious, handsome, devious, has trouble with the truth, he's boyish, adorable, ruthless, and I love him. Like you do. Maybe I just understand him a little better. I've known him longer." Also knelt on the chevron-patterned floor, which Kingman had fired three workmen over in getting the parquet designed the way he wanted. "He's gotten himself into a terrible mess. He's hundreds of millions of dollars in debt." Her voice was soft as she sat face to face with her best friend, the stepmother who was only a few years older than Also, suddenly the reluctant Park Avenue Ann Landers. "He's fighting to keep his stupid empire together and he'll do anything he has to do. Don't fall apart, will you? If you want him, he'll be back."

Fling hugged Also. When had this mopey-faced, chubby-cheeked child, whom she'd sat next to at the Fling! launch, turned into such a lovely creature of wisdom and kindness? A gentle woman with courage and grace? Suddenly Fling wanted to be just like her.

"I had no idea. I thought business was great. Carmen is breaking records."

"It is. Dad just wants to own the whole universe! Come with me to Watch Hill. Bunny and her parents and some Yalies will be there. We'll play tennis, swim. It'll be fun."

"Oh, those are *your* friends."

"And your fans. I won't leave you for a minute. I'll be your shadow, like two summers ago in Greece, remember?" They both giggled. Also had followed every move, every gesture, every habit of Fling's, watching her so intently she had accidentally walked right off the ship, falling overboard. Fling had dove in to save her.

"No, you go. I need to be sadder before I can get better. And then I'll be me again, you'll see." Fling kissed Also on the cheek.

"You know, Fling, you're too good for him. Men don't really respect women who sacrifice for them."

"How did you get so smart about men, Also? I didn't even know you had a boyfriend."

"I've learned from the masters." She picked up her father's Pasha pen, holding it between her fingers as if it were Dr. Corbin's pipe. "Dr. Corbin, he was a pretty groovy teacher. Corbin gave me enough insight to scare me off men for years. I think I was thirteen when he told me that men give you crabs. I had nightmares about going out on a date and finding lobsters hanging onto me, and, of course, Dad always sent me those lobsters from Lutece. Somehow I began to associate men with crustaceans. Then there's Dad, the psychiatrist's nightmare. He's good for a wholesome model of the opposite sex. Then to really retard myself, I've read everything on the male mystique in Vassar's library. I know plenty."

"Ooh, Also. I'd love to be as educated as you."

"I'll get you the books, Stepmother dear. Just take charge. Don't be Dad's sacrificial lamb. Be more like a man."

Fling started to laugh.

"What's so funny?"

"I was thinking of the other man in my life, Frederick." She looked at Also with mirth and mischief returning to her clear sky-blue eyes.

"You're right. I've got to be more like a man, thinking clearly, not ruled by my emotions, not wearing my heart on my sleeve," Fling sung out, catching Also's mood.

"Absolutely. Did you ever see a man with his heart on his sleeve?" Also stood up like a soldier leading the charge at San Juan. Even with no makeup, sporting masculine garb, her short hair brushed off her face, she appeared as feminine as a turn-of-the-century valentine.

"We've got to think more like men! Here, Also. Have a cigar." Fling offered her one of King's illegal Havanas from a malachite-and-gold-trimmed humidor that once belonged to the chairman of Salomon Brothers. Kingman loved other important men's possessions. He collected these talismans so some of their power and success would rub off on him. Other rich men's knick-knacks were his icons.

"Let me light it for you, buddy." Fling flicked the snap of one of King's silver Cartier lighters, meticulously designed in the shape of the Beddall Building, with a sapphire for the roof. Also choked on the smoke. She was a nineties woman, who didn't smoke, drink, or eat red meat.

"Have a brandy!" The daughter now filled two mono-grammed glasses to the brim with Courvoisier.

"Think like a man!" They both said, charging through the library like the Light Brigade into Kingman's clothes closet, as long as a train car and with the look and smell of an exclusive men's club. Kingman's magazine covers with his arrogant, boyish face hung everywhere in wood-rimmed frames, treated to look like tortoiseshell. This had been the first room in the house to be finished, and was still the finest, with its paisley-patterned carpet stretching a hundred feet into his wood-paneled dressing room, its Biedermeier cabinet full of shirts and woolen scarves. Brass rails held hundreds of pairs of shoes. Fling took a pair off the rails and stuffed her feet into them. Her feet were bigger than King's. She dropped her terry-cloth robe, which she had been clinging to for a week as if it were a child's security blanket, and stepped into a pair of Kingman's custom-made undershorts from Sulka. The pure patterned cotton felt smooth against her baby-soft skin.

"Pick a color." Bare-breasted, she grabbed a Turnbull & Asser shirt from the rows of racks, buttoning it on the unfamiliar side. Both of them simultaneously stepped into King's trousers, baggy on his daughter but nicely cupping Fling's shapely bottom. Fling pulled an Hermès tie from over five hundred and popped a fedora on her head, the Cuban cigar dangling from the famous pouty mouth. As an afterthought, she plopped a fedora on Pit Bull's snout, who was visibly emotional about smelling the familiar scent of his master.

"Think like a man!" Also stuffed two nattily designed Sulka silk handkerchiefs into their suit jackets. Fling arranged them into three perfect points.

"So this is what it's like to get into a man's pants!" Fling giggled. "It's been a while. I was left waiting at the chapel."

"Just like a man." Also was thrilled to see Fling display a spark of humor. "It's a man's world, sister, we might as well dress for it," she stated. "It's easier to win if you know how to play their game." Kingman Beddall's daughter had figured this out a long time ago.

The Fourth of July weekend in New York. Park Avenue from the Seventies all the way to Grand Central Station was like a ghost town. Nary a soul in sight. You could have shot a cannon off without anyone hearing it. She could have walked stark naked down the middle of the street without anyone seeing her, Fling thought. New York was so dead. It was eerie. She wished Frederick were here. Maybe she should have gone with Also. Tonight was the first time Fling had ventured out of the apartment in days. She just hadn't felt like seeing anybody. Fling couldn't bear the idea of going to the cozy beach house in East Hampton without Kingman. Not alone. All of her model girlfriends would be with their rock star boyfriends, celebrating the national day of independence decked out in their rock-star-society best. The Fourth of July. Red, white, and blue rockets going off. *She* didn't feel like celebrating. *She* didn't want her independence. She wanted her husband back.

The apartment on Park was too big and too empty to rattle around in alone. Hook had gone to Boxwood for the rest of the summer to work for the Randolphs because the new live-in couple hadn't worked out. The Czech butler and his wife, who cooked, were so snooty. Fling had suggested to Jimbo, her personal security guard whom Kingman had hired for her protection, that he should spend the holiday weekend with his own family. Jimbo had been only too happy to comply. It was pretty boring for a six-foot-four-inch ex-linebacker from the Giants, with bad knees, to protect a jogging fitness-freak supermodel with great knees, when all that ever happened was that well-wishers came up and told her how much they adored her. Now she was sorry she had let everyone go. She was lonely.

In this part of town the neighbors were so sophisticated, they would let Jacqueline Onassis breeze undisturbed down Park Avenue with her grandchild, or the current first lady lunch unannoyed with her favorite designer. Yet Fling always seemed to invite well-meant greetings and friendly overtures from complete strangers, who had so frequently seen her face gazing at them from magazines, television, the backs of buses, and even their shower stalls, from Fling! bath splash, that they felt like they knew her. Her MTV promotional videos were the most requested. Her CBS environmental specials were run and rerun. She was more than a familiar face: she was their friend. Ordinarily she'd wave back and call out a chirpy hello. These past few weeks, though, she hadn't felt up to putting on a pretend smile and acting like she was just fine, thanks, when she wasn't. She felt as if someone were twisting a knife into her heart, and she was afraid if she went out in public it would show. If you were this unhappy it was better if no one saw you. Somehow it didn't hurt as much if other people didn't know how bad it really was. So when she had ventured out on this Fourth of July Saturday, she had waited until after dusk. She'd feel better as soon as Also and everyone returned.

Fling had been promising Gael Joseph for days that she would get into the office and test the five samples that Gael and her team had cooked up for their new fragrance. The last time she'd experimented with new fragrances hadn't turned out so well. Number thirteen from Annick Fourel hadn't been very lucky after all. Fling knew from the perfumers at Carmen that different smells could excite you and cheer you up, while others could bring you down and depress you, trigger memories from deep in your brain. Maybe Gael had mixed up a batch of something that would lift Fling's gloomy mood.

Pit Bull tugged on his leather leash, leading Fling from the apartment at Seventy-second and Park to the Beddall Building at Fifty-eighth and Fifth. The thick-necked dog knew the route by heart. He and Kingman took this walk almost daily, with the chauffeured silver Mercedes driving along curbside, following them per Mr. Beddall's instructions. Kingman had become very security conscious, and Pit Bull was a ferocious guard dog. Fling felt safe anywhere with Pit Bull, even on this deserted street in New York as night was falling. She turned around twice, looking over her shoulder, before she got to the Beddall Building. She had an uneasy and unpleasant sensation of being watched. She finally dismissed her anxieties as an overactive imagination heightened by three days of moping around their huge empty apartment, and lack of sleep. Last night she had been awakened three different times by hang-up calls. Twice the caller had stayed on the line, breathing heavily into the phone until Fling finally hung up. The downside of being a celebrity.

Pit Bull acknowledged the weekend watchman in the Beddall Building by jutting his jaw out at him. Louie waved a hand in greeting, unlocking the two doors as Fling signed in, writing her name in her childish scrawl, the hour, and what floor she was going to. Gael's offices were on the fiftieth floor.

"Are you going all the way up to one twenty-five to watch the fireworks? I was thinking of sneaking up there myself, Mrs. Beddall." Louie was a strong, burly man. She smiled at him. Her thoughts were somewhere else.

Fling had completely forgotten that there would be fireworks. "Oh, I might do that, Louie. Feel free to join me."

"Thank you, Mrs. Beddall." Louie turned to look at the beautiful girl, beguiling in tight-fitting jeans, a white cotton shirt decorated with smiling baby seals, and an expensive-looking patterned silk scarf looped around her narrow waist. Even in her tennis shoes she stood a foot taller than he.

On an impulse, Fling took out her key and entered Kingman's private elevator, taking it all the way to the top. It shot up like a rocket, making her ears pop. A happier Fling stared back at her from the Valeski photo in the burgundy brass-studded lift. At the 125th floor, she let Pit Bull off the leash. The dog knew his way into Kingman's office, where Fling flipped on some overhead lights.

She walked over to the window, Kingman's window, and surveyed his personal dazzlingly lit cityscape. She looked down upon the Crown Building, with its illuminated gold-leaf ornamental roof; the gaudy Trump Tower, awash in a klieglike light; and the AT&T Building, topped with its swirled pediment, which looked as though it should be sitting on a piece of antique Chippendale furniture. It was an unusually clear night, so she watched some of the airplanes taking off and landing at La Guardia, toy planes on toy runways from this height. If you stood here long enough you got the feeling you could *be* anything. From here you could *do* anything—even rule the world, so insignificant and manageable below you. That's the way Kingman said it made him feel. Like you could fly. Heights just made Fling dizzy. She sighed. The fireworks wouldn't begin until nine P.M., when it would be much darker.

She moved over to the Ruhlmann desk, running her fingers over the burled wood of its glossy surface. She picked up one of the photographs of herself with Kingman on the windowsill behind her, and placed it smack dab in the middle of the desk. Tears started smarting in her eyes. She just didn't understand what he was doing all over Europe with Cyrielle de Resnais, the bony, hook-nosed, haughty Cyrielle. Arnie and Gael had told her that he was just using Cyrielle for business, but what kind of business took you all over the world to fancy dinner parties with heads of state, without even a single phone call to your wife? *Fling* read Suki. She knew where he was. Were his airline, the world TV network, and his new business ventures in Europe so much more important than she was? Was it so important to meet European bankers and businessmen so that he could enter charging into the European Economic Community, whatever that was, the way he had charged into New York? And why was he always photographed at dinner parties on the Riviera? He had told Fling she was indispensable when he was building Carmen. Was she dispensable now that he had changed focus? Maybe she should learn French. She wiped her tears away with the back of her hand. Had she made a mistake thinking he enjoyed quiet evenings at home eating health food and making love? Maybe she should have been having royalty for dinner instead of alfalfa sprouts! If only she knew what she had done wrong, she could change it.

Good thing Frederick was coming to stay with her next week. She couldn't stand to be alone any longer. She felt so low; she just didn't know how she'd go on if Kingman never came back. She heaved a sigh, thinking she'd better get down to Gael's workrooms. It was spooky in Kingman's cathedrallike office all alone. It made her feel like a small child locked up overnight in a huge public library all by herself. She turned her back to the wall where De Resnais's "Garden Scene" hung. As an afterthought she tore off a sheet of Kingman's personal notepaper, emblazoned with KING in raised gold block letters across the top. She picked up one of his pens and scribbled in her girlish scrawl, *"Please forgive me for any inconvenience I may have caused you."* She printed *Fling*, and drew some *X*'s and *O*'s around her name and jammed the note into her jeans. She'd leave it on Gael's desk. For sure she owed Gael an apology. Fling was supposed to have tested these perfumes a week ago!

Snapping off the lights, she called out for Pit Bull. He was barking down at the other end of the hall. Maybe someone else was working late on this holiday. Pit Bull never barked without a reason.

"Louie, is that you?" Fling called as Pit Bull came weaving down the hall, wearing a funny-looking expression on his snout. If she hadn't known better, she would have thought Pit Bull had been drinking! There was no response. Evidently there was no one there. She would have to get some sleep tonight to settle her jittery nerves.

As they entered the elevator, she noticed a distinct odor that she hadn't smelled before. Was it ginger? Tobacco? Maybe Louie had come up for the fireworks after all. It was probably from his cigar. King passed out Cuban cigars like nickle tips to everyone who worked for him. When the elevator stopped on fifty, she and the dog beelined straight to Gael's office. There, on the terrazzo-topped console table, stood five vials of different golden-colored perfumes. *Real* perfumes, like Carmen and Rose. She suddenly felt a little wave of excitement. There was a typed form for her that Gael had prepared before she had gone to Nantucket with her new secret boyfriend, whom Fling suspected was none other than Arnie Zeltzer. She giggled in spite of her gloomy mood.

She felt like Goldilocks sitting before the three bears' porridge. She'd sample all five perfumes and write her responses, just as Gael had requested. Fling knew from the lectures she'd had to sit through and memorize as spokesperson for Fling! fragrance that the olfactory receptors, through which smells entered the brain, were somehow intermeshed with the lymphatic system, which controlled emotions, moods, sexual responses, and memories. Good memories and bad. She had remembered telling Kingman that even if you liked someone very much, and they were really handsome and everything, if they just didn't smell right to you, you wouldn't find them sexy. He had only laughed, sniffed around her breasts and shoulders, and then pushed her hand to his hardness, telling her she definitely passed the "sexy smell test." She loved the way *he* smelled. She wished there was a bottle of his masculine, musky scent in her hand right now, so she could drown herself in it. She bit her lip and reached for the first shiny bottle leaning on the counter, her slim ankles wrapped around the metal legs of Gael's console stool. Pit Bull stood at alert, sniffing something in the air himself.

The first bottle brought to mind pleasant images of being a little girl. There was the definite innocent smell and taste of vanilla. Ice cream, Tastee Freezes, being too tall and too thin. Texas. It all came back to her in a swirl of sweet tasty vanilla. She closed the bottle, smiling at her own little-girl memories. She'd come a long way since then! She hadn't done so bad. She was a star model. A success. She'd bought a nice house in Corpus for her mother, who had finally married the owner of the drive-in. Vanilla Tastee Freezes. She could almost taste them. She licked her lips as she neatly put the first bottle back.

The second bottle unleashed an immediate hostile reaction. It smelled French. Garden ponds, damask-hung baronial beds, snooty French shopgirls. Cyrielle de Resnais. Violets. She twisted the cap back on and roughly waved the scent out of her own space, her pouty lips forming a big silent *no!*

The third was rather intriguing. It didn't remind her of anything until she passed the scent strip under her nose for the third time. It had an introverted, dark quality about it. The notes were decidedly Oriental. She could smell the ylang-ylang oil in it. She wished she had come when Gael was there. Gael had taught Fling so much about fragrance—with such patience. She sniffed again. It reminded her of Yves Saint Laurent's Opium, or Calvin Klein's Obsession. But not exactly right.

Lavender immediately escaped from the fourth bottle. It smelled the way Fling liked to smell, clean and fresh. Gael had told her that the Greeks and Romans had burned lavender twigs to ward off "evil humors." She laughed. She'd need a lot of lavender to get her evil humors out. The bottom note was fresh and mossy. Fling put the bottle aside. It was very appealing.

The aroma emerging from the fifth bottle was delicious. It smelled white and snowy, like white baby seals, and heather on mountaintops. It was all at once warm and strong and masculine and sweet. There was a tobacco quality about it too. "White tobacco with mossy chypre notes," Gael's guideline read. Fling smelled white furry rabbits on cold clean snow. This was definitely her favorite. It smelled happy and full of promise. It smelled good. She beamed contentedly. This must be Gael's favorite too. She had left it for last. It smelled like Fling. She smiled. It was to be called Forever Fling.

She put the bottles carefully back in order in a neat row, and then dabbed some of the last fragrance around her neck and on her jeans. Promise and hope and happiness, with an undernote of innocence. "Make me to live for," Fling said to Pit Bull, who was lying on his side, not looking too well.

"What's the matter, Pit Bull?" Fling slid off the stool and gently stroked the dog's head. "Did you eat something you shouldn't have again?" she playfully scolded him. Usually the stout bull terrier had a cast-iron stomach. Once, he'd consumed a pile of poison insect repellent, ate some grass, and then was just fine. Grass in New York at night. She could hardly take Pit Bull into Central Park when it was this late. It was too dangerous! A thunder clap and then a flash of lights: the fireworks. She looked at her watch. It was already after nine.

The roof garden on ten! The Beddall Tower had a splendid grassy garden on the tenth floor terrace like the Italianate roof garden at Rockefeller Center. She nudged Pit Bull back into the elevator, forgetting to turn off the lights or leave her note for Gael. It was still jammed into her jeans' pocket.

She had to push the iron gate extra hard to pry it open. It slowly creaked back. A clap of thunder again. More fireworks. It was very dark. She didn't know where the switch was for the cast-iron street lamps that usually lit the roof park. Pit Bull jumped out of her arms, probably to eat some grass. She groped along in the darkness, occasionally lit by a flash of fireworks, which on this lower floor could be seen only in fragments around the corners of tall buildings. The night air felt muggy and heavy around her as she groped along, her eyes slowly growing accustomed to the darkness.

"Pit Bull," she called. "Come, boy!" She remembered that the Italian lights, twinkle lights, woven through the hedges automatically went on at nine-thirty P.M. It must be almost that now. She stood quietly in the shadowy garden, waiting until she could at least see outlines, her eyes growing accustomed to the darkness, her pupils enlarging.

"Pit Bull!" she cried, anxiously groping her way against the terrace wall. She heard Pit Bull, closer. Another clap of thunder and suddenly the little Tivoli lights twinkled on, casting a huge daddy long legs–like shadow of herself directly in her path. She jumped back in fright. Another shadow behind her seemed to spring back, too. Tricks of an overactive imagination. She heard another sound to her left. A branch snapping? She felt she wasn't alone up here. She could feel her heart thumping wildly in her chest.

"Pit Bull," she pleaded. "Come back." The dog was at her side again, but a low growl was emanating from his throat and, then, a big terrifying bark. She heard a fluttering of wings. It stirred her heart to terror. She turned. A pack of ordinary pigeons. She put her hand on her famous chest.

"Pit Bull, you and I are just two chickens! Barking at pigeons!" She laughed nervously. She bent to gather up Pit Bull in her arms. She could barely lug the animal, King's prize-winning best of breed. She just wanted to get back home. She had a new fragrance to launch, a husband to claim, a case of nerves to calm. She heard the iron gate creaking and a thrashing through the trees. For sure she wasn't alone. Suddenly the twinkling lights dimmed.

"Who's there? Louie, is that you?" Fling was frightened. Pit Bull rushed to attack a fleeting shadow. His barking was vicious. He was running toward the Fifth Avenue side, chasing something. She could hear the deep clenching growl that meant he had something in his mouth. With those jaws he could kill a cow, King always said. Fling was a strong girl. If there was a mugger up here, she could fight. The barking got louder, closer. Suddenly, she felt something cold brush against her cheek. She swung out frantically with her fists. She couldn't see, it was so black! Fling stood frozen in terror, trying to find Pit Bull, trying to fight jumping shadows, trying to get her legs to move. She'd run. She turned in the blackness toward the light creeping from the darkened building, feeling with her fingers, groping in the dark.

"Pit Bull!" she shrieked as another flash of fireworks exploded and lit up a small corner of the sky. Raining bursts of light momentarily revealed a darkened outline hovering near the low terrace wall. Pit Bull gave out a hideous cry and then a whimper, until he mysteriously sounded far away and fallen.

"Pit Bull!" Fling screamed and rushed straight into a silent shadow that held a wire taut across her throat. She swung out, sweat trickling down her shirt. There was light now but she couldn't see the shadow choking her. The wire bit into her neck, her sweet perfumed neck sprinkled with innocence and hope and promise. Forever Fling. She lashed out at the boxing shadows, kicking and screaming, savagely pulling at her throat with her fingers. Somewhere below she heard Pit Bull barking. Surely she was going to die. She could feel her eyes bulging from the pressure at her throat. Her fingernails dug fiercely at the garroting cord. She skidded her heels as she was pulled and pushed closer to the sounds of the dog and the lights of the city streets below. Her knees skinned and bloodied as she was pulled along, flailing her arms, frantically kicking the deadly shadow with such unexpected force that she finally heard another human sound. She'd struck her invisible assailant. Desperately gasping for air, panting, the hot wind just escaping her lungs, a rush of consciousness, and adrenaline charging her up for one last, feeble attempt. Her long arms and legs pushed out, kicking, tearing at anything, the horrible sensations of blood at her throat, her fingers tearing at the steel band, a wad of something woolen shoved into her silently screaming mouth. A fingernail caught in the wire. She was going over. Someone, something, was heaving her over the shoulder-high wall! The arms gave out before the high kicking legs, one tennis shoe falling before her, whizzing into a wicked spiral.

"Please, Kingman, save me" was mumbled only into a muting rag.

"Count on it," she could hear him say, from somewhere far and long ago. Suddenly Fling's long neck snapped back and she never saw who flung her over the tenth floor garden roof of the Beddall Building—hurtling through the stifling air, failing to fly, slapping into the fountain, dead, only her face untouched and intact on the Fifth Avenue side of the tallest building in New York. The 125-story Beddall Building, across the street from Bergdorf Goodman, where life-sized Fling! mannequins were elegantly arrayed in the windows.

# 14

Buffalo Marchetti studied Kingman Beddall's every move from the eighth pew of St. Patrick's Cathedral. He had thrown a sports coat over his chambray shirt and jeans in deference to the solemn occasion. Suki, who hadn't left her apartment in years, was seated next to him, giving breathless color commentary the way a former ballplayer would at a televised sporting event. Suki wanted to cover Fling's funeral in person. This was too important an event to assign to one of her spies. Her assistants were outside, talking to pedestrians to see who was entering the church and who was being turned away. She would turn out two full columns on the service. Suki was overdressed for the midday funeral, in a black satin brocade cocktail suit topped by a black-and-yellow turban with a bright yellow jewel glittering in the center.

Kingman and his dog were peering into the open casket. Buffalo had paid his respects to the beautiful corpse earlier. He couldn't figure out these high-profile rich people. They were treating the holy cathedral like the family funeral parlor. Buffalo felt very sad as he had viewed the deceased, even though he had met her only in pictures. She was just as beautiful in person. Now Buffalo was straining his neck, trying to read the emotion on Beddall's face. From where he sat, it looked like genuine grief. He and Suki had come two hours early to get good seats. He wanted to watch Beddall, what he did, to whom he talked. Later he'd walk around and observe him from the Lady Chapel behind the altar, where he'd have an unobstructed view of Kingman's face.

Billionaire financier Gordon Solid was sitting in the row behind Buffalo with an all-male army of world-class deal makers. They could be heard discussing business in hushed, respectful tones. Solid sat in the center. The row directly in front of Marchetti was an all-girls aisle. Skinny models in skimpy little black dresses, weeping and shredding their Kleenexes, dabbed at their high taut cheeks and their trickle of tears.

Suki, her own cheeks hillocks of fat, identified the lady carrying on to beat the band as Baroness von Sturm, royal drag queen and giddy toast of Europe. Heaving and wailing, her trim, flat-chested figure was extremely handsome in a custom-cut suit of some kind. At one point the high-strung baroness confronted Kingman and shook a puce-colored gloved fist at him. Kingman seemed not to care for her funereal antics and angrily dismissed her. His secretary, Joyce Royce, appeared to be riding shotgun. Big, really big, security guys were everywhere, with walkie-talkies and big bulges beneath their dark jackets. For all Buffalo knew, they could have been carrying Uzis.

There was something depressing, shallow, and sickeningly contrived about the whole thing. Buffalo felt like throwing up. Suki was in people-watching heaven. Everybody was there, and the attention to detail was insurpassed. She particularly liked the bunches of ylang-ylang and jasmine, the floral ingredients of Fling! festooned and garlanded around the pews. Purple and yellow billbergia, queen's tears, and baby's breath woven with fragrant fresh heather and white roses created a colorful floral blanket arranged over the bronze and silver coffin. Suki said it was a Hurlitzer for sure. Hurlitzers, Uzis, ylang-ylang, queen's tears, business barons, and mannequins. Buffalo wondered where the mourners were.

Out in the street holding hands and one another, thousands of women and girls were mourning one of the few really good and honest things that had been thrust down their throats by Madison Avenue. A sensation who really was sensational. A Cinderella who really married the Prince. A golden girl who was pure gold. Sweet and unaffected. Fling.

Women who had worked with her side by side at the zoo mourned her, remembering how she had birthed the young sea lion calves and conducted tours for the schoolchildren herself. The nuns who ran the Beddall Home for the Aged wept quietly for their personal angel, who spent Thursdays talking in her sunny Texas twang to the Alzheimer's patients.

Cabbies, doormen, and joggers who knew her by sight called out her name in the street now. Fling! Fashion designers' assistants who had pinned her for fittings and draped her for shows and whom she made feel so important, wept. Secretaries and housewives who had somehow gotten prettier, taller, better, after wearing Fling's fragrance, stood there and shook their heads sadly. Fling! Young girls who had worn Fling! Colors as their first makeup cried for their idol. Teenagers who had "found meaning in their lives" after watching Fling's environmental *National Geo-*

*graphic* videos mourned her like the last of an endangered species. Little girls who clutched Fling! dolls on their pillows at night wondered what dead meant. Women who had been hurt and jilted by men asked themselves aloud how Kingman Beddall could have left her.

There were others who mourned her. Out on the street, among the others, stood Tandy, who had stolen away from Edgemere for Fling's funeral but wasn't allowed into the church. It was already full when she got there and she wasn't a recognized somebody to be squeezed in at all costs. She wore a simple black dress and jacket. She had been taking "simple" and "tasteful" lessons from Anne. Her blond hair was mousy brown and her face relatively free of makeup. Kingman would have been hard pressed to recognize her. She stood there alone in the crowd. She had come to pay her respects to someone else Kingman "Carney Eball" Beddall had hurt. She thought he deserved to die. *Fling was never her enemy.*

Buffalo Marchetti watched Kingman carefully at the service for his wife in the elegant cathedral on Fifth Avenue with all the high and mighty in attendance. Carney Eball had climbed to the top using corpses and women as rungs in his ladder to success. Buffalo shook his head solemnly from the eighth pew in St. Patrick's Cathedral. The guy is evil. What's he doing in church? he wondered. The moguls, the models, the cop, and the mourners were all sitting a stone's throw from the tallest tower in the world, the architecturally award-winning Beddall Building. With his glacial gray eyes, broad brainy forehead, and chiseled nose, Kingman Beddall's face was in itself a memorable piece of architecture as he bowed to accept condolences from a social friend or nodded to receive congratulations from a business associate who cracked him on the back in homage to his big KingAir Ways coup. He had done it! He was a player. He turned the handsome head in another direction. He was a widower. How tragic. What a terrible accident.

A small man—Buffalo could see only the top of his jet-black, sleek head as he swiftly flew past him—stopped to speak to King. The mogul reeled back in shock. Instinctively, Buffalo sprang into action, trying to shove his way through the crowd as the magnificently constructed face of "King" Carney Eball fell a full 125 floors to the bottom, and looked as if it would shatter.

By the time Buffalo got to King, the dark-haired figure was nowhere in sight, and the shocked, grieving husband was being escorted from the side entrance of the church into a waiting limo. The few witnesses who saw the intruder said he was a small, well-muscled Asian fellow who moved through the crowd like an Olympic hurtler.

As far as Buffalo was concerned, the mourning period was over. He was allowed to ask questions. He had another murder on his hands. He checked off his list in his head: Jimbo the body-guard, Louie the night watchman, Arnie Zeltzer, numbers cruncher, Garcia the makeup man, and the wacky baroness, who insisted that Fling would never kill herself, had already been questioned. The Baroness needn't have ranted and raved so at their meeting, trying to convince him Fling could *never* have committed suicide. Buffalo had seen the preliminary coroner's report: the windpipe was collapsed and the neck raw with the rubbings of the strangling wire. A cotton rag was stuck in the back of her throat, water soaked because she had landed in the deep fountain in Beddall Plaza.

The coroner and Buffalo kept their discoveries secret, knowing full well this *was* New York, where secrets were never sacred. It was a total zoo. Newspaper guys were still taking pictures from helicopters and aiming telephoto lenses from roofs adjoining the

Beddall Building. Buffalo and the department were doing their best to keep the facts surrounding Fling's death out of the papers until they could be verified and deemed 100 percent accurate. The official autopsy was totally confidential, practically top secret. Marilyn Monroe's death had been obfuscated by mystery. Fling's would not. Buffalo would see to that. Had Marilyn committed suicide or had she been murdered? Had Fling jumped or had she been pushed? The papers were having a field day. So far they had Fling jumping off the 125th floor of her husband's Beddall Building with Pit Bull in her arms and a suicide note pinned to her blouse. There *was* a note, but it had been jammed into her jeans' hip pocket. Now it was in Marchetti's.

Sergeant Buffalo Marchetti knew, and the commissioner would know tomorrow, that nobody would strangle herself with a ninja-type wire, tear off a fingernail, stuff a gag in her mouth, and then jump off a tenth-story roof garden, remembering to toss a seventy-pound dog onto the terrace one floor below. Fling Beddall had been in a battle for her life. There was physical evidence all over the roof. The signs of the struggle were documented and cataloged. Hard evidence was in the plastic bags the cops were still collecting. Buffalo had wanted to have Pit Bull immediately put to sleep, to inspect the contents of the dog's stomach. Pit Bull probably had bitten Fling's assailant or at least taken off some skin. The murderer's blood would have still been inside the dog's stomach after a few hours. If he could have slit open the dog's stomach, at least he would have had the murderer's blood type. A piece of skin, not Fling's, had been found on the balcony, and bore traces of a tattoo. The Beddall security man who found Pit Bull on the balcony had conscientiously bundled the prize dog off to the veterinarian and thereby to safety, the security guy making points with the King of New York. Dammit! Right now secrecy was the investigation's best protection. Buffalo heard Rodney's voice in his head: corpse, weapon, and motive. He had already spoken twice to the medical examiner this morning. There was a weapon—traces of piano wire—but practiced killing hands had done the real job. Now what the hell was the motive? He had to do this one totally by the book. Kingman Beddall was too powerful to mess with without having all your ducks in order. The fewer people who knew the real facts, the better. Alibis couldn't be created when the facts were still under wraps. Too bad Pit Bull couldn't talk. Although if he could, Buffalo shook his head, Pit Bull would probably lie, perjuring himself for Kingman. Man's best friend never made ethical judgments.

The daughter, the next one lined up for questioning, was Anne Randolph Beddall II, the reluctant debutante. Probably another rich brat. He was really beginning to hate rich people. Why was a dollar amount allowed to be a measure of a man's worth? When he went to keep their scheduled appointment on the fiftieth floor of the Beddall Building, he was told she wasn't there. Figured. He'd probably have to interview her through a legion of Kingman's lawyers. But then he was told she was waiting for him on the tenth-floor roof garden. How dare she! It was supposed to be sealed off. He hustled himself down to ten. Damn these Beddalls. He charged up to the slim figure.

"Don't you know this place is off limits? What the hell are you doing here?" He grabbed her shoulder, turning her around. He would liked to have punched her in the nose.

"Can't you read or are you so important that you can walk right past a police barricade? What's your nickname? Princess!" Buffalo couldn't have been more surprised to see the fragile, pain-filled eyes looking up at him, if he had been trapping for a killer bear in the woods, only to find a wounded fawn caught in his snare. It was that girl, the pretty one from the elevator. He had seen her the day of his first visit to the Beddall Building. He hadn't forgotten her.

"So arrest me," she said defiantly.

"Are you Anne Beddall?"

"Anne Randolph Beddall II, commonly referred to as Also."
She jutted out her chin.

"Is this where Fling went off the roof?" she asked in a sad
whisper. A crisscross of yellow police tape cordoned off the five-
foot-high wall on the Fifth Avenue side of the garden.

"Why do you want to know?" Tough cops only *asked* questions. "About, about there." He pointed anyway.

"I should never have left her alone. I should have stayed in
the city with Fling." Also burst into tears.

"When did you last see her?" He reluctantly began his interview. Suddenly, tough cop Buffalo Marchetti felt sympathetic.

"I saw her last Thursday night. We had dinner at the apartment before I left for the holiday weekend. I stayed over with
her."

"Where did you go?" That wasn't one of the interview questions.

"Watch Hill," she offered, "in Rhode Island. I stayed with
my college roommate and her parents. I shouldn't have gone. I
should have *made* her come with me."

"What did you do there?"

"Is this a part of the questioning?" When Also got angry her
hazel eyes were flecked with gold.

He stammered, "I mean, what did you do the last time you
saw Fling?"

"I went over to the apartment late Thursday to cheer her up.
I thought she was starting to come out of her gloominess. We
stayed up practically all night discussing Dad, her career, the
future, and girl talk. She said she'd be fine. She just needed a
little more time alone." Her voice was full of genuine grief.
Buffalo wanted to console her, not quiz her. "She was depressed
but she was coming around, finally deciding to take charge of her

life. She realized she was more than just my dad's possession. I don't see how she could have killed herself." She turned her tragic face up to Buffalo for answers. She needed answers as much as he did.

"Maybe she didn't kill herself." He communicated the message to Also without actually going into his classified information.

Also held her small hands up to her face in relief. "I knew it! I knew she'd never do such a thing. She was a survivor. She wouldn't have hurt all the people who loved her by doing that! It was an accident, wasn't it?" She was waiting for him to set everything right. A half dozen emotions registered on her face.

What a lunkhead he was. Suddenly Buffalo remembered Suki telling him how Also's mother had tried to commit suicide, devastating the teenager. She must be going through hell, he thought. He wanted to put his arms around her slender shoulders.

"No," he said instead, without emotion. "Fling was attacked before she went off the roof."

"Attacked? How could she be attacked with all the security around the Beddall Building?" Also was stunned.

"Not mugged, murdered."

Also was visibly shaken. She staggered back toward the roof wall. Buffalo wanted to take her in his arms and hold her.

"Were you very close?" he asked instead, his hands stuffed into his pockets.

"She was like my sister."

"Did she have any enemies?"

"Everybody loved her."

"Wasn't there somebody who was jealous of her that would want to hurt her?"

"Fling didn't inspire jealousy." Also's voice trembled. "You wanted to be like her, you wanted to imitate her, maybe copy the

way she looked or the way she walked. She was very kind." Also
stared out over the garden and thought of Fling's smile, her
goose-honk laugh, her kindness to her from the very beginning,
when she was an overwrought, overweight teenager.

"What about your mother? I bet your mother didn't like
her."

The fierce look of defiance returned to Also's childish face.

"My mother lives in her own universe. She doesn't get involved in this world. New York and my father's life here are
totally alien to her. She tends to her own simple garden."

Marchetti pushed on. "Why would Fling come to the Beddall Building on the Fourth of July?"

Also was sincerely trying to be helpful. "On Friday we spoke
for just a moment. She sounded very low." She paused. "I was
concerned, so I called again on Saturday. I thought maybe I
should come home but Fling sounded much more up. She told
me that she was going to go down to the office and make her final
decision about the fragrance."

"What fragrance?"

"We have been working on a new fragrance at Carmen."
Also bit her lip. "Gael was thinking of calling it Forever Fling."

Buffalo recoiled as he remembered the *New York Post* headline: FLING, FLUNG, SPLAT!

"We had been waiting a week for Fling to approve the new
fragrance. Her contract stipulated that she had final say. We had
created recycled packaging just like she requested. No animal
essences, only natural floral ingredients and fruit extracts. Very
environmentally friendly." There was a momentary spark in Also's pretty eyes. "We were all very excited about the new fragrance. It just needed Fling's approval. Somehow she just
couldn't bring herself to the office with everybody there. Fling
felt very badly for causing Gael any inconvenience."

The suicide note. Bingo!

*"I apologize for any inconvenience I may have caused you. XOXO Fling"*

The handwriting analysis had already been done. It was Fling's handwriting, all right. But not a suicide note after all. Just an apology note.

"Where would she sample these fragrances?" quizzed the cop.

"Gael's office, on the fiftieth floor."

"For what reason would she come to this tenth-floor roof garden?" Other than to jump, as the papers were saying, or be savagely murdered, as Marchetti knew.

"Sometimes Fling or Dad would walk Pit Bull down here. It's nice—it used to be nice." She looked around the manicured garden, a bucolic setting in the middle of the noisy city.

"Do you know if your father was planning on divorcing Fling?"

The daughter shrugged. "I never know what my father is going to do. You'll have to ask him." Marchetti had been warned as early as this morning that Kingman Beddall was off limits. He had been out of the country when the suicide/accident/murder, pick one, had occurred, and he was privately grieving, according to the police commissioner and his buddies in the mayor's office.

"When King's on a specific project, like expanding Carmen abroad, overseeing his European cable network, or refinancing KingAir, he tends to forget about the little things, like wives and daughters." She looked a little unsteady. "I'm used to it." Her shoulders shook. "Dad can be a little cold sometimes. Very insensitive. When he's concentrating on a deal, it's like he has blinders on. He doesn't notice insignificant things, like human beings." She suddenly looked very pale.

"Would he have wanted her out of the picture?"

Her armor was on again. "In the immortal words of Fling, 'You're barking up the wrong lamppost, buster.' "

"Look, I didn't mean to offend you. Somebody threw Fling off this roof and I need to know as much as possible. Do you think your father might have been involved in any business deals in which a sore loser might have wanted to hurt him through his wife?"

"I don't know. You'll have to talk to King. If you don't mind, I'm tired. I'd like to go home now. It has been a long couple of days." She couldn't get the smell of the funeral flowers out of her nostrils.

"Do you know anyone with a tattoo?"

She shook her head no. She looked faint.

"My motorcycle is parked illegally on Fifth." He gave her a Buffalo grin. "I'll give you a lift. Where do you live?"

"In the Nineties."

Good, thought Buffalo. He was sick of the eighties.

Tandy got the messengered letter from Arnie Zeltzer three days after Fling's funeral service. Kingman was divesting, selling off Tandy's Nail Emporiums, her only achievement, her one solid foundation. The girls who worked there were her family. King was letting her down again, pulling the rug out from under her feet, making a mockery of her entire life, everything! So what if she wasn't a classical pianist? She was in the beauty business, just like Kingman Beddall, wasn't she? He had taken everything else from her, now he was taking her identity. How dare he take the business away from her?

It turned out that it never really had been *her* business at all. She had thought she was her own boss and that Kingman had been her financial backer, her partner. Actually, she was just *Tandy*, the name on the door. The ugly reality was, Kingman's interests had been traded off to some Japanese bank in a mumbo-jumbo deal. Now Tandy discovered she was just an employee, a salaried manicurist who punched a time clock for a foreign company. What if they decided to retire her? What would she do? She'd called Arnie. Could she come in and sign some papers, as long as she was in New York? Expedite matters? Sure. Why shouldn't she? She'd get some cash for her interest and separate herself from any ties to Kingman Carney Eball Beddall. *How she wanted her revenge.* Giving Sergeant Buffalo the tapes hadn't been enough. Evidently, old murders didn't matter. Cheating carny barker, sawmill murderer, provoker of suicides, homicides, extortionist, liar, seducer who bedded all Beddall, smuggler of illegal cigars, stock manipulator, woman beater, income tax evader, master of bribery, and inside trader—*that* she knew about. Why, he was the Dirty Dozen all by himself.

"I hate you. I hate you," she sang to herself.

*Revenge would smell so sweet.*

"Bad man," she whined in a sing-song voice that sounded childish and crazy at the same time.

He'd hurt her friend Anne. He'd hurt Fling. She didn't exactly *know* Fling but she used her Fling! cologne, so that was like being best friends, wasn't it? Anne wasn't her enemy. Kingman / Carney was her enemy. She had to get revenge. She had to get even. Death was too good for him.

"That's okay. I'll come in, Arnie. Just do me a favor: don't tell Kingman I'm coming in. I don't want to see him. I don't want him to see me. I've been very ill, you know." *That's what Dr. Corbin says. I'm supposed to be at Edgemere still. My friend Anne is covering for me. She was never the enemy. I called you, Arnie, when I saw the papers at my office. Didn't you know I was crazy, Arnie, that I'm at Edgemere? Kingman owns Edgemere. Kingman owns Anne, Kingman owns Boxwood, Kingman owned Fling, Kingman owns me, it's got to stop.*

Kingman was pale in spite of his Mediterranean tan. He and Cyrielle had been at Villa des Jardins when the call had come about Fling's accident. At the funeral, one of Mishima's men had swiftly passed by him and told him in a nasty hushed hiss that Fling had been "offed," that strange expression in a Japanese accent. Fling had been murdered. She had been "taken away" because Kingman had taken away Mishima's honor by selling him a set of forgeries instead of real De Resnaises.

Mishima didn't want Cyrielle de Resnais killed. Then, how would he get his "Garden Scenes" so easily? He didn't want Kingman dead. King owed Mishima too much money. He had to be alive, allowed to pay back his debts. By law, a foreign citizen wasn't allowed to own an American airline, so they were stuck with each other. Fling had to die. Wasn't she King's prize possession? It had been so meticulously logical to Mishima. Mishima's man had to kill that manicurist, too. She was in the salon that night when Mishima's goon was conducting his own inventory, before a loan was made to Kingman Beddall. *That* death had been an accident.

Tandy picked up the *Daily Sun* and read Suki. Suki had the exclusive story that the police were going to investigate Fling's "accident" as a murder, even before the front pages or the television news had the story. Ah, they must be carrying on like Chatty Cathy talking dolls at Tandy's Nail Emporiums. How dare Kingman sell *her* nail salons? How dare he be selling Boxwood? Anne had told her all about Boxwood over the phone this morning. Anne was still covering for her. Tandy was still supposed to be at Edgemere doing gardening therapy. Over the edge. Near the water. Virginia Randolph and her lawyers were meeting with Kingman's lawyers in New York today, too. Kingman was turning over the deeds and mortgages on Boxwood to a Japanese corporation—Iosha, headed by a Mishima Itoyama. According to her daughter, Virginia was ballistic. According to Dr. Kronsky, Corbin's assistant, Tandy was dangerously homicidal.

Dr. Corbin didn't agree. But of course, Anne had told her Edgemere was on the block, too. Dr. Corbin himself was feeling slightly psychotic this afternoon.

Tandy skirted in surreptitiously to the elevator block leading up to Gael Joseph's office on the fiftieth floor of the Beddall Building. On fifty, she was turned back by security. Nobody could get to the executive offices on the 125th floor without a visitor's pass and an ID badge clipped to their clothing.

"Dad, you can't sell Boxwood." Also was leaning like a rag doll over her father's desk.

"Don't *Dad* me!" Kingman's face was a dark scowl under bushy brows.

She had never seen her father in such a black mood. There was a frantic force driving him.

"King, it's not morally right. You have no authority to sell my mother's home and my grandparents' heritage. Boxwood has been the Randolph legacy for centuries. It's just not yours to throw away!"

"I hold the mortgage. I foreclose. *Finis*." Kingman was learning French.

"King, please reconsider. Boxwood can't make even a small dent in your *king*dom." Also couldn't contain her own sarcasm. People she loved were hurting. Fling's funeral had been only a few days before. Wasn't there supposed to be a grace period? What was the hurry? Why the garage sale? He was divesting desperately.

"Lots of small dents add up to big bumps." Kingman busied himself in the mountain of paper and files that were laying helter-skelter across his vast desk. He'd have to sell or mortgage anything or anyone he could to keep his airline and cable network. The debt to Mishima had to be paid. Mishima wasn't a man to mess with. Without telling her, Kingman had beefed up the security around Also. Kingman thought his daughter would be safer if he put some distance between them. Mishima was a madman.

Arnie kept marching in and out like an animated rabbit/man borrowed from the Energizer batteries commercial.

"It's not fair, King!"

"This is not about 'fair.' It's about finance. And the legal wheels keep whirling in motion, kiddo."

"No, Dad, the laws can't be so unfair!"

"Law has nothing to do with fair. Law has to do with the interpretation of rules already on the books." He used that old saw on his daughter: "The guy with the best lawyer wins." Arnie nodded and was out the private door that adjoined their two offices. Tandy Love was due any minute in his office to sign off on Tandy's Nail Emporiums. They were being sold off like yesterday's news.

Virginia Randolph's lawyers were using every legal strategy on the books, from the original land deed issued by King James in the 1600s to an old Virginia territorial law on squatters' rights from the eighteenth century, to prevent the Boxwood sale. Virginia had dubbed it "the rape of Boxwood," on a par with the burning of Atlanta, when she called in Buzzy Cohen, who had successfully defended an old friend of hers in the "Canasta Murder" in Newport, Rhode Island, and won, as well as the lawyer Alan Dershowitz, who was making appeals for both Leona Helmsley and Michael Milken. Virginia had even threatened to shoot Kingman in front of her husband, her son, and Eva and Hook before allowing Boxwood to fall into the hands of one Mr. Mishima Itoyama! Anne, puppetlike, quickly echoed her mother's sentiments from her gardens at Boxwood and Edgemere, where she pruned her roses and cut them with her sharpened garden shears.

Tandy, her brassy bleached mane of hair now a mousy shade of brown and shorn to her shoulders, and an extra twenty pounds added to her lower torso, was totally unrecognizable as she moved through the green marbled lobby of the Beddall Building and a phalanx of security guards, some plainsclothed and some sporting Beddall security uniforms. She was signed in and given a plastic security pass to clip to her somber summer clothing, per Arnie Zeltzer's instructions. She had an appointment. She was escorted by a short, stocky security man, a holstered gun pulling at the seam of his blue gabardine suit, before being whisked up to Arnie Zeltzer's office, right next door to Kingman Beddall's.

Solemn-faced, she walked into the blizzard of activity that was control central for Kingman Beddall's *de*acquisition program. He was selling off most of the Beddall empire to keep his two jewels, KingAir and World Network News. Even the uncollateralized shares in the Beddall Building were quietly being transferred to Gordon Solid in return for quick, cold cash. Carmen was on the block. King was moving his headquarters to London, where Cyrielle would be at his side. He hadn't actually spoken to her since Fling's death, or, for that matter, since his whirlwind trip to Japan to deliver the fake De Resnais. The debt to Mishima and his gang of yakuza money lenders was being paid off frantically in full. The Tokyo-based Mafia of murderers and thugs had settled their score. A fake suicide for a fake masterpiece by De Resnais painted by Otto Ubelhor!

Kingman had danced with the Devil once too often. Fling had been murdered as a warning and an act of revenge by the principled yakuza, whose henchmen wore their tattoos like fine raiments to be envied. Fling's picture stared innocently at him. *An eye for an eye, a wife for an act of fraud:* the yakuza Hammurabi Code!

Tandy was motioned into Arnie's office by another guard. Security was very tight. She sat down, Bic pen in hand, to sign the necessary papers for the swift dissolution of her popular nail emporiums, created, it seemed, almost a million years ago, in her increasingly fuzzy memory. Arnie barely acknowledged her plain presence. He was busy carrying out a barrage of barked commands from the adjoining office, which Kingman hadn't left since Fling's funeral, showering and sleeping in his barracks like Hitler in his bunker during the last days of World War II. The granite-marbled and burgundy-carpeted hallway outside his locked doors looked like central command for a major military invasion, as troops of security guards changed positions in precise round-the-clock shifts in front of his outer door. The skylighted roof, the five lower floors immediately beneath Kingman's office, and the heavy bronze elevator doors were rendered impenetrable.

Kingman, handsome in spite of the new lines etched into his tense face, worked bent over his Ruhlmann desk, a De Resnais "Garden Scene," with its thick impasto of vibrant post-impressionist splashes of color, at his back, his sleek and showy Brancusi skypointing sculpture on its teakwood pedestal at his side.

When Arnie whirly-dervished out the front door of his own office on yet another urgent mission, Tandy, still wearing the same pair of inexpensive black short gloves she had worn to Fling's funeral, put down the Bic. "You didn't have to know her to love her," Suki had said in the *Daily Sun* this morning. "She struck a chord in an entire nation. She shall be sorely missed. She will be happily remembered. She is in every whiff of Fling! fragrance and her murderer will be caught and punished. Forever Fling!"

Tandy silently stood and steeled herself for what she had to do. She looked around. There was no one to stop her. She quietly moved from Arnie's outer office into Kingman's private sanctuary, passing through the connecting door that lately was always ajar. Kingman never heard Tandy as she crossed the threshold, unobserved. She stood for a moment watching the man who had jilted her, who she'd been faithful to for over a decade. He looked up in surprise, momentarily failing to recognize her. When he did, he waved her aside like an unpleasant memory. He had something important to finish.

"Oh, Tandy, it's you. You look terrible! How'd you get in here? I'll be with you in a minute." Kingman turned his back on her to read the stock quotes flashing across his computer terminal.

She was devastated. He hadn't even recognized her! What was she? His Barbie doll! A toy to be tinkered with and then tossed aside?

"I'm a person, Kingman. Not something to be used up and thrown away," the angry words burst out of her. He ignored her.

"How can you sell off my company?" she shouted at his back.

"My company, *not* your company, Tandy. Sit down and shut up. I'm busy."

Busy. He'd always been too busy. Too busy to talk to her. To marry her. To spend time outside of bed with her. She, who had given all her time. She'd lied for him, embezzled for him, slept with other men for him. Been his secret love and the keeper of his darkest secrets. I'm a person. You're a selfish user, she thought hysterically. You've hurt me. You've hurt my friend Anne. Use you up and throw you away! That's the Kingman Beddall motto.

She looked at the back of his soft black curls. Somebody has to stop him before he uses anymore people. He made Anne try to kill herself, he hurt Fling so bad she jumped off his building, hadn't he done that? Or did he have her murdered? He'd murdered that guy in Canada, Roy Beddall Jr. Hadn't Kingman killed him, too? Tandy's vision was blurred by tears, her thoughts confused by hatred and hurt. Any logic diminished by a stronger emotion. Revenge.

He had hurt her. Beat her up. He had even trusted her with his terrible secrets because she had loved him so fiercely. All he had to do was throw her a bone once in a while. All he had to do was touch her. He had the touch, all right. Every deal he touched turned to gold. Every person he touched turned to nothing.

She could never get well as long as he was around. She could never feel good about herself as long as he was in the papers, on the news, on the same planet. She wanted to make him just go away. Then, maybe she could stop loving him.

Tandy picked up the smooth-surfaced Brancusi bronze, marshalling all her strength in her cotton-gloved hands, and violently crashed the modern museum masterpiece down upon the back of Kingman Carney Eball Beddall's head, cracking open a gash the size of a vivid red stroke of paint in the De Resnais "Garden Scene" behind him. One crack, a heavy blow, another, and then a third was all she could wield before she absentmindedly, but carefully, replaced the artist's pride upon its wooden base.

Kingman was making inhuman sounds and gurgles, although no decibels higher than the usual rants and raves that customarily came from his office. His fingers involuntarily twitched in spasms, his eyes widened open, practically pushing his bushy brows up into a horrifying look of surprise. Tandy turned on a midsized Chanel heel and resumed her signing of the dissolution papers.

When Arnie returned, Tandy finished signing some new documents, witnessed by one of the secretaries who was notarized. She rose to shake hands with Arnie. Her gloves were in her new Chanel shoulder bag, neatly stuffed into the zippered section of her farm-grown crocodile purse. After she was escorted out of the building and into the sunny plaza, she paused to look into the Beddall fountain, where Fling had been flung, stopping to toss some loose change into the water and make her wish: Tandy hoped she hadn't killed him. She taxied the rest of the way to Pennsylvania Station, where she caught the train to Washington and then on to Edgemere. Surely Anne would approve and understand. Surely they had all been revenged. After all, maybe she had just knocked some sense into Kingman's head.

Sergeant Buffalo Marchetti picked up Also at her Fifth Avenue apartment on his motorcycle, and rushed her down to Manhattan Hospital, where her father was being monitored in the intensive care unit. His condition was critical. Kingman had lain in his office almost two hours before Arnie realized that he hadn't left the building, but had fallen unconscious behind his desk.

Buffalo was used to ugly ICU dramas. Also wasn't. He felt someone should be with her. She'd need someone to help her through this. She was alone in the world. Also had been shocked to find her vital father on life support systems, trembling in uncontrolled spasms, involuntarily curling up into a fetal position. An ashy-gray pallor was swiftly replacing the healthy Mediterranean tan of the dynamic and feared tycoon. He looked helpless and vulnerable, so unlike the master manipulator who could strike terror into an adversary's heart with an arch of his heavy brows, now dark, forbidding precipices under which his hollow eyes lay sunken.

The lack of privacy in the trauma unit was startling to the uninitiated. Thin walls of sheets separated wealthy "heart attacks" from homeless "knife wounds." All the patients, only hours before well and hearty, no matter from which economic class, were lying in varying degrees of careless nudity in soiled bed linens, amid cries and moans and confusion. Exhausted interns and trauma unit nurses hurried from patient to patient, trying grimly to match their understaffed skills to the overcrowded battlefield of an urban emergency room.

Buffalo Marchetti watched at her elbow as Also conferred with doctors, signed papers, made life and death decisions, and called in outside specialists from all over the country all throughout the endless night and into the morning. Frantically trying to get surgeons, a private room, clean sheets, anything! Also, the devoted daughter, was doing everything humanly possible to pull her father through.

As morning nudged into the narrow window of the hospital's cafeteria, Buffalo watched, concerned, as Also took her first sip of something liquid in over fourteen hours. Having just lost her stepmother and best friend, the girl was now consumed in fighting for her father's life. Murder seemed to hang over the head of the Beddall economic empire like a curse. For some reason, Buffalo was starting to worry about what would happen to this girl. He didn't see how the sparrowlike beauty was holding up. Only twice during the long night had she rested her weary head on Buffalo's strong shoulder. It had felt very comfortable to the cop, who usually used his shoulder to break down doors.

"I know Dad will survive. He's a fighter." She bit her lip. "I'll stay here as long as necessary to make sure he gets the best care." Once during the long night, the doctors thought they had lost him and were ready to give up. Also had been unrelenting in forcing them to persevere. Buffalo, watching her, abstractly found himself admiring Also for her courage and quiet strength.

"Also," he took her hand across the counter, "I want you to know exactly what's going to happen. Tandy is going to be picked up and charged with attempted murder. Even though there were no actual witnesses to the crime, she had motive and opportunity. Once you press charges, I don't see too much difficulty . . ."

Also's glare stopped him cold. The enormous nearsighted doe eyes were turned on him like a five-hundred megawatt spotlight.

He went on. She might as well know everything sooner than later.

"The Brancusi is down at forensics. The only fingerprints on it are Fling's. All over it." He looked annoyed. "Tandy must have had on gloves."

Also lowered her lashes and thought, *the blood on the Brancusi, only Fling's fingerprints, almost as if Fling's ghost had done the deed.*

"Sergeant Marchetti," Also addressed him by his police detective's title, "there won't be any charges. My father was very overwrought from Fling's death. He was acting irrationally, divesting himself of profitable companies and old friends. We were all very puzzled. He was bereft, grieving. It's no wonder he fell against the sculpture, cracking his head." Her tone was dead calm.

"Also, don't do this. Tandy is guilty!"

"Is she? Tandy loved my father. We all did. None of us would ever hurt him." Her voice was clear and strong. "I think enough harm has been done in my father's name." She pulled her hand out of his to fold it resolutely over her slender wrist.

"Would you please properly take care of my father's accident for the police reports? Enough damage has been done in the Beddall name, Sergeant Marchetti. We wouldn't want anymore people hurt because of this terrible accident." Her own hurt and angry eyes were flecked with gold.

## STURMHOF

"I can't decide where to put it. I could keep it in her guest room. But the last time she stayed there, she was so depressed. If I put it on one of the mantels downstairs, it will probably just get cataloged and sent to one of the other castles." Freddie was sitting crossed-legged on the floor of Wolfy's malachite-walled dressing room at Sturmhof, holding the priceless art nouveau silver and jade urn created by Lalique at the turn of the century. The two delicately fluted silver handles were adorned by twin beauties rising like swans out of identical silver filigree lilies. Within the smooth, cool, silver surface lay the ashes of Freddie's best friend, Fling.

"Darling, you can't sit there holding them forever," Wolfy said kindly. "They should be laid to rest."

Freddie sighed. He looked forlorn, sadly sitting there in his jeans cinched in with a Barry Kieselstein Cord belt, and one of Wolfy's pinstriped shirts with Bulgari Roman-coin cuff links.

"I'm just not sure where she'd be the happiest."

"Well, dear, I can't believe that awful husband, Kingman, let you buy her from him."

"It's not like he was putting her up for sale at Sotheby's. I sort of maneuvered her away from him. There isn't even a Kingman Beddall family plot. He was going to bury her with strangers, in the dark, in a coffin."

"Didn't the mother want her in Dallas or wherever she's from?" The Baron smoothed two monogrammed silver brushes over both sides of his noble head, grooming his thick steel-gray hair.

"No. Her mother said I was more like a sister and she figured I'd know best what Fling wanted. Fling and I made a pact a long time ago that if either one of us died before the other, we would have the other one cremated and put in a beautiful urn, or scattered to the wind. Both of us had this horrible fear of the dark and both of us made cross-your-heart-hope-to-die promises that we'd never let the other one be put into a box in the ground. But I was always so high in those days that I can never remember which one of us wanted to be scattered and which one of us wanted to be urned."

"Well, do you not want to scatter some of Fling's ashes and

keep some in the urn to travel with?" He laid his brushes down on the dresser.

"Imagine," Freddie pouted, "the most popular woman in the whole world in an urn, sitting on my lap in Germany."

"I can't think of a nicer place to be." The Baron smiled sincerely.

"Oh, Wolfy, you are so sweet."

Freddie could not allow Fling's public grave to become a tourist attraction like Elvis Presley's Graceland or Marilyn Monroe's burial plot, to be trod upon and photographed by curious trespassers and fans with Polaroids. The unveiling of the grave site would be another hideous media event. The kind Fling hated.

Freddie figured cremation was the proper thing to do. He had even mixed some of her fragrance with the ashes. King and Carmen Cosmetics were going to build a huge gaudy monument to Fling, designed by Philip Gladstone, in Woodlawn Cemetery in the Bronx, in the pie-shaped plot between the graves of Fiorella La Guardia and Edward Kennedy "Duke" Ellington. Her gaudy tombstone would read Sue Ellen "Fling" Beddall. The real Fling would reside safely and privately in the woodsy gardens at Sturmhof, with Freddie to look over her. He sat there clutching the vase, rocking back and forth. Staring into space.

### TOKYO

Cyrielle de Resnais watched as the actor jumped out of the shadows and into the view of his audience. A centuries-old art transformed the thick-necked man into a willowy, reticent woman whose neck was too slender to support her own head. His skin was powdered a poreless porcelain in the ancient Kabuki tradition, in which male actors played all the parts on stage, portraying women with more femininity than the modern Japanese girls hurrying past on the Ginza strip outside. Shy and lovely in his richly textured kimono and silken wig, the dancing actor held as much grace in his unfolding fingers as a flower opening its petals. Cyrielle was transfixed by the metamorphosis and the illusion of the art.

Mishima Itoyama reached for her hand. She reluctantly let her fingers rest in his palm, just as she had reluctantly sold him her grandfather's "Tranquility" masterpiece as well as De Resnais's greatest "Garden Scene." These *authentic* paintings were the ones Otto Ubelhor had copied, the De Resnais forgeries Kingman Beddall sold to Mishima to keep his ego and airline aloft. Kingman might have carried off a perfect crime were it not for the fact that Mishima had broken his gentleman's word to Kingman, calling Cyrielle at Villa des Jardins to tell her how magnificent "Tranquility" looked on the wall of his house, overlooking his own exquisitely designed Japanese garden.

Cyrielle had laughed. What a sense of humor Mishima must have. She had been staring at the famous "Tranquility," the first one from the series, directly across the room from her, exactly where De Resnais had hung it himself. Surely someone was having fun at his expense? She could almost feel the cool anger that carried over the transcontinental call. A chill snaked down her spine as she suddenly had realized what Kingman must have done and what Mishima would carelessly kill her for. She had scrambled to save her own neck. How silly to make a joke, she had pretended to tease, her blood chilled to ice. The painting was with her, as was the "Garden" series masterpiece he had admired at Villa des Jardins! All her "children" were in their proper place, she had laughed. Perhaps someone was playing a little fun on him! If the paintings were real, they would carry the De Resnais seal, she had told him, and that was impossible.

When Mishima had informed her in a voice as sharp as a dagger that his picture bore the De Resnais stamp, she had been more angry than scared.

"*Un moment.* I know the seal is here." She ran to the wine cellar and pushed the *faux* brick in the wall, pulling out the metal box that contained her grandfather's seal—the seal that had not been used for twenty years. She was more furious than frightened when she lifted the heavy stamp out of the velvet-lined box. There was fresh ink on it. She struggled to compose herself. Kingman had committed an international art crime. Forgery. Theft. Fraud. Larceny. And he had made her his unwitting accomplice.

Mishima clearly had murder in his voice as Cyrielle promised to make good on King's deception. He promised to let her destroy the forgeries that carried the official stamp . . . if she would sell him the *real* pictures. This way, they both knew they could prevent a scandal that would make Mishima look stupid, taint Cyrielle's credibility, and send the price of De Resnais's paintings spiraling in a downward plunge. She couldn't allow this to happen. Kingman Beddall would get off scot-free. They struck the deal.

Now she and Mishima were sitting in the darkened Kabuki theater with their honor intact. The pictures would be deprived of an appreciative audience, as Mishima kept his collection entirely for his own private pleasure. Cyrielle was determined not to become one of those. She had kept her end of the bargain, thereby preserving her grandfather's reputation and the rest of his estate.

The seal was in a bank vault. She and she alone would control any future sales. Mishima squeezed her hand as the actor unfurled two yellow silk scarves, transforming them into two fluttering butterflies. She gave Itoyama an enchanting smile.

## BOXWOOD

There were more glorious sunsets in Monet's masterpieces hanging on the walls of the Musee d' Orsay in Paris. Van Gogh had certainly painted more vibrant suns vividly falling behind Avignon's haystacks, and De Resnais had captured the most dazzlingly sunsets of all in his ethereal post-impressionist pictures of dappled mauves and violets, with thick, sensuous strokes of indigo blues streaking across his evening skies. But the tranquil dusk viewed from the back veranda of Boxwood, overlooking the James River, eclipsed them all, in the eyes of the close-knit Southern family lazily enjoying day's end in the quiet comfort of contented domesticity.

Virginia Randolph sat serenely enthroned on her green wicker chair, at peace in the center of her secure domain, her pale cashmere shawl lightly thrown around her patrician shoulders against the chill of a Southern fall, balancing a Meissen cup of camomile tea on her lap. Boxwood had not been turned into a Japanese Disneyland, after all, with turnstiles and ticket takers, carny hawkers tracking dirt and selling Nikko beer and frittered corn dogs on her gently terraced lawns. Her ancestors were *not* on display like freaks and notables in Madame Tussaud's wax works. They were comfortably ensconced in Boxwood's wood-paneled library and hallways, staring down severely but approvingly from their ungarnished frames, illuminated only by the quiet glow emanating from the Waterford crystal chandeliers hung throughout the house.

Virginia's son, Jamey, was seated on a wicker foot stool beside her, animatedly regaling her with his equestrian adventures from today's Atoka Hunt, of which he was huntmaster. His horsey sports talk was punctuated with the applause and croakings of Boxwood's bullfrogs in the dozen ponds that sprinkled the property, occasionally harmonizing with the symphonic titterings of crickets. As dusk receded into the rustlings of weeping willows, the scent of magnolias and heliotrope enveloped the air around them with Boxwood's own fragrances. The well-bred family gathered on the antebellum porch appeared to have been sitting there sipping tea, mint juleps, and pitchers of old-fashioneds on the same stage set for hundreds of years. But things were far different at Boxwood this evening than they had been even a year earlier.

Uncle Cyrus was huddled with Also and Rodney at the far end of the Georgian brick house in hushed but dramatic conversation, the light from the library window casting shadows about them. It was the first time Rodney, son of Eva and Hook, who had lived all his childhood in the servants' quarters, was enjoying the Boxwood sunset from the veranda of the main house, watching day fall into night, casting a dozen purplish hues onto the gently flowing river.

"I don't understand the legal implications of all this. How could the New York DA's office just drop *all* charges against the nail woman?" Cyrus gruffed. Also dropped her needlepoint and looked up at Rodney, curious to see how he would respond.

Rodney answered in his most emotion-affecting, Manhattan assistant district attorney's courtroom voice, which carried only a trace of a black gentleman's Southern accent. "No charges pressed. Clearly an accident."

Rodney motioned to the other side of the porticoed veranda, where Hook was carefully covering Kingman's wheelchair with a vicuna blanket and tying a bib decorated with little horses around his chin before he spoon-fed him his evening tapioca. A customized metal halo was pinned to Kingman's skull, a cushioned plastic vest supporting his spinal column. He was paralyzed from the neck down, unable to speak.

Cyrus cast a cool eye at Rodney's father wiping tapioca dribble from Kingman's drooling mouth, his wobbling head supported by an uncomfortable steel neck brace connected to the other apparati that imprisoned Kingman Beddall.

Skylar was busy lapping up the sticky spilled pudding from the brick terrace. Cyrus took a sip of his espresso.

"Well, if those are the kinds of accidents you all have in your offices up north, I'm glad to practice law down here! All we ever do is fall off our horses." Cyrus's first reaction to Kingman's "accident" had been alarm that his cousin Virginia might have cracked him over the head with the Brancusi. He carried his cup over to Virginia, giving Kingman's wheelchair wide berth. If the family was engaged in a little cover-up of some sort, so be it. He'd always hated Kingman anyway.

"Also," Rodney said after Cyrus was clearly out of earshot, "it's important for you to understand that you really did make the right decision. And it's something that should never be discussed ever again."

Also jabbed at her needlepoint.

"Buffalo Marchetti did you, your family, and Carmen Cosmetics a big favor: he adhered to your wishes. No charges were ever made against Tandy. He personally denied the tabloid readers a big juicy circus of a trial. By putting that little tart on the stand, we would've been putting your father on trial as well. There were guys in my office planning to build careers, big names for themselves, by putting the noisiest tycoon on Wall Street since J. P. Morgan and his ethics on trial. They would have finished off the eighties with the crucifixion of Kingman Beddall."

"How so?" Also stopped him with a look. It was a cross between a Beddall scowl and a Randolph sneer.

"There were tapes, Also, that Buffalo brought to my attention in an unofficial investigation he had been conducting. Prosecuting Tandy would have brought all that to the surface. There were crimes, ancient and recent, that would have been brought to light. It would have made Milken and Boesky look like a couple of Boy Scouts!"

"My loyalties are to my father, whatever little laws he may have broken." Also was defensive.

"Little laws! Come on, Also! Your father was the Ivan the Terrible of Wall Street!" Rodney knew that Kingman not only had been cooking the books for years, and had committed tax fraud through his Japanese dealings, he had also committed *murder* in Canada thirty years earlier. He looked at the former financial titan, ashen-faced and caged in a metal contraption that was far worse than any prison. Maybe justice had been served after all.

"Are you sure?" Also looked puzzled.

"Yes, Buffalo had enough evidence for a grand jury indictment and a possible extradition. But he burned his file. Buffalo didn't see the point of putting a paralyzed man on display. He would have become just a symbol, anyway."

Also blushed and lowered her eyes to her needlepoint.

"Here, Skylar, here Pit Bull." Scudder Clay Randolph III, Also's second cousin, tossed a rubber ball across the sloping grassy lawn of Boxwood. Pit Bull came charging up to the white-columned back porch with something big and gray in his mouth. He barked at Kingman's wheelchair, dropping a lifeless bushy-tailed rabbit at his master's inert feet. The dog sat down, wagged his tail, and barked, expecting to be rewarded for his gruesome present.

Virginia was as horrified as if the crazy animal had just dumped Thumper dead on her impeccably maintained porch. She rose to her feet and stood perfectly erect, as if she were addressing an entire assembly of the Society of Colonial Dames.

"That animal has got to be removed from the premises. Next it will be trekking up my veranda with stray pedestrians." She threw back her dignified shoulders, her Fabergé peacock brooch bobbing at her breast.

Hook picked up the bloody bunny and carried it by the ears off to the smokehouse.

Scudder cried, "Where are you taking my bunny?"

"Don't worry, son. I'm going to fix him up and bring him right back," Hook called out. He was going to bury the dead rabbit behind the smokehouse and return with a look-alike bunny from the rabbit hutch for young Scudder.

"Now, Grammy," Also kissed her grandmother on the cheek, "please bear with me. We still don't know how much Dad can hear or understand, but I'm sure it is very important for him to have his dog around. We never know, it might help."

Virginia gave Kingman an icy look that would have sent shivers down the spine of any person who wasn't suffering from irreparable nerve damage.

"More tea?" Eva came hurrying out to fill Virginia's translucent china cup.

"No, thank you." Virginia's response was as cold as the ice in the pitcher of old-fashioneds that her husband was mixing.

"James," she ordered, "pour me one of your drinks."

"I'll get it for you, Mother," Jamey said. After James Randolph Sr.'s three o'clock cocktail hour, he was about as quick on his feet as Kingman Beddall.

"Now, Grammy," Also stroked Virginia's silver hair, "you have been so lovely and patient. Please try to be your true-blue self a little longer. I don't want my father in an institution, relying on the kindness of strangers. He can't speak or move or fend for himself. It's not like mother, who can come and go as she pleases and order everybody about."

There was total silence on the veranda, except for the wind stirring up a weeping willow.

Edgemere. Nobody mentioned that place around here these days. That dreadful Tandy was residing there, being treated by a team of doctors for a "nervous breakdown," thought Virginia.

There were certainly some flawed diamonds in the Randolph clan, but her granddaughter wasn't one of them. She was a real gem. Virginia nodded.

"Good. After all, Grammy, this is Dad's home."

A slight look of annoyance flashed across Virginia's eyes, but her body English remained impeccably the same. Thank goodness she and her granddaughter had been represented by real lawyers this time and not by her idiot husband and her cousin Cyrus. Boxwood had been one of Kingman's few properties to remain intact, still totally owned by Kingman Beddall. The courts had appointed a group of trustees to administer the debt-ridden empire. Joyce Royce was the secretary and day-to-day administrator of the living trust. The trustees were to preserve and guard Kingman's remaining holdings and assets until he "recovered," which was highly unlikely, or until Also turned twenty-five, six years from now.

When Hook returned from pulling a rabbit out of the hutch for little Scudder, Also drew him aside in a manner more befitting the mistress of Boxwood than a sophomore at Vassar.

"Hook, I would be very, very pleased if you would continue reading *The New York Times* and *The Wall Street Journal* to Dad everyday. The doctors seem to think he can understand certain things, and the only news he will hear around here otherwise is who won the steeplechase!"

"Certainly, Miss Also. It will be my pleasure. I'm kinda fond of the old scoundrel. You know, I always got the feeling he *really* liked me."

"Liked you?" Also threw back her head and laughed, showing her perfect teeth. "You were his best friend!"

# 15

To some, Le Cirque is the finest restaurant in New York. To others, it is the only place to lunch, see, and be seen, all at once. The cream of New York society liked to eat and watch, their backs to the beige-colored walls decorated with trellises and painted with a mélange of monkeys garbed in eighteenth-century court costume. The room was star studded with slim blond-streaked ladies who took their social lunching seriously, gingerly pushing fresh white truffles, foie gras, and grilled fishes swimming in colorful vegetable sauces around their wide-rimmed plates.

This was not a place where people chowed down, but rather politely picked at their exquisite food before experiencing the delicate flavors through their anorectic gullets. At Le Cirque, the circus was in the caliber of the customers, and the art of the meal was in the seating. Sirio Maccioni stood at the door of his restaurant, frantically rearranging his last-minute seating. He did the only thing he could do for the most interesting collection of "guests," as he referred to his high-paying customers, since the first lady, the Soviet premier's wife, Sophia Loren, and Allen Grubman, Madonna's and Michael Jackson's lawyer, his client shyly in tow, had all stopped in unexpectedly and unannounced for a little lunch. Sirio sent to the back room for another table.

Four waiters carried the table out over the heads of the startled diners. A white tablecloth was magically dropped to the ground, practically in syncopation with the laying of four elaborate place settings and two slender silver vases filled with red, yellow, and burgundy roses, which had fully opened about twenty minutes before. Anticipation was everywhere in the air as two shimmering silver ice buckets were placed on either side of the extra table, one holding Evian water and the other Cristal Roederer 1985. Who could be coming that *had* to be squeezed in? Four striped chairs were shoved into place.

The chairman of Revlon, lunching at the next table with Regis Philbin and Kathie Lee Gifford, had to pull in his seat to the waiter's plaintive apologies as the new arrangement was set up. There had to be enough room for the small three-tiered wedding cake on the table, too! It was Sirio's surprise for Mrs. Arnie Zeltzer, one of his favorite customers and a first-time bride at forty-something. Everything was attended to, a seat with arms for Suki, just a little bit higher than the others, to accommodate her pocket-sized height. Princess Yasmin Aga Khan, daughter of Rita Hayworth and Prince Aly Khan, tossed her mane of hair over in the direction of the newly created table setting from the first corner banquette, the best table for two, where she was lunching with the porcelain-skinned, china-blue-eyed heiress Ala von

Auersberg Isham, talking animatedly about her Brain Research Foundation.

A veritable smorgasbord of social and fashion lights filled the banquette seating running around the front of the restaurant, the correct place to be seated. Was Princess Di coming to lunch? *Quel* commotion! What suddenly exploded through the door was better than anything they could have wildly conjured up or hoped for: Suki, round and ruffled, a yellow chiffon turban wrapped around her head, was escorted into the restaurant on the arm of Gael Joseph Zeltzer, the new chairman and president of Carmen Cosmetics, which had been founded by her father in Suki's early days. The inimitable Suki had not been seen in public since Fling's summer festival funeral at St. Patrick's. Was it October already? The entire restaurant went into a tizzy. Several of the guests stopped chewing and talking as the heavily powdered museum piece, who could make or break any one of them in this room with a written word, was majestically swept to the table. Sirio was on her other side, helping her effortlessly along. Trailing behind impatiently, looking like she was late for an appointment with the Mad Hatter for her unbirthday, was the scandalous but extraordinarily beautiful Baroness Freddie von Sturm, her perfect chin pointed to the chandelier.

"Darlin'," the sunny Texas blonde two tables backstage whispered to her over-Chaneled luncheon partner, "Baroness Freddie is married to the world's *wealthiest*, no, honey, just plain *richest* man in the world! Why, he bought her Carmen Cosmetics the way Bobby bought me this little ole charm bracelet!" The Houston blonde dangled her wrist over her crème brûlée. Texas girls actually ate. "Look at that skin, her carriage. Why, I could fall in love with her myself! Look at her bone structure! I read in 'Suki' that she's really a princess, who married down by consenting to be the Baron's wife." Texas put on her glasses. "Holy shit!

Look at the size of her diamond ring! The diamond is supposed to be one of the cuttings of the great Mogul of India. The original eight-hundred karat stone belonged to Shah Jahan, you know, the fella who built the Taj Mahal! It's been missing *forever*. Stolen! I heard the Baron bought two cuts from it and the Baroness has one of them on her finger. That sucker's got to be at least fifty karats!''

Also, quietly bringing up the rear, wore a simple navy-blue pants suit and a single string of her grandmother's pearls.

Some of the guests ordered second desserts of robin's nests spun from the world's finest chocolates and filled with colorful spoonlets of raspberry, lime, and blueberry sorbets. They couldn't get up and leave now! They could dine out on this Le Cirque lunch for weeks.

Every head in the room turned or bobbed up as the party of four paraded into the public restaurant that was managed like an exclusive private club.

The Queen of the Columnists, the obscenely rich Queen of International Society, the fabulously successful newly married Queen of Cosmetics, Gael Joseph Zeltzer, slimmed down to a *size ten*, and sweet-faced quasi-orphan Also Beddall, an American Princess. Daughter of a strange fate that had taken both parents away from her, one by genteel madness, and the other by a tragic accident that had happened during tycoon Kingman Beddall's period of intense mourning for his beautiful beloved wife, the legendary Fling. Every person in the room knew this version of the somewhat-altered fairy-tale history because everyone in this room was an avid reader of Suki. The present hubbub and commotion on the part of Sirio and seven of his best waiters was as much for Gael Joseph Zeltzer as for the three legends. The Zeltzers were regulars, and although stars were good for business, regulars were even better. These days, Carmen Cosmetics was doing as much worldwide volume as Estée Lauder and Revlon.

Suki climbed into her chair with a lift from Sirio. She patted his belt buckle. He was too tall to kiss.

"Business looks fabulous, *caro*, absolutely fabulous. Who'd have thought you could crowd so many rich people into one room? You're a maestro, *il capo di cibo*, but they're so quiet, dear. Look at them. Have you put Halcion in the inmates' arugula to keep them from table hopping, darling?" Suki pointed a yellow sapphire-ringed finger around the seconds-ago buzzing room, which looked as if its leader had just called out "freeze!" in a game of Statue, or was appearing in an ad for E. F. Hutton, the brokerage firm that advertised everyone was struck silent when their firm was giving out financial advice. Suki controlled an impulse to turn around and wave to her audience. She'd do it later in her column, after luncheon, and after her nap. Gael was ecstatic, a mogulette, a bride, a married lady, a cosmetics Sadie! If Max could see her now! Thank you, God, I'll never think an insincere thought again. Her eyes rolled up to the heavens to thank the Lord. She used the third finger of her left hand, displaying an eight-karat brilliant cut white diamond, as much as possible in her animated, happy gestures. She and Arnie had consummated their marriage every night this week, leaving her skin with a glow no combination of Carmen cosmetics had ever achieved. Oh, love! Ah, *L'amour, l'amour*! If only she could bottle it! It was only at Freddie's insistence that she had created this *other* new, unveiled fragrance in the Carmen-logoed bag beneath the table. The Zeltzers were too happy in the present to dwell about the past.

"Champagne for everybody! Champagne for my adorable competition." She waved cheerily to the owner of Revlon. "Just Diet Coke for me—in a champagne glass," she instructed Antonio, who was pouring. Antonio was smiling; everybody liked *happy*. Only Baroness Fredericka von Sturm was fidgety and perturbed, her people-stopping beauty more pronounced than ever. Only her eyes were lusterless. They had been like that since Fling's death.

"Oh, this place has become so, how do you say, *provincial,*" Freddie finally declared in a newly acquired German accent.

"Cut the crap, Frederick." Gael Joseph Zeltzer grabbed one of Le Cirque's homemade cheese toasts. She'd work it off later, she thought with a smile. Gael was allowed to put the Baroness her Bossiness into her/his place. The Baron's money had acquired Carmen from Kingman's crumbling estate, but the Zeltzers were running it day to day and held a 40 percent equity interest themselves. Good old Arnie, proficient sex expert and numbers cruncher. The smile on Gael's face never even left her mouth while she chewed.

"Gael, dear, are you sure that Carmen hasn't invented something that could help put a bit more bloom into my cheeks?" Suki patted her own hillocks of fat and buttered a sourdough roll. "You're looking positively radiant! As the newest member of Carmen's board of directors, I should be privy to these little scientific secrets." She looked about the room, out of habit, for any column tidbits. All heads were turned in the direction of her own table.

"No, Aunt Suki, there's nothing in the scientific world of beauty that I haven't tried before or let you experiment with." It was true. Suki had been Carmen's guinea pig since the days of Carl Joseph and Max Mendel. Probably her old friend Lucky Stiffingwell of Newport had gotten it right when she'd advised Suki in her rich whiskey voice, "If you want color in your cheeks after sixty-five, babe, get a Greek sailor." Suki beamed over at Gael. That's what *she* had sort of done. She was thrilled for her "adopted" daughter. She was thrilled that she *herself* was an even more worldwidely read columnist than she had been twenty years earlier, and she was beyond thrilled that all the stocks and bonds

Max had acquired for her had outperformed the rest in this "guess who's going bust next?" economy. Why, that piece of the water-purifier company, Aqua-Chem, that Max had speculatively bought for her had been acquired by Coke twenty years ago, and Suki now owned three hundred thousand shares of Coca-Cola. It was worth losing a little hair over. Max had been blue-chip all the way! So was his daughter. It had been not only good business but a charitable heart that had compelled Gael to cover up all of Kingman Beddall's filthy-dirty linens, reinvent twenty-five years of his history, and throw her lot into the shark-infested financial seas. Nothing would have been gained by condemning a brain-dead man to his deserved crucifixion, heaping disgrace instead upon his daughter and ruining Carmen. *Her* Carmen. A white knight had emerged in the unlikely guise of Baron Wolfgang von Sturm, led by his wild, revenge-seeking Baroness. Freddie was determined to keep the memory of Fling pure. The only way this could be done, she knew, was to buy up Carmen before someone more exploitive could gobble it up, selling everything from Ghost perfume to Fling! embalming fluid!

Suki, Gael, the Baroness, and Also all picked up their first fork for their salads of watercress, wild mushrooms, walnuts, and fresh herbs lightly doused in red-wine vinegar. They had just come from a directors' meeting of the newly re-formed board of Carmen Cosmetics. The profits were as dazzling as the diamond on Gael's finger or the one-legged pink flamingo Cartier brooch perched on the lapel of the Baroness's jaunty leather-and-lace peplum jacket. The Mogul of India on Freddie's finger was so big, it carried no shine at all.

"I don't know why we have to have all those Wall Street stuffed shirts on our board. There isn't an innovative or good-looking man in the bunch. Why, Garcia knows more about makeup than anyone other than *me*!" Freddie pouted.

"Dear, the world is run by women but turned by men. We

need them to oil our parts, don't you know," pronounced Suki, and wondered if she had got it just right.

"Wolfy is so business smart that we don't need other, lesser mortals." Freddie peered cautiously over her oversized sunglasses, finally pulling them off. She was *sure* she had slept with the pretty Cuban busboy in another, earlier life. She gave the boy a coy smile. The room audibly responded to any gesture made by this German royal, as famous and written about as Princess Caroline or Prince Charles.

"Baroness," Also softly joined in, "I thought your point about the new fragrance for Europe was really wonderful! There *is* a whole different woman in Europe. Different levels of taste. How did you say it, 'different animals on different continents'?"

"Thank you, Also." Freddie shook off a stubborn platinum wisp of hair.

"And I loved your idea for a fragrance called Wildlife. It's wild and sexy and environmental all at the same time." Also blushed.

"Ah, wild sex," Suki reminisced. "The animal life, satin sheets, scented candles—it only lasts a minute and then, poof!" She clapped her silly little hands together and examined Also. "What a pretty child you are. Is there a wild romance in your life? Men are such dears, but they can be animals. Why," Suki had an inspiration, "have you met my new best friend, Sergeant Buffalo? Now there's a man like they used to make in my day! No offense, Freddie dear."

"None taken." Freddie guzzled down some wine. She was starting to feel good. The buzz of New York was bewitching her.

Also looked down at her plate.

"Aunt Suki, he's the cop who spent all the time with Also. He was very fair with us. Quit the force for a time over the whole matter," Gael said. "He was our point man on the Carmen cover-up. At least we saved everybody's reputation."

"Also, I hope you do have good taste when it comes to picking men. Come to my New Year's Eve ball in St. Moritz," the Baroness tempted. "I'll have all the best young men in Europe!" Freddie said in a voice all the restaurant could hear and love. A tray of oversized crystal goblets was overturned by a harried Cuban busboy somewhere in the room. Also giggled.

"Broken glass! Good luck! To the Zeltzers." Suki picked up her champagne glass in a toast. The people at the next table lifted their glasses and sent over a second bottle of champagne to the celebrating table. There were broad smiles all around.

"To the Zeltzers. Hear! Hear!"

Gael reached under the table to present each one of her friends and business associates with a small gift, somehow signifying the single tie that held them all together.

"My dear friends, I thank you for sharing in my happiness and joy. I have created something myself, just for you. Carmen will not market this special fragrance. This is only for us."

"From Gael's personal *laboratory*," the Baroness chimed in with her thick accent as she started to unravel the bright red wrapping paper.

"For us alone, then." Suki loved secrets. Gael lifted the stopper from a superbly cut crystal flacon shaped like a slim diamond skyscraper, multifaceted, with ruby-red lettering carved and painted vertically across the bottle. The smells of anise, myrrh, oleander, and Northern pines whirled to the olfactory parts of their brains, inducing different sentiments in each person at the table. The perfume had the volatility of New York, and nuances of mystery. There was a dash of pepper and a masculine, leathery middle note. The bottom note, as each lady observed as the fragrance settled on their wrists and other pulse points, was ethereal and sweet. Gael's masterpiece.

Fredericka, with tears in her eyes, knew the sweetness was extract of vanilla.

"Sweet Revenge," Gael announced. "My darlings, this is *my* gift to you. Now it is captured in a bottle and can be put on a shelf, where it belongs. It will not be sold, but you must remember, you may use it only for yourselves."

They all sniffed simultaneously. There were spirits in the room. Each one had her own personal memories and revenges. Somehow, Gael had captured it and lured it like a troubled genie back into its beautiful bottle.

*"Sweet Revenge!"* they all echoed Gael. *"Sweet Revenge."* They clicked their glasses together. *"Sweet Revenge!"* They all stood up with their glasses in the air. They would be exorcised of their demons. Life would go on. The main course was coming.

The ladies kissed and waved good-bye in an emotional, slightly tipsy after-luncheon farewell.

Fredericka was a basket case. Her driver and her footman helped her into the silver-gray Daimler, where her fluffy Maltese terrier, Fling, was bouncing and yapping all over the lush leather seating area like a human yo-yo.

"New York is so uncivilized." She waved a lace handkerchief at her friends. "In Paris, they let me take my dog to all the best restaurants." Tears of love, sadness, and joy were streaking down her face. She'd pop an Ecstasy and douse herself in Sweet Revenge. Suki was slipping into the backseat of the Baroness's car, unaided. By the time the automobile got to her apartment on Central Park South, she'd have two weeks' worth of scintillating European gossip for the column, and dog leaks all over her yellow satin coat.

Gael trundled herself into the Carmen limo. She was hurrying back to the office and Arnie. She was all smiles.

Also kissed and waved and promised her dear sweet busybody "aunts" she'd try to find time for a personal life. "Aunt" Suki, "Aunt" Gael, "Auntie" Freddie! Also laughed aloud. Who needed a mother with "aunts" like these? She pulled up her collar to the edge of her short-cropped hair and stuffed her glove-less hands into the pockets of her tweed jacket, striding quickly down Park Avenue against the afternoon chill. She barely noticed the huge Harley-Davidson careening up toward her. She looked up, startled, to hear a roar of engines and a tough cop's voice call out, "Get on, Also. Not smart to resist arrest."

Without hesitation she slipped onto the leather seat behind Buffalo.

"How'd you know where to find me?" Also asked, wide-eyed.

"Your 'aunts' beeped me from the restaurant. It's almost four o'clock. That musta been some lunch."

"I didn't touch a bite. I'm starved."

"Wanna go for a pizza?"

"Yes. That's exactly what I want to do."

Also tucked her arms around his waist and pulled her knees up to her chest as the powerful machine took off like a rocket. He smelled very good to her.

She had left her bottle of Sweet Revenge under the table. She had really left it there a very long time ago.

Her body was thrown against his as she hung onto him for support as they made their way up Park Avenue to the Nineties.

ABOUT THE AUTHOR

Chicago-born and Sarah Lawrence–educated, prominent so-cialite/philanthropist SUGAR RAUTBORD is internationally noted for her beauty, energy, glamour, and ebulliant wit. A media darling, she has appeared on major national TV talk shows, and is featured regularly in fashion and social magazines as a subject, model, and contributing journalist. Sugar is co-author of the bestseller *Girls in High Places*. She lives on Chicago's Lake Shore Drive.